WITHDRAWN

To my family—
Tony, Alex, and Zoë

Prologue

SNYDER LOOKED DOWN AT THE tiny screen and watched the action unfolding on the other side of the world. He had positioned himself in the shadows between two of the streetlamps that punctuated the Arlington Memorial Bridge with annoying regularity, but even without the extra glare, the video feed flickering on the cheap cell phone was dark and blurry.

He adjusted his silk scarf against the biting wind and leaned his arms against the railing to steady the phone. Peering closer at the screen, he could make out a hallway with doors on either side. That must be from inside the hotel, just as planned. He felt like a player in a video game, watching the jerky forward motion as the camera moved slowly along the corridor, occasionally turning to focus on the numbers on the doors. He hoped this guy was as good as everyone said.

Snyder took a deep breath to calm the pumping of his heart. He prided himself on thorough preparation, but that didn't stop the inevitable last-minute jitters. Everyone who cared about their work suffered the same thing: the sprinter before the race, the politician before the big speech, the general before the battle. The trick was to make the energy work for you, but at this point there was little left to do. He had spent a long time setting this up—his efforts commensurate with the importance of the task—and now all he could do was watch through the playing-card-sized window into the distant continent.

His concentration was pulled from the screen as a figure came striding along the bridge toward him. With a quick glance he took in the silhouette of protruding ears, broad shoulders bundled in a heavy coat, and swaying gait. The senator was punctual, as always.

Snyder returned his attention to the phone. The screen showed a hand reaching for a door handle before the unmistakable outline of a gun's silencer blocked the field of view. He felt the tiniest smile tug at the corners of his mouth.

He looked up and greeted the new arrival with a quick nod. "Good evening, Senator Brennigan. How did the vote go?"

"Bunch of imbeciles. No vision whatsoever." The senator leaned heavily against the railing. "I hope you have some good news for me."

"Soon. Very soon." Snyder held out the phone toward the senator. The silencer had moved to the bottom of the image and was now pointed forward toward the dark shape of a person in an expanse of white sheets. "That's our guy."

Brennigan peered down at the image. "I'll take your word for it. When was that taken?"

Snyder looked down at his watch. "There's about a two-second delay."

"You mean it's live?" Brennigan jolted upright.

Snyder allowed himself a real smile. Brennigan was a typical politician: he wanted things done, with no thought of the work that went into making them happen. It would be a pleasure to share this special event with him.

"Yes, live action from the Grand Hotel Kinshasa."

Brennigan stared at him open-mouthed for a second, then turned as if mesmerized back to the screen. Snyder held the phone between them as they squinted at the blurred outline on the bed. The silencer was still pointed toward the figure, but nothing was happening.

"Why doesn't he shoot? What's the matter with him?"

Snyder was wondering the same thing, but couldn't expose his own anxiety to the senator. A small movement of the silencer told him the image was still live, but something was wrong.

Abruptly the camera focused down on the gun. With a blur of motion, the gun's magazine ejected before the screen went suddenly black. The two men stared at the dark screen for several seconds until the senator's voice cut shrilly through the silence.

"What's happening? Why doesn't he shoot him? What's up with your phone?"

Snyder took a deep breath and checked the signal on his phone. "The connection's still good. It's the other end."

"Then why did they stop filming? What happened to the cameraman?" Brennigan sucked air through his teeth. "You told me this wouldn't be a problem."

Snyder felt the senator's hand grab at his arm. Maybe it hadn't been such a good idea to invite him along. Some people didn't have the temperament to appreciate the finesse of a task like this.

"There's only one guy," he explained quietly as he lifted the senator's hand away. "He has a small camera mounted on his earpiece. My guess is, his gun jammed and he's fixing it. I have no idea why his camera stopped broadcasting."

Brennigan was watching him with narrowed eyes. "I need the Congo. If we don't get those mining rights soon, someone else is going to figure out what's under Lake Tanganyika and the bidding will go sky high."

Snyder raised himself to his full height—a head taller than Brennigan—and looked down at him. He wanted to remind the senator that he, Snyder, had been the one to tell him about the coltan find at Lake Tanganyika. He'd spent hours explaining how the tantalum that could be extracted from coltan was used in just about every electronic device on the planet—the gold of the twenty-first century. Sometimes it seemed that the senator took their relationship too much for granted, forgot who was doing the favors. Snyder's work for Brennigan was far from an official part of his job at the Agency, though he liked to think of it as an extension of his duties to his country.

But Snyder knew that one-upmanship was a shallow victory. It played no role in long-term results.

"You're quite right, Senator," he responded, forcing himself to relax his posture. "Don't worry, you'll get your mining rights. Tanzania is all signed up. Burundi is falling over itself for the money. That just leaves the Congo. I told you I'd get it for you, so you get the contracts ready, and I'll do the rest."

Brennigan's reply was cut off as the screen flickered back to life and drew the attention of both men. The figure in front of the camera was now sitting up in the bed with hands outstretched in front of him. His mouth formed unheard words. The silencer was in partial view at the bottom of the screen. It jerked one, two, three times. The figure flattened back against the headboard before pitching forward face down onto the bed, the jerky image making it look like a slow-motion movie effect. The camera moved toward the figure and lingered on the sprawled shape. A dark stain seeped slowly across the white sheets.

Snyder felt a warmth spread through his body despite the rawness of the night air. He realized how tense he had been—having the senator here had turned out to be an unpleasant distraction. These things were best experienced as a solitary pleasure.

He looked over at Brennigan, who was clutching at the railing with both hands. His face was pale and the skin around his eyes and under his chin seemed to sag even more than usual.

"You've got the Congo," said Snyder.

The senator let go of the railing, but his eyes were still staring out over the river.

"Well, good. That's that then," he said. He brushed his hands together and turned his back to Snyder. "I'll be in touch."

Snyder watched him go, hurrying off to the familiar streets of Georgetown to boast with his colleagues of deals and battles fought and won for the good of America. But tonight's deal was one he knew the senator would keep to himself.

He leaned against the railing and felt the coldness of the metal spread into his arms through his raincoat. The screen on the phone was blank now—the video feed gone. He turned the device around once in his bare hands and then let it slide through his fingers. Seconds later, the screen slipped silently, untraceably, into the murky waters of the Potomac.

1

Part I

Chapter 1

Lenny Driver looked at the code he had created and knew that it was perfect.

He glanced around at the other job candidates, huddled together in two groups, talking occasionally in low voices as their pens scratched against paper. It looked as though neither team had finished the assignment yet, so he leaned back into the ergonomic mesh contour of his chair and cupped his phone against his crossed legs. He'd selected a clean pair of jeans and the only jacket he owned for the interview, but now he noticed that the sole at one side of his sneakers was starting to peel away. No worry, he thought. Blahst would be hiring him for his coding skills, not his dress sense.

He brought up *Plants versus Zombies* and resumed his attack against a particularly ferocious lair of undead ogres. A pointed cough from one of the other candidates alerted him to a roomful of glares. He waved a hand in apology and plugged in his earbuds.

He was unleashing bombs against the final zombie assault when he felt a hand tap on his shoulder. He glanced up to see that Clayton Malloy, the Blahst employee who was conducting this part of the interview process, was back in the room. Lenny thought about ignoring the intrusion until he'd pounded the last few zombies, but then he remembered that his roommate, Roy, had admonished him not to upset anyone if he really wanted this job. Which he did. He pulled out his earbuds, poked at the curls of his hair in an attempt to smooth them back into submission, and smiled stiffly at Clayton.

"Two minutes until we start the code review." Clayton's precise British enunciation rang out as he looked across at the two teams of applicants gathered at the assigned tables. Then he frowned and looked back at Lenny, who still had his chair pushed off to one side.

"Your team... haven't you been... why aren't you working with your team?" Clayton's thin lips worked to articulate the question. His fine blond hair, parted in the middle, fell forward and settled on either side of his gold-rimmed glasses.

"I had an idea I wanted to follow up," Lenny explained, waving the sheets of paper he'd been working on. Clayton's frown deepened. He had explained to the group in great detail how it had been his idea to run a mock design-and-review session as part of the job interview. He'd stressed that this was the first time they had tried it, but that was what Blahst was all about—innovation. Now Lenny was getting the distinct impression that Clayton wasn't happy about Lenny's own little innovation in abandoning the other three members of his team.

"Interesting idea to have us write code on paper instead of the computer," Lenny offered in an attempt to make amends. "Never seen that before."

The muscles around Clayton's eyes tensed behind his glasses. He peered down at Lenny's phone before turning to watch over the shoulders of Lenny's erstwhile teammates.

Lenny was not impressed with Clayton. Most of the other Blahst employees that Lenny had met earlier that day had talked to him like normal human beings. The discussions hadn't felt like job interviews—they conversed at length about the relative benefits of scripting versus dynamic programming languages, and reminisced about their first Game Boys. Clayton, on the other hand, had asked about his prior work experience and grilled him on his greatest strengths and weaknesses. Lenny tried to interest Clayton in the video game he had sold in his junior year of high school, but Clayton insisted on discussing where Lenny wanted to be in five years' time and other questions that had left Lenny semi-coherent with the effort of introspection.

Lenny looked around the meeting room. The seven other job applicants were scribbling, mostly in silence except for the occasional whispered question to a teammate. This part of the interview process had been more to his liking. Clayton had assigned them to two teams, given them a design and programming task, and, to Lenny's relief, disappeared from the room for an hour. Another Blahst employee, who had been introduced as the Associate Something-or-Other of Human Talent Management but hadn't yet spoken a word, sat in the corner taking notes on a laptop balanced on her knees.

Lenny ruffled through his sheets of paper to check his code. It was still perfect. He wondered whether he should add another feature to his program. He decided against it—there would be plenty of time for that once he got the job.

He looked around the white walls of the meeting room, which were decorated with pictures that looked at first glance like abstract images but on closer inspection morphed into a close-up of a microchip, the profile of a keyboard, and the frayed ends of a fiber optic cable. On the fourth wall, a row of large windows framed the view of a frozen lake next to the steady flow of traffic that streamed in both directions along Route 128. Lenny imagined what it would be like to come here every day, to tell people that he worked for the coolest web company in the world, to see his code launched on the Blahst site to millions of people. He leaned back and mulled over what he should propose to Blahst as his first project.

As the hands on the metal wall clock reached two o'clock precisely, Clayton clapped his hands together and collected the papers from the two teams. He stared at Lenny's proffered contribution for a moment before taking it with a loud sigh.

"Okay, let's circulate the designs and start the critique. You should have worked on the designs..." Clayton paused to look at Lenny. "... as a team, and on the code samples individually. Let's start with the red team's design."

Lenny pulled his chair up to the table where his team was inspecting the documents from the other four applicants. The room was silent as they read through the design sketches and the code. One of the code samples was far better than the rest, and it was written in the same hand as most of the design. He glanced at the name—Mari Velasquez—and matched it with a poised, dark-haired young woman who was wearing too much makeup for a programmer. He vaguely recognized her as one of the self-absorbed, condescending students he'd had to attend freshman classes with at Boston University.

A skinny guy to Lenny's right, who had introduced himself as Bernie McNee, asked Mari's team a couple of tentative questions. As the discussion picked up, Lenny caught sight of his papers at the edge of the red team's table.

Perhaps I'll add that feature after all, he thought. He reached over to retrieve the pages and smoothed them out in front of him. The feature would make it a little more user-friendly, and might even support a better—

"Lenny, the time's over for you to be correcting your work." Clayton's voice rang from the front the room.

Lenny's pen froze in his hand, held captive by the weight of eight pairs of eyes staring at him.

"I wasn't correcting it. I was making an enhancement," he explained. Nobody spoke as Clayton smirked around at the other candidates, his eyebrows raised in an exaggerated *yeah-right* arc. Lenny's skin prickled hotly as he pushed the paper back onto the other team's table.

"Do you have anything to add to the discussion before we finish up with the red team, Lenny?" Clayton folded his arms and flicked at the plastic clip of the ballpoint pen he was clutching in one hand.

Lenny picked up the page that had looked the worst during his cursory review.

"You mean this?" Lenny had been wondering why nobody had pointed out the error in the second line. They must have been saving it for him. "There's a loop—the subroutine will never end.

You can see it easily if you run down a couple of levels of function calls. It's a basic error."

The young woman next to Mari Velasquez flushed a deep red. The only sound was Clayton's thumb *flick-flick-flicking* at his pen clip.

Clayton cleared his throat. "Yes, well, thank you, Lenny, for your critique. Now let's take a look at your contribution." Clayton joined Mari's team in staring down at the pages that Lenny had written out in small print.

"I have a question for you." Clayton didn't look up from the pages. "Did you understand the assignment?"

"Sure. Take a user's calendar and location information and create updates for Twitter, Facebook, Blahst, and the like. Do it automatically, so the user doesn't have to write it."

"Unless I'm missing something, that's not what you've written." Clayton prodded his pen at one of Lenny's pages.

"There was no point," said Lenny. "Blahst already does that. Everyone does. What's the use in writing it again?"

"It was an exercise."

"I had a better idea. Instead of generating the same text every time—you know, 'Joe entered Starbucks'—why not make it sound like the user would actually say it. For one person the system might post 'OMG, I so need a skinny mocha Frappuccino!'" Lenny rose to his feet and did his best Valley Girl impersonation. "For Clayton here, it might be, 'I say, chaps, just popping in for a nice cup of tea.'"

Lenny's British accent was less impressive and drew chuckles from around the tables.

Clayton did not look amused. "That's nice in theory, but users aren't going to bother typing in all their favorite phrases."

"They don't need to. The system can learn from all their other posts, and their texts, and their blogs, and whatever else they've written." Lenny felt himself becoming more animated as he warmed up to his audience. He picked up one of his pages. "See? I wrote an algorithm that parses out emotional indicators like interjections and—"

"Okay, thank you, Mr. Driver. That's very inspired, but I don't think we have time for the details right now. How about we do the code review and move on so the blue team can have their turn. I didn't actually plan for *three* different designs." He looked deliberately at the clock. "Now, who can find an error in the code sample?"

Lenny sat back in his seat and leaned forward on the table, facing his jury. The room was still as the applicants looked down at the pages spread out in front of them. The silence continued as, one by one, they looked back up, glancing at Lenny, at each other, and around the room.

"Looks good." Mari Velasquez spoke first. Her wavy dark hair was pulled back in a ponytail. "Great idea. Would love to see it in action."

Clayton smiled at Mari and nodded before turning back to Lenny's work. He leaned forward and waved his pen toward one of the pages.

"Well, I'm surprised nobody else spotted it. You're going to get a buffer overflow. Right here," he pronounced, stabbing his pen on the page. He straightened back up and stood with arms crossed over his chest.

Lenny looked at where the pen had challenged his code and quickly realized Clayton's mistake. It looked like things were going in his favor—an opportunity to point out a Blahst employee's error, to really show how smart he was.

"No, it's a string."

Clayton's brow furrowed. His thumb flicked a rapid beat against his pen clip.

Lenny shrugged over at the other interviewees in case any of them wanted to help explain. Nobody else spoke, so Lenny realized he had to be the one to state the obvious.

"Strings are immutable. Any moron knows that!"

Clayton's pen clip snapped off its pen and flew across the room, catching Bernie McNee on the cheek. Bernie raised his hand to his face in surprise and sent an open bottle of Evian skittering across the table. The bottle deposited its contents in a neat stripe down the front of the young woman opposite him. She gasped and jumped to her feet, hands swatting at the cold liquid as it seeped into her blue silk blouse.

For a second the room was still, and all eyes were on the woman clutching at her top. Mari was the first to move. She pulled a handkerchief out of her purse and offered it across the table. Clayton raced around the table, grabbed the handkerchief from Mari, and dabbed at the woman's chest.

Mari pried the handkerchief out of Clayton's fingers and handed it back to the young woman.

"Thanks, but I think she can manage now," Mari said.

Clayton retook his position at the front of the room. He ignored Lenny as he led the rest of the group through the review of the blue team's work. That suited Lenny. He'd come up with the best design and shown he could find other people's mistakes, so he didn't have anything else to prove. He knew the job was his. He itched to get back to *Plants and Zombies*, but again restrained himself in deference to his promise to Roy that he would behave. Once he got this job, Roy would finally be off his back about paying his share of the rent. The money he'd made from selling his high school video game had been sucked dry by college fees, and he had to admit he'd been sponging off Roy for a good few months now.

But it wasn't really about the money. Lenny knew he belonged here. He knew he'd find his home among the people who lived for the rush of the brilliant algorithm and the elegant twist of code. He wondered fleetingly how Clayton had managed to get himself hired, but Clayton seemed to be in a minority of one based on the other employees Lenny had met. He relaxed back in his chair with his hands crossed behind his head as his attention drifted to the fattening snake of cars that marked the beginning of rush hour on Route 128.

The blue team's review ended with a reshuffling of chairs. Clayton closed with a short speech about what wonderful candidates they all were and how sad he was that there was only one opening at the moment. He didn't look in Lenny's direction once; Lenny figured he was still too embarrassed at the mistake he'd made about Lenny's code. Still, no hard feelings. Lenny could maybe even coach him a bit once he started work.

As he watched the candidates leave the room, Lenny saw the young woman with the drenched blouse say something to Mari Velasquez that made them both laugh. Mari's laugh was deep and smooth and Lenny felt a sudden urge to talk to her. Striking up conversations with women wasn't his strong point, but his satisfaction at how well the interview had gone sent a swell of confidence through his body. Mari seemed like a competent programmer, and her praise of his code during the review hadn't sounded as patronizing as he'd expected. Maybe he should return the favor.

He crossed to where Mari was gathering up her coat and took a deep breath.

"Your code was really good."

She turned to face him with a smile. A slight flush spread down the line of her cheekbones.

"Thanks. It's nice of you to say so."

It was Lenny's turn to feel the heat rising to his face. She was watching him, apparently waiting for him to say something more, but he hadn't thought past the opening. He should pay her another compliment.

"If I hadn't been here, you probably would have got the job."

Her smile faded into the open-mouthed, eyebrows-raised expression that all too often terminated his conversations with the opposite sex.

"Thanks a lot." She threw her coat over her shoulder and left the room.

Lenny stared after her and sighed. That hadn't gone how he intended. As he pulled on his jacket, he noticed Mari's handkerchief draped soggily over the edge of the desk. He scooped it up and ran out the door, but she was nowhere to be seen.

He pushed the handkerchief into his pocket and looked around the empty corridor. The feeling of well-being gradually returned at the thought that he'd soon be back, coding for the biggest, smartest web company in the world. Right here at Blahst, where he belonged.

Chapter 2

LENNY WATCHED WITH GROWING TREPIDATION as his roommate, Roy, brought them both to a halt in front of the building that would be Lenny's new workplace. The gentrification and renovations that had been driving up rents around Cambridge for the past decade seemed to have skipped this little corner of Central Square. Barely a block away from the eclectic shops and even more eclectic population that collected around the subway station, the side street was deserted at nine o'clock on a Monday morning.

As Roy fished out a key, Lenny approached the door and peered between the wrought iron bars that covered a small window. The thick glass was heavily textured and reinforced with a diagonal mesh of wire, blocking Lenny's view of what lay beyond.

He stepped back onto a small snowbank at the side of the cleared path and looked up at the building. Faded blue paint was peeling off to reveal the stark grey concrete beneath. A few of the dark, streaked windows still had the metallic grills of air conditioners sticking out, each with its own pyramid of snow on top.

"It's not exactly Blahst," he grumbled.

"At least it's a job. Told you I could get you in. The professor needs someone to help with the computers." Roy held the door open for Lenny before starting up a flight of concrete stairs. Lenny watched him ascend, his dark pointed sideburns visible beneath a black woolen hat. His stylish Patagonia jacket and Timberland boots looked out of place in the dingy building.

"Can't stand the thought of you lounging around at home all day littering the place with pizza boxes," Roy continued. "And you'll finally be able to pay the three months' rent you owe me. Some gratitude would be nice."

"I just don't get it—why would they choose Mari Velasquez?" Lenny didn't expect an answer. He'd regaled Roy with the same question for the past two weeks. "Blahst's the best web company, so why wouldn't they hire the best programmer? I told them I got a hundred on the finals. Nobody's ever got a perfect score before. Mari only got a ninety-eight, so why would they give her the job?"

"Perhaps she's a nice person," Roy suggested.

"That's bullshit. Companies like Blahst don't care about nice. They want the best brains on the planet."

"Apparently not. Anyway, I thought those scores were confidential."

"Yeah, right. It's a computer science department. You think anything on that server is confidential? It's a rite of passage to hack into the exam scores." He glared at the worn staircase rising in front of him. "Plus, I graduated six months early. Doesn't that count for something?"

"Didn't Mari graduate early too?"

Lenny didn't dignify the question with a response. He followed Roy up the stairs, watching his boots deposit a muddy puddle on each step as he went. He knew he should be grateful to Roy for helping him get a job, but the resentment churning inside of him seemed to choke any other worthier emotion before it could gain a foothold. "Anyway, it's all that jerk Clayton's fault. If it wasn't for him, I would have got that job. Now I'm going to have to wait for another opening."

"Well, that'll teach you to start a fight in a job interview." Roy rounded the corner on the third floor and started along a corridor of pale plaster walls and a beige flecked linoleum floor.

"It wasn't a fight. It was a peer review."

Roy stopped in front of a heavy-framed wooden door and fished out another key. A business card was taped to the door with the name "Healthway Research International" printed on it.

"Peer review?" Roy held the door and turned to face Lenny, eyebrows raised skeptically.

"Yeah, peer review." Lenny held Roy's stare a second, then couldn't help but smile. In the two years they'd been sharing an apartment, Roy had always been able to shake Lenny out of his moods. Lenny gave him a back-handed slap on the chest as he stepped past into the office.

An open door on his right revealed a wooden desk with a tumble of papers and journals flowing onto the floor. Shelves on every wall were jammed with books.

"That's Professor Ramsey's office. We're over here." Roy waved to an open area with two desks at opposite ends of the space. The walls were covered with color prints—proud African women adorned with elaborate bead necklaces, naked children with serious expressions and large eyes locked on the camera, and thin-chested men squatting in earnest conversation. Lenny knew that Roy had majored in digital photography before working here at Healthway, but he realized he hadn't seen much of Roy's work until now.

One of the desks had a large screen flanked by two smaller ones. A table next to the desk supported a printer several sizes too large for it. Lenny drifted over and picked up a camera from a chair.

"Neat stuff. Did they buy all this just for you?"

Roy shrugged. "Yeah. I applied for some grants. I do all the publicity brochures, so I need some decent equipment. I got the printer for free—it's awesome—just look at this resolution."

Roy thrust a photo at Lenny. A baby lay on a grimy sheet. Irregularly shaped patches of cracked red flesh flared over most of its body, leaving only a few patches of brown skin beneath. The baby's eyes were crusted half closed. One hand was raised a few inches off the sheet, as if in a futile plea for help.

"That's terrible."

"What do you mean?" Roy snatched the photo back. "That's forty eight hundred dpi. You can't get much better resolution than that."

"No, I mean the kid. It's awful."

"Yeah, well, that's why we're here." Roy studied the photo in his hand. "The incredible brain of Lenny Driver is going to help us bring safe sex to Burundi. I told Professor Ramsey you're the best programmer since Bill Gates, so I'm sure he'll put you to good use. Your desk is over there."

Lenny looked over at the other wall. A small, stubby monitor and keyboard sat in the middle of an otherwise empty desk. He walked over and peered under the desk at a large white computer tower.

"I'm not going to do much with this dinosaur. My phone's got more power than this thing."

A booming voice pulled Lenny away from his inspection. "Hello, anybody home?"

He turned around to face a man nearly as large as the doorway. The man started shedding clothes onto a nearby hook—green, hooded parka; fleece hat; scarf; and gloves. A tweed jacket stayed on over an open-necked shirt.

"I'm Professor Ramsey." He bent down to remove his rubber boots and slipped his feet into a pair of moccasins that had been left next to the door. "You must be Lenny Driver."

Lenny looked at his new employer, still dwarfing the doorframe even without the piles of outerwear. Dark-brown skin, a bald head, and prominent features were softened by a neatly trimmed grey beard.

Professor Ramsey strode over to Lenny's desk. His large hand grabbed Lenny's and pumped enthusiastically. "Very pleased to meet you. Roy's told me all about you."

Ramsey turned to greet Roy, then clapped his hands together. "Let's get you started, Lenny." He bustled into his office and rummaged through the piles of documents. He emerged with several inches of papers and folders. "First, some background so you know what we're here for. These are brochures on Healthway. Also, a couple of white papers on AIDS prevention. And you must read Davenport's article on the psychology of prostitution, most insightful, and this one from the National Intelligence Council on Burundi's political situation. But most of all..."

Ramsey paused and looked around the office until his eyes settled on a plain white box sitting by itself on a shelf above a small coffee machine. He took the box and dropped it on top of the pile of papers. "Most of all, it's about these." He stared almost reverently at the box for a second and then motioned for Lenny to open it.

Lenny peered inside and felt his neck become warm under Ramsey's gaze, as though his mother had caught him in an embarrassing act. He tried to look suitably serious.

"Condoms," he managed to announce.

"Exactly," said Ramsey. "It's the best defense we've got. We ship them out by the crateload, but it's not enough. The tricky part is persuading people to use them."

The professor added a thick book to the pile on Lenny's desk. On its cover, concentric circles in deepening colors spread outward behind the title *Viral Diffusion* and the name *James M. Ramsey.*

"That's my life's research. It's everything we know about how new ideas spread among groups of people," he continued. "Unfortunately, it's usually too slowly. Did you know that it took seventy years for surgeons to start washing their hands between patients, despite incontrovertible evidence that it reduced infections? And the British Navy let their sailors die of scurvy for two hundred years after one of their sea captains showed how lemon juice could prevent it?" His broad chest heaved with a deep sigh. "We still know so little about how to help people do what's good for them."

Lenny surveyed the mounting pile of literature on his desk, and looked around once more at the vivid, alien images on the wall. The problems of the third world seemed very far away from the ice and cold of the New England winter. How could a tiny organization like Healthway hope to make a difference? He felt a wash of relief that he wouldn't have to worry about that side of things. He could earn some easy money here—and add a programming job to his resume—until he could go back for a real job at Blahst.

He cleared his throat. "What exactly would you like me to do?"

"Ah yes, of course." Ramsey's wistful expression snapped back into a smile. "Gladys usually comes in every morning to keep everything in order, but she's been ordered on bed rest until the baby arrives. She left very detailed instructions, though." He opened the top drawer of Lenny's desk and took out several pages of large, friendly handwriting. "You'll need to enter the expenditures into the accounting system, print out the fundraising letters, check the e-mails every day, that sort of thing. If there's anything really important, print it out and leave it on my desk, and I'll write a response for you to send. Otherwise, just use your initiative."

Lenny felt his mouth fall open. "You want me to—"

A sharp kick on his ankle from Roy's direction made him clamp his mouth shut. He started again, trying to keep his voice calm.

"You'd like me to print out your e-mail?"

"That's right. I'm sure you'll pick it up in no time. And Roy can help show you the ropes." Ramsey beamed proudly at Roy, who was now avoiding meeting Lenny's eyes. "Now if you'll excuse me, I have a conference call with Washington and Burundi— they're seven hours ahead out there. Washington's threatening to pull our funding."

He strode into his office, pulling the door closed behind him. Snatches of his voice escaped as he began a phone call, muffled by the wood and glass.

"Data entry and printouts?" Lenny felt the exasperation of the last few weeks threatening to burst.

"Sorry, dude, I didn't know what he wanted. He does all this awesome research, so I thought..." Roy trailed off and shrugged.

Lenny sighed. He was falling further and further behind on his bills and loans. He needed to do something, and at least it wouldn't be flipping burgers.

"Hey, it's a job." Lenny tried to sound enthusiastic, but his words echoed with unintended resentment.

They sat in silence as Lenny stirred a finger among the box of condoms on his desk. "There must be a hundred in here," he said, plucking out one of the flat packages. "That'd keep me going for a whole month."

Roy snorted. "You wish." He opened one of the packages and started blowing into the rubber until it inflated into a small balloon. He smacked it toward Lenny's head.

"That's ugly." Lenny grabbed at the makeshift balloon and inspected the thick translucent rubber. "No wonder nobody uses them."

"You might have a point there." Roy crossed to his desk. He was soon engrossed in the images on his screen, leaving Lenny to his own devices.

Gladys's instructions turned out to be extremely clear, and in less than an hour Lenny had brought everything up to date and even added a couple of new screen displays to speed up the data entry. He wondered what he was supposed to do next.

He flipped open the copy of Ramsey's book and started skimming the introduction. He expected a dry, academic tome, but the professor had an engaging style, and Lenny quickly became engrossed in the story of how cell phones went from an esoteric technology to one adopted by billions of people all over the world. Lenny kept on reading, learning how some innovations, like cell phones, were adopted relatively quickly, while others, like the discovery that lemon juice prevents scurvy, could languish for decades or even centuries. Whatever the speed, they all followed a common pattern that Ramsey drew out skillfully from the examples: the initial slow growth of adoption, followed by a gradual ramping up of interest until the new idea or technology reached a magical point where it took on a life of its own. After that point there was no going back; the adoption levels surged as the innovation spread rapidly through the population like a virus.

Engrossed by descriptions of the ways that researchers had tried to make ideas go viral, Lenny began to lose all sense of time. He reached for his phone—a closer look at the computer under his desk revealed that his phone really did have a faster processor—and started jotting down some notes. Professor Ramsey's research predated the Internet, the most viral of all communication channels, and he had an idea or two about how to put the research findings into software. He was going to have to fill in his time here somehow, so perhaps he could help with the professor's research after all.

At least until the job with Blahst came through.

Chapter 3

MARI'S NOSE WRINKLED AS THE smell of Axe aftershave wafted into her cubicle.

"Hi, Clayton," she said, without turning from her screen.

She heard the squeak of a spare chair being rolled in from the next cubicle, where she'd put it earlier to make her space look less inviting. The hint had clearly been too subtle, and Clayton pulled the chair up beside her with a cheery greeting. She acknowledged his presence with a half-smile and was slightly alarmed to see his eye twitch in what she hoped wasn't a wink.

At first it had seemed natural to Mari that Clayton would spend most of his time in her cubicle, helping her figure out passwords and payroll and all the other administrivia of a new job. But as the days passed and Mari settled easily into her role, the excuses for his constant attention became flimsier. Particularly as he seemed to be clueless about the integration testing he was supposed to be managing. Every time she asked him a question, he told her he would get back to her. He never did get back to her, so she ended up figuring it out for herself or finding someone else to ask.

That was another problem. Clayton always seemed to come by when Mari was talking to anyone else, as though to protect her from the subversive influence of the other employees. Mari figured he could hear everything from his own corner cubicle. He'd stroll over, butt into the conversation, and remind them,

"We all have work to get on with." She'd taken to walking the long way round to the kitchen to get a coffee, so that she could at least have a conversation without him following her.

Her concern had escalated rapidly over the past week. Instead of his usual frayed khakis and blue polo shirt, Clayton started arriving at work in dark pants, a white shirt, and a tie that stayed around his neck until at least lunchtime. His fine blond hair was trimmed back above his ears and parted on one side. And then there was the aftershave. None of which she would have cared about in the least, if it hadn't been for a slowly rising sense of dread that she might be the cause of his transformation.

"Okey dokey. Mari, why don't you show me where you've got to?" Clayton cracked his arms behind his back and settled in to inspect Mari's screen. Mari started to describe what she'd been working on in the simplest terms she could manage. Beside her, Clayton became increasingly fidgety.

"Hey, Mari, want to hear some news?" He stretched his arm along the back of her chair and leaned in close, his voice pitched conspirator-level low.

She couldn't imagine any news from Clayton that she'd be interested in, but she nodded dutifully and wondered, not for the first time, whether she could ask to be transferred to another team.

The trouble was, it seemed too soon to be making a fuss. She'd been stunned when she found out she'd got the job, and she didn't want to give Clayton or the other managers any reason to decide they'd made a mistake. The job meant too much to her, and to her family. Her mother was thrilled that Mari was working for a high-profile company and setting a great example for her two younger sisters. And for reasons that Mari only half comprehended, her mother was also ecstatic that for the first time since the family had come to America twenty-five years earlier, a Velasquez would be paying taxes and contributing to the country's well-being. The families her mother nannied and cleaned for always paid cash, off the books.

"You know how I haven't been around as much this last week or so?"

Mari could feel Clayton's breath on the side of her hair as he spoke. She hunched forward over folded arms to gain a few inches of distance.

"Uh huh." She nodded again even though she hadn't noticed any letup in Clayton's visits.

"I've been talking with Doug over on Version 6. They want me to join the team."

Mari spun to face Clayton, dislodging his arm from the back of her chair.

"Wow, Version 6? Congratulations!"

She was genuinely impressed, and more than a little surprised. She knew Blahst was developing the next generation of its site, and the development team was handpicked by the CEO, Andrei Simenov, himself. Had she underestimated Clayton?

A sudden thought hit her. "Is that why the... I mean, I noticed you've been dressing..."

Clayton's chin jutted forward and he held up one arm so that the four small buttons on the sleeve of his jacket faced Mari.

"You like this?" A beam spread across his face.

Mari closed her eyes in relief. Clayton's change in behavior wasn't about her after all. He was just trying to make the right impression inside the company.

"Will you be moving to the other building?" She tried to keep the hope out of her voice.

"I told them I'll still need to be project manager over here— can't desert my team now, can I? I'll just split my time between the projects. So don't you worry, I'll still be able to keep a close eye on how you're doing."

"Yeah, that'll be great."

"Thing is..." Clayton placed a hand on the arm of her chair and inclined his head toward her. "I may have a chance to bring someone over with me."

Mari's relief froze in its tracks.

"I think you're pretty... uh... good at what you do," he continued. "So I was wondering if you might be interested in following me over. I mean, nothing's certain yet, but I like to encourage talent when I find it."

Mari's first instinct was to tell Clayton there wasn't a chance in hell she'd follow him anywhere, but she forced herself to consider the option. Clayton had told her outright that he'd been instrumental in hiring her. What if she was assigned to a new manager who didn't think she was good enough to work here? Plus, the opportunity to work on Version 6 would be huge for her career. She might even get a chance to work with Andrei Simenov himself. All logic pointed to joining Clayton in Version 6, so why was every fiber of her body screaming that it was a bad idea?

"Thanks," she mumbled. "I'll think about it."

"Excellent. Perhaps we could... uh... have a little drink after work. You know, to celebrate our new project." Behind his glasses, his eye squinted closed in what was unmistakably a wink.

A drink after work? Her breath caught in her throat as she realized that her earlier fears about Clayton's intentions were completely, revoltingly justified. On top of that, he seemed to have taken her vague response as an agreement to follow him to Version 6.

"I kind of have plans tonight," she lied.

"Oh." He didn't hide his disappointment. "Are you dating someone?"

Mari felt her eyes widen, caught off guard by the bluntness of the question. But suddenly she saw her way out.

"Yes," she lied again. "That's it."

"Oh. Well, maybe another time, we could plan—"

Mari was saved from Clayton's plans by a small foam ball, which flew over the cubicle partition, bounced off her screen, and landed on the floor by Clayton's shiny leather shoes.

"Hey, Mari!" a voice yelled from beyond her cubicle wall.

Mari rose from her chair and peered over the top of her cubicle. An angular face topped with short black hair jutted over the partitions a couple of rows down. Paolo, one of the other team leaders, was six feet two with a goofy smile and, to Mari's initial disappointment, a wedding band on his finger.

"I need a favor from you," Paolo called across the office. "We've got an indoor batting tournament tonight and need one more woman on the team or we'll be penalized—any chance you could play?"

The offer rang in her ears like a school bell announcing the beginning of recess. Finally, a chance to socialize with some colleagues outside of work. And Mari's home run record had helped her college softball team finish third in the nationals.

"I'd love to play. Thanks for inviting me," she called over to Paolo.

The words were out of her mouth before she remembered she'd just told Clayton she was busy tonight. She glanced back to see his face puckered in a tight frown.

"I mean, I did have plans, but this sounds like an emergency." Her mind raced to try to undo the snub. "I can rearrange my plans so I can play. This does sound important, so I can change the plans." As she listened to herself babbling, she decided she had better stop talking if she wanted any chance of redeeming a working relationship with Clayton.

"That's great—there are never enough women on the team. It's the place in Woburn, seven o'clock. Oh, and by the way, I used one of your test routines yesterday. Good stuff."

Paolo's head disappeared behind the dividers. Mari stared at the empty spot, relishing the unexpected praise. She didn't think Clayton had ever looked at her code, let alone figured out whether it was any good or not.

"That's right; we always need more girls." This came from another voice, which Mari didn't recognize, its owner hidden in the line of cubicles. "Hey, Clayton, maybe you could come too."

Mari heard a couple of snickers and felt a pang of guilt. She turned to see how Clayton was taking it, but he was gone.

Chapter 4

"SHIT, LENNY, WHAT HAVE YOU done with the budget?"

Lenny was just about done with level seven of *Glory Days*. With Professor Ramsey away in Burundi, he was having a harder time than usual finding useful ways to contribute to the smooth running of Healthway International. His fingers punched at the screen of his phone and a photorealistic gloved fist connected with a skeleton's head. A shower of crimson blood splattered across the display as though thrown at the inside of the screen. It slowly drained away to reveal the gloved crusader marching up the steps to a bejeweled door, the hard-won entrance to level eight.

"I can't believe they did that." Lenny pushed his phone to the middle of his desk, now piled high with papers, printouts, and books. "Started out good, but everyone knows skeletons don't bleed."

He felt a rough shove in the back of his shoulder and turned to face Roy. He'd barely noticed him coming into the office, he'd been so absorbed in the game.

"You got coffee?" he asked hopefully.

Roy waved the palm of his hand across Lenny's face. "Hello, are you listening? You've blown through our next three months of funding. What the hell did you do?"

Lenny stared at Roy in surprise. Roy was usually the calm one, the voice of reason. He seemed a little uptight today.

"No sweat. I was playing with some ideas from Professor Ramsey's book. You know how he talks about personalization as the key to spreading—"

"You were playing? You think what we do here is a game? There was thirty thousand dollars in that account. What, did you buy yourself some shiny new gadgets?"

Lenny looked into Roy's face, red with anger, and felt a surge of indignation. Surely his friend knew him better than that.

"What if I did?" he heard himself say.

"Then I hope you enjoy them, because there's no more money where that came from. Including our salaries."

"What do you mean?" Lenny felt a chill spread up his back.

"Washington's shut down our funding, and you spent every last nickel in the bank account. Actually, that's not true. There's about forty bucks left. Maybe you could get yourself a new game."

"But I thought that account was..." Lenny frowned. What had he thought, exactly? "I thought that money was just for supplies. That there were other accounts for..." He shrugged, trying to find words that would explain his actions. "For other stuff," he finished lamely.

Lenny slid down in his chair until the back of his head rested on its curved top. "If you must know, I spent it on condoms. They should be arriving in Burundi tomorrow."

Roy looked at Lenny incredulously. "You spent thirty thousand dollars on condoms?"

"You told me to take care of the order, so I did. But I thought we could try something... special."

Roy folded his arms and waited for Lenny to continue. Skepticism was etched across his face. Lenny sighed and closed down his game.

"Here, look at this." He brought up a window on his laptop that showed a chart with scattered patches of small dots.

"You know Professor Ramsey's theory is about hubs, right?" Lenny said. "You make ideas spread by persuading one person—an opinion leader—then that person acts as a hub to persuade others. But the trick is to find the right person. It's got to be someone who people respect."

"Yeah, I know this stuff. So what?"

"So, I built a computer simulation of how it works. Each hub reaches a different audience, with a different message. If I'm a fourteen-year-old girl, I'm not going to listen to the local midwife—I'm going to watch what the cool sixteen-year-olds around me do. Which means we have to find the coolest sixteen-year-old of all and persuade her first. The professor's been figuring out how to target the message for all these different groups. Like in those brochures you design—that's why there's twenty different versions."

Lenny pointed at a patch of dots on the screen. "This is what Healthway has been doing." He hit a key and the patches spread and darkened, then gradually faded back to their original size.

"Each group of dots is a hub. We're getting the word out, and it's helping," Lenny continued, "but it's not taking hold. It's not enough. Now take a look at this."

This time when Lenny hit the key, the patches spread as before but kept on growing and intersecting until they merged into a single mass of dense black dots. "See?" Lenny stepped back triumphantly so that Roy could better admire his work.

"Big deal," said Roy, arms still folded. "You made some nice charts."

"It's not just charts—it's a model, a simulation. All those dots are people, people who listened and understood."

"You mean all those dots are having safe sex?" Roy peered more closely at the screen.

"Yup."

"I'm jealous—how come they get all the action?"

Lenny glanced across at Roy, but the humor was wry, not forgiving. It was a start, though. Lenny was sure that if he could make Roy see the potential in his idea, his roommate wouldn't be so angry.

"That's where Healthway needs to get to," Lenny explained. "That's where all of Burundi needs to get to. We need to make the idea go viral. So I made some investments based on the model."

"What did you do?" The cynicism had returned to Roy's voice.

"We're finding the opinion leaders, and we're personalizing the messaging through your brochures. But it's not enough just to personalize the message— that's just words—you have to personalize the whole experience. That's where these come in."

Lenny picked up a brown envelope and emptied out a small pile of condoms, each in a different package. "See? Each one's targeted to a specific hub. Here, smell this."

Lenny pulled a neon-pink condom out of its cover and held it out. Roy leaned away and wrinkled his nose.

"Cotton candy?"

"Bubble gum, actually. That one's for those fourteen-year-olds. See, the names say it all. *Confidence*—that's for happy couples. *Discretion*—that one's for the hookers. *Stud*, *Endurance*—they're all different."

Roy stared down at the packages. "You sent these to Burundi?" he said evenly.

"Yeah, last week." As Lenny described what he'd done, a little of his confidence began to return. "When I worked on the computer models, they said if we could just improve condom usage by five percent, we'd get a ripple effect and there'd be a ninety-six percent probability the whole thing would go viral."

Roy picked up a black packet with a picture of a penis transforming into a gun. *Weapon* was written in silver along the barrel of the gun.

"That's a gay thing." Lenny paused. "I got half the packages translated into Kirundi, too, as an experiment. That cost extra."

"How much extra?"

"Well, with the different varieties... and it was a special order..." Lenny drew in a deep breath. "About five times as much as the old ones."

Roy crunched the package in his fist and threw it down with the others on Lenny's desk.

"Lenny, you've finally flipped out. We're talking about Africa here. These people are starving and their crops are failing. They don't have enough money for seed or fertilizer. Their kids catch malaria because they can't afford a piece of netting to protect them. And you're worrying about bubble gum flavor? This isn't Saturday night in Vegas."

The silence hung heavy and long. Lenny knew that Roy was right. He'd become so involved in his simulations he'd lost touch with what they really meant. What did his computer model know about poverty and passion, about disease and desires? Models weren't the real world. They were just like his games—skeletons that couldn't really bleed.

"What do you think Professor Ramsey will say?"

"I don't suppose it matters if he fires us or not." Roy slumped into his chair. "He can't pay us anyway."

"I'll tell him it wasn't your fault."

"He left me in charge. I know I said you should put the usual condom order in, but I didn't mean... Why didn't you talk to me first?"

"I might have if you hadn't been missing in action. You were a little preoccupied last week if you remember."

"Oh, yeah." A faint smile came over Roy's face. "That was Mandy."

Lenny shook his head. In the two years since he'd answered Roy's ad for a roommate, he'd watched a steady stream of girl-friends drift in and out of Roy's life. Mandy was the latest infatuation—a postgrad whom Roy had met at an Emerson College poetry slam.

"The Burundi team was screaming for supplies." Lenny stacked the sample condom packets into a small pile on his desk. "They've got a big community education thing next week, and they said they couldn't do anything without the condoms. So I used my initiative like Professor Ramsey told me to."

"Thirty thousand dollars is a lot of initiative." Roy exhaled deeply. "I don't know how we're going to break it to him. He'll fight to get our funding back, of course. But it could take a while, and he won't be back from Burundi for a couple of weeks. At least he's already got his return ticket, not that you would have bothered to check before you made your investments."

Lenny's forehead furrowed. "Maybe I can get the money back by then."

"Good idea," Roy laughed bitterly. "You could sell a few thousand slightly used condoms on eBay. 'Only one previous owner.' That should work."

Lenny sank further down into his chair and rotated it slowly from one side to the other. His eyes stayed fixed on his desk and the brightly colored square packages that seemed to jeer at him with their festivity.

Roy suddenly looked over at Lenny with a puzzled expression. "How did you get at the funds, anyway? There are preset limits on all our orders. Isn't there some kind of password protection on the bank account?"

"Yeah, there was."

The sound that escaped from Roy's throat was halfway between a snort and a groan.

Lenny tried to focus on the row of books in front of him, searching for the title the professor had asked him to get before his return, but his mind kept returning to the look of accusation in Roy's eyes. Lenny knew how much Roy loved his job at Healthway. He'd interned there since his junior year, and started full time the day he graduated. He lived for the field trips to Africa and was always talking about the professor's exploits. Roy had put his own reputation on the line in recommending Lenny, and it had taken all of four weeks for Lenny to blow it for both of them.

The book was supposed to be here somewhere; the Barnes & Noble computer said they had one in stock. He usually ordered online but had wanted to get out of the office. There was something calming about a real-world bookstore—the ordered shelves and the respectful, muted voices—that Lenny needed right now.

Thirty thousand dollars. What was he thinking? But he hadn't been thinking; that was the problem. He'd been so focused on proving that his simulation worked, he hadn't thought about the consequences.

Now he'd be out of a job. And if Roy was fired, they wouldn't be able to pay the rent. A gnawing sensation spread up from his stomach as he thought of another possibility. What if the professor pressed charges? Misappropriation of funds or dereliction of duty or something? He ran his fingers along the row of book spines in front of him, trying to ground himself and slow his pounding heart.

"Lenny?"

He turned sharply to the source of the voice, momentarily blinded by a stream of light.

"It is you! Hi, Lenny."

A young woman was silhouetted at the end of the aisle. Bright sunlight from the window framed her dark, wavy hair in a halo of white. She was dressed in a baggy, grey sweatshirt over a pair of faded jeans. She took a tentative step toward him and, as the bookshelves blocked the glare of the light, he recognized the face.

Mari Velasquez. Just when he thought things couldn't get any worse.

Chapter 5

LENNY HADN'T MEANT TO INVITE Mari for coffee. The words had just blurted out in the awkward silence that followed their hellos. But now that she was sitting in a straight-backed chair in front of him, he realized he had been presented with a perfect, serendipitous opportunity. If he wanted another chance to land a job at Blahst, wouldn't it be a good idea to know someone who worked there?

Quickly looking around, Lenny noticed that the Barnes & Noble café was almost deserted. He regretted his choice of an armchair, which seemed to be trying to lure him into a relaxation he didn't feel.

As he contemplated how to raise the subject of a job, Mari took the lid off her coffee and blew into the froth. She said, "So, I saw on your Blahst page that you're doing some work with Africa. That sounds cool. What have they got you doing?"

Lenny paused before answering, unsure if she was patronizing him. How cool could third-world healthcare be, next to Blahst? He decided to give her the benefit of the doubt.

"We design campaigns on AIDS prevention for third-world countries. We're doing some work in Burundi. I work on... ah... I'm writing some programs for the finance department at the moment."

"Yeah? Fundraising and stuff?"

"That kind of thing." Lenny decided not to mention that he seemed to be better at spending funds than raising them.

"Do you get to go to Burundi?"

"I don't know," said Lenny. "My roommate's been there a few times for photo shoots. He got me the job." Lenny pushed himself upright on the armchair as he saw an opening for his question. "Speaking of jobs..." He took a breath and tried to make his interest sound casual. "How's it going at Blahst?"

Mari shrugged. "It's okay, I guess."

"It's okay? You're working at Blahst, and it's just *okay*?"

"I think it'll get better."

"As long as they're not all like that guy running the interview." Lenny shook his head. "Remember him?"

"Clayton."

"Yeah, Clayton. Couldn't program his way out of a paper bag."

"He's my manager."

Lenny spat out a laugh. "I wouldn't work for that shithead if you paid me."

He sensed Mari's body tighten as she sat upright in her chair.

"Good thing they didn't offer you the job then."

Lenny felt heat rising to his face. He tried to think of a sarcastic comeback, but the sight of Mari glaring across at him, her arms folded across her chest, made him clamp his mouth shut against further damage. He wondered again at his inexplicable skill for pissing off women.

"I'm sorry, that was low." Mari looked down at her coffee. "You're really good. You just... had a bad day." She ran a hand through her hair. Lenny noticed how the dark waves draped over the shoulders of her sweatshirt, so different from the slicked-back ponytail of the interview.

"Yeah, well, at least I learned something for my next job interview," he mumbled.

"What's that?"

"Not to call the interviewer a moron."

Lenny watched Mari's dark lips relax into a smile. He liked the way they looked without makeup.

"Actually, he *is* a moron." Mari's smile faded. She paused and seemed to be deciding whether to say more. "He follows me around. Doesn't like me talking to anyone else."

"He's a micromanager." Lenny had never had a manager, but he'd read the word somewhere and it seemed to fit here. "I know the type."

"Yeah, maybe." Mari clasped her slim hands around her coffee cup as if for warmth. Her air of vulnerability inspired a sudden and uncharacteristic flash of gallantry in Lenny.

"Well, if he ever bothers you, give me a call." Lenny leaned back onto the cushions and enjoyed the way the words sounded. "I'd be more than happy to finish the argument."

Mari laughed. "Thanks. That's an argument I wouldn't want to miss. But it's okay; he's being transferred to another project, so hopefully I won't see him as much." She leaned forward on the table. "You know, I'm glad we did this. Had coffee I mean. Especially as I know you don't... that is, I know you didn't like me much at school."

"What makes you say that?" Lenny was genuinely surprised. Mari had always seemed disdainful toward him during the four years they'd spent in Boston University's computer science department, so he'd never had much to do with her. Why would she think he hadn't liked her, even if it was true?

"Just that time in our freshman year, I suppose. You remember."

Lenny racked his brains for an encounter with Mari in his first year at BU, but nothing came to mind. He could remember passing her in the hallway after class sometimes, seeing her in the middle of a group of girlfriends and often a couple of guys, but he hadn't paid much attention.

"Not really. Remind me."

"In Professor Siegler's class the first semester. He called on me for an answer—it was Shannon's Theory—and I hadn't read the homework, so I made something up. Then you gave the right answer and proved to the whole class how mine was totally impossible. You must have thought I was pretty dumb."

Lenny frowned. He couldn't remember the incident, but it sounded exactly like the kind of thing he would have done that freshman year. He'd been intimidated by the friendly, confident students as they discussed the world affairs and student politics that he was oblivious to. He'd aced every science and engineering class in his path but he still felt like a fraud as he tried to fit in with the intellectual campus atmosphere. He remembered how he had tried to impress the professors whenever the opportunity arose—it hadn't occurred to him that he might intimidate other people along the way. Had Mari been scared of him, not disdainful at all?

"I guess I used to be a bit of a jerk sometimes," he admitted.

"Yeah, good job you've changed." Mari raised her eyebrows but continued before he could respond. "It taught me a lesson, anyway. I always read the homework assignments after that. In fact, I probably owe my good grades to you."

Lenny wondered whether that was another jab about her getting the job instead of him but decided to let it go. As they sipped their coffee in silence, he thought about how to broach the favor he wanted to ask.

"I was wondering..." He cleared his throat and swallowed. "Do you think you could introduce me to a couple of the guys at Blahst? I thought it might help, you know, if I apply again." He dropped his eyes. "But I understand if you don't want to. I mean..."

He felt Mari's gaze probing his face. "Sure, why not," she said finally. "Do you play softball?"

"Meh." Lenny wrinkled his top lip. Sports had never been his strong point.

"I'll find some way." Mari pushed her coffee cup aside and leaned forward on the table. "Tell me more about Burundi."

Lenny told her about Healthway and about Professor Ramsey's work on hubs and opinion leaders. He told her about the simulations he'd created and how he'd applied his ideas on personalization, although he stopped short of telling her about his snafu with the budget. That wasn't something he'd be including in his next job application to Blahst.

When the server came over and told them the store was closing, he walked her to her car. Watching her drive away in a sky-blue VW Beetle, Lenny reflected that she wasn't quite as bad as he'd thought. It wouldn't be too terrible if he had to see her again. Just as a way to get a job at Blahst, of course.

"The trouble with Burundi is, they don't have enough cell phones." Lenny sat on his desk and kicked his chair round in slow circles with one outstretched leg.

"What, now you're going to buy them free nights and weekends to go with their designer contraception?" Roy peered intently at his screen and traced the outline of a blurry arm that had encroached at the edge of the photo he was editing.

"What I mean is, there's no way to spread the message. The villages are too remote. You can find your opinion leader, you can personalize the message, but it doesn't spread far. They're just not connected enough."

"You finally noticed. Welcome to Planet Earth."

Roy cropped the arm out of the photo and blended the area seamlessly into the background. In the center of the image a mother held her baby tight against her chest, its head leaning against her cheek as she looked down at it with eyes that were beyond despair. Behind her, the grey dirt faded in the distance to a range of low mountains.

Lenny picked up his phone and idly brought the screen to life. He opened the browser and checked out his Blahst page—five invitations to friend people he'd never met and a bunch of photos and video links from people he didn't care about.

"See, some YouTube video of a surfing warthog gets fifty million downloads all over the world, but in Burundi most of the population can't even text their friends." He shook his head. The more he researched, the more he realized how little he really knew about how things worked on the other side of the planet. He tried to imagine living a whole day without his phone. Or even an hour.

Roy looked up from his terminal. "Surfing warthog? Haven't seen that one." Lenny pulled up the short video snippet and held it up for Roy to watch.

"Crazy." Roy chuckled and returned to his photo. He circled the cursor carefully, and a glaring reflection of sunlight on the woman's forehead faded to a light brown. With a few more clicks, the picture cycled through the color spectrum before settling into a crimson hue that made the sky behind the mountains glow with blood-red streaks.

Lenny watched in admiration. "That looks just like a sunset."

"A little bit of Photoshop, a whole lot of talent," Roy replied. He stepped back to check his work, then clicked once more and the printer started humming.

Lenny felt a wave of frustration as he thought about what would happen when Professor Ramsey returned in a few days. He'd resigned himself to the fact that he was going to be fired, but it sucked that he might be taking Roy with him, too.

Lenny wondered if perhaps they could both apply for jobs at Blahst. It would be a long shot, but Roy was great at what he did and had an excellent track record. Lenny—well, he didn't have to mention everything that had happened here at Healthway. He could just tell them the bare essentials and they'd come to their own conclusions, like Mari Velasquez had done when she'd thought he was fundraising...

He sat bolt upright and his chair shot across the linoleum.

"Roy, I can get the money back."

Roy rolled his eyes and carried on inspecting the printout of his photo.

"Fundraising," explained Lenny with growing excitement.

"That's a hell of a big bake sale."

"I mean it." Lenny jumped off the desk. "We can't reach people in Burundi, but we can here."

Roy turned to face Lenny. "Look, I know you're trying to help, but it takes money to raise money. You've got to pay for advertising, call centers, printing services—"

"I know a better way. I'll write some programs based on my simulation. I can search people's blogs and Facebook and Twitter feeds and Blahst pages to find the ones that might care about helping Africa. I can analyze all the links and pointers to see who's the most influential—I can find the opinion leaders, Roy. I can figure out what kind of people they are and personalize the messages. All the information's already there."

Roy frowned. "If you've got to look at everyone's Facebook and Blahst pages, that's a shitload of work."

"I'm not going to search it all myself, you dork." Considering how good Roy was at digital photography, Lenny was constantly surprised by how little his roommate knew about what was going on behind the screen.

"I told you, I'm going to write programs—algorithms to analyze it automatically. That way it's completely scalable. I can hit thousands of people at once. Then they'll tell their friends and I can make it go viral."

"Is that legal?" Roy eyed Lenny with suspicion.

"Why wouldn't it be?"

"I don't know. Aren't there anti-spam laws or something?"

It was Lenny's turn to frown. "I don't think that would apply, because I'll personalize the messages. But you're right, the spam filters might block it, so I'll have to... let me think." He pulled his laptop closer and typed himself some notes.

"We usually get money through grants, but we have some sponsors in the Boston Marathon," Roy mused, "so I suppose it would be okay to do some fundraising. But you'll have to wait until Professor Ramsey gets back from Burundi."

"The whole point is to get some of the money back before he comes home. That way he won't be so mad, and you might still have a job."

Roy looked dubious, but Lenny could see that his last comment had hit home.

"Are you sure it won't cost anything?" Roy asked.

"Not a dime. Everything we need is right here." Lenny patted his keyboard. "Anyway, I already put some extra security on the purchasing software so I can't spend any more money without you or the professor approving it. It needs at least two digital signatures to write a check."

"You're protecting the bank account against yourself? That sounds like one of those fox-babysitting-the-chicken deals. Are you sure you didn't leave some kind of backdoor?"

"It's solid," Lenny replied. "I used two-hundred-and-fifty-six-bit encryption—I can't hack that."

"That's the best protected empty bank account I ever heard of."

Lenny jumped back into his chair and pulled it up to his desk. "If I can figure this out, it won't be empty for long."

As he pulled up the code for his simulations, Lenny sensed Roy's hesitation.

"Don't worry," Lenny reassured him. "Even I can't screw up good old-fashioned fundraising, can I?"

Chapter 6

"DUDE, IF IT'S NOT OPEN source, I don't want to know."

"Just wait till you try their new platform. You'll change your mind."

"No way. You should take a look at what the Open Friday group's doing. They've got fifty thousand developers..."

Lenny heard the conversation drifting above the low, synthesized beat of the music. All around him, Blahst employees and their friends and families mingled beneath the giant crystal chandeliers, filling the grand ballroom of the Four Seasons almost to capacity. Some were in business suits, some wore the business casual uniform of khaki pants, and a few, Lenny was glad to see, were dressed as he was in jeans smartened up with a respectable shirt. At the front of the room behind a large podium, the Blahst logo rotated slowly across an array of screens that stretched across the wall.

He tried to focus on what the woman in front of him was saying, even though he was dying to set the guy behind him straight about the programming platform they were discussing. He'd tried it himself recently and it really wasn't—

"So, Lenny, you were at Boston University too?" The woman was tall, with hair pulled up into a bun. A heavy turquoise pendant lay over a high-necked sweater with no sleeves. Lenny forced himself to listen to her as he puzzled over the functional logic of the sweater. She said, "I got my Masters in International Relations at BU. Do they still have that amazing frozen yogurt place—what was it, Angora?"

"I don't know... yeah, I think it's still there."

Lenny's brain raced for something more to say, something impressive. Mari, true to her word from their meeting in Barnes & Noble, had called yesterday and invited him to Blahst's launch party for Version 6 so he could meet some people from the company. Lenny had accepted with more than a little trepidation, which had intensified when they'd arrived to the laughter and swirl of a party in full swing. After a few minutes of peppering Lenny with questions about Burundi, Mari had noticed they were standing near the Head of Human Talent Management and had taken the opportunity to present Lenny and his credentials. Now he could feel Mari beside him, waiting for him to stun this woman with his intellect so that she'd want to hire him on the spot.

"I think I had a sandwich there once," he said.

"Oh yes, those wonderful wraps." She nodded at Lenny and took a sip from her wine glass. Lenny nodded back and tried to think of what to say next. Mari finally broke the silence and started chatting with the woman until several newcomers drifted up and Lenny found himself at the edge of the group, straining to hear the conversation.

Mari spoke softly in Lenny's ear and tugged at his shirt sleeve. "Come on, let's get a drink."

She greeted several people by name as they made their way over to the bar. A waiter blocked Lenny's path and held out a silver tray filled with small pastries. Lenny tried to find one that didn't involve fish roe and failed. He declined and hurried after Mari. She was already holding two bottles of Sam Adams, each · wrapped in a napkin to mop up the dripping condensation.

"The only decent beer they had," she said, handing him a bottle. "Unless you wanted wine?"

"No, this is great." He took a long drink and felt the cold liquid start to soothe the embarrassment of his last encounter. "Sorry about... back there with the human resource lady, I wasn't very..."

"You were fine," Mari reassured him. "At least she knows who you are now." She raised herself up on her toes and peered around the room, frowning. "I don't see anyone I know. Wait, there's a guy I played softball with. I guess we can say hi to him."

Lenny trailed behind Mari as she wove her way through the crowds. He nodded and smiled and tried to look like he belonged there.

Mari joined a group of twenty-something men and women lodged around one of the buffet tables, straining the waiters' ability to replenish the sushi platters.

"My softball colleagues," she said to Lenny, before introducing him to each of the group in turn. He shook hands, smiled, and instantly forgot everyone's name. A platter of shrimp appeared in front of him and he shook his head.

He looked around the room at all these people who had made the cut to work at Blahst. What did they have that he didn't? They were no smarter than he was, Lenny was sure about that. So how come they got to eat shrimp and caviar in a fancy hotel while he and Roy made do with pizza in an office building that should have been condemned?

He watched Mari talking with her colleagues. She looked stunning in a fitted purple blouse with black pants that flared at the ankle over slim black boots. She tried a couple of times to include Lenny in the conversation, but he couldn't think of anything interesting to say. He felt himself zoning out as the topic turned to the latest management reorganization. He finished his beer, excused himself, and headed off for a refill.

Before he reached the bar, he noticed a bank of computer terminals off to the left, stretching down to the podium at the end of the ballroom. A couple of them were in use, but most were idle. Lenny approached the nearest one and saw the familiar

Blahst site with a pop-up window offering to give a tour of the new features.

Lenny sat down to give Version 6 a test run.

Mari looked around for Lenny and saw him engrossed in a computer screen over by the wall. *No surprises there,* she thought. She'd been a little worried about bringing Lenny to the launch party, and she was starting to feel that her fears were well founded. It was a strain to keep introducing him to people she didn't know that well herself, and even more of a strain to keep the conversation going when he stood there like a piece of furniture. At the coffee shop he'd seemed kind of cute, but now she couldn't think why she had felt that way.

She decided to relax for the rest of the evening with her new colleagues. At the office, Paolo's team had seemed to adopt her like a little sister, especially now that Clayton's assignment to Version 6—an assignment that he had chosen not to share with her after all—was keeping him away from her area for most of the day. She would spend the rest of the evening with them. She'd delivered on her promise to Lenny by bringing him here; now the rest was up to him.

Mari was excited to hear a voice over the loudspeaker introduce Andrei Simenov, Blahst's President and Chief Executive Officer. The room lights darkened, and Andrei Simenov strolled on the stage to loud applause, cheering, and a few whistles. His slight frame somehow seemed to fill the stage, and the room grew quiet. Everyone had heard of this legend of the high-tech industry. His was the archetypal American success story: the penniless immigrant who had turned his PhD thesis into one of the largest corporations in the world.

Mari looked over at Lenny and was surprised to see that he didn't even look up from the screen—not many people had seen Andrei Simenov in the flesh.

Andrei started off hesitantly in his accented English, seemingly shy of the attention as he welcomed everyone to the event. A brief recap of Blahst's meteoric rise followed, highlighting the way the company's fast-paced innovation had headed off Google and Facebook. He spoke of some recent deals with major retailers that would cement their position as the only social network that really mattered.

Andrei paced to the front of the podium and expounded on the powerful personalization features of Version 6 that would keep them well ahead of the competition. His accent grew more pronounced as the passion flowed into his words, and Mari felt herself captivated by a sense of pride at the phenomenon of which she was now a part. The respect she'd been receiving from the other programmers was helping her feel more secure in her job, and she knew she would have other opportunities to advance her career that didn't involve Clayton.

"Hey, Mari, I need to talk to you." The whisper belonged to Lenny.

"Sure. Let's wait until after the speech," she whispered back.

"No, we need to talk now. It's important." His voice rose slightly, and the woman in front of them, whom Mari recognized as the VP of Marketing, turned her head to frown at him.

Mari leaned over to Lenny's ear and whispered as quietly as she could, "Can't it wait five minutes? He hardly ever talks in public."

"Come on, Mari." He was no longer even attempting to whisper. More heads turned and Mari looked away to avoid their annoyed glares.

Lenny was tugging her agitatedly in the direction of the exit. She was torn between ignoring him to hear Andrei's speech, and going with him to avoid a scene. As she hesitated, Lenny turned to look her full in the face and spoke loudly and urgently.

"They stole my fucking algorithm, Mari."

A sea of heads turned to look at them, and Mari felt like melting into the soft pile of the carpet. Why was Lenny doing this to her, in front of her new colleagues, and just when she had a chance to hear Andrei Simenov in person? The VP shushed them sharply, and the heads gradually turned back toward the stage. Mari let Lenny lead her toward the back of the room. The guests shifted to let them pass without taking their eyes from Andrei.

As they reached the exit, Lenny pulled Mari through the open doorway into the wide hallway. Mari looked at him in exasperation as she waited for him to explain. *This had better be good*, she thought.

"Version 6 uses my algorithm," he exploded.

"What are you talking about?" Mari felt her heart pounding as she realized how little she really knew about Lenny. Was he using her to come here and stir up trouble because they hadn't given him a job?

"You remember that algorithm I wrote for the interview? The one that personalized automatic status updates?"

"Sure."

"It's there, in Version 6."

Mari's brain scanned through what Andrei had just said about the features of Version 6. He had mentioned something about new levels of personalization—could he be referring to Lenny's algorithm? But that made no sense. Blahst was famous for its innovation, and it had thousands of developers. They didn't need to steal ideas from anyone.

"Lenny, they've been working on this product for a year. It's just a coincidence."

"Bullshit. I can't get inside the code to see if they did it exactly the same way, but it's so..." Lenny's words trailed off and Mari saw his focus shift to something in the hallway behind her.

Mari turned to see Clayton plodding out of the banquet hall with an empty glass. He peered at the signs around the walls and headed in the direction of the men's restroom. As he caught sight of Lenny and Mari, he straightened the front of his jacket with a downward wipe of his hands and started toward them with an enthusiasm that reminded Mari of her neighbor's Jack Russell closing in on a squirrel.

Mari felt an involuntary groan inside her throat. She glanced around to see if they could escape with a quick, "Hey, how's it going," but Clayton had them trapped.

"Mari, how are you?" Clayton greeted Mari like a long-lost friend. She was afraid he might hug her, but instead he thrust out a hand toward Lenny.

"You must be Mari's... oh." Clayton's outstretched hand froze as recognition passed over his face. "From the interview, right? Let me see... Larry?"

Lenny ignored the hand.

"This is Lenny," said Mari.

"Oh right. Did you, uh..." Clayton paused and looked around the empty foyer behind him. "Did you get a job here or something?"

"He came with me. He works at Healthway; they're a not-for-profit. They do amazing work in Burundi. He's written this whole suite of fundraising software..." Mari trailed off, not liking how defensive she was sounding. She didn't need to justify herself to Clayton.

"Charity work, how admirable." Clayton seemed to relax as he addressed himself to Lenny. "It's probably for the best. Blahst doesn't seem like a great fit for you—no offense—but you know what I mean." He chuckled lightly. "Mari's settling in just great here. I've been helping her out, but she catches on quite quickly. We have put in some late nights though, haven't we, Mari?"

Clayton squinted a wink and Mari wondered what on earth he was talking about. Late nights? She'd stayed back once with another teammate when they'd had a tight deadline, but Clayton had fallen asleep in his office until they were done. With a thud of realization, Mari remembered telling Clayton that she had a boyfriend. He'd obviously come to the wrong conclusion about why she was here with Lenny.

"Don't feel bad about the interview, Lenny," Clayton continued. "We have pretty high standards here, so not everyone makes the cut. Still, perhaps you could try another time. When you've got a bit more experience—"

Lenny grabbed Clayton by the collar and swung him round against the wall. Clayton's head banged onto the embossed silver wallpaper and his mouth opened sharply, but no sound came out.

"Lenny, what the hell?" Mari tried to pull Lenny's arm away but it was locked tight against Clayton's chest. Was he trying to completely ruin her reputation at Blahst? She looked around to see if anyone had noticed. A couple of guys she didn't know were watching with interest, but thankfully most of the company was still listening to the speech inside the ballroom.

Lenny held his grip and pulled Clayton toward him before releasing him roughly and sending him thudding back against the wallpaper. From the corner of her eye, Mari saw a uniformed security guard striding toward them with his head cocked to one side as though unsure of what he had just seen. Before the man could reach them, Lenny stormed across the hall toward the staircase.

The guard followed Lenny a short way down the staircase. He stopped to speak with muffled tones into his walkie-talkie as Lenny disappeared toward the hotel exit. Clayton straightened his collar and scurried away to the restroom.

Mari was left alone at the edge of the foyer. She realized her body was rigid, her fists clenched against her legs. She forced herself to relax as she figured out what to do next.

She could hear the applause for Andrei's closing words echoing from the ballroom. She should go back in with her colleagues and forget about Lenny before he caused any more trouble in her life. But his words bothered her—was it possible that the personalization in Version 6 was the same as his algorithm from the interview? She pictured Lenny sitting in the interview room explaining his idea, his eyes blazing with enthusiasm. Should she go after him and try to find out more?

She shook her head. She couldn't believe Blahst would take his idea—she'd received a whole day of ethics training during her first week, and everyone seemed genuinely concerned to "do what you know is right," as the company motto bade them.

Lenny must be mistaken. Or possibly even delusional. He certainly seemed unstable, the way he'd gone after Clayton.

She resolved not to let the episode ruin her evening. She suddenly craved normal conversation, sushi, and another beer. She took a deep breath and strode back into the ballroom, letting the energy of the music and laughter drive away any more thoughts of Lenny Driver and Clayton Malloy.

Chapter 7

"YOU HAVE TO SUE THEM. That's not right." Roy twisted the tops off two bottles of Michelob Light and handed one to Lenny.

Lenny took the beer and sank back sideways across the armchair, his head and shoulders leaning on one threadbare arm and his legs dangling over the other. He'd had a couple of beers before Roy arrived back at the apartment, and his head was starting to buzz.

"Hell yeah, I'll sue. Andrei Simenov has a few billion to spare."

"You're sure it's your idea, though?" asked Roy.

"Check for yourself." Lenny nodded over at his laptop, which sat in a small clearing on the kitchen counter. Around it, a mismatched collection of used plates, mugs, and silverware fought against piles of unopened mail and catalogues for possession of the precious surface space.

"That's my Blahst page." Roy peered at the text and images on the screen. "Hey, I didn't post all that stuff."

"It's the new Blahst autofeed feature they released today. Part of Version 6."

"It says here, 'I'm having a wicked good time at the Joshua Tree.' How did it know I was there? And how did it know I wasn't having a shitty evening?"

"I enabled auto-locate and auto-post in your Blahst settings. You must have posted from the Joshua Tree other times you were there, and the system learned that you usually have a good time."

"Yeah, I do. But I never say 'wicked good.'"

"Yeah, you do."

Roy pushed his beer onto the counter and folded his arms. "You could have asked before you changed my account settings. And hacked my password." He read through the rest of the postings. "Anyway, you still don't know that Blahst didn't come up with the same idea themselves."

"I didn't hack your password. You use the same one for everything. Mojo0412."

Roy's face fell pensive. "Mojo was my dog growing up."

"And your birthday, that's real secure. Anyway, that's not the point. See here..." Lenny pulled himself out of the chair and crossed to the laptop. "These two posts—'Chilling on Highland Ave' then 'Chilling on Elm St.' That's exactly what I used as a placeholder in my algorithm. If it's a new location, just post 'chilling.' What are the chances of Blahst coming up with that too?" Lenny dropped back sideways across the armchair.

"Not likely." Roy shook his head. "That's not a coincidence." He flopped into the sofa opposite Lenny and chugged his beer. "By the way, we got a couple of checks today at the office. I stopped by this morning."

Lenny raised his head enough to take a drink of his beer. "It's Saturday."

"I know. I needed to finish something up for the brochure."

"Who were the checks from?"

"Don't know. Looks like your fundraising is working. One was for a thousand dollars."

Lenny tried to sit up straight but his back was trapped in the seat of the chair. "A thousand dollars?"

Lenny's astonishment was interrupted by his phone buzzing on the coffee table. He reached out one arm out to pick it up and the screen announced a call from Mari Velasquez. As his brain debated whether to answer it or not, his finger moved to touch the green *Answer* button.

"Hope I didn't wake you," Mari's voice greeted him from the other end.

"I'm not feeling sleepy," he replied.

He heard Mari take a deep breath before she spoke again.

"I talked to the product manager. Of Version 6."

Lenny waited.

"I mentioned the thing about the interview," she continued. "How you thought it might be your algorithm."

Lenny's fingers drummed slowly on the arm of the chair as he waited out the silence. He didn't see why he should make this easy for her. She clearly hadn't believed him earlier.

"He says he'll look into it."

"That's it?" Lenny burst out. "Why do they have to look into anything, when they know they stole it from me? Fuck them." He was just about to end the call when her next words caught his attention. He lifted the phone back to his ear.

"There's something else," her voice was saying. "Even if it's true about the algorithm, I'm not sure there's anything you can do. Lenny, are you there?"

"I'm here."

"Remember the papers we signed going into the interview?"

"Sure." Lenny remembered several sheets of small and nearly illegible font that had required his signature and a date at the bottom.

"Did you read them?"

"Course not."

"Well, I did." Mari paused for a second and Lenny heard her draw another deep breath. "Lenny, you signed away your rights to anything you created during the course of the interview process. I'm sorry."

Lenny felt a wave of anger course through his body. He'd been joking about suing them, but he'd thought he might be able to get something out of it. Even if it was just public recognition that he was the author of the idea. That was only fair. But Blahst obviously had other plans, ones that didn't include him. How could they think that Lenny Driver wasn't good enough to work at Blahst, yet his idea was good enough to launch to millions of people in Version 6?

"Lenny, you okay?"

"Sure." Lenny didn't trust himself to say much. Perhaps Mari was in on it too—she'd read his algorithm at the interview. Her and Clayton. They were all in it together, them and their precious Andrei Simenov. Fuck the lot of them.

"I'm sorry," she repeated. "Don't do anything stupid, okay?"

"What, me?" said Lenny softly, and disconnected the call.

As Roy knocked an empty beer bottle off the edge of his desk for the third time, Lenny swept up an armful of empties and dumped them into the recycling bin in the cramped nook that passed for a kitchen. He grabbed a couple of fresh beers as he passed the fridge and returned to see what Roy was creating on the screen.

The photo showed a smiling Andrei Simenov standing next to a slightly more serious Osama bin Laden. Andrei was reaching across to shake bin Laden's raised hand. A Kalashnikov rifle was resting at his feet.

"That's awesome." Lenny took a drink of beer as he pulled up a chair to admire Roy's work. "Show me the rest."

Roy flipped through the images on the screen, his hand able to move freely around the mouse pad now that the empty bottles were gone. A series of smiling Andrei Simenovs paraded across the screen—Andrei passing an uneven, hand-rolled joint to a wild-haired teenager at his side, Andrei brandishing a chainsaw in a dense rain forest, Andrei reaching out to put a dollar bill into a waitress's panties at a topless bar.

Lenny felt laughter building through the blackness of his mood. The tensions of the day dissolved as he cracked up at the images. Roy clicked to a full-color photo of Andrei naked in a field of sheep, and Lenny felt himself slide off the chair, clutching his stomach as a fresh spasm of laughter took control.

"How about these," Roy continued enthusiastically. The smiling face was replaced with a frowning Andrei in a series of grainy photos. Andrei raising his hand to strike a cowering child, Andrei thrusting his finger at a policeman's chest at an anti-abortion rally, Andrei on the podium at a white supremacist meeting.

Lenny sat on the floor for a moment longer and looked at the sinister images.

"The world needs to see these," he decided. "Andrei Simenov, finally unveiled."

"Everyone would know they were fakes," Roy pointed out.

"Course they would. But if people thought they were funny and passed them on, it would still embarrass him."

"You'd be better off getting a lawyer. At least you might get something out of it."

"What's the point? They've probably got hundreds of lawyers. I wouldn't stand a chance." Lenny picked himself up and swayed over to his own laptop on the kitchen counter. The room was rotating in an uncomfortable way, so he took another drink of beer to ward off the feeling. "You said the fundraising was starting to work, right?"

"Yeah, why?" Roy sounded dubious

"I could do something similar with these pictures."

"No, I don't want these going out. I've got my profshh... professional reputation to think about." Roy enunciated the words slowly but couldn't stop the slur in his speech.

"Nobody would know it was you. That's the whole point of what I did with the fundraising, remember?" Lenny looked impatiently at Roy, but Roy's expression remained blank.

"Look, I'll show you again." Lenny clicked an icon on his laptop screen and waited while the cursor flashed busy. "Step one. We find opinion leaders. The hubs, remember that? People who influence other people, because they're cool, they're smart, they're persuasive, they're fun, whatever. People who are connected. We're looking for the people with the most followers or friends or the most links to their blog, stuff like that. I'll start with Blahst accounts, but I can do Twitter, Instagram, all of them."

Lenny could feel the excitement start to cut through the fog of the alcohol. He punched some keys and broke into the file the program was creating. It listed a couple hundred account names. That was enough to get started—he would add more later.

"Step two. We're going to find what these people are into," he explained. "Where they've lived, where they went to school, where they go on vacation, what organizations they donate to, what they spend their money on."

"You're going to hack their accounts?"

"Will you stop assuming I'm hacking everything?" Lenny spread his arms in exasperation. "This shit is all over the web. It's all public. Even if it's not on Blahst, it's out there somewhere—the soccer results from the local high school team or some tagged photos from a concert." He put a hand on his stomach to settle a faint ripple of nausea and realized he hadn't eaten since lunchtime. "Hey, you want to drive over to Wang's and get some takeout?"

Roy frowned. "No, I don't. We've had a few beers in case you hadn't noticed. I'm not driving anywhere and neither are you." He wandered into the kitchen nook and poured two bowls of Frosted Flakes with milk. He put one bowl on the counter next to Lenny, who grabbed the spoon with his left hand while continuing to work the mouse with his other.

"This part of the program right here... it creates groups of opinion leaders who are interested in the same topic. Say we did want to send out your photos—one of our targets would be opinion leaders who cared about the environment. We'd send out your photo of Andrei cutting down the rainforest to them, and they'd post it for their gazillion followers to see. It's the personalization that makes it sticky."

"Sticky?"

"Sticky. It's a technical term," said Lenny, taking a mouthful of cereal. "It means the message sticks."

"Sticky," said Roy again, and broke out laughing. His mirth was infectious, and Lenny found himself joining in mid-mouthful.

Half-chewed Frosted Flakes splattered out over the keyboard, and they laughed even harder.

A beep from Lenny's computer drew their attention back to the screen. Lenny wiped the keyboard with his shirt sleeve and started typing again.

"Step three is the real genius. I built on the idea I had at the Blahst interview about mimicking someone's online voice. You know, *wicked good*. The idea those jerks stole."

"I don't say *wicked good*."

"We want to plant the seed, but let these people—these opinion leaders—discover the idea for themselves. So I just point them to other people's postings and conversations. Fake ones. I make it look like their friends are talking about something. They can take it or leave it, but if we do step two right, they won't be able to resist. They become a hub, and the whole thing goes viral."

Lenny saw a frown of concentration cross Roy's forehead. Roy said, "So if I saw my friends talking about a great new camera, I'd go and check it out for myself, then tell other people if I liked it. A buzz marketing kind of thing."

"Exactly. You'd jump in and take up the cause, and you'd never know it was a fake conversation that got you started."

Roy leaned back in his chair. "Man, that's... that's..."

"Wicked good?" offered Lenny.

"Screw you." Roy raised his cereal bowl to his lips and finished off the milk. "I'm going to bed. Have fun with your hubs."

As Roy stumbled into his bedroom, Lenny turned back to his computer and brought up a new screen. The code he'd written for the fundraising had been really good, but he had to admit that Blahst had expanded on his original idea when they'd implemented Version 6. Perhaps if he used their auto-posting function, he could make the third step of his program even better.

Lenny was soon engrossed in matching Roy's photos to groups of opinion leaders. As he worked, he started to wonder what people would think of Version 6. Would they actually like to have postings that sounded like them, but that they didn't write? Or would they react like Roy when they discovered how they came across?

Another idea started to stir in his mind. He remembered catching a recent news report where a red-faced pundit railed against the social media companies' invasion of people's privacy. What would the electronic privacy organizations think about Version 6? He grinned. Wasn't this automatic personalization just the tip of the iceberg, the slippery slope of corporate tyranny, the specter of Big Brother? He wrote out a little conversation between two concerned friends discussing the issue. A fake conversation he could insert into people's Blahst feeds in their own unique online voices. A conversation that might galvanize others into action.

Lenny settled himself down for a long, fun night of programming.

Lenny woke to a pounding at the door, then realized it was coming from inside his head. A sharp pain in his shoulder urged him to move his position, but he couldn't seem to find the space to maneuver. He half-opened his eyes and saw light flooding in from the window next to the old armchair he was draped across.

He raised himself slowly to his feet and felt a wave of nausea. He steadied himself against the armchair and shuffled over to the sink. He found a glass that didn't look too dirty, filled it from the cold tap, and took a gulping drink. His tongue no longer stuck to the roof of his mouth, but the thumping in his head didn't let up.

Heading toward his bedroom, he peered through the door of Roy's room and saw him splayed face down across the bed, his dark hair plastered to his head. A sudden need to talk with Roy overcame him.

"Hey, Roy," Lenny leaned heavily against the doorframe. "I sent out those photos. And some other stuff. Serve 'em right, huh?"

Roy's face twisted free of the covers and turned to the other side, letting out an incomprehensible mumble as it went. Then he lay still, mouth open and snoring lightly.

"Right," replied Lenny, finishing off the conversation to his satisfaction as he lumbered to his room and flopped onto his own bed.

Chapter 8

"WELL, LENNY, WHAT DO YOU think I should do with you?"

Lenny stared across the desk at Professor Ramsey's face but found him hard to read. Ramsey stared right back, his mouth a straight line tucked inside the clipped grey beard.

Lenny had given quite a bit of consideration to this question. He had been prepared to justify why Professor Ramsey should let him and Roy keep their jobs. Especially Roy. But he hadn't really expected Ramsey to ask the question flat out, just like that. Something about the professor's calm tone made him think, really think, about what he would do if he were in charge of Healthway.

"I think you should fire me, and ask me to pay back the money over a period of time," he finally answered. "But not Roy. He had nothing to do with it."

The corners of Ramsey's mouth gave a barely perceptible twitch upward, but he didn't relax his stare. "That seems very fair. How long do you think you would need to pay it back?"

Lenny slid down in his chair and relaxed for the first time since arriving at the office that morning. He realized that he had already resigned himself to losing the job, and in a way it was a relief to have it over with. And if Roy could stay, at least they'd be able to pay the rent, assuming Healthway could get more funds.

"I have no idea. It depends how quickly I can get another job. I would think a couple of years at least—thirty thousand's a lot of money."

"Indeed it is," agreed Ramsey. "But it looks like you've been successful in raising some funds while I was away. Perhaps we should deduct the proceeds from the amount you owe."

Lenny sat up straight. He'd forgotten about the checks that had come in. A couple of thousand dollars would be a good start on paying back the money.

Professor Ramsey reached into a drawer in his desk and pulled out a messy pile of papers of different sizes and shapes. Lenny saw that they were letters, some typed and some handwritten, interspersed with checks.

"Have you got fifteen dollars on you?" asked Ramsey, his eyebrows raising into a bushy arc.

Lenny stared at the checks, not quite understanding the significance of Ramsey's words. "Those are all donations?"

"Twenty-nine thousand, nine hundred, and eighty-five dollars at the last count. There's probably more that arrived today. They're from all over the country, some from Europe, one from Australia, and about twenty from Japan. And there are a whole lot of e-mails asking how to send us money electronically."

"So we got the money back?"

"We're fifteen dollars short."

Lenny fell back against the hard wood of the chair. The fund-raising was a success. He might not have a job anymore, but there was a cool satisfaction in knowing that his algorithms were really working. He let the realization wash over him.

"Did you say Japan?" he asked.

"Hmm?" Professor Ramsey was reading one of the letters.

"You said there were a bunch from Japan. I didn't send anything to Japan."

"Yes, you've got quite an international showing here." Professor Ramsey slipped the letter he was holding back into the pile and pushed the envelopes across the desk toward Lenny. "I want you to sort through these this afternoon and deposit them at the bank before you do anything else," he said.

"But... I thought..." Lenny looked at the letters in bewilderment. He'd expected Ramsey to ask him to leave immediately, and now he was trusting him with all these checks?

Professor Ramsey leaned forward, his shoulder muscles rounding out his ribbed sweater. He was a powerful man for his age. For any age, Lenny corrected himself.

"Listen, Lenny. I'm not going to fire you. You're obviously very smart, and we need all the smarts we can get. But we're a team here. You have to think about how your actions affect everyone, not just yourself."

Lenny stared at Ramsey's neatly manicured nails and felt like he was eleven again, back in the principal's office after he'd broadcast the exam answers to the entire class through a system of secret hand signs.

"It's a tough time for all the not-for-profits. When the economy's bad, people stop giving." Ramsey paused and looked down at the pile of checks. Lenny noticed the dark creases around his eyes and thought he looked somehow older than when he'd met him just a few weeks earlier. "But you seem to be onto something. Roy tells me you wrote a special fundraising program."

"Not just fundraising. It's a general-purpose algorithm that finds opinion leaders and targets them with personalized messages. It uses a lot of your ideas from *Viral Diffusion*, and a couple of things I added."

"So, a viral algorithm?"

"Yeah, you could call it that."

Ramsey sighed and massaged his left arm. "That sounds like it has potential. I want to learn all about how you did it, but it will have to wait until tomorrow. I'm afraid the jetlag has really gotten to me this time."

Professor Ramsey pushed himself up from his chair. His large frame swayed slightly and he steadied himself with one arm against the desk.

Lenny felt like running around the desk to hug Ramsey. Not only were he and Roy going to keep their jobs, but Professor Ramsey was actually interested in *his* work. He settled for a mumbled thank-you as he watched the professor pick up his coat and shuffle out of the office.

"You are one lucky guy." Roy lined up a condom packet on a stretched elastic band and flicked it at Lenny. It landed on Lenny's legs, which were crossed and propped up on his desk.

"It's not luck. It's epic genius," Lenny replied. "Professor Ramsey says he wants to learn all about my viral algorithm."

"Your what?"

"That's what he called it. I think it's a good name."

"It's the jacket. I told you a jacket would help."

Lenny looked down at the one jacket he owned, the blue blazer that he'd bought for his high school graduation.

"It makes a difference, how you look," Ray continued. "Hirings, firings, and weddings always need a jacket."

Lenny grunted. "Didn't do me much good at the Blahst interview."

"I said that it helps, not that it works miracles. Anyway, the professor told you we can both stay?"

"Yup." Lenny dodged a condom that flew past his head. "I mean, I didn't even send anything to Japan, and someone's just launched a huge campaign there. The messages are reaching opinion leaders I didn't target."

Roy held up a fistful of letters. "There's more here."

"And that's in ten days. Thirty thousand dollars in ten days!" Two more condoms hit him on the shoulder. He grabbed one and flicked it back. The corner of the packet caught Roy just above his eyebrow and bounced off to land on his desk. A small bead of blood appeared above Roy's eye.

"Shit, Lenny!" Roy's hand flew to his eye. He pulled it away and looked at the smear of blood across his fingers.

Lenny laughed, thrust the condoms from his lap into his jacket pocket, and pulled out a handkerchief. It was Mari's, from the interview. He balled it up and threw it to Roy.

"You could have taken my eye out." Roy dabbed at his forehead and inspected the handkerchief for signs of fresh blood. When it came away clean, he threw it back at Lenny.

"And what about the photos?" Roy demanded.

"What photos?"

"You know, my photos of Andrei Simenov. The ones you sent out on Saturday night. Without my permission."

"I told you what I was going to do. I explained how the whole thing works. You didn't say I couldn't use them."

"I didn't say you could. I thought it was all theoretical. I didn't know you were really going to do it." A note of alarm sounded in Roy's voice. "If the fundraising's going so well, the photos could be all over the Internet by now."

"Probably not. Like you said, they're obviously fakes." Despite his words, Lenny started to feel a faint sense of unease. He had to admit that he hadn't even thought about Blahst since the weekend. It was as though the all-nighter on Saturday had purged him of the need for revenge. He'd spent most of Monday and Tuesday playing video games and waiting for Professor Ramsey to return from Burundi and fire him.

He leaned over Roy's computer and typed in a search for images of Andrei Simenov. Thumbnail-sized pictures filled the screen, and Lenny's hand froze on the keyboard. He recognized at least a quarter of the photos as Roy's handiwork.

"Uh-oh." He glanced sidelong at Roy.

Roy's mouth fell open, and he grabbed the mouse from Lenny. He scrolled through the thumbnails, becoming more agitated each time one of his photos flashed by.

"See who's posting them," said Lenny.

Roy clicked through to one of the websites and read the headline aloud. "*Social Networking Giant Seeks Antisocial Prankster.*"

"See, they know it's a joke."

"But look at this one. *Immigrant CEO Accused in Moral Turpitude Scandal.* They're demanding the government take away Andrei's visa."

Lenny read some of the ranting text. "That's just some extremist crazies' blog. What the hell is moral turpitude?"

"No idea. Maybe the photo of Andrei and the sheep." Roy followed another link. "Shit, Lenny. It says here that Blahst's stock price is down."

Lenny took the mouse and brought up the stock listing for Blahst. A chart filled the top half of the screen. It showed a steep and jagged upward trend over most of the chart, followed by a sharp downward turn on the right-hand side. They both leaned in to scan the list of news headlines on the lower half of the screen.

"Huh. Nothing about the photos." Some of the panic drained from Roy's voice. "Looks like there's some privacy problem with their new version. That's why the stock price is falling."

Lenny stared at the headlines and back up at the stock chart. A cold knot gripped his stomach.

"That's a relief," continued Roy. "At least the photos aren't what's making the stock fall. People aren't that dumb. I was worried there for a second."

Lenny listened to Roy chatter on. Should he tell Roy about the other messages he'd sent out on Saturday night, the ones accusing Blahst of violating the nation's privacy with Version 6? A glance at Roy's face, still puckered with anxiety, told him that now might not be the best time.

"They won't find us, will they?"

"Huh?" Lenny's eyes were drawn back to the trajectory of the stock price, the sudden downward trend starting even before the markets had opened on Monday morning.

"It says that Blahst is looking for the sources of the photos."

The knot tightened in Lenny's stomach. He hadn't had to break into anyone's account to make his algorithm work, so he was fairly sure what he'd done was legal, mostly. But there had to be laws against trashing a company with enough lies to bring its stock price crashing down. And he'd read somewhere that there was a whole department at the FBI that hunted down hackers.

"They won't even know it's coming from a single source. It will look like it started spontaneously all over the place. And even if they did figure it out, they won't know where to start looking." Lenny rubbed his hand across his eyes. "I used anonymous forwarding."

"So they'll never find us?"

"No." Lenny's response was a little too rapid as his mind started formulating scenarios that he didn't want to pursue. He had covered his tracks well, and it should, theoretically, be impossible to work backward from the messages to find their origin. But it might just depend on how hard and for how long someone was prepared to look.

Chapter 9

MARI HAD ACCEPTED THE NEW assignment without a single question. Being pulled away to work on a new project for a new manager—in fact, to work for anyone besides Clayton, whose full attention had returned to her after the launch of Version 6—felt like being rescued from a prison cell. But, as the newly assembled team received its first briefing, a growing disquiet buzzed at the edges of her mind. She tried to push aside the idea that she might already have the answer to the question her company was so desperately investigating.

She shivered and pulled her jacket more tightly across her chest. Her liberator was Pierce, Blahst's Chief Security and Privacy Officer, a stern man with a buzz cut, and his first action had been to gather Mari, Paolo, and two other employees in an unused and so far unheated corner of the tenth floor.

"Before I start, I must stress that you are not to discuss anything outside of this team." Pierce locked on Mari's eyes with a frown. Frozen by his penetrating stare, Mari could believe the rumors that Pierce had once escaped Taliban forces in Afghanistan. She wondered why he didn't trust her before realizing that he was treating each of her three new colleagues to the same warning stare. Once he had done the rounds, his expression relaxed and he beckoned them all inside a cubicle, which was bare except for a single computer.

"Gather around and make sure you can see the screen." Pierce shuffled his chair toward the desk so that Mari and the others could fit inside the cubicle. "As you know, we're trying to find the origin of the photos that were used in the hate campaign. We're running the photos through an image analysis program, but we need your help to sort through the results."

The screen on the desk showed a photo of Andrei passing a joint to a girl of about fifteen. The girl's head was tipped back and her eyes were half closed in an expression of rapture. Behind the two figures, a sea of blurred heads faded into the distance.

Pierce shook his head as he looked at the image. Mari had been surprised by how offensive the others found the photos. Now she was beginning to sense the depth of loyalty these people felt to Andrei. Two of the team—Lance and Debra—had been with the company almost from the beginning. Mari had already heard their lectures about how Andrei's intellect, integrity, and sweat had grown the company from nothing to the powerhouse it was today. They viewed the photos as a personal affront to the man who was their daily inspiration. The sneaking feeling that she might know the source of that affront ran through her again.

"We can get rid of the fake part easily enough," Pierce continued. The photo of the stoned girl appeared with a dark silhouette where Andrei had been. "The images of Andrei were all pulled from the Blahst website, so they don't tell us anything. But we're hoping to find where the backgrounds of the photos came from to see if we can learn something about the perpetrators."

"You mean the perps might have used their vacation photos?" Lance's ruddy face was framed by a silver-grey ponytail pulled back from triangular sideburns.

"It's a long shot," nodded Pierce. "They probably pulled the backgrounds from public sources too, but we might get lucky. The image analysis program looks for matches across millions of web and social media sites. It uses multiple cues—shape, color, texture—to compare the images, and it brings back anything that matches."

"Sounds straightforward." Debra leaned closer to the screen. She tugged the edges of a woolen hat over her short-cropped hair, and buried her chin deeper in a scarf wrapped several times around her neck. "What do you need us for?"

"The software throws out a lot of matches. Most of them are false alarms, so we need human eyes to take a final look through and see if we've caught the real match." Pierce handed a different photo to each member of the team. "You're each going to take a photo and check the matches that the computer throws out."

"Great. We get to do the part that's too boring for the computer," complained Paolo. Mari was fairly sure it was Paolo who had recommended her to Pierce. He'd hinted a couple times that he'd look for an opportunity to get her away from Clayton. And he'd used several of her library routines in his team's code, so she knew he liked her work. But she couldn't help feeling intimidated as she looked around at the heavy-hitting team.

She took the photo from Pierce and studied the image. Andrei was raising his hand to strike a cowering, dark-skinned boy who was squatting over cracked dirt. Behind them the sky glowed in streaks of red and orange, its vibrancy mocking the squalid scene in the foreground.

"We found the match for this one last night." Pierce pointed back at the photo of the stoned girl. "It's from the movie *Woodstock*. It's too broadly available to tell us much about the perpetrators, but we've established that the approach works."

"How many matches did you have to search through to find this one?" asked Lance.

"We started out focusing on the face, but we got millions of hits," said Pierce. "Turns out the expression on her face shows up in a lot of, well..." Pierce flushed and looked down at his feet.

There was a moment of silence. Mari looked around at the puzzled faces of her colleagues until Paolo pumped his fist in the air and whooped.

"Dude, you're telling me I'm getting paid to check out porn? I love this place."

Pierce shuffled his feet and looked back up at his team. "Actually, we changed tactics and tried to match the marijuana cigarette. Again, a lot of matches, but nowhere near as many as the face, and we finally found it in the Woodstock still. We started working on this on Sunday afternoon, after the photos hit early Sunday morning. Then we started getting all the pushback that Version 6 was violating our customers' privacy, and Andrei pulled me onto that instead. He doesn't want us spending time on the photos, but I told him I'd pull together a small skunkworks with some of our best people. That's you."

Early Sunday morning. Mari gnawed at her bottom lip as the buzz of disquiet grew to a roar that demanded attention. The timing was too close to be a coincidence. She replayed her parting words to Lenny on the phone on Saturday night. *Don't do anything stupid.* Had he done something stupid, after all? Something really, really stupid? She looked around at the group, the earnest defenders of Andrei Simenov's reputation, and wondered how to broach her suspicions.

"Do you have any hunches about why the... um... perpetrators would do this?"

"I know, it's hard to understand these people sometimes." Pierce shook his head again. "We're checking out competitors, hacker organizations, traders who have sold our stock short. We know it's an organization with global reach, based on all the different places the photos have been appearing."

"How do you know it's not an individual? Like a..." Mari chose her words carefully. "Like a disgruntled employee?"

"No, this is a coordinated campaign. The postings are coming from all directions at once. Usually these things get posted on one site and everyone else picks them up. But with these photos there's no single point of origin. It's not the work of an individual."

Mari closed her eyes and exhaled slowly. She wasn't sure why she felt quite the level of relief that she did. She had been spared confessing her suspicions to Pierce and her new teammates, but it was more than that. She thought she had written Lenny Driver out of her life after he embarrassed her at the launch party, but she had to admit she'd found herself replaying their meeting in Barnes & Noble on more than one occasion. There was something about those unruly curls—and his earnest, intense expression when he talked about his work—that kept drawing him into her thoughts.

"If it's international, will we be able to prosecute them when we do find them?" asked Debra. She tucked her legs up onto her chair and hugged her knees.

"There's the rub," answered Pierce. "We're not sure that we have any legal remedy, even in the United States."

"But the photos are all fake," said Lance. "Isn't that libel?"

"That's usually reserved for publication by the mass media," explained Pierce. "The courts have found that individual material on websites is protected by constitutional freedom of speech, particularly if they can claim parody or satire."

"Satire my ass." Lance emitted a short grunt. "This is a smear campaign. Andrei should go after them."

"I just wish I had as much fun as the Andrei in the photos," a clipped voice sounded from behind their backs. They jumped around, startled to see Andrei Simenov leaning on the edge of the cubicle. His arms were folded across his chest, his slim wrists poking from an olive-green sweater.

"Hey, Andrei." Lance looked a little sheepish. "I didn't mean—"

"I appreciate your concern." Andrei waved a hand toward Lance. "I wanted to stop by and thank you for helping out. Pierce is right; it is an important task. We need to understand how and why these things happen, even if we can take no action." Andrei nodded at each of the team in turn. "I am sorry to pull you from your other projects, but we want to clear this up as soon as possible. You can contact me any time if you have questions. Pierce is going to be busy with this other problem we are having with Version 6."

Pierce shook his head. "It's getting worse. Someone's even started a website claiming that Blahst personal profiles are the mark of the Beast—they're calling it Version 666."

"Stock's down three percent," added Debra. "Our first drop ever."

"People don't have to use the personalization features if they don't want to." Andrei's shoulders slumped as he leaned more heavily against the edge of the cubicle. "We ran it by the privacy groups before we launched, and they had no problems. Now they're all over it. I don't understand why we hit such a nerve. We're being attacked from all directions."

Mari felt her eyes narrow in recognition. Now that she was reassured this had nothing to do with Lenny, she was paying full attention to the discussion. *From all directions.* There was something very familiar about the phrase that Andrei had just used. Should she say something? She didn't want to say anything dumb in front of the top brains in the company. But surely the others had made the same connection? She glanced around but saw only blank expressions. She cleared her throat.

"Could the photos be part of the privacy backlash? A way to get back at Blahst if they feel we're invading their privacy?" she asked.

"No, the privacy issue is different," said Pierce. "It's some kind of grassroots campaign. It's coming from all over the place."

"Isn't that what you said about the photos? And they both started spreading at the same time."

The group fell silent. Mari looked between Pierce and Andrei and watched the possibility register on their faces. Andrei was the first to speak.

"Yes, yes. It is a very similar pattern." He unfolded his arms and tipped his head toward Mari. "Well observed, Mari. That will give us a new path to pursue."

Mari bit back a smile as she saw Paolo giving her a thumbs-up behind Lance's back. She didn't want to appear too self-satisfied at Andrei's compliment.

"In the meantime, Pierce, I am afraid I have to steal you away to discuss another matter that has just come up," Andrei continued. "It never rains but it pours."

Mari could have sworn Andrei's eyes were looking at her as he spoke, but before she could fully register it, Andrei and Pierce disappeared down the hallway together.

"Come on skunks, let's get to work." Debbie rallied them to move a pile of equipment from the elevator foyer to their corner, where they helped each other set up more workstations in the cubicles. Mari's new colleagues included her in the banter and jokes, and the warmth she started to feel was not just the effect of the heating that finally kicked in to take the chill off the tenth floor.

Chapter 10

LENNY ARRIVED AT THE BLAHST headquarters in Waltham ten minutes early. He pulled into a parking spot marked *Visitors*, which was close to the main entrance. *Perfect for a quick escape,* he thought.

He squinted up at the tower, dazzled by the sunlight reflecting off the glass and surrounding snow. Bare twigs poked out of the snow drifts that stacked up like foothills around the base of the building. At the edge of the parking lot, a lone, hardy jogger plodded along a cleared path, his heels kicking up salt crystals as he ran. The man's breath formed jets of steam from a mouth that was barely visible beneath sunglasses, neckroll, and hooded sweatshirt.

Lenny had received the phone call late the day before. It was from Andrei Simenov's personal assistant, inviting him to please come and discuss a matter of a sensitive nature at 3:30 on Friday afternoon, if he was available.

Lenny hadn't thought it would happen this way. He had imagined being called into Professor Ramsey's office again, this time with a policeman standing behind the professor's chair. Or being pulled over as he drove to work, waiting with his hands spread-eagled against the side of his battered Explorer while they checked in with headquarters before bundling him away in handcuffs. He had even imagined the FBI knocking his door down in the middle of the night.

His initial reaction had been to decline the invitation. Maybe they were only guessing at this point—maybe they wanted to talk to a whole bunch of suspects and they were waiting to see how they each responded. Then he thought about making a run for it. Grabbing a few things and driving back to his parents' house in Albany. Or staying on the road and driving somewhere far away where nobody knew him. None of it held much appeal, but then neither did jail.

In the end, he couldn't resist the lure of the invitation. The prospect of meeting Andrei Simenov was too enticing. He was also intensely curious about how they had managed to find him, a reaction he recognized as entirely inappropriate, but he still couldn't help wondering. If it was a trap, then so be it—he was sure they could find a way to arrest him if they wanted to, even if he didn't come. He wished he could have talked things through with Professor Ramsey first, though. He felt a need to come clean about the way he'd used his viral algorithm against Blahst, even though the professor would have no choice but to ask him to leave Healthway. It would have been worth losing the job to gain the professor's advice about what to do next. But Ramsey hadn't been to the office since their meeting on Wednesday.

Lenny's heart was already pounding as he pushed through the revolving door into the reception area. He recognized the woman at the desk from his interview. She signed him in, handed him a plastic badge, and offered him a seat on one of the curved, red leather sofas scattered through the grey-tiled lobby.

The woman was friendly enough, but Lenny wondered if she knew why he was here. The top management certainly would have to know, but how many other people at Blahst had been told that he was the cause of their problems? The stock had dropped another ten points since Wednesday—ten point in two days. Would Blahst want to make a public example of him, or would they try to cover up the fact that one person could do so much damage? He wondered if anyone would take his side if they did try to prosecute. After all, they had stolen his work, so was it any wonder he had struck back? He just wished his retaliation hadn't been quite so effective.

He couldn't bring himself to sit down. He waited a few steps away from the reception desk and played a round of *Angry Birds* to occupy his hands and mind.

Within a few minutes, a tall woman in a brown pantsuit emerged from the elevator and crossed to greet him. He shook her hand and realized that his palm was damp.

She introduced herself as Andrei's personal assistant. She would take him up to Andrei's office, she explained, but he might have to wait a few minutes because Andrei was finishing up another meeting that had started late. Lenny figured she must know all about him, and he couldn't look her in the eye.

In the elevator the woman put her ID card into a slot and punched the button for the fifteenth floor, the top of the building. As Lenny stepped in past her, he saw that the elevator had glass walls that were open to the central lobby. His heart thumped even harder—he had never been good with heights. Even before they reached the second floor, his feet started to tingle in a way he remembered too well from the forced marches along the diving boards at YMCA swimming lessons. He turned to face the elevator doors, which were a substantial and reassuringly solid metal.

By the fifteenth floor, Lenny's feet were screaming for the soft, black carpet that greeted them as they stepped outside the elevator. The woman led them along a corridor to a corner office with a seating area outside it. Lenny refused the offer of a drink, but he accepted one of the chairs that would keep him tucked out of the way of the door to Andrei's office. Several people marched past in the corridor, singly and in groups, and snatches of conversation and laughter drifted into the seating area.

Lenny wiped his palms on the sides of his pants and checked out his phone. He had no new messages, so he flicked through some news headlines, carefully avoiding the financial news.

After a few more minutes he heard Andrei's door click open, and two men and two women came through the door in a bustle of purpose. They didn't see him sitting there and headed down the corridor still deep in conversation.

A face poked around the door of the office, one that Lenny recognized all too well from staring at Roy's doctored photos: Andrei Simenov.

"Lenny? Come on in. Sorry to keep you waiting."

Lenny wiped his right hand on his pants again and followed Andrei inside. The large corner office continued the red-and-grey color scheme of the public areas—a tribute, Lenny assumed, to the colors of the distinctive Blahst logo. The office looked out on two sides over the icy expanse of the lake. On the back wall, a row of bookshelves was cluttered with papers, toy robots, antique cameras, and comics as well as a considerable collection of technical books. The other wall held framed photos of spectacular mountain views. One showed Andrei smiling from a sheer wall of rock, suspended by one foot and one hand as the wind blew his hair horizontally back from his head.

Andrei sat down at a small, round table in front of his large desk and gestured Lenny to join him. He leaned back in his chair and crossed one sneaker-clad foot across the knee of his jeans.

"Lenny, I think you know why I invited you here, so I will not play games with you."

Lenny felt his whole body turn cold. He didn't know what he had been expecting from the meeting—the invitation had seemed so surreal. Now that he was here with Andrei Simenov, he had no idea what he was going to say in his own defense.

"I am in a very difficult situation. Blahst has achieved its place in the industry because we did many things right. But to me, nothing is as important as our reputation."

Lenny was entranced by the way Andrei's words melted into one another in a blur of rolled "r"s and softened "t"s. "Without our reputation, we are nothing."

Lenny nodded, but his jaw was frozen shut.

"Some people might say I take things a little too far sometimes. *Anal* is the word they use, actually." Andrei gave a wry smile. "But that is okay. It is true that I am a little compulsive on this matter. I just don't think it is right to take the easy route at someone else's expense."

Again, Lenny could only nod.

Andrei uncrossed his legs and leaned forward on the table. His bright-blue eyes locked directly on Lenny. "That is why I will do whatever it takes to protect this company's reputation."

Lenny swallowed. He had to say something. He had to let Andrei know that he hadn't meant for things to go as far as they had. His brain raced as he tried to come up with the right opening.

Before Lenny could respond, Andrei leaned back in his chair once more. "I hear we have your friend Mari Velasquez to thank for bringing it to our attention. She is an impressive person. Smart and tenacious."

Lenny's forehead furrowed. What was Andrei talking about? What did Mari have to do with anything? She had no idea what he had done—he hadn't spoken to her since their phone call on Saturday night. He and Roy were the only ones who knew about any of this. Surely Roy hadn't been in touch with Mari behind Lenny's back?

"Your program is brilliant," Andrei continued. "A simple idea, well executed."

Lenny's confusion deepened. Was Andrei such a technology geek that he could actually praise the software that was destroying his company?

"I was led to believe that one of our own employees had come up with the idea," said Andrei. "I take full responsibility, though. I should stay closer to development, but running a company... it can be..."

As Andrei trailed off with an apologetic wave of his hand, Lenny nodded numbly as though he knew all about the challenges of running a multibillion-dollar company. He felt he was drifting further away from the conversation with every word that Andrei spoke.

"Anyway, I checked the records from your interview, and our solution does draw heavily on your code. There is no doubt Version 6 uses your approach to personalizing the automatic Blahst postings."

Lenny's tension burst in a relief so intense he felt like his body was deflating onto the chair beneath him. *That was what this meeting was about.* He expelled his breath with an explosive sigh that reverberated around the room.

"Are you okay?" Andrei looked at him quizzically.

"Yes, yes, I'm fine." Lenny spoke his first words to Andrei Simenov. "Really fine."

"Good." Andrei nodded. "I invited you here to offer you three things as a result of our error. First, my personal apology. We broke the trust of someone who wanted to come and join us here, and for that I am most sorry. You can be assured that the employee who took credit for your work is no longer with the company."

Andrei reached across to retrieve an envelope from the top of his desk. He handed it to Lenny and continued. "Second, we would like to offer you this token of our appreciation for your work. A significant token, as Version 6 is a significant part of our strategy."

Andrei looked expectantly at the envelope. Lenny was obviously supposed to open it. It was not sealed, and Lenny pulled out several sheets of printed paper with a check attached to the front one. The check had the Blahst logo in the top left-hand corner and was made out to Lenny Driver for the amount of seventy-five thousand dollars.

Lenny stared at the check. He looked again at the amount, thinking he must have misread it. There was no mistake. Andrei had just given him a check for seventy-five thousand dollars.

Andrei reached over and touched the corner of the printed documents. "I have to explain this to you. Our legal department wanted the check to be contingent on you signing this document. It says that by cashing the check you relinquish all rights to pursue legal action against Blahst. But I say that is no way to right a wrong." He opened his arms toward Lenny. "This check is a gift to you, Lenny. You do not have to sign anything."

"Thank you. It's very nice," Lenny stammered before he could catch himself. He winced inwardly. *Nice?* What kind of an idiot said a check for seventy-five thousand was *nice?*

"However, if you were to sign it, my legal counsel would be very happy, and she would stop beating me up." Andrei smiled apologetically. "It is up to you. If you do not think we are being fair, then you should not sign the document, and you are free to pursue whatever recourse you see fit. The money is yours in any case."

Lenny looked at the document and tried to make sense of it, but his eyes wouldn't focus on the words. Should he sign it if he didn't have to? How could he refuse, when Andrei was paying him for his work? And anyway, what difference would it make—he was hardly going to sue Blahst over his algorithm now.

"Have you got a pen?" Lenny asked. Andrei handed him a blue ballpoint. Lenny found the dotted line on the last page of the document and scrawled his signature.

As Andrei placed the document back on the desk, Lenny's eye was caught by a series of photos in matching red leather frames standing out against the light polished wood. The largest showed Andrei with one arm around a young woman and the other arm holding a toddler at his waist. Other photos showed facial shots of young children of different ages and skin hues, some smiling brightly, some with what Lenny now recognized as the haunted look of hunger.

"They're not all mine; don't worry," said Andrei, following Lenny's gaze. "Those are some of the children we sponsor. We worked out a way for our employees to contribute pre-tax through a payroll deduction—these kids need it more than the IRS. Which brings me to my third offer."

Andrei turned back to face Lenny across the small table. "I talked with Estelle from our talent management department—you remember, she was taking notes at the interviews—and it sounds like your peer review session was... well, I must be honest... quite entertaining. They made a very sensible decision in hiring Mari, and her ability is unquestionable. But somewhere in becoming a large corporation we lost our ability to take a risk on talented people who may be a little more—shall we say—rough around the edges." Andrei paused. "What I am trying to say is that I would like to offer you a job here at Blahst."

The room suddenly felt claustrophobic. Lenny looked out of the window at the open space below and longed to be out in the cold air. He was being offered everything he'd ever wanted, and all he could do was sit here and nod like a dashboard ornament. He opened his mouth to speak and his words came out as a croak.

"I'm not sure if I—"

Andrei raised his hand. "It is okay. You do not have to decide right now. But if you do want to join us, just call or e-mail me anytime. Here is my card."

As Lenny pushed the business card along with the check into his coat pocket, he felt Andrei watching him thoughtfully.

"You know, you remind me of myself a few years back. We are a lot alike, you and me," Andrei said.

Lenny glanced at the photo of Andrei hanging off the side of a mountain and doubted deeply that they were anything alike. This was not a man who was afraid of glass elevators, nor one who would wreak silent revenge from his computer terminal like Lenny had done. But he managed a weak smile of agreement.

Andrei stood to bid Lenny goodbye and good luck and repeated the offer to contact him at any time. He led Lenny out to his assistant's desk, and she escorted him back to the elevator. On the ride down she made small talk about the freezing weather and the Patriots' chances at the Super Bowl. Lenny grunted what he hoped were appropriate responses and tried not to think about the open space beneath the elevator.

As he handed his plastic name badge back to the receptionist, he wondered if he should try to find Mari. He should probably thank her for talking to the product manager.

He asked the receptionist if he could call Mari at her desk. She checked her computer screen and pointed over at a large cardboard poster displayed on a stand next to the elevators. The poster showed smiling workers in matching red t-shirts climbing up ladders with hammers and paintbrushes. "She's out all day at the Habitat for Humanity event. She probably won't be in until Monday."

Lenny pushed through the revolving door and headed to his car. The Blahst tower cast long, cold shadows across the parking lot, and he thrust his hands into his pockets for warmth. His fingers connected with the hard edges of Andrei's business card next to the smooth paper of the check.

He pushed his car into reverse and shot out of the parking spot before he noticed the car coming toward him. The other car braked sharply, and Lenny braced for the inevitable honk of reprimand. But the car waited silently for Lenny to finish reversing. Lenny quickly worked his way toward the exit of the parking lot and pulled onto the highway. He melted into the frantic rush of Friday evening traffic with one hand still resting against the check in his coat pocket.

Chapter 11

"I'M TELLING YOU, ROY, I feel like I've screwed Mother Teresa. This guy is a saint."

Lenny sat on a stool in the kitchen and kicked at a cupboard door under the counter. The door flapped open and closed with a rhythmic thudding.

"Nobody's all good." Roy pulled the fridge door open, hauled out a plastic-wrapped package, and sniffed it. He wrinkled his nose and threw it back in the fridge. "It's your turn to get food, you know."

"He sponsors orphaned kids and lets his employees do Habitat for Humanity on company time. He's as good as it gets."

"No moral turpitude?" asked Roy, staring blankly into the fridge.

"Not a turpid bone in his body." Lenny watched Roy open and close cupboard doors. "I shopped already. It's in those bags on the floor."

Roy rustled through one of the bags and pulled out boxes of macaroni and cheese. He stashed them in the closest cupboard and returned for the next bag.

"This is all carbs," he complained, tipping packages of ramen noodle soup onto the countertop. "You've got all that money; you should buy some decent protein."

"I didn't cash the check."

"And where are the Frosted Flakes?"

"I don't like them anymore."

Roy sighed noisily. "It's going to be okay, Lenny. You said it yourself: nobody can find us." He ripped open a package of ramen noodle soup and lit the stove under the kettle. "And anyway, the fuss about the photos is dying out. I mean, they're still being posted, but nobody cares. It's the privacy thing that's driving the stock price down. Blahst has more to worry about than a few photos."

Lenny kicked harder at the flapping cupboard door. Roy had never questioned Lenny's assurances that they wouldn't get caught, and the burden of Roy's faith was weighing him down as though it were a physical load.

"Hey, I've got something that will cheer you up." Roy jumped over the remaining shopping bags and landed in front of his computer. He brought up a screen of videos and peered at them, searching. "You're going to like this. It's about Burundi."

"Fuck Burundi."

Lenny's welling frustration exploded and he met Roy's gaping surprise with a glare. It wasn't right that Roy should be so carefree while Lenny was wretched with guilt. Roy was supposed to be the sensible one, the one who worried so that Lenny could reassure him—and himself at the same time. He felt a sudden need to set Roy straight about the reality of the situation.

"That privacy thing you're so pleased about? The one that's keeping Blahst from caring about the photos? It's not some happy coincidence." Lenny let the sarcasm ripple through the last two words.

Roy was silent. He tipped his head to one side and studied Lenny.

"It's because of what we did?" he asked.

"It's because of what I did. After you went to bed. I sent out messages to privacy groups."

"With your viral algorithm?"

"Yes, I sent—"

A blast of distorted rap music sounded from the coffee table. They both looked down at the flashing screen on Roy's phone. Roy reached down to answer it without taking his eyes off Lenny.

Lenny turned away and continued to kick at the cupboard door. The knob had come loose and he could see the dark core of the metal screw that held it in place. As the kettle whistled its readiness from the stove, Lenny glanced at Roy to see if he was going to take care of it. Roy's face had drained of color.

"When was this? Where is he? Can we see him?" Roy listened a little longer, then thanked the caller and dropped the phone to his side. He looked at Lenny, his eyes and mouth round in alarm and disbelief. The kettle's whistling rose to a wail.

"Professor Ramsey's had a stroke. Late Wednesday night. He's at Mass General."

"Is he going to be okay?"

"He's doing fine, but they're keeping him in. That was his sister."

Lenny pictured Professor Ramsey at the end of their conversation on Wednesday. His drawn face, his shuffling gait as he left the office. "Roy, that was after I spoke with him about the funding. I think I might have... his stroke... it was because..."

"Don't be dumb; it has nothing to do with you." Roy had to raise his voice over the shriek of the kettle. "It's because he's seventy-eight and still clocks a hundred thousand miles a year on his frequent flier program. He had a heart attack three years ago, but he still jets off to Africa every few months. Don't flatter yourself that you're the cause of all the world's problems." Roy marched across the kitchen and removed the kettle from the stove. The open package of noodles remained untouched.

"We have to go and see him," Lenny mumbled into the sudden silence.

"His sister said we can go after the weekend. We should get him some flowers or something."

"Books. He'd like something to read, if he's stuck in the hospital."

Roy nodded briefly and sank onto the sofa. After a few moments he leaned forward and pushed his hands between his knees. "The privacy... thing," he said. "Are you sure it's not a coincidence? The media's saying it's a grassroots backlash."

"That's what it would look like if it's my algorithm."

"But you can't be sure?"

Lenny didn't answer. He picked up his phone and pulled up the stock quotes page for Blahst, now firmly established at the top of his favorites list. Its stock price was still falling, and some of the other big social media companies were starting to drop as well. Three analyst firms had downgraded Blahst's stock from *buy* to *hold*, and one was already advising *sell*, based on a flurry of blog postings and news articles calling for stricter online privacy policies.

Could his algorithm really be causing all this activity? Perhaps Roy was right and Lenny was just being arrogant to think that he could have this much influence on such a big company. Like on his first vacation at the beach, when his parents had let him believe that he had successfully instructed the waves to turn back before they destroyed his sandcastle. It took a week for him to realize the tide would turn without his intervention.

"No, I can't be sure." Lenny flopped onto the sofa next to Roy. "Maybe my algorithm isn't that powerful."

Roy leaned back against the cushions and hugged his arms across his chest. Lenny felt a wave of remorse for dumping his latest round of problems on Roy, especially now that they'd heard the news about Professor Ramsey's stroke.

"What was it you wanted to show me about Burundi?" he asked in an attempt to divert their conversation to something other than the professor and Blahst's ills.

"Oh." Roy looked across at his computer, where a video image was frozen on the screen. "It's... um... nothing."

Lenny inspected the picture. A female newscaster was pointing a microphone at a girl of about ten.

"You said it was good news."

"That was before. I mean, it's really not..." Roy rose from the sofa and lurched toward his computer. "You don't want to see it right now."

Lenny lunged forward, a fraction of a second faster than Roy, and hit the *play* icon on the screen.

"... at my school." The girl spoke clearly into the microphone. She was holding out a small stuffed bear, which was white, green, and red. Three red, embroidered stars adorned its chest. "We raised over two thousand dollars for Burundi."

"What made you decide to help?" asked the anchor, with a toss of her long hair. A smile was fixed onto her face as she pointed the microphone down at the girl.

"We heard about the fighting there, and all the kids who are hungry because their parents have AIDS. We want to buy them food and medicine so they can go to school."

"Well here's one more donation," said the anchor, handing the girl a ten-dollar bill. The girl handed her the bear in return.

The anchor turned to face the camera with the bear held beside her head. "This is Maria Colthwaite and the Burundi Bears reporting from Clearwater, Florida." She locked in an even broader smile that froze as the final frame of the video.

"That was the national news." Roy returned to the sofa and sank slowly into the cushions. "That's not a coincidence, is it?"

"I seeded a whole bunch of teen forums with fundraising ideas—bears were one of them. 'Hey, Geena, my Burundi Bear looks so cute on my desk!' 'Peter gave me a Burundi Bear last night. He's soooo hot!' That kind of stuff."

"How did you make the bears?"

"I didn't have to. I sent a bunch of messages to some of those gift bear companies, so they were ready for the demand when it came."

"I guess bears are sticky," said Roy.

"I guess so." Lenny crossed to the armchair and dropped onto it from the side so that his head rested on one of the arms.

"None of it's a coincidence. Your algorithm's gone viral. First Burundi, now Blahst."

Lenny stretched his arms beside his head and let them flop over the edge of the chair toward the ground. He'd really done it. A sense of awe rose inside of him. He was influencing the actions of thousands of people, maybe tens of thousands. And there was no denying that the Blahst situation was his doing as well. His heart accelerated in a sudden flash of panic as he thought of what he'd done to their share price. He had to find a way to reverse it before it got worse. Because there was no doubt, based on the success of his fundraising, that it would get worse if he let it run its course.

He slid his head further back on the arm of the chair. From his upside-down vantage point he surveyed Roy, who was clutching his knees to his chest in the corner of the sofa. Roy's eyes were looking at Lenny but seemed glazed and unfocused

"Don't worry; I'll find a way to fix Blahst." As Lenny slipped back into the role of reassuring his worried friend, his confidence grew. If he'd managed to create a viral algorithm, surely he could find a way to control it. "At least Burundi's all good."

"Yeah." Roy looked across at the frozen image of the news-caster holding her Burundi bear. "At least there's that."

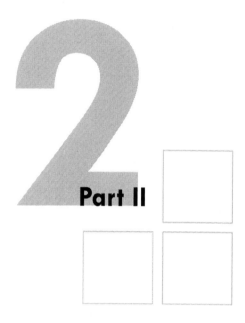

Part II

Chapter 12

SNYDER TASTED BILE AS HE swallowed back his anger, trying to push it to a deep place where he could store it, where it would grow like an investment until he could put it to good use.

He wasn't looking forward to telling Senator Brennigan the news. Like most politicians, the senator enjoyed a good, self-righteous rant at somebody else's expense, and Snyder wasn't sure he had the patience to be on the receiving end today. He hoped to diffuse some of the explosion by meeting the senator on his home ground, where it would be harder for him to cause a scene.

He drummed the back of his fist on the broad, wooden doorframe of the Senate chamber and watched the huddles of lobbyists, interns, secretaries, assistants, and assistant secretaries talking in muted voices, waiting for their senators to emerge. As he listened to them—the older ones joking and laughing, the younger ones frowning as they debated the finer points of some draft legislation, all of them aglow with their self-importance—he remembered why he avoided coming to the Capitol building whenever possible. These people believed it was their bottomless well of prattling opinions that made the world advance. Snyder knew that real progress demanded a different approach.

He'd worked with the senator several times now, always on projects of mutual benefit to America's security and the senator's career. Brennigan seemed to be following this latest coltan mining deal with particular intensity—an intensity that Snyder had only observed in relation to the personal half of Brennigan's motivations. A successful outcome was going to be critical to Snyder's own plans as well. If they could bring in the coltan deal for the U.S., then Brennigan would be in a position to get Snyder a spot on the Intelligence Action Network, a group that few knew existed and even fewer were invited to join.

Brennigan had first approached Snyder three years earlier, on the day that Snyder had delivered a prepared speech to the Senate Select Committee on Intelligence. Throughout the critical session on the threat of China's investments in Africa, half the senators had dozed, and most of the others had looked distracted, as though Snyder were discussing the weather. Brennigan had slipped up to him afterward to compliment him on his presentation and ask if he would join him in a stroll around the West Lawn. Now Snyder recalled their conversation as clearly as if it had happened yesterday.

"Are you a patriot, Captain Snyder?" Brennigan asked as they walked between rows of red and yellow tulips. The smooth petals were perfectly formed, each plant an equal distance from its neighbors, like rows of brightly helmeted miniature soldiers.

"Of course," Snyder replied.

"How far would you go? For your country?"

Snyder stopped to look at Brennigan, whose eyes gave nothing away. Still, Snyder knew what he was asking. The senator had a reputation as someone who got things done, a reputation that Snyder admired.

"I'm a military man, Senator. I do whatever it takes."

Brennigan nodded. "Good, good. That's what I like to hear. You come highly recommended, by the way."

It was Snyder's turn to nod. It was no secret that he'd been one of the Defense Intelligence Agency's most successful field agents for many years before being called to the Pentagon.

"Sometimes we have special problems," Brennigan continued, "that need special solutions. Shall we say... fast-track solutions. You know how slow official channels can be."

"I understand."

Brennigan smiled. As the two men resumed their stroll along the neat pathways, the conversation turned to the perils of China's increasing ownership of U.S. corporations. Snyder felt warmed by the early spring sun and by the sense of a growing bond with the senator.

When they reached the edge of the park, Brennigan bent down to touch one of the tulips, his fingers caressing the silky red petals.

"My wife loves flowers," he said. "For her, that was the hardest part about coming to Washington. Leaving her garden."

Snyder leaned over the flower bed and let his own hand brush along the row of resplendent blooms. As he touched a particularly tall and vivid bud, he slid his hand deep into the succulent foliage at the base of the plant and, with a twist of the wrist, freed the stem. He presented the flower to Brennigan with a bow of his head.

"For your wife."

Brennigan glanced around, instinctively nervous at the breach of protocol. A few other people strolled along the paths, but nobody was paying them any attention. He looked at Snyder and threw his head back with a loud laugh.

"Why not?" he said, taking the flower and slipping it carefully under his jacket.

The buzz of the first group of senators emerging from the chamber jolted Snyder back to the present. The politicians were quickly surrounded by a crowd of attendants jostling them with documents and questions.

Brennigan followed soon after and immediately attracted his own swarm of aides. He snapped out an instruction to a woman with grey hair swept back into a bun, who deftly tapped notes with a stylus into a tablet computer.

Snyder took a step forward and fell in with Brennigan's group as they walked along the hallway. It took several seconds for

Brennigan to register his presence, and when he did, his face slipped immediately into a scowl.

"Excuse me, I need a moment," Brennigan said to a young woman who was handing him a cell phone. He crossed to walk alongside Snyder and held up his hand to ward off his staff. They all dropped back to a respectful distance except the woman with the bun, who joined them with her stylus expectantly poised above her tablet.

"It's okay; I'll handle this one." Brennigan touched the woman's arm. She examined Snyder under raised eyebrows before she too backed away.

"What are you doing here?" demanded Brennigan. Snyder knew that the senator was always nervous about them being seen together, even though there was no reason why Brennigan, as a member of the Intelligence Committee, shouldn't associate with a member of the Defense Intelligence Agency.

"Something's come up with the coltan mining deal."

Brennigan glanced over his shoulder at his staff, still keeping their distance. "Well?" he hissed.

Snyder took a deep breath. "It's Burundi. They've pulled out."

He watched the small capillaries on Brennigan's nose and cheeks fill with blood, signaling an impending eruption.

"What do you mean, pulled out?" Brennigan's voice echoed around the corridor, drawing several stares. He caught himself and moved closer to Snyder, continuing in a more controlled voice. "You told me they'd signed over their rights already."

"They agreed to. The final ceremony is supposed to be tomorrow in Kinshasa. We've got five Silicon Valley CEOs on a plane right now."

"Don't tell me Burundi signed with China instead?"

"The Chinese still don't know about the find, we think. The local mining contractor managed to..." Snyder recalled the photos he'd seen from when the coltan deposit was first discovered. The tangled bodies, including the smooth frail limbs of children, piled at the center of the squalid huts that passed for a village in that part of the world. It had been blamed on the rebels, of course. "They kept it under wraps."

"They can't just change their minds. It's a verbal contract. It's enforceable." The capillaries merged into a solid band of red across Brennigan's face. "We'll sue their government for breach of contract. They'll have to sign."

Snyder bit back a sarcastic response. Sometimes the senator's legal background wasn't an asset. "That's one approach," he said patiently. "But perhaps first we should find out why they changed their minds."

Brennigan took off his glasses and rubbed at the bridge of his nose. "Yes. I thought you said they were desperate for the money?"

"They are," Snyder nodded. "Or at least, they were. There's a sudden flow of money into the country."

"What are they selling? Drugs? Women?"

"Nothing like that. It's coming in through agencies and charities and direct donations to the Burundi government. People are just giving them money."

"That makes no sense." Brennigan pointed a finger at Snyder, a move that Snyder recognized as the onset of a lecture. "You'd better work out what's happening. It's our duty to protect the people who live in these places. The minerals are their birthright, their way out of poverty." The redness spread from Brennigan's face out to his ears and down to his neck, disappearing beneath the stiff, white collar of his shirt. "You saw what happened in the Democratic Republic of Congo. We can't let rebels from all over the place just waltz in and steal the stuff to fund their wars. We've got to stamp out the abuse and give them a fair price."

Snyder let the words fade into a drumbeat, a rhythm of sound and energy that pulsed but had no soul. Snyder had given Brennigan the words as ammunition to drive his deals; now the senator was shooting them back as though they were his own.

Snyder knew that it wouldn't matter to the local people who won. China, the U.S., or the rebels—all would become mired in a web of exploitation that would lead to thousands more deaths and millions more refugees. Tantalum, the precious grey metal that came from the coltan, was needed for the capacitors in the billions of cell phones, medical devices, and other electronics the world demanded every year. Because of silent heroes like himself, Snyder reflected bitterly, neither the fashion-enslaved consumers nor the money-hungry corporations knew or cared that the miracle metal for the twenty-first century was mined from poverty and corruption.

Snyder watched Brennigan's face stretch and grimace its way through the predictable arguments, his finger waving more emphatically with each new point. Eventually, the movements slowed and ended in an expectant silence.

Snyder realized that Brennigan had asked him a question.

"Of course, Senator, you're absolutely right," he said quickly.

"The American people won't stand for more bloodshed," Brennigan continued. "Remember all those Hollywood types protesting about the people being slaughtered in the Congo?"

"Actually, that was about the gorillas."

"What?"

"The miners were killing gorillas for food. That's what caused the protests."

Brennigan stared at Snyder. "Well, I'm sure they cared about the people too."

The two men had arrived at the door to the senator's office. The trailing entourage caught up and Brennigan waved them inside.

"One more minute," he said with a quick smile to the woman with the bun. He waited until she disappeared through the wooden door, the senator's gold nameplate flashing as the door closed behind her.

"There's something else." Brennigan lowered his voice. "I heard that Shenyang Electronics is working on a takeover bid for Capacitron. They want to announce it at the global electronics show in March."

Snyder drew in a breath. "Where did you hear that?"

"I have my sources too."

Snyder tasted the anger returning to his throat. Sometimes he felt he was trying to stave off the Chinese invasion single-handedly. Now they wanted to buy the biggest U.S. manufacturer of capacitors? His frown deepened as another thought occurred to him.

"Doesn't Capacitron have a plant in your—"

"Yes," snapped Brennigan. "I'm going to have four thousand unhappy constituents if they close that plant. Plus the hourlies that flip their burgers and mow their lawns."

"But if we can claim a new source of tantalum for the U.S., we can drive Capacitron's stock price up enough to ward them off." Snyder felt a puzzle piece fall into place. The reason for the senator's special interest in this deal was becoming clear. He wondered if the good senator was also a Capacitron shareholder.

"Exactly." Brennigan paused as a woman in a navy-blue suit walked past, her skirt showing barely an inch below the thigh-length jacket. "I'm counting on you, Snyder. You said this deal was all sewn up after the... incident... at the Hotel Kinshasa."

"It's just a delay. It won't take long to sort it out."

"That's good, because the final decision on the new appointment to the Intelligence Action Network is three weeks from now."

Snyder studied the senator's face, its redness now faded to a residual pink. "It's in both our best interests to have me in that network. Think of the connections I can—"

"Yes, yes." Brennigan waved a hand impatiently. "You get that coltan, I'll get you on the IAN. I'll tell them how you single-handedly saved the U.S. electronics industry."

Snyder felt a burning desire to reach out and crush the soft flesh around Brennigan's neck. One day, perhaps. But for now, he needed the senator's influence. "I've already got intelligence alerts out on Burundi," he said evenly. "I'll step it up a level."

"See that you do." Brennigan straightened his shoulders and flung open the door to his office. Inside, a flurry of aides scuttled toward him.

"Because we have to help those people over there," he called over his shoulder. "No more exploitation."

"Of course, Senator." Snyder forced his lips into a smile. "We wouldn't want that."

Chapter 13

"I JUST THINK WE SHOULD tell someone, that's all," said Roy. "In case they can help you fix it faster." He stopped and peered up at the large white map outside the entrance to Massachusetts General Hospital and compared it to the room number scrawled on the Post-it note he was holding in one hand. In the other, he held a basket of yellow flowers that he and Lenny had bought from the stand outside the supermarket,

"Who do you suggest?" Lenny snapped. "You want me to tell Andrei Simenov how I'm wrecking his company, and ask if he can lend me a few engineers to sort it out?"

For all his sarcasm, Lenny had actually considered this idea briefly. He had dismissed it just as quickly—he was still hoping there was a way to put everything right without Andrei Simenov or anyone else from Blahst finding out. Then he could cash the check they'd given him and walk in with his head held high to accept Andrei's job offer.

"What about the FBI? They have some kind of cyber division."

Lenny groaned. Roy's suggestions had been getting more preposterous as the weekend progressed. Why couldn't Roy leave him alone? Lenny was sure there was a way to stop his viral algorithm from spreading, although so far, he had to admit, the exact solution had eluded him. And he didn't need to look at his phone to remind himself what was happening to Blahst and its high-tech competitors. The steeply declining stock charts were burned into his retinas. But telling the FBI?

"I thought you were worried about getting caught?" Lenny lowered his voice as the automatic doors slid open and they walked into the busy hospital lobby. "Now you want us to turn ourselves in to the Feds?"

"You keep saying we didn't break any laws." Roy lowered his eyes to the white floor tiles. "Probably."

"You know they just put that hacker in jail for five years. Made an example of him. And he didn't even steal anything."

"Neither did we," said Roy.

"You didn't do anything, okay? I was the one that sent out the messages. It's my problem, so quit bugging me."

Lenny wondered what they might be able to prosecute him for if he did turn himself in. The Blahst postings claimed to be from other people, even though he was the one who had created them. Did that count as identity theft? What about photos of Andrei? Did doctoring a photo count as forgery? He hadn't researched any of it because he didn't really want to know the answers.

"We don't need to go to the FBI, because I'm going turn this thing around." Lenny pulled Roy to one side as an orderly wheeled an empty bed past them. They continued along the corridor until Roy pointed at a room number that matched the one on the Post-it note. Lenny paused outside the door.

"I just wish Professor Ramsey hadn't had a stroke right now," he said morosely.

"We agreed, remember?" Roy spun to face Lenny. "Not a word. He needs to rest."

"I know, don't blow a fuse." *It was just such bad timing,* Lenny brooded. Not that there was ever a good time for that kind of thing, but he was sure the professor would know what to do. Now Lenny had no idea how long it would be before Ramsey recovered enough to help them out.

Roy knocked and pushed open the door of the professor's room. The neatly made bed had a TV mounted on the wall to one side, and a chest of drawers was covered with vases and baskets of flowers. The walls were papered with an abstract pastel fleck.

Ramsey was sitting in a chair next to the bed. His silky, maroon dressing gown was covered from the waist down by a navy blanket. He greeted them with a smile and a wave.

"Professor, you look great!" exclaimed Lenny. From the doorway, Ramsey actually looked better than he had the last time Lenny had seen him at the office. But as Lenny got close enough to shake the professor's outstretched hand, he saw that one eye and one side of his mouth were dropped and motionless. Lenny looked away quickly. The heat of the room felt suddenly stifling.

Roy cleared a space on the drawer unit for the flowers while Lenny shook off his coat and pulled up one of the hard-backed chairs that lined the wall.

"They've got me in a treatment program," said Ramsey. His voice was his usual booming baritone, though Lenny detected a slurring of his words that hadn't been there before. "Physical therapy six times a day. It's my left side." He raised his left arm a few inches up from his lap before it flopped back down.

"We brought you some books," said Lenny, pulling them out from a plastic bag. He placed them on the professor's lap and tried not to stare at the limp arm. Ramsey smiled broadly with the right side of his face while the left side stayed defiantly immobile.

"Thank you. How wonderful." Ramsey picked up the top book with his right hand and held it out at arm's length in front of him. "Would you mind reading me the titles? There's something up with my eyes—I can't quite get the words in focus."

Lenny held the book in front of his face to hide his dismay. He couldn't imagine being unable to read. Ramsey clucked and smiled appreciatively as Lenny read the titles, complimenting him on his selection even though Lenny was sure he must already own some of them.

"So, how's it going at the office?" asked Ramsey once he had finally finished thanking Lenny and Roy. "Managed to burn the place down yet?"

Lenny and Roy both answered at once.

"It's going fine."

"We're doing great."

"Glad to hear that's unanimous," chuckled Ramsey. "If the physio goes well, they tell me I could be back in a month, but I need you two to keep things going until then. Oh, and how's the fundraising going?"

"Ah..." Lenny hesitated. At the last count they had just over two hundred thousand dollars in contributions at Healthway, and Roy was hearing through the grapevine that other charities were being flooded with donations too. He didn't want the professor to suffer a relapse from shock. "We're over fifty thousand now."

"That's marvelous, just wonderful work, Lenny." Ramsey was beaming lopsidedly again. "And I don't think I told you this before, but your condom selections were quite popular in Burundi. They became something of a collector's item. I'm not sure that's exactly meeting the goals of the program, but we certainly learned something about product marketing."

Ramsey looked thoughtfully at Lenny before he continued. "Roy showed good judgment in recommending you. I have to thank you both. I know things are in good hands while I'm tied up here."

Lenny felt heavy heat rise to his face. "Sure, thanks," he mumbled.

The professor selected a book from the bed and opened it up, moving the text toward and away from his eyes. After a few tries he sighed and closed the book, setting it back onto the bed.

"I was just wondering, Professor. In your work, have you found a way to..." Lenny considered how to phrase the question without giving anything away. "Once an idea starts taking hold, is there any way to stop it?"

"Why would you want to do that?" Ramsey shrugged. "Let's enjoy it while the going's good."

"But what if it was moving too fast? How would you slow it down?"

"Is there something you're not telling me, Lenny?" Ramsey's right eye narrowed and his shoulders leaned forward.

Lenny flinched as he felt Roy's knuckle dig into the side of his thigh.

"I mean, just in theory. It's for my research."

Ramsey held Lenny's gaze for a moment longer, then relaxed back against his chair. "As you know, ideas have their own life cycle. If it doesn't hit critical mass, it will just fade out by itself eventually."

"And if it does hit critical mass, what then?" Lenny persisted. "What if it's already gone viral?"

The professor rubbed at his left cheek gently with his right hand. "In that case, you'd probably want to introduce an idea that countered the first. Something that would change people's minds."

Lenny began to feel a trickle of hope. It made perfect sense. A counterattack of good press about Blahst to undo the negative messages he'd been sending around. It was so obvious, he should have thought of it himself. The trickle of optimism gave way to a rush of urgency. He had to start working on it as soon as possible.

"The trouble is," added Ramsey, "these things are so unpredictable. The counter message would have to be even stronger than the original. But changing people's mind once they've accepted an idea is more difficult than persuading them in the first place. Your new message might be adopted by a new set of people, but ignored by the ones you influenced the first time around. Then you'd end up with two strongly held but opposite opinions by two different groups, which isn't what you're trying to achieve."

Lenny nodded as Ramsey spoke, trying to focus on the words and not the professor's slackened cheek. In Blahst's case, he couldn't see that it would matter if a few people still didn't like the company. If his new campaign was powerful enough, if he sent messages to even more people than last time, it would be enough to cancel out the decline in the stock price for Blahst and the other social media companies. They might even end up better off than they were before Lenny had set his algorithm loose. At least he would be doing something.

Lenny ignored the dark looks that Roy was giving him and pulled out his phone. He watched the spinning circle tell him it couldn't find service and shut it off again. Ramsey and Roy were running through the minutia of Healthway's needs for the next four weeks, but Lenny couldn't summon up a shred of interest in the topic. His legs felt charged with energy. His muscles ached to run out of the room and out of the hospital, to a place where he could be alone and get online. He couldn't wait to put things right.

Chapter 14

SNYDER STARED AT THE BLACK smudge that was growing like a cancer over the center of Africa and felt the corner of his right eye twitch. Something big was happening here, and his host wouldn't stop rattling on about the processes and best practices he had created for his department, the CIA's Office of Predictive Analytics.

"Could you tell me what's going on around Lake Tanganyika, Colonel Egham?" Snyder asked the question for the third time and tried not to let his impatience show. "The intensity of the activity around that region, particularly Burundi, seems to indicate..."

"Ah, yes, you notice how well these screens showcase the visualizations." Egham's Texas drawl extended each syllable by an unnatural length that further frayed Snyder's nerves. His circular, boyish face looked out of place between the starched precision of his military uniform and cropped grey hair. "Ms. Mahoney here is our expert at this," he continued. "Angie, why don't you show Captain Snyder how it all works?"

The third person in the conference room jumped up from the edge of the table where she had been perched, staring vacantly at the screen on the opposite wall. Angie's straight brown hair was gathered loosely at the back of her neck, and she wore straight-legged brown pants with a beige sweater and flat shoes. She stepped into the center of the room and cleared her throat, but before she could say a word, Egham launched into an explanation of how he'd finagled the intricacies of the CIA budget cycle to procure the latest in gesture-activated, wall-to-wall display technology for their incident room. While he spoke, Angie raised her palm slowly and deliberately to the right, sending the African continent sliding over to a side wall. The center display was filled with the familiar outline of the Americas.

As Egham recounted how he had convinced the procurement officer to change the purchasing guidelines, Snyder sighed and wiped a bead of sweat from the side of his forehead. It amazed him that they could manage to overheat these old offices when it was below freezing outside. The Office of Predictive Analytics was housed in the deepest basement of the old headquarters building, as though to fool the enemy into thinking that nothing as high tech as this department could exist in such a forlorn corner of Langley. *Probably just some drywall separating us from the furnaces*, he thought.

Snyder had spent all day yesterday, and half the night, hunting down any information on the subject of Burundi. Now that he'd found what looked like his first real lead, he was faced with a gatekeeper who was turning out to be the biggest bore in the CIA, an honor that in Snyder's view had plenty of contenders. In another time and place, Snyder might actually have been interested in the mapping technology as something he could duplicate in his own offices at the Defense Intelligence Agency. But right now Snyder didn't care if the map was rendered on an Etch A Sketch—he just had to know if whatever was causing that dark stain across Burundi was the reason his plans with Senator Brennigan had been shot to hell.

At least his host seemed to be drifting closer to the question at hand as he boasted about the department's activities.

"All of the information from the other agencies is fed into our system here at the Office of Predictive Analytics, or OPRA as we like to call it." Egham pointed at the acronym emblazoned at the top of each screen. "Pronounced like Oprah. Because we know all the gossip, see?"

A disturbing braying sound came from Egham's mouth, and Snyder realized he was laughing. "All the military intelligence, criminal activity, financial markets, that kind of thing. Millions of petabytes of information a day flow into our system. Angie, let's show Captain Snyder what we do here."

Angie picked up the thread seamlessly. "We're looking for trends, for changes in the patterns. As long as things continue on a predictable path, we can ignore them, which is how we manage to keep up with so much input. What we're looking for are hotspots of activity that indicate major changes. See this slightly darker blue area over here, for example."

Angie indicated toward the screen with her hand. "This is Madrid, and we're seeing an unusually high level of police activity. I happen to know that there's a summit there this week on the shark fishing treaty, and there are major protests. If we didn't know that, it's something we would check out, because the area is darker than normal."

"Tell him about the butterfly part, Angie," Egham beamed.

Snyder detected a slow intake of breath from Angie, so slight that an untrained ear would have missed it. It seemed as though Angie felt the same frustration with Egham as Snyder did.

"A large part of what we do involves trying to predict the effects of change," said Angie. "The Madrid conference is having some effect on the local economy as workers are staying away from the center. It's impacting the world's opinion of Hong Kong, as they are refusing to sign the treaty. We estimate how far each of these effects will go, and how long they will last." Angie made a circle with her index finger and thumb and moved it toward the screen. The map on the wall rippled with a spiderweb of pale lines radiating out from Madrid.

"This is an influence network—that means you can see the connections between the cause and the effect. The stronger the effects, the darker it shows up on the map."

Egham nodded his head. "It's called the butterfly effect. A butterfly flaps its wings in Brazil, and there's a hurricane in Texas, right Angie?"

"Um... yes, that's right." Again the intake of breath. *Not impressed with her boss's presentation of chaos theory,* Snyder surmised.

"In fact, most direct effects die out very rapidly," she continued. "If we fast-forward Madrid by two weeks, the models predict that things will be back to normal, just a little residual anti–Hong Kong sentiment." On the map, the colors and lines around Madrid faded away. Egham was still smiling and seemed oblivious to the fact that Angie had just contradicted his butterfly homily.

Since Egham appeared determined to talk about everything except what Snyder wanted to know, Snyder decided to try another tack. He had homed in on the Office of Predictive Analytics late last night, when his private search network had yielded a daily briefing report with multiple references to Burundi. The name on the OPRA report had been Egham's, but Snyder was getting the impression that he could never have penned it. Angie Mahoney was the more likely author, and the one more likely to have the answers that Snyder needed.

"Your report said something about Burundi." Snyder knew exactly what the report had said. *Burundi is exhibiting unprecedented levels of converging influence from disparate, unidentifiable sources.* "Tell me about that."

"Yes, well, that may have been a little premature. We don't quite understand..." Egham's voice was tinged with disapproval as it tailed off.

Snyder walked up to the map of Africa on the side wall of the meeting room and jabbed a finger at the edge of Lake Tanganyika. "This is it, isn't it? This dark spot over Burundi? It's not like the rest of it." He swept his hand over the pastel lines and shading that covered the map. "What does it mean?" He fixed his eyes directly on Angie.

Angie looked down at her feet. "We're investigating it, Sir. There are some unusual financial flows that seem to be having some broader repercussions. We haven't quite identified the source yet."

"Have you seen anything like it before?" asked Snyder.

"Well, actually, I have a research project..." Angie looked across at Egham, who gave a small shake of his head.

Another bone of contention, thought Snyder.

"I would love to hear about that." Snyder smiled at Egham. "It's admirable that you encourage your people to pursue their own research. We need more of that type of inspired management in our intelligence organizations, if you ask me."

Egham glanced hesitantly between Snyder and Angie. Finally he nodded, although his annoyance was still evident.

"I've been recreating historical influence networks from the twentieth century." Angie pointed at a small image on the far edge of the side screen. She drew both hands apart slowly, and the image formed into a series of animated slides. She enlarged each one in turn as she described it. "This one's a world map from 1911. These are the waves of revolution spreading throughout China and beyond. This next one is Hitler's Germany." Angie's hand tracked the thick lines radiating out to engulf Europe and Asia in blackness. Another sequence showed an intense but self-contained red circle flaring over Cambodia's killing fields. To finish, she ran through slides with solid blocks of color mapping out the long stalemate years of the Cold War.

"What about more recent examples?" asked Snyder.

"There don't seem to be any of this strength since 1989. The Arab Spring showed up as a series of dramatic but short-lived influence networks, but nothing that persisted over time."

Snyder thought for a moment. "1989 was the fall of the Berlin Wall." He nodded to himself. "Why did that change things, do you think?"

Angie glanced at Egham, who stood to one side with his arms crossed. Angie swallowed and continued.

"The pattern changed after the fall of communism. Those heavy influence networks you saw were the results of governments imposing their will, of driving and maintaining their influence networks. But if you remember, the 1980s were the

Reagan and Thatcher years, when they started revitalizing the free market economy and limiting the role of the government."

"Go on," said Snyder.

"It's all down to globalization," Angie continued. "Governments don't control their economies anymore. The markets do. All governments can do is set up guidelines to keep everybody honest and let the international markets do their thing. Which means the role of the government—"

"Yes, well, I think we can assume our government is still firmly in control," interrupted Egham. "So, Captain Snyder, as you can see, we perform some of the most important work in the agency here in this department."

As Egham ran through a list of near crises averted by OPRA's keen insights, something on the center screen caught Snyder's eye. He felt himself drawn closer to the map until he reached out and drew a small circle with his finger around the East Coast of the United States.

"There's another one."

Angie was by his side in a second. Egham stopped talking as he realized he'd lost his audience.

"It wasn't there yesterday," said Angie.

The three of them inspected the small black dot over Boston, Massachusetts. Angie pointed a finger at the bottom corner of the screen and looped it around until a window popped up with a stream of text.

"I never saw an influence network develop this quickly. Look at this! There are some sociopolitical indicators around privacy issues, and..." Angie paused and glanced nervously at Egham. "Colonel Egham, perhaps we should wait..." She indicated their visitor with a nod of the head.

"No, no. This is a great chance for Captain Snyder to see how the department works. We can show him some real action instead of those historical theories."

Angie shrugged and continued. "The other driver is financial. Abnormal levels of trading activity in the high-tech sector. Seems to be related to the privacy issues. Let's do a drill down." With an open-handed gesture, she pulled up another window on the wall display, and company names started appearing in different colors.

"Is it the same as Burundi?" asked Snyder.

"Different drivers, same result." Angie looked between the two black areas on the map. "I've never seen anything like it."

They watched in silence as the company names swirled slowly around on the screen until they came to a standstill, radiating out from bright red in the center to shades of orange at the edges. One name stood out in the center of the window, highlighted in scarlet font.

"Anybody heard of Blahst?" asked Colonel Egham.

Chapter 15

"HE'S FROM THE FBI."

"I heard it was the CIA. They think foreign agents are trying to bring down the U.S. economy."

"I don't think a few photos are going to wreck the economy." Mari pushed away a Coke can so that she could lean against her desk. She'd been surrounded by curious colleagues all day, because her cubicle offered the best view of the corner office and its new occupant, a tall man in a dark-blue suit who was causing intense speculation among her teammates. Lance and Paolo were the latest to stop by with contributions to the rumors swirling around the company.

"Not the photos, the privacy backlash. It's hitting our competitors as well," Lance reminded her.

Mari felt mildly embarrassed that she had become so engrossed in her work with the photos, she had almost forgotten about the other, more serious, attack on Blahst.

She peered round the edge of her cubicle as a Blahst security guard wheeled a dolly with a sealed plastic crate on it toward the corner office. Paolo and Lance crowded behind her to get a look.

"There's only one person," she whispered, wiggling to one side to get some space. "If it was the government, wouldn't there be hordes of them?"

"Maybe he's getting everything ready before the rest of them come," suggested Lance. "Anyway, there was that other guy in earlier, the one with the Yankees cap." He reached up to touch his own Red Sox cap as though to comfort it against the affront.

"I spoke to him in the elevator," said Paolo. "The Yankees guy."

Mari and Lance looked up at him expectantly, but Paolo suddenly feigned interest in the photos lining Mari's cubicle walls—row upon row of sunsets that the image analysis software had flagged as potential matches for the fake photo of Andrei.

Mari poked Paolo in the ribs. "Well? What about the guy in the elevator?"

Paolo turned with a smile and leaned toward his audience.

"I was on my way to the soda machine when I saw him go in the elevator, so I managed to catch the door and jumped inside. I asked him if he's with the guy in the suit, and he said, 'Sys admin.' Then the elevator doors opened and he bolted away. Didn't even look at me."

"He's a system administrator? That's it? Couldn't you find out anything else?" said Mari. "Some spy you'd make."

Mari had quickly adopted the style of teasing banter that was the standard communication mode of her new team. Although the work was dull, she found herself enveloped in the camaraderie created by the long hours and Pierce's constant reminders about the importance of their work.

"Well, if he needs his own sys admin, he must be—"

"Did you hear?" A newcomer with red-rimmed glasses and gelled hair skidded to a halt in front of Mari's cubicle. It was Yefim, a young man who had been part of Paolo's team before Paulo was transferred to Pierce's sleuthing project.

Finally some real news, she thought. Yefim was always well informed with the latest office rumors.

"Well, who is he?" she asked.

A frown spread on Yefim's face for a second. "Who's who? Oh, that guy?" he said, glancing at the corner office. "No idea. I mean, did you hear about Clayton?"

Mari had to admit that Clayton had barely crossed her thoughts since she'd been assigned to Pierce a week earlier. He hadn't stopped by in all that time. She had been so enjoying the freedom from his constant supervision that she hadn't paused to think that might be a little odd.

Yefim stepped closer to his colleagues. He straightened his glasses in a way that reminded Mari of Clayton, but the dark arms beneath the tight-fitting black t-shirt were nothing like Clayton's physique.

"They fired him." Yefim paused and looked round at his colleagues. "He stole some code and said it was his."

Paolo and Lance looked suitably impressed at the news. Mari felt frozen to the spot.

"Who did he steal it from?" asked Paolo.

Mari closed her eyes. She didn't want to hear Lenny's name. They'd all seen her with him at the launch party, and she wasn't in the mood for an interrogation.

"Some guy Clayton interviewed," Yefim replied. "Turns out Clayton went to the product manager for Version 6 and said he'd developed a new feature, already had the code. They took him onto the team and put it right in the product."

Mari remembered how Lenny had looked at her at the launch party—the absolute certainty in his words, the expression of betrayal on his face, the slight pleading in his eyes for her to believe him. She should have thought of Clayton right away—he was there with them in the interview. How could she not have made the connection? The truth was, she'd never really believed Lenny's accusation, not even as she was relaying it to the product manager. She couldn't conceive that Blahst would deliberately do such a thing, so she hadn't stopped to think through the scenarios of how it might have happened.

"When did they fire Clayton?" she asked quietly.

"They put him on paid leave last week while they investigated. Then they fired him on Friday, but they've been keeping it quiet because of this other mess. Don't want the stock price worse than it already is. But here's the thing..." Yefim glanced up the corridor and continued in a low voice. "They say he might be the one who caused all the trouble. He knew he'd been found out when they put him on leave, so he decided to get back at the company."

Mari frowned and glanced at her colleagues. At least once a day, Pierce repeated his instructions not to talk about the investigation, so she wasn't sure they should tell Yefim that they knew it was some kind of global organization, not an individual. In any event, she couldn't imagine Clayton staging anything as sophisticated as this. Now that his invitation to join the Version 6 team had been explained, Mari figured that Clayton was as clueless as she had first thought. Trying to claw his way up the corporate hierarchy on the back of someone else's work seemed much more his style.

Yefim was still waiting for a reaction, but Paolo and Lance were also looking uncertain of how to respond.

"That doesn't seem likely," she mumbled.

"It's true. It's all over the company," insisted Yefim. "You guys are so out of it up here. Once they confirm it was Clayton, you can stop this secretive shit and come back and do something useful." He looked around at Mari's sunsets, shook his head, and bounded off down the corridor.

Lance stretched his hands behind his head. "Shame it couldn't be Clayton. I'm going bug-eyed from sorting through this crap."

"At least you got rain forests," complained Paolo. "I've been staring at Osama bin Laden's face for a week. It's giving me nightmares."

"Pierce called that meeting for this afternoon, so maybe we'll hear something then." Lance removed his baseball cap, fluffed his hair with his fingers, and put his cap back on. "So Clayton is 'no longer with us.'" He spoke the words with a tone of officialdom. "Can't say I'm too surprised. I never saw the guy produce anything, and there he was, promoted to Version 6."

He pushed pretend glasses up his nose and fell into a British accent. "Paolo, could you help me here. I put my Java code into the coffee machine but it clogged up the filter."

Paolo laughed and leaned back against Mari's chair.

Mari felt a flash of irritation at the cheerful way her colleagues were discussing Clayton's demise. Clayton had not only got himself fired, he'd also messed with Lenny's career chances by not giving him credit for the work. No wonder Lenny had been so angry. She was feeling steadily worse for not believing him right away.

"They haven't told us to stop working yet, so you guys should get back to your own cubes," she said, pulling the chair from Paolo and sitting down in front of her computer.

She could feel their surprised stares boring into the back of her neck. She clicked her mouse and pretended to focus on the pink and orange sunset image on the screen.

"Sure," said Paolo. The two of them shuffled out of the cubicle.

She heard a whisper from the other side of the divider. "What's up with her?"

"Don't know. Maybe she really liked Clayton."

After the excitement of the day, Pierce's team meeting was an anticlimax. Mari saw Paolo and Lance exchange disappointed glances when Pierce announced that the man in the corner office was a consultant working for Southridge Partners, Blahst's biggest investor. Pierce told his team to cooperate fully with the consultant, as their investors were concerned about the damage to the stock price and wanted to help in any way they could.

There was a brief surge of interest when Pierce announced that he had serious news about a Blahst employee. Eight pairs of eyes watched expectantly as Pierce cleared his throat and shuffled his feet with obvious discomfort. Mari felt sorry for him. Clearly he didn't know that his team had already heard the news.

They didn't learn much that was new. It was just as Yefim had told them. Clayton Malloy had been asked to leave the company because he had made a serious error in judgment regarding intellectual property. Pierce spoke for several minutes on the need for integrity and the highest ethical standards, and eight pairs of eyes slowly glazed over.

The third piece of news was unexpected. Pierce announced that the company was awarding stock options to all of its employees, with the amount varying according to seniority.

"Not worth the paper they're written on," mumbled Debra.

Pierce turned to face her, one eyebrow raised.

"Actually, it's a pretty smart financial move for the company," Pierce said. "We're conducting a stock buy-back from investors while the price is low. That means we can buy a lot of stock for our money. And we have every faith in Blahst's ability to rise again, which will make the employees who stick around very rich. And by the way, the trading window is open for employees, so you might want to think about buying up a little extra if you have the cash."

Mari saw approving nods from Paolo and Lance.

"Talking of rising again, do we have any leads on the perpetrators yet?" asked Lance.

"No," said Pierce. "I realize everyone else is convinced it's Clayton, but you guys know better. I'm trying to figure out how to squash that particular rumor without revealing all the details of our investigation. If we find the real culprits soon, that will certainly do the trick. So, back to work."

Mari returned to her cubicle and flopped down in her chair. She let her eyes wander over the images pinned around her wall, scanning instinctively for the differences between each one—differences in shade, intensity, or cloud pattern. She was actually enjoying the work in a way the others didn't seem to be. She'd taken the pattern-matching code and started to feed it back its own search results, annotated in detail as to which elements matched what she was looking for and which didn't. She was teaching the software as she went along, making it smarter with each new data set.

But even though the results were a little closer each time, none of them quite matched the sunset on the outsized image hanging above her terminal. There, a small, dark-skinned child looked up with terrified eyes at a black outline where Andrei Simenov had been cropped out of the doctored photo. Behind the child, crimson and orange streaks splashed across an endless expanse of navy sky.

She started marking up the latest set of search results for a new run she was planning for the morning. Outside her cubicle, she heard others leaving for the day. Snatches of conversation and laughter floated over as she worked, and she heard Clayton's name more than once.

She was focusing mostly on the sky and landscape, as she'd found the image of the child too unsettling. It might not have been Andrei Simenov towering over him in the original photo, but the child was clearly terrified of whoever or whatever was there. From the blank outline where Andrei had stood, a thin line of silver was pointing toward the child. A knife perhaps? She shuddered at the thought of what she might see if she did find the original.

Mari didn't realize there was anyone standing behind her until she heard a slight cough. She spun her chair around and leapt to her feet.

The man in the blue suit who had been the subject of her colleagues' earlier discussions was standing at the entrance to her cubicle, the lights from the corridor silhouetting his face. Mari could make out a prominent nose and cheekbones splashed with the reflected scarlet from her computer screen. She felt herself recoil from the intensity of his stare, but before she had taken more than half a step back his face relaxed into an apologetic smile.

"I didn't mean to startle you." The man's voice was smooth and reassuring. "I'm working over there in the corner office and didn't realize anyone else was still here."

Mari put a hand up to her pounding heart. "That's okay; you just made me jump." She held out her other hand toward the man. "I'm Mari Velasquez."

"Pleased to meet you." Mari felt her knuckles squeezed together as he shook her hand and looked around the cubicle. "Ah yes, the photos. Are you making any progress?"

"I haven't found a match yet, but I'm narrowing it down."

"Good. And I hear you may even have a suspect."

Mari looked up at the man in surprise. Had he heard something from Blahst management, something they weren't sharing with their employees? Or had he just heard the rumors about Clayton?

"Well we don't know... I mean..." Mari tried to think of something noncommittal to say.

"That's okay. I know you can't discuss these things outside the company." The man smiled again and inspected the walls of the cubicle before stepping back into the corridor. In the light, Mari could see that he was in his late fifties, with grey hair swept back from a point in the center of his forehead. A fleeting vision of old vampire movies floated through her mind.

"Keep going. This is important work," he said. He nodded to her firmly and strode away along the corridor.

Mari shivered and grabbed her sweatshirt from the back of her chair. As she pushed one hand into the baggy sleeve, she closed down her computer with the other.

She'd had enough of rumors and investors and intrigue for one day. She needed to find Lenny Driver and apologize.

From the door of the corner office, Snyder watched the young woman zip up her sweatshirt as she hurried down the corridor toward the elevator. He was nearly done for the day himself—just a couple more areas of the building to visit.

The microphones he had selected were so high powered that he only needed three or four to cover each floor, although he'd put some extras in the executive suite just in case. The brand was one favored by those involved in industrial espionage, so even if the bugs were discovered, it would be impossible to link them back to government activity.

Not that he was here on official government business. Nor did he care about Blahst, or their stock price. But if he could find out what was causing the influence network around Blahst, it might give him some leads on the Burundi situation.

He'd found a local resource here in Boston who was unconnected to any of his usual support network, a man who was ready to take action as soon as Snyder could point him in the right direction. Snyder had assumed that it would take days—maybe even a week or more—of painstaking listening and analysis to find any useful needles in the haystack of corporate blather, but now it seemed possible that he might not even need the listening devices at all.

Sometimes the employee rumor mill was a far more efficient communication channel than any number of executive meetings.

Chapter 16

"WANT ME TO MAKE UP a photo of Andrei singing round the camp-fire with some Boy Scouts?" suggested Roy.

"No photos this time. I'm doing another campaign around privacy." Lenny squinted at the blurred words on his screen. He hadn't slept much last night, or for the last few nights since he'd visited the professor. He'd researched everything he could find in the marketing and psychology literature on the topic of persuasion, so that he could target his messages perfectly. "Only this time it's all good—it's about how Blahst is working with the other social media companies to drive standards for privacy protection."

"Is that true?" Roy crossed from his bedroom and peered over Lenny's shoulder.

"I'm hoping it will be after the messages go out," Lenny shrugged. "Blahst will have to do something because everyone's going to be expecting them to. And in the meantime it should start to cancel out all the negative press they've been getting." He frowned at the words he was preparing, suddenly doubting whether, even after all his careful preparation, they had the power to stem the tidal wave he had started.

"Dude, you need a break. It's Saturday night and you've been slaving away all week. Why don't you come with me to the party? It's a black-and-white theme. How do I look?"

Lenny pushed his chair away from the computer. Roy stepped back and spread his arms. He was wearing a white, button-down shirt with a skinny black tie above black jeans and heavy Doc Martens. Lenny envied his friend's compact frame, which seemed to infuse anything he wore with a certain style. Lenny didn't worry about his own looks too much, but sometimes next to Roy, he felt distinctly ungainly.

"You look black and white," said Lenny.

"You could bring Mari," said Roy, picking up his wallet from the counter and searching through a wad of receipts stuffed inside. "If you ever decide to return her calls."

Lenny looked down at his phone on the kitchen counter. Mari had been texting him and leaving him voicemails for the past two days, but he had ignored them all. His impulse to visit her when he was at the Blahst offices had been replaced with a much stronger desire to avoid her. He needed to repair the damage he had done before he could face Mari again. Or anyone else from Blahst.

Roy threw his wallet back on the counter. "You got any money?"

"Dunno. Try my North Face."

"Still not cashed that Blahst check?" Roy rooted in the pockets of Lenny's jacket and pulled out a folded ten-dollar bill. "Can I borrow this?"

"Sure. If it's for gas for your car, just borrow mine. I won't be using it."

"Thanks, but no car tonight. It's an open bar and I have no intention of being in a fit state to drive." Roy pulled on a belted black leather jacket. He paused at the front door. "What you're doing now... you think it will really work?"

"Sure." Lenny answered with no hesitation. The last thing he needed was Roy hanging around worrying for the rest of the evening. "Go party."

"I still think some nice pictures would help—Andrei helping little old ladies across the street, that kind of thing," Roy called over his shoulder before slamming the door behind him.

Lenny tried to settle back into his work, but he kept finding himself staring at the screen with no recollection of what his next step was. He really did need a break. The nights of napping on the sofa between mammoth work sessions were catching up with him.

His eyes were drawn back to his phone with its unanswered messages from Mari. He wondered how the conversation would go when he did call her back. Would she gloat that she'd got him credit for his work? Would she apologize for not believing him? Or— his heart sped up at the thought—did she have an inkling that he was behind the Blahst attack?

Perhaps he should just call her back and get it over with. He pictured the waves of her hair falling over her face as she bent over her phone, picking out the letters of her text messages with the purple nail polish she'd worn to the launch party. He was so close to finishing—just a few more hours—it wouldn't do any harm to call her now. He was sure his new campaign would turn things around for Blahst so that he could face her with a clean conscience. Besides, when he did finish, it would probably be the middle of the night, and he couldn't exactly call her then, could he?

He picked up the phone and scrolled down his contacts until the name *Mari Velasquez* lit up the small screen. He ran his thumb slowly across the letters of her name before hitting the *Call* button.

"Hi, Mari." He tried to keep his voice casual.

"Oh, hi, Lenny. What's up?"

"I... um..." Lenny ground to a halt. He hadn't thought beyond his opening words. "You called me," he said finally.

"Oh yeah. Uh... hold on a sec."

There was silence. She'd put him on mute. He drummed his fingertips against his keyboard until her voice came back on.

"Lenny? Now's not a great time, actually."

He felt a flash of annoyance. He wasn't the one who had been calling every day. Now she was blowing him off? As he opened his mouth to speak, he heard a muffled crack and a gasp from the other end of the phone.

"Mari, are you okay?"

"Yeah, it's just... oh!" Another crack.

"What's happening, Mari?"

"It's Clayton. He's outside my apartment. I think he's throwing something at my window."

Lenny jumped to his feet. "Did you call the police? Is he threatening you?"

"No, no. He's... uh... singing."

Clayton. Lenny felt a wave of loathing. It was Clayton's fault this whole thing had happened. If Clayton hadn't passed off Lenny's work as his own, Lenny would never have needed to get back at Blahst.

"Mari, stay inside, lock the door, and I'll be there as soon as I can."

"No, Lenny, I don't think that's a good idea. I can handle—"

"I'll be there."

Lenny snatched up the North Face jacket that Roy had dumped on the floor and grabbed his car keys from the counter.

Lenny heard Clayton before he could see him. He had remembered the directions to Mari's street from when he'd picked her up for the launch party and managed to squeeze into a permit-only parking spot around the corner from her apartment.

The sidewalk was slick where the snow had melted and then refrozen into a solid sheet of ice. As Lenny slid his sneakers along the ice, the sound of loud and tuneless singing drifted through the cold air. His foot slipped sideways, and only his flailing arms kept him from falling. He climbed up onto the ploughed rocks of ice piled between the sidewalk and the road, which offered at least a small amount of traction.

As he rounded the corner he saw Clayton holding onto a waist-high wall outside Mari's apartment building and bellowing at the top of his lungs. Lenny recognized the words of a recent pop hit.

"*Don't wanna say goodbye, Marie.*" Clayton was gazing up at the windows of the four-story building. "*This was never...*" His feet slid backward and he landed on his knees, his hands still holding the top of the wall. He sunk his forehead against the brick and stayed there.

Lenny tried to hurry his pace, but the uneven lumps of compacted ice beneath his feet made it slow going. As he got closer, he saw Mari's face in a second-floor window. She caught Lenny's eye and waved quickly, then disappeared from view.

"*... never my idea. But now our choice is binary...*" Clayton was pulling himself back up the wall to a standing position as he resumed his singing. "*And I know I need you here.*"

Lenny stopped a few feet away from Clayton. He could see the air puffing out of Clayton's mouth in small clouds as he gazed up at the window where Mari had been.

The large front door of the apartment building opened, and Mari stepped out. For a second Clayton kept staring up at the window, but then he saw her and started moving along the wall toward the opening to the building's front courtyard, one hand steadying himself on the wall. He reached the stone lion that was mounted at the end of the wall and moved onto the path that led to the front door.

"Mari, my sweet flower, you came!" Clayton reached out his arms toward her and shuffled his feet along the ice. The effect reminded Lenny of an extra in a zombie movie.

"Clayton, you should go home." Mari turned toward the mound of ice where Lenny was standing. "Hi, Lenny."

Clayton swung around to where Mari was looking. His eyes stared blankly at first as though he was having trouble focusing. Then he blinked, and his face transformed into a twisted smirk of recognition.

"What do you know. It's Lenny the Loser."

Lenny scrambled down from the ice and picked his way toward Clayton.

"Hi, Mari. Is this guy bothering you?" The cliché felt good on Lenny's lips.

"Come to save the fair princess? What you gonna do, try and hit me again?" Clayton flung his arms apart. "Come on then, let's see what you can do." He wobbled precariously and grabbed for the stone lion on the wall.

Lenny crossed carefully to the opposite side of the opening and held onto the other stone lion. "Clayton, go home."

"Oooh, I'm so scared." A drop of spittle landed on Clayton's chin as he spoke. "Big tough guy, can't get a job, has to go around beating on people. Well, guess what—I'm one of you now. The great unemployed. But I didn't get fired. No, no, no. I resigned for personal reasons, no thanks to you, dorkface."

Clayton lunged across the opening, reaching for Lenny's jacket with one hand and pulling the other back into a sloppy fist. He flung the fist, palm first, toward Lenny's head. Lenny caught the fist easily in his left hand, but he lost his grip on the lion as he did so.

Clayton's feeble momentum was enough to propel the two of them toward the ground. Lenny managed to twist out from underneath Clayton as they fell, but Clayton was still holding his jacket. There was a crack as Clayton's head hit the ice, and a grunt as Lenny landed heavily on top of Clayton, his shoulder and arm sinking into Clayton's stomach.

Lenny heard Mari gasp and start down the path toward them. Lenny rolled off Clayton and felt his elbow connect painfully with the ice.

Before Mari could reach them, Clayton managed to raise his shoulders off the ground and grab the back of Lenny's jacket.

"We can be losers together, you and me." Clayton's fingers groped along Lenny's arm, and Lenny winced as they dug into the elbow that had hit the ground. Lenny swatted Clayton's hand away and raised himself to his feet. He yanked Clayton off the ground and pinned him against the end of the wall. Clayton made no move to pull away. He looked back at Lenny with the same leer on his face, as though daring Lenny to react. The lion's mouth gaped in a growl above his head.

Lenny drew his fist back and felt the energy building in the muscles of his arm. He paused for a moment, savoring the sensation. He had been waiting for this moment for a long time. The smirking face in front of him was the cause of all his problems. And Clayton had attacked first, so Lenny could legitimately claim self-defense if anyone called the police.

He was vaguely aware of Mari standing a few feet away. Clayton noticed too and turned his face in her direction, the full moon glinting off his glasses. Lenny found himself wondering if he should let Clayton take off his glasses before he punched him, as the guy probably couldn't see a thing without them. He shook his head against the distraction but dropped his fist slightly. Another thought tugged at his concentration—what if the police did come? What if they dragged him and Clayton off to the police station and made them stay in a jail cell for the night? Lenny would never get his new campaign started. If he could be rid of Clayton, he'd still be able to get back to work tonight and set the good publicity for Blahst in motion.

Lenny relaxed his fist and thumped it against Clayton's shoulder.

"Clayton, you should go home."

Clayton looked from Lenny to Mari and back to Lenny again. A tear appeared from behind his glasses and Lenny watched it wind its way down the side of his nose. Clayton's smirk had been replaced by a frown of confusion, or maybe disappointment.

Clayton pulled away from Lenny's grasp, rounded the corner onto the sidewalk, and immediately slid sideways. He grabbed clumsily for the wall.

Lenny shook the tension out of his arm and sighed deeply. "Let's call him a taxi."

Sobs sounded from the other side of the wall, interspersed by a reprise of the song. *"You're breaking my heart, Marie..."*

"I don't think a taxi would take him, in his state," said Mari. "Perhaps we should drive him. It's somewhere in Porter Square, only about five minutes away." She shivered and tugged the sleeves of her sweatshirt over her hands.

They watched Clayton sink down into a sitting position on the sidewalk, still snuffling. His head lolled back against the wall.

"I'll do it." Lenny was beginning to enjoy his role as the gallant defender. Mari hesitated, but then looked down at the slippers on her feet and nodded her agreement.

Lenny made his way back to his car, now practiced at the sliding motion he needed to make headway. He pulled it up outside the entrance, and he and Mari bundled Clayton into the back seat. As Lenny climbed into the driver's seat, Mari reached for his hand and gave it a squeeze.

"Thanks," she said. "I'll put some coffee on for when you get back."

Clayton was mostly silent in the back of the car, occasionally bursting into mournful singing or muttering something involving the word *loser*. Lenny couldn't be sure whether Clayton was aiming the insult at Lenny or at himself, so he kept quiet except to ask Clayton for directions.

Within a few minutes they were pulling up at a small two-family home. Lenny opened the car door and Clayton heaved himself out of the vehicle and up the path without a word. He stopped to retch twice as he stumbled toward the left of the two identical front doors. Nothing came out of his mouth, but Lenny was glad he had saved it until he was out of the car. He watched Clayton pull a key from his jeans pocket and jab it repeatedly at the lock. Eventually it made contact, and Clayton disappeared from view into the darkness.

The warmth of Mari's apartment relaxed the last of the tension from Lenny's body. He could feel the soft velvet of the sofa caress his arms as he stretched them along the back cushions. His muscles ached as though he had been in a fight rather than walked away from one, and his elbow was swollen where it had hit the ice. He rotated his forearm slowly and decided nothing was broken.

Mari's apology for not believing him hadn't brought him the pleasure he'd anticipated. He just felt embarrassed and had moved on quickly to tell her about his visit to Andrei, skipping over his fears that they had invited him there to arrest him. Mari kept his coffee mug filled as he talked, and she insisted on putting ice on his elbow. As their conversation tailed off, she reached across and gently stroked one finger over a fresh scrape on Lenny's wrist. The feel of her touch stayed as a trail on his skin.

"Why didn't you hit Clayton?" she asked. "I'm glad you didn't, but why?"

Lenny shrugged. "I guess I have more important things to do." He glanced past Mari at his phone. Ten fifteen. Still time to send out the new postings tonight.

"Oh Lenny, that's so sweet." Mari shifted her body sideways on the sofa. He felt her hand move up and settle against the side of his neck, sending a soft shiver through his whole body.

Lenny realized she had misunderstood him. He started to correct her, but as her other hand reached out and pulled his head gently toward her, he decided to let it ride. He felt the soft pressure of her lips gliding across his cheek. Their lips connected and all worries about Blahst, viral algorithms, privacy campaigns, and Clayton Malloy melted away. He closed his eyes and turned to face her, burying his hand deep into her hair.

The postings could wait a few more hours.

Chapter 17

LENNY KNEW HE HAD FOUND the right house by the column of cars parked along one side of the street. He drove past slowly, trying to see inside to where Mari and her family were celebrating. Several fuzzy figures were silhouetted in the windows of the single-story house.

He pulled past the last car in the line, eased up to the snowbank now passing for a curb, and cut the engine. He'd promised Mari he would come to the graduation party that her mother was throwing in her honor, but his mouth was dry at the thought of walking into a house full of strangers. He didn't know what had possessed him to accept the invitation.

Actually, he did know. He could still smell the rich, salty scent of Mari's skin and taste the musky flavor of her kiss. The cup of coffee had turned into a bottle of wine, accompanied by lingering kisses and animated discussions about music, books, family, and professors at the university. In the early hours of the morning, Mari had persuaded him not to drive home after so much wine and offered to make him up a bed on the sofa. The offer was fine with Lenny, and he had spent the night sleeping deeply and chastely in her living room.

Lenny picked his way along the front path in the pair of leather shoes he'd found in Roy's wardrobe. A clean white shirt was topped with his blue hirings-firings-and-weddings jacket, but neither garment offered much protection against the frigid air. He rapped on the door with a brass knocker that was shaped like a pineapple, and let himself in when there was no response.

He nearly didn't recognize Mari. He thought at first that the young woman with her hair swept up into a cascading spiral of flowers and ribbon above a stunning turquoise gown must be one of the many cousins he had heard about. She was one of a group of dark-haired, immaculately dressed teenagers and twenty-somethings who were chatting and laughing on the opposite side of the open living area. The chairs had been relegated to the sides of the room to make space for a collection of mismatched wooden tables in the center, every inch of them covered with bright plates of food on white lace mats.

Lenny caught Mari's eye. She leaned in briefly to say something to the group and then crossed to greet Lenny with a hug. He noticed the other young women eyeing him with unabashed curiosity.

"Wow, you clean up well," she said with a smile, her hands resting on the shoulders of his jacket. Her lips and eyes had the dark, glossy makeup of a magazine cover. "Come and meet some people." She pulled him by his sleeve toward the kitchen.

The kitchen was a blur of hospitality—uncles, cousins, neighbors, all of whom greeted Lenny like they'd known him for years. The men moved in and out of the kitchen quickly, picking out a beer or two from the fridge and heading back to an all-season porch behind the kitchen, where a TV was broadcasting a soccer match in Spanish. Lenny gathered from the frequent groans that the favored team was not doing well.

A large woman in a blue, floral dress entered the kitchen from the hall and frowned at a teenage boy, who was squashing a tomato against a chopping board in a failed attempt to slice it. She handed him a sharp knife and started showing him how to cut the tomato with smooth strokes. Mari put her arm around Lenny's waist and guided him toward the woman.

"Lenny, I want you to meet my mother, Rosa. Mama, this is Lenny."

Rosa turned to face them. "Mari tell me so much about you." Her English was halting but clear. She beamed and cupped the palm of one hand against Lenny's cheek. "Such a nice boy," she said to Mari, who looked proudly between Lenny and her mother.

Another older woman ran into the room with a phone and held it out to Rosa, talking rapidly in Spanish. Rosa took the phone and spoke excitedly into the mouthpiece. After a minute, tears started to stream down her face, but she continued her animated conversation, smiling and laughing at the same time as the tears fell.

"That's my grandmother in Hermosillo," explained Mari. "They're having a graduation party for me there, too."

Rosa passed the phone to Mari, who took up the conversation in fluent Spanish. Lenny watched her for a minute, not understanding the words but entranced by the way her mouth formed the unfamiliar syllables. He reminded himself that he had unfinished business and pulled himself away.

The bathroom was unoccupied, so he lowered the lid of the toilet to form a seat and settled down to do some work. The small browser window on his phone wasn't ideal, but it did the job. He'd spent a couple more hours that morning thinking up good publicity for Blahst, but he still needed to post the messages to the opinion leaders. He set up a search to find investors, small business advocates, and online startups that might have been hurt by the privacy backlash that Lenny had triggered through the attacks on Blahst. He was anxious to set the positive wave in motion by creating a surge of activity and buzz around how the social media companies were working to enhance their customers' privacy.

A sharp rap on the bathroom door distracted him momentarily, but he was able to ignore it, pleased that he'd thought to turn the lock. As the list of names started to flow, Lenny cross-referenced them with Blahst accounts and began to stream out Blahst postings. He'd targeted half a million opinion leaders in the attack, so he figured double that number should counteract the three-week head start of the old messages. Nothing too direct, just hints and half-formed ideas that would inspire readers to form their own opinions, all written in the unique online voices of a million strangers.

"Ola? Hello?" Between the knocking on the door and the jiggling of the door handle, Lenny was finding it increasingly hard to concentrate. It looked like he would have to find another spot to finish things up.

He nodded politely to three people waiting in a line outside the bathroom and wandered back into the dining area. The sight of the food displayed in the center of the room reminded him that he'd eaten hardly anything all day. He crossed to the tables, picked up a plate, and surveyed the dishes in front of him. He scooped some rice and burritos onto his plate, then peered dubiously at a meat dish with a vivid green sauce. A serious-looking woman opposite was carefully selecting some prawns while continuing a nonstop discussion with two women on either side of her. They were all dressed similarly, in light-colored suits with bright silk blouses. The teenage boy, who had apparently given up on the tomatoes in the kitchen, was ladling a little of everything onto his plate as an older man beside him kept nudging him and pointing, none-too-subtly, at one of the girls chatting in the corner.

Lenny decided that the teenage boy had the right idea and reached to sample one of the meat dishes. Before he could pick up the spoon, the serious-looking woman opposite scooped some cocktail sauce onto her plate a little too vigorously, and red splatters flicked up onto the lilac lapel of her jacket. All three women gasped at the deep-red stains.

Lenny remembered that he still had Mari's handkerchief in his jacket pocket. Inspired by Mari's good deed at the Blahst interview, and pleased to offer a service that transcended the language barrier, he whisked the handkerchief out and passed it across the table to the woman.

Unfortunately, the handkerchief was not the only thing to emerge from Lenny's pocket. Two condom packets arced gracefully across the table and plopped into the middle of the food—one in the rice and one in a bowl of guacamole. For a moment Lenny stared down at them, wondering where they'd come from and marveling at the coincidence that they were the same brand as the ones in his office. Slowly, a vision of Roy flicking condoms at him stirred in his head, followed by a memory of stuffing them in the pocket of his hirings-firings-and-weddings jacket.

Lenny risked a look across at the woman in the sauce-splattered jacket. Her chin had risen into the air, and she was looking down at the packets with distaste. Her two companions seemed to be waiting for the serious woman to take the lead in figuring out how to react to this unexpected addition to the menu. The teenage boy watched with a broad grin until the man next to him pulled him away from the table toward the porch.

"I'm sorry, I didn't mean..." Lenny felt heat rise to his face as the serious woman looked up from the condoms and glared at him. His mind groped for a way to explain the situation.

"Don't worry. They're for my work."

The woman on the left whispered a translation into the serious woman's ear. As she spoke the words, Lenny realized his explanation wasn't going to have the reassuring effect he intended. The serious woman's eyes opened wide. She turned, clutching her plate of prawns, and marched toward the hallway, with the other two women a half step behind her.

Lenny fished the packets out of the food and dabbed at them with the handkerchief before pushing them back into his pocket. He looked furtively around the room, but nobody else was paying attention except the still-grinning teenager, who was at the back of the porch, trying to peer around the heads of the men between him and Lenny.

Lenny retreated with his food to a small wooden chair at the far end of the dining room and pulled out his phone. It took him less than five minutes to finish the run of postings, and he felt a momentary wash of relief when the confirmation scrolled onto his screen. The relief was rapidly followed by a nag of doubt. Would these messages change anything? His approach had worked twice before, so there was every reason to believe it would work again. But could it really be so easy to undo the damage he'd done?

"Qué estás haciendo?"

Lenny looked up and saw a small girl in front of him. She was wearing a pink satin dress with matching hairclips, and she clasped a plate of cookies and brownies in one hand.

"I'm sorry, I don't speak Spanish," he said in a slow, clear voice.

A frown crossed her round face. "Why not?" she asked in perfectly accented American English.

"I just never learned."

Her eyes narrowed suspiciously. "How do you talk to people from Mexico?"

Lenny opened his mouth and closed it again, not sure how to answer her. She climbed up on the chair next to him and poked a finger toward his phone.

"What are you doing?"

"Just some work."

"Do you have *Moshi Monsters*?"

"No, but we can get it from the App Store if you like."

"What kind of apps are you showing this girl?" Lenny looked up at the sound of Mari's voice. "I see you've met Daniela," Mari continued. "She's my cousin's daughter, just turned four. Daniela, this is my boyfriend, Lenny."

My boyfriend. Lenny rolled the words around inside his head. He liked how they sounded, and the casual way she had spoken them.

"You have to eat some vegetables first." Mari was inspecting Daniela's plate "What kind would you like?"

"Chocolate."

"Daniela, chocolate isn't a vegetable."

"Yes, it is. It's a bean, and it grows on a bush. I saw it on TV. Anyway, *he* isn't eating any vegetables." She pointed at Lenny's plate of rice and burritos.

"Well, that's true," Mari said. "Maybe you should both have some." She picked up a platter of crudités from the table and held it out toward them. "How about some broccoli?"

Lenny turned up his nose, and Daniela giggled.

"Asparagus?"

Lenny pretended to gag. Daniela howled with laughter.

Mari cocked her head to one side and looked down at Lenny. "You're not exactly helping, you know."

Lenny looked at the plate of raw vegetables and picked up a baby carrot. "If I eat this, you have to as well," he said, pointing the carrot at Daniela.

"Deal," said Daniela and scrunched her fist around three of the carrots.

Lenny doused the carrot in creamy dip, but before he could take a bite, Daniela let out a small shriek.

"Look, it's Matthew." She dropped the carrots onto Lenny's plate and ran off to greet the new arrival, a fair-haired boy of about six or seven

Lenny abandoned his own carrot now that he was no longer a role model and slid his plate under an empty chair. Mari was ladling a soup-like mixture into a bowl. She sat down on the wooden chair next to him and handed him the bowl and a spoon.

"Try this," she said. "It's ceviche."

Lenny carefully sampled a prawn and a piece of avocado and then started to devour the rest indiscriminately. It tasted exquisite. As he ate, he remembered there was something he ought to tell her.

"Who's that woman in the purple suit?" he asked. "With the two clones?"

"That's Senora Constanza. She's my mother's landlady. She and her sisters own half the street. Why, what's up?"

Lenny decided the confession could wait. "No reason," he shrugged. "Oh, I have something for you."

He reached into his pocket and found Mari's handkerchief. He pulled it out carefully and folded a dried brown stain and a fresh green smear to the inside before handing it to Mari. "You left this at Blahst."

Mari's face spread into a smile of delight. "Thank you! I thought I'd lost it. My mother gave it to me when I started college."

"A handkerchief?"

"And a can of pepper spray. She said the handkerchief was for good luck—it belonged to my great aunt. And the pepper spray was in case the luck ran out."

Mari wriggled down in her chair and placed her head on Lenny's shoulder. The warmth of her touch spread through his body. He closed his eyes and leaned his cheek against her hair. In the kitchen and the hall, he could hear gentle chatter and laughter, and a jubilant roar from the porch indicated that the soccer team had finally managed to score.

Chapter 18

MARI KNEW SOMETHING WAS WRONG as soon as she pulled into the Blahst parking lot on Monday morning. Four police cars were lined up along the usually deserted fire lane outside of the main entrance. Two policemen loitered next to them, shoulders hunched in their black anoraks and hands pushed into their pockets against the icy wind.

The area where Mari usually parked her car was full, so she kept heading toward the back of the lot, looking for an empty space. She was later than usual—she'd allowed herself an extra hour in bed to sleep off the effects of the party the day before. There had been many margaritas, many toasts. They had toasted Mari's degree, her new job, and her future. They had toasted her mother for raising such a wonderful family. They had even toasted Lenny, once Mari had convinced her neighbors that he wasn't a pimp or a gigolo.

She maneuvered into a parking space and retrieved a large baking sheet from the trunk. It held the remains of the graduation cake her mother had insisted she take with her. She picked her way carefully across the icy parking lot to the cleared pathway. She wasn't worried about showing up late. Blahst was the kind of place where the managers didn't look too closely at the hours their employees kept, as long as the work got done.

The policemen outside the entrance seemed to turn away slightly as she passed them, so she resisted the temptation to ask them what was up. Norma in reception would fill her in. She shuffled awkwardly through the revolving doors, trying to fit the large, square baking tray into the triangular space.

"Hi, Norma, what's up?" she asked as she passed the curved wood of the reception desk.

"I.D. please," said Norma.

Mari stopped and looked at Norma. This was the first time since she'd started work that anyone had asked to see her employee I.D.

Norma's eyes darted toward a policewoman standing on the opposite side of the lobby, then back to Mari. She gave a small shrug.

Mari looked down at the huge tray in her arms, at the bag hanging from her shoulder, and at the tiny shelf that surrounded Norma. The bare lobby offered no resting place for a large, half-eaten cake. She balanced one end of the tray on the shelf and held onto the other end while she groped in her bag for her badge. Her hand connected with the plastic card, and she pulled it out to show Norma.

"What's going on?" she whispered.

"They'll tell you inside," Norma answered. There was no trace of the usual cheer that greeted the employees every morning.

Mari crossed to the elevator with a growing feeling of trepidation. Could they be announcing layoffs? There had been some rumors that it would happen if the stock price kept falling, but nobody had really believed it. If there were serious layoffs, they might want to play it safe by having police around in case anyone turned violent. She closed her eyes and sighed as she waited for the elevator. Last in, first out—wasn't that how layoffs worked? She'd been with Blahst exactly three weeks. It would be too embarrassing if she lost her job the day after her family had been celebrating her success.

On the fourth floor she headed straight for the kitchen to put down the cake. Her arms were aching, and she felt embarrassed to be walking around with it when something important was going on.

Paulo and Yefim, who were in the kitchen, stopped talking immediately when she came in.

"What's happening?" she asked as she deposited the cake on the counter next to the coffee machine.

Her colleagues looked at each other. Finally, Paulo said, "We're not supposed to say anything. You've got to go and see Pierce."

Mari opened her mouth to persuade Paolo to give her some hint of what it was all about. But his eyes weren't crinkled in their usual teasing smile. Relieved of the cake, she headed straight to Pierce's office.

Pierce was on the phone when she arrived, so she hovered by his open door.

"He's your consultant! You must have some contact information. He's not in today, and the police want to interview everyone who was in the building last week." Pierce raised his hand in frustration as he listened to the response. "Well, *somebody* sent him over. I suggest you find out who."

Pierce disconnected his call and gestured for Mari to come inside. She sat in one of the two chairs facing his desk.

"These investors. One hand has no idea what the other hand's doing." He shook his head and drew in a deep breath. "Did anyone tell you yet?"

Mari shook her head.

"It's Clayton."

Mari felt dread rising inside of her. She'd read about employees who were fired and then came back to blow away their old colleagues. There was that incident in Wakefield a few years back. But surely not Clayton. Not here.

"What's he done?" she asked quietly, not wanting to hear the answer.

"He didn't do anything." Pierce rubbed his hands over his face and leaned forward on the desk. "Clayton's dead."

Mari tried to make sense of the words. How could Clayton be dead? She'd just seen him on Saturday...

The temperature in the room seemed to rise by ten degrees. She felt the skin under her arms prickle as she remembered the cracking sound that Clayton's head had made against the ice. She and Lenny hadn't even looked to see if he was bleeding before they bundled him off home. Yet even as the guilt started to form, she felt some small part of her mind rejoicing that this wasn't about layoffs, that she still had a job. She shook her head to lose the unworthy thought.

"I didn't know he hit his head so hard." Her words sounded as though they had come from somebody else's mouth.

Pierce frowned. "What do you mean?"

"On Saturday night. He was singing. And then..." Her mind replayed the scene. Clayton losing his footing and going down—that crack—and Lenny landing on top of him. "When they were fighting he hit his head on the ice. Well, they weren't really fighting, it was more—"

"You saw Clayton on Saturday?"

"Yes."

"Mari, I think you should come with me." Pierce stood up and came around his desk. He took her lightly by the arm, helped her to her feet, and then guided her out of the office.

"Where are we going?" Her own voice seemed to be getting fainter.

"The police are interviewing anyone who worked with Clayton. It's going to take all day, at least. But I'm sure they'd like to talk to you as soon as possible if you saw him on Saturday."

Mari let Pierce guide her to the elevator. He put his card in the slot and punched the button for the fifteenth floor. As the elevator lurched into action, Mari's confusion grew. Why would detectives want to talk to Clayton's colleagues? And why were detectives involved at all? She would have to make it clear to the police that it was all a terrible accident.

On the fifteenth floor, Mari followed Pierce to a corner office with Andrei Simenov's name engraved in black on a brass plate. At a nearby desk, a policeman was reading a copy of the *Boston Globe*.

Pierce knocked on the door and disappeared inside without waiting for an answer. Thirty seconds later, he came out with the office administrator for Clayton's department. Her eyes were puffy and red. She reached out and patted Mari on the shoulder as she went past.

Pierce beckoned Mari to come inside the office. "This is Detective Plummer and Detective Yu," he said with a wave at two men behind the desk. "Please tell them exactly what happened on Saturday night." He pointed Mari to a chair in front of the desk and then left the office, closing the door behind him.

Mari sat down in the chair and looked at the two detectives, her anxiety growing by the second. One was in his fifties, with bushy grey eyebrows. The other was about twenty years younger, with dark, slicked-back hair.

The dark-haired man leaned forward and pushed a button on a small, electronic device in the middle of the otherwise empty desk. A red light glowed on the recorder as he leaned back and spoke to Mari.

"I'm Detective Yu. I'm going to ask you a few questions. Just relax and answer as best you can. How long have you been working at Blahst?"

Mari stared at the detective. She tried to think when her first day had been, but the dates swirled in her head. Why did it matter how long she had worked here, anyway? She had to tell them what had happened on Saturday.

"Clayton was outside the apartment and he was singing to me. Then Lenny came over, and Clayton tried to hit him, and—"

"Whoa, slow down." Detective Plummer's eyes creased into a smile beneath the canopy of his eyebrows. "I know you want to tell us about Saturday, but first we want to figure out how long you've known Clayton, stuff like that. Just humor us."

Mari took a deep breath and tried to focus on Detective Yu's questions. He asked about the work she did at Blahst. What was

Clayton like as a manager? Why had she been transferred? As she answered, the sound of Clayton's head cracking against the ice played over and over in her mind.

"How was Clayton regarded by his colleagues?" Another pointless question. Mari remembered the snickers, the jibes from the other employees.

"I guess he was a bit of an outsider." She shrugged. The two detectives exchanged a look.

"Any particular enemies?" Yu asked.

Mari felt as though she was going to explode with frustration. "Why don't you ask me about Saturday?" she burst out. "That's what matters, isn't it?"

Yu leaned forward in his seat and pushed the tiny recording device an inch or two closer to Mari. "Okay, tell us what happened on Saturday."

Finally. Mari recounted the evening's events carefully: Clayton showing up, wanting to come inside, declaring his love for her from the street, Lenny's arrival.

"Tell me about Lenny," interrupted Yu. "Is he your boyfriend?"

Mari frowned. What business was that of theirs? She tried to glare at Yu, but the detective was obviously used to staring down much harder cases than Mari. She let her eyes drop.

"Yes, but he wasn't on Saturday. I mean..." She wondered to herself what their relationship was. She'd called him her boyfriend and he hadn't objected—did that mean that he really was? She sighed again and continued with her story.

She told them how Clayton had tried to punch Lenny. That he had fallen and dragged Lenny on top of him. She told them about the loud cracking sound Clayton's head had made against the ice, and she felt another surge of guilt invade her chest like a plague of skittering insects.

"When did they find him?" she asked. Now that she had told her story, she needed some answers from the detectives.

"How did Clayton get home?" Yu continued as though he hadn't heard her.

Mari felt a rising annoyance at the way the detective was treating her. She was answering all his questions, and they hadn't told her anything about Clayton's death. She decided that two could play at that game.

"How did he... I mean, did he bleed... was he unconscious?" She couldn't bring herself to ask the real question: *Could we have stopped him from dying?*

"Did you see him leave?"

Mari heard the studied patience in the detective's voice. This was just a job to him. She could never win a battle of wills. She needed another approach—maybe the truth.

She took a deep breath and fixed her eyes on Yu. "We didn't look at Clayton's head. He stood right up and started talking again, so I didn't think it was a big deal at the time. But now he's... I have to... I need to know if there was anything I could have done after he fell."

Yu looked across at the other man, who pursed his lips, then nodded. Yu stood up and looked out of the window. Mari followed his gaze out across the featureless landscape, the snow reflecting the grey of a gunmetal sky.

Yu turned back to Mari and leaned his hands on the desk.

"Clayton didn't die because he fell."

Mari looked up at Yu. Hadn't he heard anything she had said?

"No, I saw it happen. He hit his head on the ice."

"Mari, Clayton didn't die from a head wound." Detective Plummer's deep voice cut across the desk for the first time since she'd entered the room. "On Saturday night, Clayton Malloy was shot dead. Murdered."

The two detectives seemed to fade from Mari's view. She saw Clayton's proud face when he was pulled onto Version 6, Clayton trying to run his team meetings, Clayton's eyes ogling her body, Clayton serenading her. Clayton, alive. How could it be otherwise?

She heard Detective Plummer's voice tugging at her thoughts. She looked at his face, tipped to one side in an expression of concern, but the words were a river of sound washing over her.

"Mari, are you okay?"

She finally made some sense of the sounds and nodded her head.

"You might experience some shock reaction; that's normal." Detective Plummer reached his hand across the desk toward her, but stopped short of touching her. "You should stay here with your colleagues for a while. The company has arranged for counselors to be available."

Mari nodded again and looked down at the detective's hand spread out on the desk. Raised veins on the back of the hand gave way to soft grey hairs sprouting from the wrist. The nails were short and neatly manicured. Next to his hand, the red light glowed on the tiny recording device.

"There are still a couple of details we need from you," Detective Plummer continued. "Please try to help us out. Then we're all through here."

Detective Yu leaned forward on the desk. "Clayton was found murdered in his home. We need to know how he got back there."

Mari blinked and tried to concentrate on what she was being asked. She saw now that the questions were anything but pointless. *How was Clayton regarded by his colleagues? Any particular enemies?* Somebody had killed Clayton, maybe somebody he knew. Somebody *she* knew.

"Was he driving when he left your apartment building? How did Clayton get home?" Yu repeated the question patiently.

Mari opened her mouth to tell Yu that Lenny had given Clayton a ride home and froze. The detective's face snapped back into focus as she realized the implications of the question. If she told them that Lenny was alone with Clayton, they would think that he was the killer.

Mari's heart accelerated as though it was trying to escape up through her open mouth. What if it really was Lenny? What if Lenny had gone inside with Clayton and shot him? "*Why don't I give him a ride home?*" Lenny's suggestion after the fight had sounded so casual. But hadn't he turned down her offer to come with them? Maybe he wanted to be alone with Clayton, wanted to finish off the fight when they were alone together...

She looked down at the desk to avoid meeting the detective's eyes. The sound of blood pounding in her ears was deafening; she hoped the detective couldn't hear it. She saw Lenny arriving back at her apartment that night—his cheeks flushed from the cold, his wavy hair rumpled, and his lopsided smile showing just a hint of shyness. She saw him on her sofa cradling the hot coffee to warm his hands. She remembered him telling her the story of how he and a friend had put a live chicken in the bottom drawer of the math teacher's desk. When the teacher opened the drawer, she looked for a few seconds and simply closed the drawer and kept on teaching. Lenny was so impressed with the math teacher that he claimed his love of numbers had begun at that point.

That wasn't the behavior of someone who had just shot another human being.

"Mari?" Detective Yu's voice was calm but insistent.

Mari took a deep breath and looked the detective squarely in the face. "Yes, I'm sorry." She held his gaze for a second before she spoke again, slowly and clearly.

"After he hit his head, Clayton got up and walked away up the street. Lenny and I went inside my apartment. Neither of us left again until morning."

Chapter 19

LENNY CRANKED THE VOLUME UP on his iPhone, hooked in his earbuds, and set about clearing a space on his desk for the pile of mail that had been building up at Healthway. He was planning to visit Professor Ramsey later in the day, and he wanted to be able to report that things were in good shape. He hummed along to the pulsing beat as he settled down to rip open the first envelope.

Most of the mail was still donations for Burundi. His awe at the power of his viral algorithm grew with each check he added to the pile. If this new set of postings worked, if they stopped the Blahst stock price from falling, then maybe he could try his algorithm on something new, perhaps even... He forced his mind to slow down and focus on the desk in front of him. It would take a couple of days for the messages to spread until he knew for sure.

He put the letters of support into a separate pile, not sure who was ever going to read them. A few of the envelopes contained bills, and some were letters to the professor from colleagues at other universities. He sorted them into separate manila folders and wondered why anybody would send a letter when they could post it on Blahst. One of his favorite songs kicked in on his iPhone, a rapper alternating English and Spanish, and he found his mind drifting back to Mari's party the day before.

A tap on his shoulder made him scatter a handful of envelopes onto the floor as he spun his chair around.

Roy was standing behind him. He had on black jeans and a white shirt, and the angles of his chin were accented with dark stubble. Lenny pulled out his earbuds, pleased to see his room-mate for the first time since Saturday night.

"Dude, remind me not to let you be the lead singer of my band," said Roy.

"You'd better learn to play guitar first," Lenny retorted. "Where have you been, anyway? Wait... let me guess. Mandy?"

"Can I help it if she locks me away to be her love slave? Just because your idea of a hot Saturday night is stroking a keyboard." Roy looked down at the pile of letters spread across the desk. "Looks like you had the same idea I did. We still on to visit the professor this afternoon?"

Lenny nodded as Roy pulled a chair up next to him. Lenny let him sort a few letters before speaking.

"Actually, I spent the night with Mari."

Roy slapped an envelope down on the desk and turned to stare at Lenny. "That was quick work, man. Congratulations."

"We didn't... it wasn't..." He felt the blood rise to his cheeks. "I slept on the sofa. It's different with her—we talked a lot. I met her family, and they're really nice."

Roy raised his eyebrows. "Man, you worry me sometimes. You didn't even sleep with her yet, and she made you meet the family? That's not right."

Lenny shook his head and turned back to the pile of mail. He knew that Roy regarded him as a hopeless case.

The two of them drifted into a rhythmic sorting. Roy exclaimed each time he pulled out a check for Healthway, and they watched the pile grow. Roy kept a running tab on a calculator, and within half an hour they had added another fifteen thousand dollars to their department's budget.

"When you going to tell her about Blahst?" Roy asked, leaning back and stretching his arms up.

"Huh?" Lenny looked up from a letter asking the professor to give a talk the following month.

"You know, tell Mari you're the one screwing up her company? Or were you planning on keeping that a secret?"

Tell Mari? Lenny realized he hadn't even thought about telling her. It was as though that part of his life was stashed in a separate compartment. But if their relationship kept moving as fast as it had been doing, he wouldn't be able to keep such a big secret from her forever. He felt a momentary flash of panic. Then he remembered the messages he had posted the day before.

"It's okay. I've fixed the problem. I sent out a whole bunch of positive press for Blahst yesterday. If it works, Mari will never have to know what happened."

Roy raised his eyebrows skeptically. "Just like that? Fix a few billion dollars off their market cap?"

Lenny shrugged. "Why not? If the first messages worked, why wouldn't these? You heard the professor—the messages just have to be stronger than the original ones. We'll have to wait and see."

Lenny picked out his phone and keyed in the stock ticker symbol for Blahst. The markets had been open only a few hours, but he was curious to see how quickly the stocks were still falling. A graph appeared on the small screen, and Lenny stared at it in disbelief. The steep downward line had suddenly flattened out across the chart. The stock had stabilized, with only the usual minor ups and downs since trading had started that morning. He checked some of the other high-tech giants. The picture was the same. The downward trend that had started after Lenny sent out his messages was finally slowing down.

"Is it working already?" Roy peered over Lenny's shoulder at the charts.

"Couldn't be. It's way too soon. Must just be settling down by itself." Lenny clicked through to the discussion forums for Blahst, the part of the financial site where the day traders, company PR flacks, and scam artists tried to pump up or talk down the stock to send it in the direction that would make them the most money. He read a few of the postings with a growing thrill of anticipation.

"Roy, this is it. This is my stuff they're talking about. See this one here." He pushed the screen toward Roy. "It says that Blahst is leading an alliance of search companies to set standards for customer privacy. That's mine. I made it up over the weekend." He took a deep breath and put his phone down on the desk.

He realized that he had never fully accepted that he was the cause of the Blahst stock crash. There was still a nagging hope that it was all one big unhappy coincidence, that his little prank was just bad timing that made it look like he was to blame. But now there was no more doubt. He was making it happen.

"That was fast," said Roy. "But it's a good thing, right?"

Roy's question hung as Lenny checked out more of the forum postings.

"What happens when everyone finds out it's not true?" asked Roy.

The same thought was on Lenny's mind. Would the stock crash even faster than before if the news was exposed as fake? He shook his head slowly as he read the postings about some of the other search companies.

"They might not find out," said Lenny. "A couple of Blahst's competitors have already signed up for the alliance. Blahst really might have to do it."

"But then it's like you made them do it. You're calling the shots." Roy leaned back and regarded his friend with admiration. "Just think what else you could do with a viral algorithm. You could rig this year's music awards. Get all our favorite bands to win."

"Yeah, and the Oscars, too. But that's little stuff." Lenny mused on the possibilities. "I could pick the next president."

"You could depose despots, get free healthcare for kids, outlaw Christmas Muzak." Roy jumped to his feet and punched Lenny on the shoulder. "Shit, Lenny, you could sit right here and rule the world."

"Yeah." Lenny leaned back and locked his hands behind his head. "Yeah, I could."

A buzz sounded at the office door. Lenny watched Roy disappear from view into the corridor. His mind mulled on the possibilities that the success of his algorithm offered him, now that he had sorted out the Blahst problem. On the one hand, he could be grateful he'd averted a near-disaster, clean things up here at Healthway, and take the job at Blahst. He'd leave the influencing to the academics and politicians. On the other hand, if he had created something this powerful, didn't he owe it to the world to put it to good use?

He heard Roy speak into the intercom, and a man's distorted voice replied. A moment later, Roy was back beside the desk, trying in vain to speak. He caught his breath and tried again.

"It's the police. They're coming up, and they want to talk to you."

"Ms. Mahoney, may I have a few words?" Snyder had to raise his voice to be heard over the buzz of excitement in OPRA's incident room. He looked around and estimated that there were close to twenty people scattered around the wall displays in small groups, examining an assortment of lists, charts, maps, and scrolling data feeds. Colonel Egham was at the center, directing his orchestra of analysts and displays with expansive gestures of his arms.

"Captain Snyder, good to see you again." Angie Mahoney looked up from a small desktop display.

"Looks like you have company."

Angie smiled. "It's been like this for a few days. Since we discovered the Blahst influence network, actually, so you can take some credit for that." Angie closed the chart she'd been working on and gave her full attention to Snyder. "What can I do for you?"

"All working on Blahst? Any leads?"

"The power and speed of these influence networks are causing quite a stir. You've probably seen, it's spreading beyond the tech sector now. We've got the State Department here, and the Federal Reserve, as well as counterterrorism."

"So, a deliberate attack on the U.S.?"

"That's one theory," answered Angie. "Though it doesn't explain how—"

"Tech sector's up!" An excited yelp from the far side of the room drew Egham and several others into a new huddle.

"That's the first positive indicator we've seen in two weeks," said Angie.

"Why the change?" Snyder inspected the wall displays for any sign of the African continent, but all attention seemed to be on Blahst and the U.S. economy.

"Something happened over the weekend. Seems to be a new influence network, all kinds of positive press about Blahst."

"Could it be coming from Blahst itself?"

"Doesn't look that way. It's like the others: the influence is coming from everywhere at once and converging."

Snyder looked around the room at the hubbub of activity. "Is there anywhere quieter we might speak?"

"Sure. Let me get Colonel Egham and we can—"

"No."

Angie's eyebrows registered surprise, and Snyder realized he'd spoken too emphatically. He lowered his voice. "I'll catch up with him afterward. It's just..." He tried to think of a justification for peeling her away from the chaos of Egham's command center. "I had some follow-up questions on the project you talked about last time. The historical influence networks."

Angie's face lit up with enthusiasm. "Yes, of course. We can go to my office." She gestured for him to follow her out of the incident room.

The unadorned plaster walls of the corridor were painted an unusual shade of eggshell blue that Snyder recognized from a recent Pentagon visit. Probably a surplus paint lot from an over-zealous GSA procurement officer, he mused. With a small rush of adrenaline, he realized he'd be spending a lot more time at the Pentagon once his appointment to the Intelligence Action Network came through. It had been a long path of service—official and unofficial—that had brought him this far. If the last few steps meant getting Senator Brennigan his coltan, then Snyder would deliver that coltan by whatever means necessary. Snyder prided himself on always delivering what he promised.

They arrived at an office with just enough space for two desks set back to back and room to sidle around them. Angie rolled a chair around from the vacant desk opposite her own and invited Snyder to join her in front of the three screens that spanned her desk.

As she logged in and started to pull up information, Snyder watched enviously. He would love to have access to OPRA's data analysis over at his own office in the DIA headquarters, but even with the supposed interagency cooperation of the post–9/11 intelligence community, the CIA would never let something of this value be networked outside the building. He thought of his cell phone, banned like all the others from the premises, tucked away in one of the rows of lockers in the lobby in the interests of security. The only way to keep up with the latest and greatest on Burundi was going to be by making friends with the right people, which Snyder was quite capable of doing when the need arose.

"Here are the two Blahst networks overlaid." Angie pointed to the screen in the middle. "And over here is a set of influence networks I modeled from the 1960s. You can see there are some similarities, even though each network has its own unique signature pattern based on how it spreads. See right here..."

"Can we look at Burundi, too? That was the first of the current set, wasn't it? It might be interesting to compare that one as well." Snyder leaned back in his chair, trying to sound as though his interest was purely academic. In fact, he was desperate to learn whether Angie had any further insight into the flood of funds into Burundi that was still holding up the coltan deal. The fiasco with the Clayton Malloy kid on Saturday night hadn't yielded any progress on the source of the influence networks, and the police involvement would impede his investigations at Blahst for a while.

A few seconds later, a map of Africa appeared on the screen. Tiny Burundi, already dwarfed by Democratic Republic of the Congo to the west and Tanzania to the east, was completely obscured by the radiating black lines of the influence network. But Snyder knew the geography of the region like the way home to his apartment.

"Captain Snyder, may I ask what your interest is in all of this?"

Angie's question struck Snyder as impertinent, but he kept his face expressionless. His paperwork requesting access to OPRA's systems was all in place, and there was no need for Snyder to justify himself even to Egham, let alone one of his minions. But he was well-practiced in the honey-over-vinegar school of social interaction.

He forced his mouth into a smile. "You used to be a field agent, didn't you, Ms. Mahoney?" His smile grew as Angie dropped her eyes. He knew she couldn't respond, but it didn't matter whether it was true or not. He'd found that line to be as effective with analysts, male or female, as telling a woman it was obvious she did Pilates.

He shuffled his chair closer to Angie and tipped his head. "I'm part of a special task force looking at methods for disseminating misinformation to enemy forces. We want to see whether someone is deliberately starting these influence networks and—frankly—how we might do the same."

"Interesting." Angie nodded thoughtfully. "If you could combine the deliberate initiation of an influence network with our predictive modeling—well, that's a killer combination."

Snyder's skin began to tingle with the promise of a half-formed insight. "Because..." he prompted.

"Because whatever or whoever has set those influence networks in motion probably has little or no idea of what the end results are going to be. OPRA's predictive capabilities are unique—we can roll forward based on various prediction scenarios."

Snyder remembered how Angie had looked ahead at the lingering effects of the Madrid demonstrations in their first meeting. "Can you show me what that might look like for Burundi?"

"Certainly," said Angie. She turned to the screen showing Burundi's rippling network of radiating lines. "If things continue as they are with an inflow of capital into Burundi, then this is the most likely path. You can see that there will be significant socio-economic shifts in the region, with a slow but steady increase in business partnerships with neighboring countries, likely some Asian alliances."

"What about if the money stopped?"

"Well..." She made adjustments to some data points at the bottom of the screen. "In that case, we see that there is a permanent improvement in Burundi's economic status based on available capital."

Snyder realized he was frowning at the news and relaxed his face into an expression of curiosity. "What would it take for them to end up like they were before?"

He watched Angie manipulate the models to explore the outer bounds of the scenarios.

"Wars or natural disasters, which do occur periodically in that region."

Snyder's eyes were fixed on the screen, but his mind had traveled far beyond. What if he could start an influence network, and use these models to track it and see where it would lead? What if he could manipulate it step by step until it took him where he wanted to go? He'd been thinking in terms of undoing his problems in Burundi, but now he realized that he'd completely underestimated the potential. If he could figure out how these networks were starting, and keep his access to OPRA's systems... He realized his heart was racing and took a deep breath to retain his calm.

"Is that something OPRA's working on?" he asked. "Starting influence networks?"

"Hah. Not a chance. There's a couple of century's worth of collective experience back there in the incident room, and nobody has a clue what's going on. And even if they did..." Angie paused and shook her head. "OPRA doesn't make things happen. We just watch. And run scenarios of how things might turn out, so that the decision-makers can formulate plans."

Snyder heard the edge of frustration in Angie's voice. Maybe she really had been a field agent.

"And even if we did try to start something, you saw how the influence networks fade out over time," she continued. "You can't keep an influence network going long enough to make anything major happen."

Snyder's finger traced the thickest black line from the edge of the screen toward the red flashing *Burundi* in the center.

"Somebody can," he said.

Chapter 20

"Now, Mr. Driver, there's no need for hostility."

Lenny glared at the policeman sitting in Roy's chair. He felt perfectly entitled to his hostility. Detective Yu had been baiting him since the two policemen arrived and was obviously reveling in Lenny's discomfort. Lenny had quickly figured out their good-cop/bad-cop routine, but Detective Yu was far too good at the bad-cop role for it to be entirely an act.

Lenny's plan was to deny all knowledge of whatever they asked. He had gone back over his tracks several times on the Blahst postings he'd sent out and convinced himself that it was impossible to trace them back to his accounts or his computer. He didn't know how the police had managed to track him down, but he was sure they were working on a hunch rather than any kind of proof.

But the detectives hadn't asked anything about Blahst, or the photos, or privacy postings. They'd jumped right in with rapid-fire questions about Mari, Saturday night, and Clayton. After sitting stubbornly silent for several minutes, Lenny had finally snapped and told them where they could stuff their questions.

Yu's face didn't waver. "We're just trying to establish the nature of your disagreement with Clayton on Saturday night."

The detective's voice had the calm, measured tones of a psychiatrist, and Lenny could feel its quiet force trying to lull him into compliance. He wished Roy were here, but the detectives had asked for privacy, and Roy had slipped out the office door, paler than Lenny had ever seen him. Lenny felt an overwhelming desire to get the two detectives out of his office as quickly as possible, if he could only figure out how.

"Why do you keep asking about Clayton? I hardly know the guy. He's just some jerk who stole my idea."

Detective Yu raised his eyebrows and looked deliberately at his older colleague. Then he turned back to face Lenny.

"Stole your idea? Can you tell us a little more about that?" Yu leaned forward with his hands on his thighs.

Lenny closed his eyes and exhaled audibly. Shit. He should have kept quiet. He really didn't want to go into the whole Version 6 thing with these guys.

Lenny's phone blared a few bars of song from his desk. He reached across to pick it up.

"Please don't answer that," said Detective Plummer.

Lenny's hand froze for a second, then he palmed his phone and brought it toward him. He glanced at the screen. It was Mari. He hit the button once to answer the call and a second time to disconnect it. One more push with his thumb switched the phone to vibrate instead of ring. Detective Plummer nodded his thanks.

Detective Yu took up the questioning again. "So you didn't like Clayton?"

"I think he's a—" Lenny was about to tell the detective exactly what he thought of Clayton, when something about the question struck him as odd.

"Didn't?"

"Huh?" It was Detective Yu's turn to sound confused.

"You said *didn't*. As in the past." Lenny looked over at Detective Plummer, who was watching the interview from a large leather armchair he had wheeled in from the professor's office. "Did something happen to him?"

Lenny had barely voiced the question when his phone vibrated in his hand—three short tones that told him he had a text message. He glanced down at the screen and locked his eyes in disbelief on the message from Mari. *Clayton murdered Sat night. Call me.*

"Clayton was killed on Saturday night." Detective Plummer's deep voice seemed to fill the room. Lenny felt a sudden sense of unreality as the same message hit his eyes and ears at the same time, as though he was caught in some bizarre 3-D, surround-sound movie. His eyes searched the office walls for something familiar to ground himself. Roy's photos stared back, stark images from another world.

"Why don't you tell us about this idea he stole?" Detective Yu's legs splayed wider apart as he rested his forearms on his thighs and thrust his face toward Lenny.

Lenny crossed his ankle over his other leg to mask his phone from Yu. He looked again at Mari's message and typed in a quick response. *Police here.* He sent the message and looked back at Yu. He wanted more than ever to get rid of these guys and figure out what was going on. Surely they had no right to be here if he didn't want them—he hadn't committed a crime. At least, not one that they knew about.

"I want you to leave now," he said, trying to keep his voice steady.

"I'm sure you do." Detective Yu didn't move.

Lenny's phone vibrated in the palm of his hand. He looked down at another message from Mari. *Killed after he walked home from my place. Remember he wouldn't take ride from you?*

Lenny tried to remember the events of the evening. He couldn't remember Clayton turning down a ride. What was Mari talking about? He closed the message and noticed he had a string of missed calls from her.

"Who are you talking to?" Detective Plummer looked disap-provingly at Lenny's phone.

"My broker," Lenny replied. "Now if you'll excuse me, I have important work to do."

Lenny turned his back on the detectives and switched on the ancient computer screen on his desk. He searched through the list of computer games he'd loaded onto the hard drive and selected one to launch. Tinny-sounding rock music crackled from the old speakers as the screen filled with a realistically rendered city street at night. An unshaven young man in a torn T-shirt, jeans, and army boots was leaning against a car in the otherwise deserted street.

"You're not doing yourself any favors." Detective Plummer's voice cut through the distorted music.

Lenny ignored the comment and focused on the screen, where a policeman with outsized shoulders and arms approached the unshaven man and shouted something indecipherable. Lenny punched a couple of keys and the unshaven man launched a karate kick at the jaw of the policeman. A grunt issued from the speakers and the policeman fell to the ground, blood pumping from his mouth.

"We could do this at the precinct if you want," Detective Plummer continued. A note of annoyance had crept into the older detective's voice.

"Don't you have to arrest me first?" Lenny's knowledge of legal procedure didn't extend beyond the TV show level, but it seemed like a reasonable bluff. In front of him, the unshaven man climbed into the car, and the image changed to a first-person view through the windshield. Lenny held down the arrow key to back the car up. Then he turned it slightly and gunned it forward over the prone policeman. Screams and a crunching sound rang out as points clocked up on the car's dashboard.

"Most suspects want to cooperate." Yu's voice sounded close behind Lenny's shoulder. "Unless they have something to hide."

Lenny's attention was jolted away from the game, but he forced himself to keep looking at the screen. Suspect? Did they think he had killed Clayton? He must have been one of the last people to see him alive, but that didn't mean he'd killed the jerk. He'd have to tell the police what had happened on Saturday—why he'd argued with Clayton—and help them understand it was nothing to do with him.

On the screen a police car was heading straight for him. He instinctively reached out to the keyboard and swerved around the car, sideswiping it as it passed. The sound of screeching tires and breaking glass accompanied more points ticking up on the dashboard.

Lenny shook his head as he realized he was playing into their hands. They were trying to panic him into talking, and they had nearly succeeded. He vowed not to say another word, no matter how they goaded him. He leaned back over the keyboard and pointed the car at a woman walking a miniature poodle on the sidewalk. He mowed them down and notched up another ten points.

He heard the two detectives talking in low voices behind him and the scraping of the chairs on the linoleum floor as they stood up.

"We'll be back, Lenny," said Detective Yu.

"Sure, I can't wait," Lenny said without turning around.

He felt a hand slam down on top of his own, squeezing the palm of his hand hard against the plastic of his mouse. He felt something brush against his hair and then heard Detective Plummer's voice close behind his ear.

"You think you're so smart, don't you? So funny? Well, let me tell you that you're nothing to us. We deal with nobodies like you every day." The words were barely more than a whisper, but they pounded into Lenny's head with the force of a hurricane. "We've got a dead guy that you didn't like, that you argued with on more than one occasion, that you got in a fight with on the night he was killed. You don't need your computer to tell you that it doesn't look good for you."

Lenny heard a raspy breath rise and fall beside his ear. Then it was gone, and the pressure on his hand was released as quickly as it came. He listened to the sound of heavy steps along the corridor and the slam of the office door closing.

So much for the good-cop/bad-cop theory.

Lenny dropped his hands to his knees. On the screen in front of him, he watched the car careening along the dark street, bouncing off the occasional streetlamp and parked car. Ahead, four police cars with flashing lights were spread across the road. Lenny knew he had to build up speed to crash the roadblock, but his hands felt glued to his legs. He watched helplessly as the out-of-control car spun into the roadblock and the unshaven man was thrown through the windshield. He landed in a splatter of blood on the hood of the closest police car, and the points reset to zero.

"Who did you kill?" Roy was panting as he sprinted into the office and skidded to a halt in front of the leather chair. He looked even more gaunt than when he'd arrived at the office that morning.

Lenny fixed Roy with a don't-be-stupid stare.

"I heard them. I was waiting in that little cubby behind the stairwell and they couldn't see me when they came down. That old policeman asked the young one if he thought you were a killer."

"What did he say?"

Roy paused. "He said he thought you were an asshole."

Lenny let out a mirthless laugh. "At least they can't put you in jail for that."

He told Roy the news about Clayton, and his own activities on Saturday night. As he recounted the events—the fight, the ride back to Clayton's—he remembered Mari's message. Something about Clayton walking home. He opened up the message again and checked the wording. *Remember he wouldn't take ride from you?*

"So you were the last person to see Clayton alive." Roy lowered himself into the leather chair. "No wonder you're a suspect."

"No, the murderer was the last person to see Clayton alive."

Lenny read Mari's message again. If Clayton had refused his ride and walked home, Lenny would never have been alone with Clayton. He felt his heart quicken as he thought through the implications of the message. Was Mari telling him she had given him an alibi?

A groan from the leather chair disturbed Lenny's train of thought. He looked up to see Roy leaning forward, his head clasped in his hands.

"Lenny, I don't think I can take much more of this."

Lenny stood up in alarm. "What's the matter? You look like you're going to hurl."

"I feel like I'm going to hurl." Roy groaned again. "When I saw those cops at the door, I thought they'd come for us. You know, because of Blahst."

Lenny frowned. "But you didn't do anything."

"I made the photos, remember?"

Lenny looked down at Roy and realized how much he took his friend for granted. Roy was always the sensible one, trying to keep Lenny in check, listening to Lenny's latest rant. Lenny had been so caught up in his own worries that he hadn't thought once about how Roy might feel.

Lenny placed a hand on Roy's shoulder. "Roy, this is all my stupid idea, and you're not going to take the blame for any of it. I'll just tell them I took your photos and did it myself. If anyone ever asks, tell them you knew nothing about it and I'll say the same."

Roy lifted his head and squeezed Lenny's still-outstretched arm. He smiled faintly and the color started to come back to his cheeks.

"What are you going to do now?" he asked

"I'm going to find Mari, then rule the world, but first I'm going to buy you a coffee."

"How about a triple espresso?"

"Sounds good to me."

Mari peered at the business card taped to the door. *Healthway Research International.* This was definitely the place. Yesterday at the party, Lenny had told her she should stop by to visit him sometime, but she hadn't imagined it would be so soon.

The thick metal of the door deadened the sound of her knocking. After a minute of no response, she pushed it with two hands and felt it yield. She peered around the door, her coat attracting green paint flecks from the peeling doorframe.

"Hello?"

No answer. She slid inside, grateful for the warmth of the office after her climb up the unheated stairwell.

"Anybody there?"

She walked past an empty, book-lined office and along a corridor covered with unframed prints of colorful scenes—marketplaces, dwellings, and people decked in bright robes and beads.

The corridor opened out into a wide space with several desks around the walls. The floor here was scattered with envelopes and piles of papers. Two of the desks and the walls behind them were covered with photos, as though the images had taken root on the desk and started to grow upward.

Mari picked up an empty coffee mug—cold, but not congealed. Perhaps she'd just missed Lenny. Or maybe he hadn't come to work and the police had visited him at his house. Or maybe the worst had happened—what if they'd taken him in for questioning or even arrested him?

She sighed with frustration. He wasn't answering her voice calls, and she didn't want to keep sending him text messages. Maybe she was just being paranoid, but she didn't want to leave a written record that she'd warned Lenny about what to say to the police. That might give away the fact that she'd lied to them.

She decided to try calling him one more time. As she pulled her phone from her bag, she caught sight of a photo mounted in a collage of images above one of the desks. It showed a small, dark-skinned boy crouching in the dirt, looking up anxiously at a medical worker. The worker wore a coat that had once been white but was now darkened with grime. His hand was positioned around a syringe as he prepared to vaccinate the boy. The tip of the syringe glowed silver against a sky streaked with a spectacular orange and crimson sunset.

Mari's breath left her body in an audible rush. In her mind, she blacked out the medical worker and replaced him with Andrei Simenov. Her eyes darted between the boy's scared expression, the cracked ground, and the spike of silver pointing toward the boy, as her mind tried to deny what her eyes were telling her. It couldn't be the same photo. It must just be a coincidence that it looked like the photo at her office—the one she'd looked at a thousand times in the last two weeks.

She selected the camera icon on her phone and held it up so that the photo was mirrored on her screen. The electronic click of a shutter was quickly followed by the thud of the office door slamming and the sound of feet moving along the corridor toward her.

The phone slipped from her hand and landed with a smack on the wooden floorboards.

Chapter 21

LENNY WAS STILL CLUTCHING THE remains of his coffee and his egg-and-bacon breakfast bagel as he and Roy walked back into the Healthway office. Roy had downed his espresso in three gulps and then insisted on getting back to the busywork of sorting the mail.

Lenny was planning to call Mari as soon as he arrived back at the office. He needed to find out what had happened to Clayton, and to learn exactly what she'd told the police about Saturday night.

"Mari!" It was as though his thoughts had conjured her into his office. She was standing in the open area between the desks. His eyes took in the lines of her fitted, black wool coat and the loose drape of her hair gathered back behind her shoulders. He tossed the coffee cup into a trashcan and took a step toward her.

"Am I glad to see you. What the hell is this about Clayton?"

Mari shuffled backward and glanced over each shoulder at the walls behind her.

"The cops were here," Lenny continued. "There was this one jerk with—"

"Sorry, I have to go now." Mari cut Lenny off and moved toward the opening between him and the corridor, turning her body sideways to stay close to the wall.

Lenny put out his arm to stop her, puzzled as to why she would want to leave when she'd only just arrived. She recoiled away sharply.

"Mari, what's up?"

Lenny watched as Mari's eyes filled with tears. Then she blinked and looked down. He reached a hand toward her shoulder, but again she maneuvered away from his touch.

"It's nothing. I just broke my phone."

Lenny looked at the spiderweb of shattered glass covering the front of her phone. "Yeah, that's a mess."

Mari pressed her eyes closed, and a tear ran down one side of her nose. Lenny started to reach out to wipe it away, but then he thought better of it. She didn't seem herself today. He hadn't known her long, but he did know she wasn't the kind of person to get upset over a broken phone.

"Are you still in the contract, is that what the problem is? It's gonna cost you a fortune for a new one? 'Cause I know this guy who can unlock—"

"Don't be such an idiot." Roy crossed to Mari and placed a hand on her shoulder. Mari opened her eyes but didn't shake off the hand. "A guy's dead—murdered—of course she's upset. And not just any guy. He was her boss." Roy guided Mari to a chair, and she sat compliantly on the edge of the seat, her phone clasped on her lap.

Lenny cursed his denseness. Roy was right. Of course that would upset anyone. Even if the deceased was a shithead. He crouched next to the chair and placed his hands gently over Mari's.

He felt his arms thrust away as Mari jumped to her feet. Tears were streaming freely down her face, but her eyes were locked on Lenny. He tried to fathom out her reaction and realized that even through the tears, she didn't look upset. It was something else. Fear?

With a flash of understanding, Lenny realized just how completely insensitive he'd been.

"Mari, I'm so sorry. You lied to the police, and all the time you didn't know..." He shook his head. *She must be scared out of her mind,* he thought. "You think I killed Clayton."

Mari threw her head back and studied the ceiling for a moment. When she lowered it back to look at Lenny, her eyes had narrowed and her mouth was a tight line.

"I didn't even go in the house." Lenny wondered what he could say that would make her believe him.

"I know you didn't kill Clayton." Mari's voice had an edge to it that he'd never heard before. As she wiped at her cheeks with the back of her wrists, he finally recognized that she wasn't sad or afraid— she was angry. And it seemed to be aimed at him.

"It did cross my mind," she continued. "But then I thought, Lenny Driver wouldn't have the guts to shoot someone. He'd just make up some lies and spread them around Blahst and Facebook. And he'd be so clever that nobody would even know it was him."

Lenny felt a coldness spread inside his chest. What was she talking about?

"Is there anything you wanted to tell me, Lenny?"

Lenny felt paralyzed with confusion. It sounded like she knew about the Blahst attack, but he realized that his defenses were on hyper-alert. First Andrei Simenov, then the police, now Mari— every time he thought he'd been busted, it turned out to be something else. He kept his mouth shut and watched Mari cross to the far wall.

"Let me tell you about the picture of Andrei Simenov I've been looking at for the last two weeks. That evil captain of industry is hitting a poor little boy. They look like they're in... I don't know... Africa? With this amazing sunset in the background. Anything sound familiar?"

"Oh, crap." Roy's words broke into the silence that followed Mari's question. Lenny looked at his friend and followed Roy's gaze across to the picture on the wall beside Mari.

It was over.

She knew. Maybe Andrei and the rest of Blahst knew, too. Lenny couldn't begin to imagine what the fallout was going to be, but right now all he wanted was for Mari to stop looking at him like that. Still the anger, but mostly... disappointment.

"I was going to tell you."

Mari raised her eyebrows.

"No, really," Lenny continued. "I've fixed it now, but I wanted to wait until everything was back to normal. The stock's not falling anymore; you can check for yourself."

"Is that why you wanted to be with me? Because you knew I was on the team looking for you? That must have been very entertaining."

"But we never talked about... I didn't know you were..."

"I lied for you, Lenny."

Lenny watched the tears coursing in rivulets down Mari's face. Then she wheeled around into the corridor and ran toward the office door without looking back. He tried to think of the words that would keep her from leaving, but he found himself speaking to the empty corridor.

"I was going to tell you."

The only natural light that reached Mari's cubicle was a slanted ray that dazzled her screen in the late afternoon, highlighting the flecks of static dust on the glass and making anything behind them impossible to read.

Mari usually took this as her cue to wind down for the day, or, if she was feeling like working late, she would walk around the cubicles to the side of the office and pull the blinds across the setting sun. Today, she watched the dust specks hovering in the narrow beam of sunlight and wondered how you could so easily miss what was right in front of you.

A fresh spasm of sobs racked her body, and she sank her head into her hands. She didn't care if anyone overheard. A few other employees had drifted past her cubicle toward the elevator to mark an early end to the day, but she supposed that nobody had thought it odd to see her crying on a day like today. She was just one of many employees who were stunned by the death of a colleague.

She pulled a tissue from a tattered box in the corner of the cubicle and rubbed it roughly across her cheeks and eyes. Fresh tears rushed in to fill the space. She'd really thought Lenny was special—a little impetuous maybe, but that was part of the attraction. Now it turned out he was a liar and a hacker. And her earlier confidence at his inability to kill was starting to trickle away. If Lenny had hated Blahst enough to attack them in secret, what festering resentment had he felt toward Clayton, the person who had started it all? What lengths would he go to for revenge? And now that she knew his secret, was she in danger too?

She dropped her tissue into the trashcan, where it landed on top of a pile that had been forming for most of the afternoon. She really should tell Pierce or Andrei about the photo. She should go to the police and tell them she had lied about Clayton walking home. But she felt paralyzed by a flood of mixed emotions. Lenny made her laugh. He had met her family and nearly eaten a carrot for her. The memory of the party brought a smile to her lips, which quickly twisted into more sobs.

The sound of her desk phone startled her, but she didn't answer it. It might be Lenny still trying to reach her. She had a dozen missed calls and messages from him on her cell phone, which still seemed to work despite the cracked screen—calls that she had no intention of returning.

A shadow rose across Mari's computer screen as the sun slipped below the top of her cubicle wall. Slowly the shadow quelled the glare, and the contents of her screen slid back into view: a photo of a crouching boy, his dark eyes seeming to plead for a resolution to his endless fear.

Mari grabbed another wad of tissues and dabbed at her face. This time the tears seemed to have dried up. She picked up her coat and bag and headed out of her cubicle toward the elevator. Perhaps Lenny Driver wasn't a killer, but a cute smile couldn't excuse what he'd done.

Chapter 22

"WHAT WILL THEY DO TO him when they find him? The attacker, I mean."

Now that Mari had made the decision to act, she was feeling calmer. Pierce was nowhere to be found, so she had headed up to Andrei's office on the fifteenth floor. The CEO's boast that his door was always open to his employees turned out to be true.

"We are not sure what action we will be able to take, particularly as we believe it is a distributed group. Maybe a political organization. There are many who dislike big businesses nowadays." Andrei moved out from behind his desk and gestured for Mari to sit in a small red armchair next to a round table. He joined her in a matching chair at the table "Why do you ask?"

"I think I might... uh... know something."

Andrei cocked his head expectantly. His blue cotton shirt sported a neat crease down the outside of each arm, but fatigue showed in the shadows under his eyes.

Mari cupped her phone in one hand and let her fingers trace the outline of the raised green-and-purple spiral on its protective cover. "What if it was just one person? You know, a hacker or something."

"Then it would be easier to go after them." Andrei straightened himself in the armchair. "Did you see that the stock has stopped falling? It even gained half a point before the market closed. I think the worst may be behind us."

"Yeah, I saw. That's great." Mari forced a smile. "Do you think that could be... deliberate as well?"

"What do you mean?"

"I don't know... say the same hacker decided to say good things about Blahst instead of bad? Would that stop the stock from falling?"

Andrei frowned as he considered the question.

"Perhaps. But it seems to be our new consumer privacy initiative that is helping. Something the marketing group has put together."

Mari nodded distractedly and tried to get the conversation back on track. "If you found out that a hacker did start it all, what would happen to them?" She looked down at her phone and pulled up the photo she had captured in Lenny's office. Tiny glass shards stuck to her finger as she drew it across the screen.

"It is a little hard to say, since we do not know exactly what they did and how they did it, so we do not know what laws they broke. Any unauthorized access to a computer network is a third-degree felony—two to ten years. If the hacker profited from Blahst's share price going down or up, then that is stock manipulation and securities fraud. And if nobody else can get them, the IRS usually finds a way." Andrei chuckled and reached an open palm toward Mari. "Now Mari, what do you know about who is behind all this?"

Mari's finger froze on the screen. What had Andrei just said? *Stock manipulation and securities fraud.* She found herself staring at a green-and-gold coaster on the table, fashioned from a circuit board. Her eyes tracked the intertwined wire paths on the coaster as the phrase played over in her brain.

Andrei said, "Do you have a name for us?"

"I was thinking that perhaps... it was more of a hunch, really... I don't know if..." *Stock manipulation.* She couldn't tell Andrei the truth. She cleared her phone's screen and slipped it into her bag. But she had to say something.

"Clayton," she blurted. "I was thinking that Clayton might have done it after all, even before he was fired, because he knew..." Her teeth chewed at her bottom lip. "He knew he'd be found out once Version 6 was launched and..."

She tried to calm her breathing and looked across at Andrei. He was watching her quizzically.

"It is possible..." he began slowly.

"No, you're right, it doesn't make sense." Mari stood up with an overpowering desire to escape. "I'm sorry. It's been a long day. I wasn't thinking straight. I'm sorry to disturb you."

As she headed for the elevator, Mari tried to calm her panicked breathing and plan her next step. Because if she wasn't very, very careful, she was going to be following Lenny Driver straight to jail.

Snyder leaned back in his chair and smiled as he watched the jagged lines of the voice recording on his computer screen. The streetlights were coming on outside the windows of his Georgetown townhouse, but he enjoyed the darkness of his home office and the comforting glow from his laptop.

It had been less than a week since he'd made the trip to Blahst to plant the transmitters, but it seemed so much longer, what with the long hours at OPRA and the fat red herring that had been Clayton Malloy. It had been risky going there in person, but his diligence was proving more than worthwhile. He reached out and zoomed his display into an area of the recording that was highlighted in red. The spiked waveform froze on the screen with the words it represented spelled out beneath.

That was the beauty of technology—it exposed more than the human senses could detect. Behind the predictable sounds of the spoken words were tiny variations in the voice signal that gave away the emotions of the speaker. There was no such thing as a foolproof lie detector, but if you knew what to look for, the right software could pinpoint the parts of a conversation where the speaker was stressed about something. It told you when someone was excited, or scared, or thinking too hard about what they were saying.

It told him the girl was hiding something.

A few minutes later he had a report of Mari Velasquez's phone activities for the last two weeks. He didn't have time for the levels of bureaucracy required to access the content of the calls and messages, but the simple list of numbers dialed was plenty for his needs. He fed each name through a database search until one came back with some very interesting results.

One of the names was a smart computer programmer who had been turned down for a job at Blahst. A programmer who was employed by a charitable organization serving Burundi that had recently deposited more than two hundred thousand dollars of contributions into its bank account.

Blahst and Burundi, the centers of the two influence networks. The more Snyder learned about Lenny Driver, the more he liked what he was hearing.

He was looking forward to calling Brennigan with some good news. For the first time since Snyder had seen the spreading black snakes of influence on the wall displays at the Office of Predictive Analytics, he felt he was making progress. He had suspected that someone was controlling those influence networks. Now he had a name.

A snatch of female laughter sounded from the street below. Snyder stood up and crossed to the large bay windows. A group of students was milling on the sidewalk, in no hurry to reach their destination. He liked the vantage point that his third-floor office provided—the way he could study the vignettes of other people's lives as they passed below. People rarely looked up and saw him watching; it was as though the world above their heads didn't exist.

Snyder opened the door of the mahogany bureau next to his window and inspected the contents. Tonight deserved a small celebration, he decided—the single-cask Glengoyne would be perfect. He poured himself a generous glass and sipped it as he watched the students slowly disappear around the corner.

He strolled back to his desk and cupped the whiskey glass as he stared again at the trace of Mari Velasquez's voice on the screen. He had two problems to focus on. The first was to find out exactly what Lenny Driver had done to Burundi, and fix it in time to rescue the coltan rights—and Snyder's appointment to the Intelligence Action Network in two weeks. The other was to find out if anybody else knew about Lenny's ability to start influence networks, apart from the girl who wasn't telling everything.

His gaze fell on a small toy bear, which was propped against the wooden tray where he kept his incoming mail. It was striped in white, green, and red and had three red stars on its chest: the colors and emblem of the Burundi flag. He'd bought it at one of the stalls by the canal, the owner buried in a hooded sweatshirt, still trying to make money from tourists even in the frigid February wind. *Charity bears* the sign had said, but Snyder doubted that any charity would see the ten dollars he had paid.

The bear stared back at him with glassy eyes. Snyder felt a wave of anger wash through him as he thought of all the work he had put into the Burundi deal, and how easily it had fallen apart. He thought about Clayton Malloy and the others who would inevitably follow before this affair was through. Such a waste. People like Lenny Driver interfered in things with no thought for the consequences of their actions.

He retrieved a silver serving tray and placed the bear in the middle. With one hand, he held out his glass and poured the contents carefully over the bear. An amber stain splashed over the fur and spread slowly downward as the liquid soaked in. Snyder pulled a packet of matches from his desk drawer and struck one. He breathed in deeply, savoring the smell of the match flare, and held the flame against the rounded stomach of the bear. A black patch formed where the flame licked determinedly at the stained fabric. As the heat touched Snyder's fingertips, he flicked out the match and lit another. This time a small hole formed in the singed fabric, its edges glowing orange and spreading slowly wider until a piece of stuffing caught alight with a hiss. The flames spread rapidly up the bear's chest and head until its vacant expression was obliterated by flickering shades of orange and blue.

Snyder stared at the flames until the heat stung his eyes. He blinked and relaxed as the warmth spread over his face, engulfing his senses so that he barely noticed the insistent shriek of the smoke alarm.

Chapter 23

"So, you're colleagues of Professor Ramsey?"

Lenny studied the two visitors. The tall one was clearly in charge. It showed in the way he'd walked into Lenny and Roy's office like he owned the place—not with the cocky authority the police had shown yesterday, but with the sleek presumption of a cat. Lenny felt the man's eyes checking him out, boring into him from their perch above a jutting nose. He carried a black raincoat draped over the arm of an expensive-looking suit. His companion wore a grey suit of thin, shiny fabric that bunched into creases under his arms.

"Make yourselves at home." Roy moved some piles of papers from two of the desk chairs and motioned for the visitors to take a seat. The stocky man sat down awkwardly, tugging at his jacket as the creases gripped tighter under his arms. The tall man ignored the chair and walked over to the table where Roy's camera equipment and printers threatened to overpower the thin metal legs beneath them.

"How do you know Professor Ramsey?" asked Lenny.

"Who's the photographer?" The man picked up one of the cameras and held the viewfinder up to his eye. He moved one hand in a fluid motion, and an outsized barrel of a lens, larger than the camera itself, zoomed out several inches, then retracted.

"Nice," he said, placing the camera back on the table.

"That's mine," said Roy proudly. "The Nikon's my favorite for daytime, but the motordrive isn't as fast as the—"

"I didn't catch your name." Lenny stepped toward the visitor. "Professor... ?"

The man turned to Lenny with a smile that looked as though it didn't get used very often.

"Excuse me, where are my manners? I'm Snyder, Bernard Snyder. James and I were at Stanford together. I'm doing some consulting for Greenpeace, so I wanted to catch up with the work James has been doing for Burundi."

Lenny nodded and relaxed a little. His nerves had been frazzled since the confrontation with Mari yesterday. When he'd first opened the door to these new visitors, he was worried that they were more cops, back to sound him out about Clayton, or the FBI to grill him about Blahst. But if they were colleagues of the professor, Lenny owed them some hospitality, even if he wasn't feeling particularly sociable. Professor Ramsey had published *Viral Diffusion* while he was at Stanford, and he still visited to lecture there from time to time.

Snyder sat down on the free chair and hung his coat over the back. "This is fortuitous. Professor Ramsey speaks very highly of you. I was hoping I might get the opportunity to meet you."

Lenny felt a surge of pride that the professor had been talking about him to his old colleagues. He wasn't sure how his boss had felt toward him after the incident with the budget, but it sounded like he was pleased with what Lenny had achieved since then. The professor didn't know about Blahst, of course. As far as he was concerned, Lenny had just come up with a powerful new fundraising technique. No wonder he wanted to share it with his colleagues at other groups like Greenpeace.

On the other hand, these two didn't strike Lenny as Greenpeace types. Not that he knew anybody from Greenpeace, but he imagined they would be young and outdoorsy, ready to chase seal hunters on Ski-Doos. Maybe Snyder was from the finance department. Lenny glanced over at the other visitor, who was sitting with one foot propped against the side of Ray's camera table, exposing an inch of hairy leg above scuffed black shoes.

"I have a simulation I can show you," said Lenny, rolling his chair over to his desk. As Snyder pulled his chair next to him, Lenny brought the model up on his screen. He talked through his approach to finding the opinion leaders that formed the center of the hubs, and they watched the screen light up as the hubs spread rapidly in all directions. Roy stood behind them and tried to throw in helpful comments, but Lenny sensed him becoming quickly out of his depth.

"So you've found a way to keep the network spreading, instead of fading out," Snyder commented. "That's impressive. Every fundraiser would love to know how you do that."

Lenny looked across at Snyder with growing respect. It was good to meet someone who understood what he had achieved. His initial mistrust began to fade—this guy knew what he was talking about.

As he turned back to the screen, he caught sight of Snyder's colleague still lounging in the desk chair across the room, picking at his fingernails with obvious boredom. Why had this man come if he wasn't interested in how the fundraising worked? Lenny shook the distraction from his head and returned to his guest.

"There are three parts to the algorithm. The first uses social network analysis to track down the opinion leaders with the most influence," Lenny continued. He paused to see if the term meant anything to his visitor. Snyder nodded his understanding, so Lenny launched into the details of how he analyzed the digital trails that people left in the online world.

As he explained his work, his eyes roved once more to the other visitor's scuffed shoes, and a dull sense of unease started to crawl in his stomach. What if these men weren't who they said they were? How could he be sure they knew Professor Ramsey? And that they worked for Greenpeace? He could hardly ask them for I.D. at this point in the conversation. He needed to catch them in a lie, something he knew wasn't true. He interrupted his own monologue as an idea flashed into his head.

"What do you think about that Greenpeace boat that sank? They lost—how many was it—ten people?" Lenny glanced at Snyder to see his reaction.

Lenny felt Snyder's eyes look him up and down appraisingly. He tried not to smile as he saw the man thinking about how to answer the question. If he pretended to have heard the news, Lenny would have caught him out for sure.

"I didn't hear about that," Snyder replied. "Are you sure it was one of ours? But then, I've been traveling. I have a hard time keeping up with the news when I'm on the road." He shook his head. "Tragic."

"No shit." Roy's voice came from behind them. "That sucks." Lenny had nearly forgotten Roy was still there.

Lenny frowned slightly. He hadn't expected that response from Snyder, but it meant the man had passed the test. After a moment's hesitation, he continued his explanation.

"The second part personalizes the message so that the opinion leader gets really excited about the idea," said Lenny.

"Find their hot buttons." Snyder nodded. "How do you identify their interests?"

"Well, I..." Lenny cleared his throat. "There are commercial services you can get that information from."

He didn't want to dwell on some of the more creative ways that he had found people's interests, so he moved on to explain how he'd categorized the opinion leaders and handcrafted a twist on the basic message that would appeal to each set. He started to relax again as he warmed to the unfamiliar sensation of an appreciative audience for his work. He went deeper into the details of the set categorization algorithm, encouraged by Snyder's thoughtful nodding. As he finished up describing how scalable his approach was, he glanced at the time in the bottom corner of his screen and realized he'd been talking for twenty minutes straight, without a word from his guest.

Snyder was watching Lenny with his mouth slightly open and head tipped forward, his eyes staring intently at Lenny. Lenny had the impression of someone waiting for the final number to match a winning lottery ticket. His sense of unease returned with an intensity that froze the flow of words from his mouth. Across the office, Snyder's colleague looked as though he had fallen asleep in his chair. His body was a straight line from the round head leaning against the top of the chair to the outstretched legs in their shiny grey suit.

"Just fascinating. Do go on." Snyder's voice was silken.

"Uh, that's all there is."

"You said there was a third part?"

"I'm still working on that." Lenny crossed his arms and leaned back in his chair.

"I thought you had that all figured out." Roy's voice cut in from behind Lenny. "What about how you make them think—ouff!"

Lenny slammed his chair backward and sent Roy flying into the sleeping visitor. Roy slid down the man's legs and crashed onto the floor with a grunt. The visitor sat up straight, his arms clenched against the arms of the chair, and looked in confusion at Roy sprawled at his feet.

"Sorry, Roy, didn't realize you were so close behind me." Lenny rose to his feet and crossed over to Roy. As he reached a hand to Roy's elbow to pull him back up, he leaned over and mouthed an exaggerated *no*. Roy glared back at Lenny as he regained his feet, but didn't speak a word.

Both of the visitors were now on their feet. The stocky man blinked groggily as he tried to make sense of the scene. Snyder crossed to Roy and spoke before Lenny could intervene.

"You were saying something about making people think..." He tailed off and waved his hand in a circular gesture, inviting Roy to continue. Lenny took a deep breath as Roy's eyes flickered briefly in his direction and back to Snyder.

"No, I was thinking of that social network stuff." Roy shrugged and looked at the floor. "I just take the photos."

Lenny let out his breath. He vowed to himself that once these visitors left, he would bolt the door and never answer it again.

"It's been a pleasure meeting you, but if you'll excuse us, we do have quite a bit of work to do." Lenny picked up Snyder's coat and handed it to him.

Snyder took the coat and reached out to shake Lenny's hand. "Thank you for your hospitality," he said. "And good luck with your research." He nodded for his colleague to join him, and the two of them headed toward the office door.

As he reached Professor Ramsey's office, Snyder stopped and turned to face Lenny.

"Have you ever modeled the actual results from your fund-raising activities? You know, tried to keep track of all of the consequences—intended and maybe unintended?"

Lenny stared at Snyder, wondering again who he really was.

"You've never analyzed the influence networks you've created?" A half smile played on Snyder's lips. "Maybe even tried to predict how they might play out in the long run? Experiment with different scenarios?"

Lenny turned the notion around in his head. If he could track the effects of his viral algorithm, instead of just launching it and hoping for the best, he'd be able to control it so much better. And if he could predict a whole range of outcomes based on different actions, then... wow.

"Is that possible?" Lenny couldn't hide the awe in his voice.

Snyder pursed his lips and shook his head slowly. "No, just an idea. Never mind." He turned and strode toward the door, calling over his shoulder as he walked. "Goodbye. I'm sure we'll meet again."

Lenny watched the two men disappear into the hallway and hoped fervently that they would never meet again.

Chapter 24

"THIS PLACE IS A MESS!" Lenny glared at the floor of his apartment, which was strewn with clothes, shoes, unwashed mugs, and plates abandoned with half-eaten food.

"It's all your mess," said Roy from under the desk where he kept his computer equipment. He pulled out a plug from the wall and replaced it in a different socket.

"No, it's not. You're just as much a slob as me." Lenny swept up a jacket and a pair of jeans from the back of the sofa. The legs of the jeans were sculpted with dried mud, as though some invisible body were still wearing them. As he passed Roy's open bedroom door, he looked morosely at the neat bed and spotless floor and realized that Roy was probably right.

"Well, you might at least help me. Mari texted me that she's coming over. I want it to look... you know... nice."

"Oh yeah, that'll make all the difference. Once she knows you put your socks in the hamper, she's bound to forgive you for trashing her company and lying to her."

Roy's voice faded as Lenny strode into his own bedroom, opened the sliding door of his wardrobe, and dumped the jacket and jeans inside. He dropped onto his knees and started picking up shoes and dirty laundry from the floor around his bed, throwing them over his shoulder in the direction of the open wardrobe.

He was relieved that Mari had finally contacted him, but he had no idea what he was going to say to her. How could he possibly justify what he had done? And what if she had told someone? Perhaps she was on her way over here now with Blahst's lawyers, or the police. He took a deep breath to stave off the welling panic and set upon his pile of not-quite-dirty t-shirts.

When the floor of his room looked passable, Lenny slammed the wardrobe door shut and started on the living room. He collected two handfuls of mugs and deposited them in the kitchen sink.

As he went back for a second round of crockery, he heard a thump and a curse from underneath the desk. He peered down and saw Roy jiggling the power cord in the back of his computer.

"Do you have to do that now? I could use some help."

"Well, if you hadn't nearly broken my arm with that chair stunt yesterday, I might have been able to help." Roy slid out from under the desk and started checking the wires that ran into the back of the monitor. "And yes, I do need to do this now. I have to print and deliver a job tomorrow morning, and I'm way behind on the design. I've got to finish it this evening, but I can't get this thing to start up."

"The monitor's working, so you're wasting your time checking the power input," Lenny said, looking around the living room. It didn't look any different from when he'd started cleaning. He could probably fix Roy's computer in thirty seconds flat, if he didn't have to work on this mess.

"How about you clean, and I'll take a look at your computer."

"Sure." Roy ambled over to a drawer and pulled out a trash bag.

Lenny checked the connections and restarted everything, but he had no better luck than Roy did in getting the computer to fire up. He realized that it might take longer than he had thought. But that was fine; it was better than cleaning.

"It might be the motherboard. I'll have to look inside." Lenny rummaged in the desk drawer for a screwdriver. He undid the casing, eased the front cover off, and inspected the inside of the computer. He checked again and knelt back on his heels.

"The hard drive's gone."

"It's broken? Piece of shit. I only had it a year." Roy was working on a collection of apple cores on the coffee table. He was trying to pick them up by the small stems, to avoid touching the congealed brown flesh as he dropped each one into the trash bag.

"No, I mean it's gone. It's not there."

Roy dropped the trash bag and crossed over to Lenny. "It's got to be there. You're just not looking in the right place."

"I'm telling you, it's gone."

Lenny looked into Roy's puzzled face and knew it was a mirror of his own.

"Do you think the police took it?" Roy's question was little more than a whisper.

Lenny shook his head vigorously, as much to ward off his own doubts as to reassure his friend. "No, that's not how they work. They'd come with a warrant and take the whole lot away."

"What about yours?" Roy asked, nodding over at Lenny's computer on the countertop.

"Why would mine be..." Lenny stopped himself and crossed to his laptop, lodged at one end of the counter.

He opened the bottom cover with the screwdriver and stared at the empty space where his hard drive should have been.

Mari pushed Lenny's doorbell for the second time and stamped her feet to loosen the snow that clumped around her boots. She glanced up at the second floor of the red brick townhouse to see if she could make out a light at the window. Lenny had acknowledged her text that she was coming, but maybe he'd changed his mind and decided to ignore her. As she readied herself to lean on the bell again, a muffled voice came from a slotted metal plate.

"It's me," she replied.

"What's your name?" The words were clearer this time, and she could make out Lenny's voice. She sighed with exasperation and leaned closer to the metal plate.

"It's me, Mari, who do you think?"

The buzzer sounded and Mari pushed open the door. A curving staircase with a decorative railing ran up one side. Mari ran her hand along the twisted metal as she walked slowly up to the second floor. Maybe it had been a mistake to come here. She slipped the other hand into her purse and felt the hard, plastic case of her pepper spray.

The front door was open slightly, and she could see Lenny's eye looking out through the crack. As she drew closer, the door closed and she heard the rattle of a chain before the door opened all the way.

Lenny's hair was even more rumpled than usual, with curls bouncing in all directions. He was barefoot beneath jeans and a plain blue t-shirt. His eyes didn't meet hers as he glanced around the hallway behind her.

She figured she'd stand outside the door forever if she waited for Lenny to invite her in, so she slipped past him and looked around the small apartment. An oversized floral sofa dominated the living area. She took a seat at one end and studied a patch of matted fringe at the edge of the rug. Now that she was here, she didn't know what to say to Lenny. Why had she even come? It wouldn't change anything.

She heard the front door close and the chain latch again. A few seconds later, Lenny and Roy were hovering in front of her, waiting expectantly.

"Did you tell anyone?" Roy was first to break the silence.

"No." Mari looked up and saw Lenny's shoulders relax visibly.

"Are you going to?" Roy didn't meet her gaze. His fingers twisted around each other in front of his stomach.

"No."

Mari saw them exchange a glance. Lenny sat down next to her on the sofa. He moved one hand toward her knee but hesitated and placed in on his own instead.

"Mari, thank you. I know I don't deserve it, but—"

"I'm not doing it for you." Mari willed the tears to stay away. "I bought a bunch of Blahst stock when the price was low. Everybody did; they all said it was a great opportunity. So now the price has gone up, it looks a bit fishy, don't you think?"

"But if everybody else was doing it too, why would—"

"Everybody else didn't have a boyfriend who forced the stock to crash and rise again."

Mari watched Lenny's face change from puzzlement to slow realization. She'd played it over in her own mind enough times, trying to find a scenario that didn't look like she and Lenny had planned it together. He would manipulate the stock; she would make the trades.

"And everybody else didn't give their boyfriend a fake alibi the night Clayton was killed."

"Mari, you don't think I—"

Lenny's body tensed beside her.

"No. No, I don't." Mari pushed her face into her open palm. Her eyes remained dry—in fact her whole body felt drained of emotion. "What did happen that night?"

"I didn't even get out of the car. He sort of threw up and then he let himself in the house. I never saw him after that. So you don't think I killed him?" Lenny sounded almost disappointed.

Mari shook her head. "Probably just some druggie burglar he interrupted."

"What about all this other weird shit?" Roy dropped into the armchair opposite Mari and Lenny. "Someone broke into our computers. Stole my old CDs, too. All my party mixes."

Lenny and Roy brought Mari up to date on the theft of their hard drives and the strange visitors they'd had at the office. Mari tried to make sense of what she was hearing but succeeded only in sharing their confusion at the chain of events.

"Do you think it had anything to do with what you did to Blahst?" she asked.

"If you didn't tell anyone..." began Lenny.

"I didn't."

"Then we're the only three that know. I don't see how it could be related..." Lenny trailed off, and Mari saw in his eyes that he didn't believe his own words.

"The professor knows that the viral algorithm works for fundraising," said Roy. "I wouldn't put it past those sketchy Greenpeace guys to steal our stuff."

Mari considered the possibility. A break-in sounded desperate for an organization that was supposed to help the world be a better place. And it didn't explain Clayton's death.

"What was on the drives?" she asked.

"Bunch of old photos mostly," said Roy. "But I've got backups at the office."

"Nothing much on mine," added Lenny.

"But what about your viral algorithm?" asked Roy. "And all the messages you sent out? Aren't there records?"

Lenny shook his head. "It was all done through online accounts. And I never store cookies or user names locally. Nothing on my machine."

Mari wished she could rewind her life back to the night of the launch party. If she hadn't let Lenny leave angry, she could have stopped all of this from happening. But reality didn't come with a reset button. All they could do now was stop things from getting worse.

"You need to delete those programs," she said to Lenny. "And all your accounts."

Lenny stared at her. "Delete them? Are you kidding?"

"She's right." Roy nodded.

"But I've figured out how to control it. Look at Blahst's stock price—I put out some good press, and it's an all-time high."

"Exactly. If you delete them now, everything's back to normal. Nobody need ever know, and nobody else can use it." The more Mari thought about it, the more sense it made.

"Look, I know you're trying to help, but—"

"It's my problem too now." Mari glared at Lenny. She hadn't asked to be a part of it, but now that she was implicated, he could at least listen to her.

"It'd be for the best, Lenny." Roy's face was glum. "Nobody should have that kind of influence."

"You're pathetic, both of you. This is the most amazing thing since... since Google, and you're ready to wipe it out just like that. Well, it's my algorithm, and I say we keep it."

Lenny stormed into his bedroom and slammed the door. Mari jumped to her feet and started after him, but Roy placed a hand gently on her arm.

"Just wait," he said.

Mari hesitated, and then sank back into the sofa. Roy's instincts proved right, and a few minutes later Lenny emerged from his room, phone in hand. He pulled a stool out from the kitchen counter and sat facing them.

"We were going to rule the world, Roy."

"I'm not sure the world's ready for us."

"It's gonna take a while to delete." Lenny propped his feet on the bar of the stool and leaned his elbows on his knees. His thumbs flew across the screen of his phone, and his forehead creased in concentration.

Roy caught Mari's eye and nodded his head toward Lenny. "You want to stay here and keep an eye on him?"

Mari shrugged, then nodded. She was too riled up to go back to an empty apartment.

"I was supposed to meet Mandy half an hour ago. Just feed him Coke and pizza every now and then." Roy pulled a jacket from beside the front door and left her alone with Lenny.

Mari watched Lenny's slim fingers working at the phone. Occasionally his mouth formed silent words as he concentrated. She was starting to doze against the sofa cushion when she heard the clunk of Lenny's phone skidding onto the coffee table.

"I hear world domination is overrated." Lenny sat down next to her and reached hesitantly for her hand. She let him take her fingers inside his own. "You were right. You always are."

"Thank you." Mari studied Lenny's face, still creased in a frown. "You okay?"

"Yeah. It's kind of a relief actually. That it's over."

She reached out and massaged the frown until his face relaxed, wondering if it could be that simple. She wanted to share his optimism that it was over, wanted more than anything to feel about Lenny the way she'd felt before she saw that photo. Could she trust him again?

"It's still in your head, you know."

The frown returned as he looked at her, puzzled.

"You could rewrite those programs anytime you wanted."

He thought for a second, then cupped his hand under her chin and pulled her face toward him.

"I swear, I will never again use my powers for evil," he said.

"How do I know that's not an evil lie?"

"I guess there's no way to know for sure." He shrugged.

"I have a way." She leaned forward and let her lips play slowly up the curve of his chin to his mouth. His hand slid to the nape of her neck and pulled her closer to him until their lips locked into a soft embrace.

"A kiss never lies," she whispered. "I believe you."

As their lips melted into another kiss, she felt his hand slide up inside her t-shirt and tentatively cup her breast. A delicious shiver coursed through her body at his touch. Her own hands hungrily explored his chest and the flatness of his stomach until her fingers brushed against the unyielding waistband of his jeans. Her body tensed for a moment as she pictured her colleagues at Blahst. What would they think if they could see her now with the person they had been hunting all this time?

Lenny seemed to sense her hesitation and rose to his feet, pulling her with him. She let him take her by the hand and pull her into his bedroom. As he pushed the door closed with his foot, their lips and bodies locked again and they tumbled onto the bed. Lenny's fingers fumbled as he unbuttoned her blouse, and she helped him release her body from its clothes. His lips caressed her shoulders and neck before working their way down her body.

She knew at that moment that whether the crisis was over or not, they were in it together.

Chapter 25

SNYDER SHOOK HIS HEAD AS the contents of the last file scrolled slowly up the screen. He'd had to unplug the desk lamp to find a power socket for his laptop, so the only source of light in the small motel room was forty watts of pale yellow glow that fought its way through the dirty lampshade. It was just enough to illuminate his keyboard and the bored features of the figure next to him.

"Are you sure this is all there was?" Snyder snapped at the slumped figure, who seemed to have zoned out into his own world. "Wally?"

Wally started upright and frowned at the screen. "That's everything from the office and the residence. I got the disks and the hard drives." He looked sideways at Snyder. "Like you said."

Snyder didn't try to hide the contempt in his voice. "I meant that you should copy them, not bring them with you. Didn't you think they might notice? And why on earth did you bring their music collection?"

Snyder waved his arm toward the silver CDs scattered across the carpet.

"They're disks, aren't they?" said Wally. "He might have... I don't know, hidden his programs on them."

He paused and licked his lips before looking squarely at Snyder.

"I can tell you exactly what you said." He pulled a small silver device out of his pants pocket, fiddled with the controls, and Snyder heard his own voice played back.

"I need all his files. Get the hard drives, flash drives, disks, everything."

Snyder stared incredulously at Wally's squat features. "You recorded our conversation?" he said, as calmly as he could manage.

"See, you said *get* the hard drives, not *copy* the hard drives. I just did what you told me."

"I meant that you should get the data from the hard drives." Snyder watched Wally's hands fiddling with the voice recorder. "Have you been recording everything?"

"No, just when I get new orders. It's just... sometimes I forget things." Wally glanced nervously at Snyder. "I always delete it afterward."

Snyder took a deep breath and tried to stay calm. It was his own fault for trying someone new, but for this job he'd wanted to avoid his usual connections. If Lenny's work turned out to be as powerful as he hoped, Snyder wanted to be very careful about who he shared it with. Using an outsider was always a risk, but Wally had come highly recommended—which just went to show that you should never rely on secondhand sources.

"At least you didn't shoot anyone this time."

"I told you, that wasn't my fault." Wally's shoulders sank as he spoke. "That Clayton dude came barging in and shouting his head off when I was at his computer. I tried to cover his mouth, but he threw up all over me. It was gross."

"You killed him because he vomited on you? Good job you didn't go into the medical field."

"He was biting and clawing, and we were slipping around in his puke. He got a lucky blow in and knocked me down, so I just grabbed the gun and..." Wally shrugged and looked up at Snyder. "You know how it is."

Snyder knew exactly how it was. He knew the surge of adrenalin as the lock clicked open and you walked into the darkness of a stranger's house. The laser focus you felt as you walked through the empty rooms to find your target. The strange sensation of floating above yourself as your arms and hands performed their task with precise, efficient movements. The sickening thrill of a sudden sound, and the burst of mental and physical agility required to evade detection. Above all, he knew the importance of staying calm, of never killing anyone except when there was no choice. A bungled break-in would be low on the list of police attention; a murder would be right at the top.

"Do you want me to go back and search his workplace?" Wally's voice was hesitant.

Snyder shook his head. He'd scanned Lenny's files and found nothing of interest—old college essays, photo archives, a few programming enhancements to online games. This approach wasn't leading anywhere; nowadays everything was in the cloud. He reached out and started closing down his laptop.

"What are we going to do next then?" asked Wally.

"Nothing. I'll give you your money. Then we're done." Snyder placed the hard drives into a heavy plastic bag and swept the CDs on top.

"You're not giving up, are you?" Wally rubbed his hand over the short spikes of his hair. "I thought you said this was something big. World-changing, you said."

"Did you record that too?"

Wally's laugh sounded forced, a little too loud in the muffled confines of the motel room. "I mean it; I can still help you. I won't mess up again."

"I know you won't." Snyder pulled out a wad of money from an envelope in his laptop case and started peeling off fifty-dollar bills. As he counted, he saw Wally glance up at him slyly and look back down at his voice recorder.

"I kept some copies, you know."

Snyder's hands froze on the bank notes.

"Copies of you talking about Clayton. When you first called me."

Snyder placed the money slowly on the desk and turned to face Wally.

"Are you blackmailing me?"

Wally shrugged and sat down on the brown nylon bedspread. "It would be nice to be a part of something big." He leaned back on his hands and looked up at Snyder expectantly.

Snyder pursed his lips to give the appearance that he was thinking, then paced across the room to stand next to the single bedside lamp. He turned to face Wally, making sure that what little light there was would be focused on Wally's features. He had his suspicions, but he had to be sure about this

"Where are the copies?" Snyder asked.

"Somewhere safe."

"What do you plan to do with them?"

"Nothing if you keep me in. Otherwise..." Wally raised his eyes toward the ceiling. "Otherwise, they might find their way to people who care about what happened to Clayton."

Snyder pursed his lips again to cover the smile that threatened to creep onto his face as Wally spoke. Now he was sure. The strain of the face muscles, the tiny pauses, the direction of the eyes. Wally was bluffing. There were no recordings.

"Well, I always admire free enterprise." Snyder nodded as though in deference to a superior opponent. He pocketed the money from the desk and handed Wally the trash bag with the hard drives and CDs. "You can start by helping me get rid of these."

Wally jumped up from the bed and grabbed the bag eagerly. "There's this guy in Chelsea—"

"No. Nobody else gets involved. We're going to take a trip to the North Shore."

Snyder gathered up his coat and laptop bag and glanced around to make sure they had left nothing behind. He'd prepaid for the room, so they didn't need to check out. Wally led the way, carrying the trash bag. Before he closed the door behind him, Snyder reached into his bag until his fingers connected with the skinny wire of his phone charger. He pulled the neatly looped coil out of his bag and slipped it into his coat pocket.

Snyder looked out at the crashing foam. Light from a half moon in a clear sky picked out the curves of the rocky outcrop around him. Further along the shore, the shallow waters of the beach had frozen into gentle ripples before being smashed into a spectacular tectonic display by the relentless motion of the tides. The jagged chunks of ice thrust across each other like an alien landscape of crystal rock. But here the ocean was too deep, the tides too strong, for the cold to still the churning waters.

They'd come in Wally's car. Snyder had stopped at his own car just long enough to put his bag in the trunk and retrieve a pair of insulated boots, which had served him well as they trudged through knee-deep snow along the shore path to the promontory. Wally's leather shoes had slipped several times as he carried the trash bag across the rocks, and Snyder had needed to steady the younger man to keep him from falling.

"This it?" Wally peered out over the surging tide.

"Yes. It's a good site. There's a rip tide that pulls everything straight out to sea, any time of day. Out and down, never to be found."

"Okay then." Wally gathered the plastic neck of the bag in both hands.

"No, empty them out. That way the salt will destroy them sooner."

Snyder stood behind Wally and watched him as he threw the metal drives out over the cliff, then flicked the CDs one at a time, Frisbee-style, after them.

"Hope we're not killing the fish, dumping all this crap in the ocean. What do you think?" Wally grinned as he pitched the last CD from the bag.

Snyder moved fast. The phone cable was already wrapped securely around both of his hands. He passed his right hand in a circular motion around Wally's head, crossed the cable at the back, and pulled it taut with two fists. Wally's hands flew to his neck, his fingernails clawing in vain at the thin wire. He tried to twist his body, but Snyder matched each move to stay at Wally's back, out of reach of the flailing arms and legs.

It always surprised Snyder how long it took for a man to die. The power of the human life force was something to be respected, which was why Snyder preferred a personal approach whenever possible. Guns were too casual, too cold. It was important to feel the connection, the awesome responsibility of taking a man's life. Even the life of an imbecile like Wally.

Snyder kept the wire pulled tight for a full minute after Wally slumped to the ground. He could feel the muscles of his own arms and chest complaining at the prolonged tension as he knelt over the body. He would ache in the morning.

His work was far from over. Wally had been no help; in fact he'd slowed the process down by forcing Snyder to take this trip this evening. He was still no closer to what he wanted than at the Healthway office, when Lenny Driver had decided to hold out on him. He needed to take a different approach to persuade the boy to cooperate. A more direct approach that would leave Lenny no room to maneuver.

Chapter 26

THE RASP OF THE DOORBELL startled Lenny out of a fitful sleep. He'd been dreaming he was back at college taking his final exams. In the dream, he was late, and he didn't know which room he was supposed to be in. Everyone he asked pointed him in a different direction, all as helpful as can be, but when he finally walked into a lecture hall, it was the wrong one. A sea of faces he didn't recognize looked up to see who was interrupting. He turned to leave, but the door had disappeared, and he searched in vain along the wall for the way out.

The doorbell rang again. He glanced at the clock on his bedside table. Eleven o'clock in the morning—he should be at work by now. He stretched his arms above his head with a smile, remembering that he hadn't slept much last night. He must have drifted off to sleep again after Mari left for work. An early staff meeting, she'd said. She'd slipped into her clothes while Lenny watched from the warm covers, which were still fresh with her perfume. Another sharp ring pulled him back to reality.

"Just a second," he yelled, blinking his eyes into focus. It was probably Roy, too lazy to find his key. He swung his legs over the side of the bed, pulled on a pair of shorts, and ambled out of his bedroom.

"Hello, Lenny."

Lenny stared at the grey eyes and ramrod nose of the man standing in the middle of his living room, and recognized him instantly as the man who had visited his office the day before. A rush of adrenaline jolted him wide awake, but his body stayed rooted to the spot. He inhaled deeply.

"You're not from Greenpeace, are you?" he said.

Snyder's mouth creased into a smile, but the eyes stayed fixed on Lenny. "No, I'm not from Greenpeace. And you were a little slow in answering, so I let myself in. Hope that's okay."

Lenny's chest swelled with indignation. "No, it's not okay. You can't just—"

"I know what you did to Blahst."

Lenny felt his throat try to swallow, but it came up dry. It had finally happened. He had been discovered. A dozen questions raced through his head. *Who was this man, and what did he want from Lenny? How had he tracked him down? Had Mari told somebody after all, or had Roy?* But amid the rising panic, Lenny sensed another emotion working to calm his pounding heart. Breaking through the fear, Lenny started to feel an unexpected sense of relief. Maybe this would be for the best. He could tell them what he'd done, pay the price, and get on with his life. Surely the penalty wasn't too bad for a bit of spamming?

"Come, let's talk." Snyder sat down in the armchair and beckoned for Lenny to sit on the sofa opposite.

"I was very impressed with what you told me about your work yesterday," said Snyder.

"Who are you?"

"I'm with the government."

"Shit." The word escaped from Lenny's lips, barely more than a whisper. It was as he had suspected. The FBI had tracked him down. He felt again that peculiar mixture of dread and relief. Might as well get it over with.

"Are you going to arrest me?"

Snyder raised his eyebrows and seemed to ponder the question.

"That would be a waste, don't you think?" he said.

Lenny looked at Snyder in confusion. What did he mean, a waste? Snyder knew what he'd done but wasn't here to arrest him?

"What you have created is remarkable," continued Snyder. "I've been watching your achievements over the last few weeks. Really remarkable."

"What do you want?"

"I want you to educate me." Snyder stood up and paced around the room, inspecting the posters and the few pieces of furniture. He picked up the two parts of Lenny's laptop, still separated where Lenny had unscrewed it the day before. "You were nice enough to tell me most of what you did when we had our little chat at your office. But then you decided to... hold out on me."

"I told you everything."

"No, you didn't." He placed the laptop pieces back on the counter. "Tell me about the third factor."

Lenny was becoming increasingly uneasy about the visitor. Surely the FBI wouldn't act this way. And why was he alone? Didn't the police always have partners? Where was the short guy he'd been with yesterday?

"I don't think I want to do that." Lenny folded his arms.

"Would you rather go to jail?"

So that was the deal. Give his ideas to this man, and he would keep him out of jail. But how could he know who this man really was, and if he had the power to make a deal?

"I want to see some I.D.," said Lenny.

Snyder shook his head. "I don't think you grasp the situation, Lenny. You don't have the bargaining power here. It just takes one anonymous call and everyone knows what you did to Blahst."

Lenny's earlier relief had completely evaporated. His hopes that his problems would soon be over were replaced with an increasing discomfort that he was alone with this man in his apartment. How could he get rid of him? Perhaps he should call

Snyder's bluff. He'd rather face Detective Lu again than spend a minute longer with Snyder.

"It doesn't matter, anyway. I deleted all the programs."

Snyder's face registered no surprise. "That's okay. It's still in your head."

Something rang familiar about Snyder's words, but Lenny couldn't quite place it.

"Yeah, well, that's right where it's staying." Lenny stood up and crossed to the front door. "I think you should leave now." His heart was pounding as he spoke the words, trying to sound more confident than he felt.

Snyder strolled over to the window and pulled a string to open the blinds. Stripes of sunlight shone through, picking out the thick layer of dust on the plastic slats.

"You know, they never found the gun that killed Clayton," he said.

Lenny blinked at the figure silhouetted against the sudden flood of light.

"Who knows where it might show up." Snyder's tone was matter-of-fact. He turned away from the window and let his gaze rove around the apartment. "And your car was outside Clayton's house, wasn't it? The night he was killed."

Lenny opened his mouth but no words came out. Who had seen his car? One of Clayton's neighbors? The police hadn't said anything about that. If they knew he was there that night, then they would have taken him in for sure. Which meant it wasn't a neighbor. One other person was definitely at Clayton's house that night—the person who killed him.

"What do you want?" The words were a croak.

"You know what I want." Snyder smiled. Lenny stared at the smooth line of his top teeth, all identical in length as though they'd been sheared off with a single stroke of a knife. "I want you to tell me the third factor. I want you to rewrite your programs. I want you to use your powers of influence."

"Who are you?"

"I told you. I work for the government. You'd be helping your country. Using your powers for good."

There it was again, a familiarity to Snyder's turn of phrase. What had he said to Mari the night before, something about not using his powers for evil? And she'd said the algorithm was still in his head. Why would Mari have been talking to Snyder, unless...

"What have you done with Mari?" he yelled.

"Huh?" Snyder looked amused.

"Where is she?"

"How should I know? Probably at Blahst, mopping up your mess. Text her if you're worried. Tell her you love her. They like that. Just don't go telling her about our little conversation here. That's our secret."

Lenny's phone was in his bedroom. He turned to get it but stopped before he reached the bedroom door. Texting Mari at Snyder's bidding made it feel cheap, unclean. And Snyder's reaction had calmed his fear. He turned back to Snyder.

"How did you find out about Blahst?"

"Let's just say I'm a good listener. And right now I want to hear that you're going to rewrite those programs." No trace of amusement remained on Snyder's face.

Lenny closed his eyes against Snyder's cold stare. He'd promised Mari and Roy he'd delete his programs and never use them again. But what choice did he have? If he didn't do what Snyder said, the man would set him up for Clayton's murder. Or worse...

Lenny snapped his eyes open. "If I give you my algorithm, how do I know you won't kill me afterward?" He paused. "Like you killed Clayton." He watched for a reaction, but Snyder's face remained inscrutable.

"If you help me, I'll take care of you. You have a talent, Lenny. And I know how to put that talent to good use."

"Why should I believe you?"

Snyder's hands shot out and grabbed the back of Lenny's hair. Lenny's face was forced up toward Snyder's as the taller man bent down and pushed his mouth over Lenny's. Lenny felt the hardness of the other man's teeth against his lips. He tried to pull away but the pressure on the back of his head was unrelenting. He tasted tobacco and bitter coffee and snorted the air out through his nose in panic. Just as he realized he would have to take a breath, Snyder's hands released their grip, and Lenny staggered backward, gasping for air.

"A kiss never lies," said Snyder.

Lenny barely registered Snyder moving toward the door. He felt vomit rising in his throat and reached his hand out to the wall to steady himself.

"I'll call you at eight o'clock tomorrow morning." Snyder opened the front door. "Don't go anywhere too far away. The police might find that suspicious."

The door slammed, and Lenny stared at the empty space where Snyder had stood.

Let's just say I'm a good listener. No wonder Snyder's words had been familiar. He'd bugged Lenny's apartment. He'd been listening to everything, spying on him and Mari the previous evening, maybe even watching as they'd talked and kissed and...

Lenny released a yell of anguish. All of the events of the past weeks seemed to be crammed inside of him, churning around and trying to escape. He could feel the pressure building as he looked around his apartment, once his safe haven, now violated.

Where would Snyder have put a recording device? Lenny picked up a plastic lamp from Roy's desk. He tried to pull the wire out from its bulbous base but it was too firmly attached. He brought it crashing down on the edge of the desk and pulled apart the cracked shards of plastic. Nothing but air and electrical wire.

You know, they never found the gun that killed Clayton. Snyder's words swirled into Lenny's head. Had he hidden the murder weapon here too? Lenny pulled the seat cushions off the sofa and felt in the creases underneath the back. He crossed to the shelves under the TV and ripped out the set-top box and the router. He tried to pull the unit away from the wall, but the wheels had sunk into the carpet. He yanked harder and the TV toppled forward, picking up speed until it landed with a crack against the coffee table. His hands grabbed the cheap black TV stand and threw it on top of the sofa. Nothing underneath but dust.

He moved to his bedroom, ripping the sheets off the bed and heaving up the mattress. He grabbed his pillow and froze as his eyes focused on the smooth pillowcase. A long dark hair was caught against the white cotton. He remembered reaching out to stroke Mari's hair as she slept, the dark waves flowing across both pillows. *Snyder had heard everything.* Lenny dropped the pillow and punched his fist against the wall. The plaster caved in, splintering off in chunks and releasing a cloud of dust.

Lenny sank to his knees, his palms flat against the wall. A thick bead of blood snaked its way from his knuckle through the white powder coating the back of his hand. Slowly, he drew back the same fist and smashed it once more through the wall.

3

Part III

Chapter 27

LENNY LOOKED AROUND AT THE polished marble columns of the hotel foyer and caught his breath, remembering the last time he was here. The Blahst Version 6 launch party. Was it really less than a month since he'd sent out those photos? It seemed like fate was conspiring to cram as much misery into as little time as possible.

Snyder's advice on the phone this morning seemed to be paying off. At exactly eight o'clock, Lenny's phone had blared out its tune, making his heart contract even though he'd been staring at the device for a full hour.

"Wear a suit," Snyder had barked. He had given Lenny the suite number, and said he would be waiting.

With a jacket and clean khakis, Lenny was blending in well with the smartly dressed crowd of people hurrying through the foyer or standing around in small groups. As he waited for the elevator, a woman's sudden laugh made him flinch and spin around. The woman continued a conversation with her colleague, taking small sips from a cardboard coffee cup and paying Lenny no attention. He slipped into the interior of the elevator, thankful that it was constructed of wooden panels rather than clear glass like the Blahst elevators, and welcomed the soothing hum of the machinery.

He found the suite easily and rang the small doorbell mounted on the frame.

Snyder opened the door and waved Lenny in with a flourish.

"There's breakfast over here. Make yourself at home."

Lenny walked into a room with floor-to-ceiling windows running along two sides to meet in the corner. On one side the glass towers of Boston's downtown shone against a piercing blue sky. From the other bank of windows, Lenny could see a snow-covered Boston Common, with dots of people moving along brown paths that cut through the landscape like an ant farm. The room itself was a study in beige—the carpet, the rich satin curtains, the sofa, the lamps, the padded chairs. Only the desk stood out with its traditional mahogany hues, juxtaposed with the sleekness of a wide-screened laptop and mouse on its surface.

Lenny crossed to a small table spread with bagels, pastries, and fruit. Next to the food, carafes of brightly colored juices were standing in a bowl of half-melted ice. He hadn't eaten breakfast—hadn't even thought about food since he'd woken up in a spasm of panic in the early hours—but he didn't think his stomach could handle anything solid. He located a flask of coffee and poured some into a beige china cup. He usually took it black, but he slowly poured some cream into it to delay the moment when he had to face the room's other occupant.

"Let's get started, shall we?" Snyder's voice sounded almost jovial.

Lenny turned toward Snyder and took a sip of his coffee.

"What do you want me to do?"

Snyder gestured over to the desk. "Show me what you did. Rewrite whatever you need to, so you can make it happen again."

Lenny looked between Snyder and the desk. He remembered the relief he'd felt when he'd deleted his programs—the sense that he could put this all behind him and move on. Now he was supposed to reincarnate them and set them loose on the unsuspecting world again? If he did that, it would never be over. But he didn't like the alternative: going to jail for attacking Blahst—and possibly for killing Clayton—if Snyder followed through with his threats.

He looked up at Snyder, poised with his half smile, waiting patiently for Lenny to take his seat at the computer. Somehow Lenny was sure Snyder would succeed in framing him for Clayton's murder, even if he tried to tell the police the real story. There was only one choice: he'd have to think of a way to make Snyder believe he had re-created his programs, but make sure they didn't really work.

Lenny placed his coffee cup on the desk and nudged the mouse. The black screen changed to a password prompt. Snyder pulled a second chair to the desk, sat down, and tapped at the keyboard until a browser window appeared.

"The world is yours," he said, patting the back of the empty desk chair.

"What do you want me to do?" Lenny asked again as he took his seat. "It's not just code. There's a whole bunch of things that need to be done. It depends what you want to make happen."

Snyder pursed his lips. "I need to fix something you messed up."

"What do you mean?" Lenny frowned. "I already fixed everything. Blahst's stock is back up, higher than before."

Snyder's lips parted to show the smooth line of teeth.

"Let's pretend you're doing some fundraising like you did for Burundi. This time it's for DRC—the Democratic Republic of the Congo."

"Where's that?"

"Right next door to Burundi. Huge country, incredible mineral resources, trying to get back on its feet after a civil war. Say I want to target the power bases within DRC, and influence them to do some good for the country."

"Is that what this is about?"

"Something like that. I need you to set it up for me. Find the hubs of influence, then find out what makes them tick—isn't that how it works? And then... the third factor. Which you still need to tell me."

Lenny wrinkled his forehead. "But in order for this to work, they've got to have computers, and blogs, and Blahst, and so on. The Burundi money came out of America, mostly, because we have all of those things. I can't do it if they don't have computers."

"The people who matter have computers," Snyder said. "And social media. Not as much as here, but plenty for us to work with. Just start writing that code."

Lenny shuffled his chair closer to the desk and brought up several more browser windows on the computer. "We'll need to set up some new accounts. I deleted all of mine. And you'll have to seed them with a real e-mail address."

He leaned back to give Snyder access to the keyboard and watched as Snyder began to create a new Blahst account.

"Do you really work for the government?" Lenny asked after a few minutes.

"Yes, I do."

"Which part?"

"That's classified."

Lenny laughed ruefully. "You're a spook. I should have guessed." He took another slow sip of coffee. "Couldn't you just have—I don't know—recruited me or something?"

"I believe I did recruit you. You're working for me, aren't you?" Snyder tipped his head to one side. "Do you mean you want me to pay you?"

Lenny thought about the check from Blahst sitting uncashed on his kitchen counter. Would this feel any less tainted? He'd be helping his government, after all. Lenny glanced up at Snyder's amused expression and decided there was no way he wanted to be on this man's payroll.

"No, that's okay."

Snyder typed an e-mail address into the first window. Before he hit the *Enter* button, he paused with his finger over the keyboard.

"Lenny, this will be untraceable, right?"

"Blahst never found me. Only you did. Somehow."

Lenny waited for Snyder to answer the implied question, but he didn't take the bait. After a few moments of silence, Lenny tried again. "You never told me how you tracked me down."

"It wasn't through your e-mail address." Snyder's thin lips curled into a smile. "We'll be fine. Nobody else has traced anything back to you, or you'd know it by now." He hit the *Enter* key and a confirmation screen popped up.

"Don't you have some fake spy e-mail addresses you can use?"

"Of course. But if it's a working e-mail address, there's always a way to trace it if you try hard enough. Always some link to the real world."

Lenny shook his head. "The postings that the opinion leaders see look like they're from their friends, but they're all generated automatically by my program. I found a way to sever the links once the fake postings are done. You can't trace it back."

"That's good," said Snyder. "But why the indirection? Why not just send the suggestion to the target directly, instead of pointing them to fake postings from their friends?"

Lenny stared at the computer screen and realized he'd blown it. He had just given away the final part of his work, the third factor, the reason the ideas spread virally. Did Snyder realize it, or could Lenny gloss over it and move on? He sneaked a look at Snyder, who was watching him with eyebrows raised. His eyes had the same look of intense anticipation that Lenny remembered from their meeting at Healthway. No chance of changing the subject. But even if Snyder knew the approach, Lenny could easily find a way to make the messages ineffective. He could send out a million useless e-mails and claim to have no idea why it wasn't working.

He turned toward Snyder. "Imagine if somebody tells you their idea and asks you to go and make it happen. How motivated do you feel?"

Lenny watched Snyder ponder the question and found himself enjoying the fleeting sensation of superior knowledge. "Now imagine it's your own idea. It's a whole different feeling."

"I can see that. The target reads the postings, and they trigger an idea. And because you targeted the power brokers—these hubs of influence—you know they're going to act on it." Snyder nodded slowly, then decisively. "Excellent." He focused his attention on the keyboard and screen, and Lenny saw multiple new Blahst accounts spring into view.

Lenny took over the keyboard, uploaded his favorite programming tools, and started re-creating his algorithm to identify the hubs of influence. Much of the code he needed was already out there for the taking—libraries of open source software he could modify, and free services he could tap into. Snyder watched closely, occasionally interrupting with a question about the purpose of some particular line of code. Lenny had a feeling it was going to be harder than he'd thought to sabotage the process. Maybe he could switch the postings at the end and send the wrong topics to each hub, so it wouldn't resonate with them. Snyder might not notice that.

As he let his mind wrap itself around the complexities of his program's logic, Lenny felt himself relaxing into the work. He thought up a few improvements along the way and incorporated them into this new version. He kept up a running commentary to head off Snyder's questions, and he felt a surge of satisfaction at this small source of power over the man who had him trapped.

The ring of a doorbell startled Lenny, but Snyder crossed the room smoothly. He heard a clatter of trays behind him as the remains of breakfast were replaced with fresh food. Snyder slid a plate with a French bread sandwich and a packet of chips next to the computer, and Lenny ate hungrily as he continued to work.

The sun had disappeared behind the curtains at the far end of the room by the time Lenny pushed back from the screen and rubbed his eyes.

"Everything's in place," he said. "Now we just need to feed it the keywords to find the right social networks."

Snyder looked up from the screen of his phone, where he had been tapping in a message. "Start with the country name—DRC and Africa—and then we'll focus in."

Lenny typed in the letters and squinted at the screen as it filled with unrecognizable text. "What's this? Something's wrong with the results."

Snyder inspected the display. "It's French. And a little bit of Swahili—see these characters here?" Snyder ran his finger across the screen and mouthed some sounds that Lenny couldn't decipher. "French is the official language, so we'll work with that."

"But I don't know any French."

"Don't worry, I'm fluent. I just need you to run me through the process."

Lenny's mouth dropped open. Snyder would have to write the messages and postings. How could Lenny make sure they didn't work if he wasn't the one sending them out? Snyder would have it all—the code, the process, everything he needed to work whatever influencing he had in mind. And then... why would he need to keep Lenny around?

Lenny crossed to the food table and stood with his back to Snyder.

"What happens? After we're done here?" he asked.

"You get to go home and forget you ever figured out this little technique. You don't use it anymore, you don't tell anyone, you live happily ever after."

"And you'll just leave me alone?" Lenny tried to sound nonchalant, but he heard the quaver in his own voice. Despite his suspicions, he'd been shocked to find a tiny electronic device taped underneath the sofa in his apartment, and another on the underside of a kitchen drawer. After multiple sweeps with a $200 RadioShack bug detector, he was fairly sure he'd found them all, and that flushing them down the toilet was an effective way to stop them transmitting, but the experience had reminded him of how out of his league he was.

"Lenny, you're a smart kid." Snyder placed his hand on the back of Lenny's shoulder, and Lenny felt his arm tense involuntarily at the touch. "If you don't trust me, think of a reason why I need to keep you around. As long as you haven't hidden any viruses or Trojan horses." Snyder's hand gripped Lenny's shoulder and pulled him around to face him.

"No, it'll work." Lenny looked down at his feet and frowned in thought. "You mean, I could write upgrades or something?"

Snyder gave a staccato laugh. "Yes, upgrades are always useful." Snyder pulled his hand away from Lenny, strode back to the desk, and took the seat in front of the keyboard. "Let's keep going."

Lenny sat beside him and began to explain how to identify the opinion leaders and their interests. As Snyder typed in lists of words, Lenny tried to make sense of them from his hazy memory of high school Spanish—wasn't that supposed to be similar to French?—but he didn't recognize anything.

Lenny felt a heaviness swim through his body. He'd hardly slept all night, and his brain had been toiling the whole day to figure out how to sabotage Snyder's efforts while appearing to help. Now it really was all over. Snyder had everything he wanted.

Maybe it wasn't so bad, running a little more fundraising for Africa. A power like this was too good to squander—it made sense that the government should be able to use it where they needed it. At least Snyder seemed to be using it for a good purpose, from what little Lenny could tell, even if his tactics were dubious to say the least.

As Snyder worked, he had fewer and fewer questions for Lenny. He didn't even seem to notice when Lenny left his chair to sink into the beige brocade of the sofa.

Lenny rested his head against the corner cushions and closed his eyes. But sleep eluded him as his brain chased after half-formed ideas for upgrades that might keep Snyder interested—and himself alive.

Chapter 28

LENNY SLID UNDER THE COVERS as he heard the front door slam and Roy's voice calling him. He worked himself down the bed so that the quilt draped over the contours of his face and sealed out the light. He lay still and felt the soft cotton against his closed eyes.

"Lenny, I know you're here."

Lenny felt a waft of air as Roy lifted up a corner of the quilt. Lenny snatched it back and pinned it shut from the inside with one hand. He pushed the covers up with his knees to form a small burrow in the center of the bed. There was silence for a moment, followed by the rumble and slap of the roller blinds being opened. The fabric surrounding him glowed faintly red before a flood of light blinded him as the warmth of the covers was ripped away.

"Lenny, you have to get up. Professor Ramsey's back, and he's talking about going to Burundi."

"So?" Lenny pulled himself into a sitting position and tugged down the hems of his sweatpants, which had bunched around the back of his knees.

"He's not well enough. We have to talk him out of it."

Lenny blinked up at Roy and smacked his lips against the sour taste in his mouth. Roy's stocky figure was accentuated by a padded black jacket that was shiny wet over the shoulders and chest.

"Is it raining?"

"It's that slushy-ice-rain crap." Roy leaned forward and ran his fingers back and forth through his hair. Drops of cold water stung Lenny's bare arms and shoulders. He turned his back on Roy and hugged his knees to his chest.

"C'mon, Lenny. You've got to help me."

"Nothing I can do." Lenny spoke without turning.

"Get dressed. The professor might listen to you. He likes you." A pair of sneakers bounced off Lenny's legs and landed next to him on the bed. "Can't imagine why."

"Why's he going to Burundi?"

"No idea. I just heard from Gladys that he's at Government Center updating his visa. We've got to find him and talk him out of it. He shouldn't be taking a journey like that, not yet."

As Lenny listened, a sense of unease began to carve its way through the fog that had enshrouded him since he'd left Snyder's hotel room. He'd managed to convince himself that whatever Snyder was using his algorithm for, it was for the good of the country, just like he'd said. But the news about the professor threatened to release the panic that he had so far managed to keep smothered.

"Does it have anything to do with the Congo?" he asked.

"What?" Roy wrinkled his face in confusion. "How should I know? And you'd better call Mari today." Roy's pointed finger jabbed toward Lenny's face. "She called me this morning, worried sick about you. Said she hasn't heard from you since... since she stayed the night. That's just not right, dude."

Lenny thought of the calls from Mari that were steadily incrementing the message count on his phone. How could he face her, after he'd promised her never to use his algorithm again? How could he admit he'd rewritten the whole thing for Snyder?

"Why are you sleeping so much, anyway? You on drugs?" Roy hurled a crumpled sweatshirt at Lenny.

Lenny swung his legs over the edge of the bed and briefly considered the idea. He'd never been tempted beyond the occasional joint at high school parties, but the idea of instant, mind-numbing escape sounded attractive.

He looked back at Roy, who was glowering at him with unusual ferocity. Should he tell Roy what he'd done, and why he couldn't contact Mari? He decided it wasn't a good time, not when Roy was already fretting about the professor.

"Just tired. What time is it, anyway?" He squinted toward the window but couldn't decide whether it was morning or afternoon. Come to think of it, he wasn't even sure what day it was. He remembered raiding the fridge several times when he was sure Roy wasn't home, and feigning sleep whenever Roy had come knocking on his door.

"It's eleven o'clock, and you've been slobbing in your room for three days. What's the matter with you?"

Lenny pulled on the sweatshirt and sneakers and ran his fingers through his hair as a substitute for a brush. Roy was right; it wasn't a good idea for the professor to desert the rehab that was getting his limbs back in motion. What could be so urgent that he needed to go to Burundi in person?

As Lenny followed Roy out of the bedroom, his legs were stiff and his stomach released a hollow gurgle of protest, but he was suddenly anxious to find Professor Ramsey.

The plaza outside Government Center looked unusually full for a Monday afternoon, especially one that was still drizzling icy rain. Lenny pulled the string of his parka hood tight around his head as he and Roy walked from the subway station across the plaza. A few makeshift stands had been erected at intervals around the plaza, each surrounded by a huddle of people trying to stay dry under an assortment of umbrellas.

Lenny's stomach reminded him that he needed to eat, so he made his way toward one of the stands, hoping for a hotdog or a salted pretzel. Roy tried to pull him back, but the lure of a potential food source was too strong. He tried to identify the end of the line, but as he approached, a young man with spiked red hair edged back to let Lenny closer to the stand.

"Sign up over here," the man said. "We're heading over to the State House in about fifteen minutes."

Lenny started at the man's hair, gamely holding its Mohawk against the water that beaded up on the surface and ran in rivulets between the spikes. He turned his attention to the stand, inspecting it for anything edible, but it contained only sheets of paper covered in plastic and small baskets of stickers. A woman wrapped in a brown-and-white blanket handed him one of the sheets. The top part of the page contained a printed list of civil rights organizations, and the space underneath was half full with handwritten signatures.

"Come under here," she said, holding an umbrella over him and the sheet of paper. She eased the plastic back from the bottom half of the paper and offered him a pen.

"What's this?"

"It's the new POP bill they're trying to pass—you know, the Protection of Online Privacy. It pretends to be giving us privacy, but it's taking away our rights to free speech. It's a front for big business."

The POP bill? Lenny hadn't heard of it, but then he hadn't so much as looked at his computer in days. Could the POP bill be a result of his anti-Blahst viral campaign? Or the pro-Blahst one? *Or*, he thought with a sudden sense of foreboding, *were the two campaigns setting off conflicts between opposing camps, like Professor Ramsey had speculated?* Lenny closed his eyes against the maelstrom swirling in his mind.

"Lenny, let's go." Roy's voice rang out from behind. Lenny picked up one of the stickers. "POP Goes Your Freedom" was written across a background of stars and stripes.

"Thanks," Lenny mumbled to the woman. He headed back toward Roy, away from her protests that he'd forgotten to sign the petition.

The cavernous lobby of the Government Center offices was milling with visitors trying to find the right office and protestors sheltering from the weather. Lenny and Roy rode the elevator in silence, and Roy led the way along the third-floor corridor, peering at the names and numbers on each office door. Lenny followed numbly until Roy pounced on one of the door handles below a pane of frosted glass.

"This is it." The door swung open easily. "Professor Ramsey's got some buddy at the African Affairs Office who's pulling some strings to get his visa renewed quickly."

Inside was a room with a dozen metal chairs organized in rows down the middle, and a few more around the edge. A man's voice, speaking in a language Lenny couldn't understand, was coming from behind a half-open door at one end of the room. The professor was sitting next to the door, alone. He looked up when Roy and Lenny entered, and a smile spread across his face.

The professor stood to greet Roy with a hug. He shook Lenny's hand, and Lenny was relieved to feel that the professor's pumping grip had returned. Then he caught sight of the professor's left arm, which was hanging limply by his side, and a walking stick that was propped against the wall.

"Good to see you both. What are you doing here? Lenny, where have you been hiding?"

Lenny realized with a surge of guilt that he had visited the professor only once at the hospital. Roy had asked him to go plenty of times, but he'd been too preoccupied—first with Blahst, then with Snyder. The professor's broad shoulders looked a little more rounded than before the stroke, but the shine had returned to his skin and eyes. His beard was neatly clipped, a little shorter than usual.

"You can't go to Burundi, Professor Ramsey," Roy got straight to the point. "You're not ready."

"It's good of you to think about me." The professor turned and placed his hand on Roy's shoulder, wobbling slightly as he did so.

"Have a seat," he continued, and gestured to the first row of chairs. He sat down heavily, and Lenny and Roy perched on chairs opposite him.

"You're not ready to travel," said Roy. "What does your doctor say?"

"I do appreciate your concern, Roy, but I'll be okay, really. I didn't lose my faculties, you know, just a little bit of peripheral sensorimotor nerve function."

"What's so important that you have to go there, anyhow?" Roy pulled his chair closer to the professor. Lenny watched the right side of the professor's face fold into a frown, the left side trying to follow but not quite making it.

"Ah, bad news, I'm afraid. The Burundi government's revoked Healthway's non-government organization status. I'm sure it's a mistake—you know how bureaucratic some of these government departments can be. But without NGO status, we can't operate or bring in supplies. Even my old visa's no good now, so I've got to... Oh, Lenny, don't worry, we'll sort it out."

Lenny realized with embarrassment that he had just launched a noisy sigh that the professor had mistaken for concern about Healthway's plight. In fact, the news that it was some government screw-up that was taking the professor to Burundi was a major source of relief. He hadn't realized how tense he had been, like a clockwork toy wound so hard that one more twist of the key would break the delicate mechanism. He mumbled an acknowledgement to the professor.

"You don't look good," said Professor Ramsey, inspecting Lenny's face.

Lenny ran his hand over the stubble on his chin and up to his hair, which he could feel was greasy and lank. "I had a stomach bug," he said, avoiding Roy's eyes. "I haven't eaten for a while."

"There's coffee and donuts on the table over there," said Professor Ramsey, nodding to the back of the room. "Help yourself."

Lenny shuffled to the back of the room and poured black coffee from a carafe. He picked up a donut soaked in syrup and took a tentative bite. The dough was heavy, cold, and cloyingly sweet as he bit into it. He washed it down with a gulp of coffee that tasted like it had been made many hours earlier, then set about devouring the rest of the donut. As the professor recounted the details of the re-approval process he would need to go through, Lenny picked up a second donut and joined Roy opposite the professor.

"We'll go instead of you." Roy nodded vigorously as he spoke. "We can file all the papers, and if we need you, we can conference you in on the phone. We can do it, can't we, Lenny?"

Lenny paused mid-bite and looked at Roy to see if he was serious. Roy's face was earnest, almost desperate, as he leaned in toward the professor. Lenny followed his gaze and was caught off guard at the pride in Professor Ramsey's eyes as he looked back at Roy. Lenny realized that Roy was probably the closest thing that the professor had to a son.

"No." The professor shook his head slowly. Lenny sighed, quietly this time, and continued eating. The dull ache of hunger was gradually subsiding.

"It's too dangerous, especially if you don't know the language," continued Professor Ramsey. "The border violence is getting worse. That's why they're kicking out the NGOs—with all the recent incidents on the Congo side of the border, the Burundi government's trying to take control of all possible distribution channels."

"Did you say the Congo?" Roy glared suspiciously at Lenny as he asked the question that was on Lenny's own lips. "What incidents?"

"Yes, that's where it all seems to have started. Some kind of uprising. Just when we were making some headway with the family programs, too. Ah, Mr. Andwele, any progress?"

A tall and impossibly thin figure emerged from the back office. He wore a baggy grey suit that looked like it might slide off if he moved too quickly.

"Yes, we are progressing. I think we'll be able to clear up the visa by the end of today." The man turned and greeted Lenny and Roy with a broad smile. "Are these your colleagues I've heard so much about?"

Lenny was half aware that the professor was rising to his feet to make introductions, but his mind was racing down a different track. Incidents in the Congo? He'd stopped believing in coincidences. Snyder must have done something wrong—he'd messed up the Congo fundraising and this was a side effect. It had to be. He needed to figure out what was happening and warn Snyder, before it got any worse. But the thought of having anything more to do with Snyder set his stomach churning again.

"Lenny? Lenny, this is Mr. Andwele." The professor's voice broke through Lenny's thoughts, and he looked up at the smiling man, who was offering a long, slim hand toward him.

Lenny's gaze shifted quickly from the man's extended hand to his own, sticky with crumbs and syrup. Mr. Andwele chuckled and returned his attention to the professor, leaving Lenny staring at his own soiled hand and longing for the dark, safe covers of his bed.

Chapter 29

LENNY CLUTCHED HIS PHONE BETWEEN his hands and ignored the polystyrene coffee cup in front of him. He'd taken a seat at the narrow bench along the window of the Dunkin' Donuts to make sure he got the best phone reception, but nothing in the world outside kept his attention for more than a nanosecond. Snyder had given him a number to call "for emergencies only." It connected to a mailbox with a metallic female voice telling him to leave a message. Lenny had left three in the last hour.

On the first note of the ringtone, Lenny leapt out of his seat, casting a quick look over his shoulder to see if anybody was watching him. He waited until he was on the sidewalk before he glanced down at his phone. *Unknown Caller.* He hit the answer button.

"This had better be good." The connection was crystal clear, and there was no mistaking Snyder's voice.

Lenny opened his mouth but was suddenly unsure of how to tell Snyder what was happening. What if he blamed Lenny for not getting his programs right when he rewrote them? What if it was Lenny who had screwed up, not Snyder?

"Hello? Anybody home?"

"I think we've got a problem," Lenny managed to say.

"Go ahead."

"The things happening in the Congo, the fighting—I think it might have something to do with what we did."

There was silence at the other end of the phone.

"You know, the fundraising. It might be having repercussions. I swear, I didn't do anything different from before. But last time, when I put out the good press about Blahst's privacy policies, it didn't cancel out the bad stuff; it made everyone take sides. So maybe the Congo fundraising is interacting somehow with the Burundi fundraising and—"

"It's working perfectly."

"But..." Lenny's voice trailed off. He'd just checked out the news from his phone. One of the attacks had made the "World" section of CNN.com. Surely Snyder had seen the reports?

"Did you really believe it was about fundraising?" Snyder gave a short bark of a laugh. "For someone who's so smart, you can be pretty dense at times."

A bus screeched its brakes at the curb in front of Lenny, its engine pumping the smell of diesel across the sidewalk. Lenny's hand tightened on his phone, and he realized he never had believed Snyder. He wanted to believe, wanted it so hard that he'd deluded himself into thinking Snyder was doing something worthwhile. If he hadn't allowed himself this fantasy, either he'd have had to acknowledge he was part of a scheme he knew was deadly wrong, or he'd have needed to defy Snyder and face the consequences. Neither had been an alternative he was prepared to face.

"No, sure, I knew it wasn't..." Lenny tried to keep his voice steady. "I just wanted to check it's going the way you wanted."

Another mirthless laugh. "Of course, always good to check on progress. Everything's fine. How about you—any upgrades yet?"

Upgrades? *Think of a reason why I need to keep you around.* Lenny remembered Snyder's words from the hotel room, and his own defensive response.

"Yes, I'm working on something you'll like." He tried to think of a plausible improvement. "An acceleration pack. It's going to take a few days."

"Very good. I like the sound of that. Anything else?"

"No, that's it."

As he ended the call, Lenny knew there was only one course of action left to him. Roy had been right all along.

He tapped an address search for Cambridge police headquarters into his phone and headed down the damp steps into the mouth of the Government Center subway station.

"Can we run through those casualty scenarios one more time?" asked Snyder, perched on an old wooden chair in the cramped quarters of Angie's personal office. The conversation with Lenny had been an interesting diversion, but it had forced a round trip outside the all-hearing walls of Langley to find a private spot for the call. Now Snyder was anxious to finish up his analysis. He wanted to share good news with Senator Brennigan before the Intelligence Action Network appointments were finalized next week, but he needed to be very sure that Burundi had returned to its natural state of financial desperation.

"Certainly, Sir."

There it was again, thought Snyder. An edge to Angie's voice, a hint of sarcasm in the way she said *Sir*. He'd been spending a lot of time in Angie's office over the past week, drawn by the dual attractions of the incomparable wealth of data feeding OPRA's analytical systems and a chance for some intelligent conversation. At first Angie had seemed comfortable with the arrangement— grateful, even, for the attention from someone who appreciated her insights and research. Snyder could imagine the frustration she must feel at working for someone like Egham. But for the last couple of days she'd been cool, almost reticent. And she'd started calling him *Sir*.

"The current trajectory is nasty." A frown creased Angie's forehead, and her tone seemed to thaw as she concentrated on the graphs splashed across her screens. "Escalating Hutu-Tutsi violence leading to tens of thousands killed within two years, and hundreds of thousands displaced." She manipulated a slider control, and the density of the graphs faded slightly. "If the impact of the influence network could be scaled back by fifty percent, then the damage could be limited to thousands of casualties and tens of thousands displaced. Reduce it by seventy-five percent and it may never reach critical mass, just burn itself out in a couple of weeks with a few hundred casualties."

Snyder felt slightly disturbed to see the dark spiderweb fade away under Angie's expert manipulation. He'd been enthralled since the first moment he'd seen the results of his work—his first influence network—making its tracks across OPRA's screens. He reminded himself that the screen was just showing future projections, that the real influence network was alive and well and spreading *a toute vitesse* in the French-speaking regions of East Africa. His man on the inside in Burundi was reopening discussions about the coltan mining rights today, and depending on the outcome he might be able to scale back...

"Funny, isn't it?"

Snyder looked up from the screen to see Angie watching him intently. *Here we go*, he thought. Had he said something to hurt her feelings? This was why he never got involved with women, especially at work. He didn't have time for this.

"What's that?" He fixed her with his most disarming smile.

"Last week. We were just discussing that the only thing that could change Burundi's influence network was a war, and here we are. Another influence network and a potential war."

Snyder felt his face twitch. He looked back at the screen with feigned nonchalance and cursed himself. He hadn't expected this, but he should have. Angie was too smart for him to drop his guard as much as he had done. He'd been too reliant on her, too impatient to wait for the bureaucracy of getting his own private access to OPRA's systems.

"You're right. It's just what I was afraid of." He shook his head as his index finger traced the lines across the screen. "May I?" he asked, one hand hovering over the slide controller.

"Uh, sure."

Snyder sensed Angie's momentary hesitation behind his shoulder. The first rule of lying: don't talk too much. It had probably taken Angie a lot of courage to make that little speech, and he needed to deflect her suspicions before she repeated them to anyone else.

He zoomed in on the familiar pattern of lines converging in a dark mass on Burundi and stared at the small but growing web radiating around its larger neighbor. How to explain his seemingly impressive foresight about an unexpected war? As his brain tried to weave together a suitable explanation, he felt the tug of a promising strand of thought. What had Lenny said about the two Blahst influence networks he'd created?

"Let's compare it with the Blahst networks." He brought up Boston on another screen and felt his confidence return as he inspected the similarities between the two patterns. "See here. First the influence is in one direction—in this case, anti-Blahst. Then there's another influence network with good press about their new privacy policy. But the networks don't cancel each other out, they..." Snyder tried to remember what Lenny had told him. "They make everyone take sides." He took a risk and drilled through to some recent press coverage of Blahst. He was rewarded with scenes of clashing demonstrators outside the White House that nicely proved his point.

"It's the same thing here," he continued, pointing at Burundi. "First the flood of charitable donations, now this second influence network working against Burundi. Any updates on what triggered it?"

"No ground intelligence. Lots of rumors that Burundi rebels backed by the government have been stealing from the Congo mines. But it's the same as the other influence networks: the original sources are impossible to trace, and it's hitting from all over the place simultaneously. No connection between the different groups involved. I see what you mean about the similarities with Blahst. Let me just compare the root cause analyses..."

Snyder relaxed his shoulders and felt his body release its earlier tension. Angie seemed to have bought his explanation.

Now she was chatting excitedly about possible explanations for the emergence of the influence networks. Shame he could never tell her the truth. But the fewer who knew, the better. Right now, he counted three people besides himself who knew Lenny's secret—Lenny, Mari, and Roy—which at some point might be three too many.

"Five million."

"What's that?" Snyder looks up at Angie's third screen, which was scrolling a stream of old news reports.

"1998 to 2003. Over five million people dead in the Second Congo war, mostly civilians." She shook her head. "We can't afford to let that happen again."

"No, we certainly can't," agreed Snyder. Conflicts of that scale were rarely good for business. If there was an all-out civil war, they'd never be able to get the coltan out of the region safely. It looked like he'd need some more coding sessions with Lenny to calm things down once he had the mining contract signed. Lenny's phone call had worried him, but Snyder wasn't confident enough that he could adjust the algorithms on his own yet. He would have to keep Lenny around for now. As long as the boy didn't do anything stupid.

Chapter 30

"LENNY, THIS IS A VERY serious accusation." Detective Plummer leaned back and scratched his chin thoughtfully.

Relief washed through Lenny now that he had finally told his story. He slumped on the metal chair with his legs stretched loosely in front of him.

A policewoman had led him from the station's reception area to an interview room almost immediately. Detective Plummer and a younger officer had listened intently to his story, with the occasional question to prompt him forward. Once he'd started, he was amazed how easily the words flowed.

"There's one thing I still don't get," said Detective Plummer. "If you're the one with all these computer programs, why did the CIA kill Clayton?"

"I think that was a mistake," explained Lenny. "He stole some of my ideas, so they probably thought he was the one using the viral algorithm on Blahst."

"Makes sense." Detective Plummer nodded. "And now you're using this viral algorithm to start a war in East Africa, as well as to control the stock market here in the U.S."

"It's mostly just Blahst and some other high-tech companies. And these privacy demonstrations, the POP bill, that's me too."

"Just you, or is the CIA involved in that as well?"

Lenny shook his head. "They're only responsible for the Congo. And Clayton's murder, of course." He paused, wanting to make sure he was being completely clear with the facts. "I'm not sure if it's actually the CIA—it could be some other agency. Snyder didn't say."

Detective Plummer let out a long, slow whistle.

"This is some serious business. Do you think you might be in danger from this guy? Maybe we should get you some protection. What do you think, Jensen?"

The second officer pursed his lips. "We could take him to a safe house."

"I'm thinking witness protection."

"A new identity would be good," Jensen agreed. "He could go somewhere warm. I always fancied Texas, myself."

"We don't know how deeply this goes into the CIA," said Detective Plummer with a frown. "We might even have to stage his death. What do you think Lenny? Would anyone miss you?"

Lenny stared at the detectives in growing horror as the seriousness of his situation dawned on him. A new identity? He hadn't thought beyond this point, past the confession that would let someone else take on the burden that had been his own. Stage his death? What would that do to his parents? A million questions jumped into his head.

As he looked at Detective Plummer, trying to decide which question to ask first, a change came over the policeman's round face. The corners of his mouth pulled up little by little, until a snorting sound erupted from the back of his throat.

Lenny leaped to his feet, shooting his chair back so hard that it crashed against the wall behind him.

"You don't believe me."

Detective Plummer dissolved into loud, whooping laughter that shook his shoulders and chest. Jensen chuckled once and shook his head, keeping a wary eye on Lenny. Slowly, Detective's Plummer's laughter subsided, and he pulled out a handkerchief to dab at his eyes.

"Oh, my." Detective Plummer adjusted himself in his seat. "I'm sorry, Lenny. What do you want us to do with this?"

Lenny was speechless. After all he'd told them, how could they not take him seriously? They'd seen the Blahst stock crashing and recovering, and they could check out the trouble in the Congo. True, he couldn't prove it was him until he showed them how his programs worked, but why would they think he'd make this up?

Jensen leaned forward onto the table. "Thing is, Lenny, we know who killed Clayton."

Lenny stared back at the detective. With his dark blond hair and slim build, Jensen looked like he could have been one of Lenny's college buddies.

"You know about Snyder, then?" Lenny's words were slow with doubt. If they already knew that Snyder had killed Clayton, why were they giving him a hard time?

"Let's see." Jensen picked up the notes he had made while Lenny was telling his story. "Six two, thin face, long nose, expensive suit." He looked across at Detective Plummer, who shook his head.

"Our guy's five six, stocky, black hair. No match there."

"Are you sure? How do you know it's him?" Lenny set his chair back in place and sat down at the table again. "Did you find the weapon?" He felt a thread of hope. Maybe Snyder had been bluffing all along about planting the murder weapon on Lenny.

"We have the gun, and we have another... shall we say... forensic match with the murder scene." Jensen leaned back in his seat. "Seems that our guy was behind on his rent, so the landlord checked inside the apartment in case he'd skipped town. Came across a nice cache of guns and knives and called in his friendly neighborhood officers. One of them found some boots and clothes stashed in a plastic bag that hadn't been cleaned up since the murder. He made the connection. Sharp lad."

"Yeah, not a pretty sight." Detective Plummer grimaced with apparent disgust.

"You found blood?" Lenny tried to remember why he had been so sure that Snyder had murdered Clayton in the first place. It wasn't just the threat of planting the weapon, there was something else...

"Not exactly. We found vomit." Jensen shrugged. "Don't you read the papers? The press had a field day with that one when it leaked out. Anyway, plenty for a warrant. Wally Busby's his name. Except nobody's seen the guy since around the time of the murder. He's taken off somewhere, but we're looking for him."

"Which means your Snyder wasn't the one who murdered Clayton Malloy," added Detective Plummer. "Unless you have any other evidence for us?"

Snyder knew that Lenny had been outside Clayton's house the night of the murder. That was how Lenny knew Snyder was involved. Lenny looked first at Plummer and then at Jensen. Perhaps it wouldn't be wise to share this particular piece of information, even if the detectives said they had the crime wrapped up. Maybe he was still a suspect, and they had made up this whole story to catch Lenny off guard.

He had to make them take him seriously.

"What if that guy was working for Snyder? You know, like a hit man. Yeah, wait—there was a stocky guy with Snyder when he came to our office—"

"Lenny, enough." Detective Plummer sighed and glanced at his watch. "Look, anything's possible, but our guy's got a history of breaking and entering and petty theft since he was twelve years old. This was all in the papers—you can go home and read up on it if you're interested. We found some electronics gear stolen from Clayton in the guy's apartment. No reason to believe anyone else was involved."

"Was it his computer? Don't you see, they must have taken it when they thought—"

"Listen, Lenny." Jensen planted both hands firmly on the table. "Me and Detective Plummer here, we're the murder squad. And right now, Clayton's case is classified as solved, with an active warrant out for the killer. So unless you have anything for us other than this... speculation, we're not going to reopen the case."

Lenny turned to Detective Plummer, who was writing on the back of a business card. His face was serious as he clicked the pen closed and handed the card to Lenny.

"As for these viral computer networks you claim to be running—I don't know which of these numbers you need, but I suggest you give one of them a call and get yourself sorted out."

Lenny looked down at the card. Two phone numbers were printed neatly in blue ink. One was marked "FBI Computer Analysis and Response Team." The other was the Boston University mental health hotline.

Lenny's mind was a blur as he stormed out of the interview room. The hope he had felt with the news that they had found the murder weapon had swiftly unraveled. Snyder had no hold over him around Clayton's murder, but what did that matter if everyone laughed at his story? He stared down at the phone numbers on the back of the business card. Would the FBI treat him any differently?

He crumpled up the card and dropped it into the trash on his way out.

Snyder had selected a 2001 Screaming Eagle Cabernet for the occasion, accompanied by Bach's Chaconne, the most challenging of the master's violin pieces. He leaned back in his chair and slowly sipped the wine as the rich notes rang out from the speakers positioned around the walls of his home office. He waited until the mournful tones of the minor key mutated to the upbeat major key before dialing Brennigan.

His contacts in Bujumbura reported successful meetings with Burundi's politicians and business leaders, and the coltan contract was once again close to completion. Even though the signatures weren't yet inked, he knew Brennigan would want to resume using the coltan source as a way to finally squash the Chinese takeover bid for Capacitron. Brennigan would be the hero who saved thousands of jobs—and the votes that went along with them.

Snyder smiled as he thought of Brennigan's rant at their last meeting. Not that the senator would ever apologize, but he'd soon be kissing back up to Snyder in gratitude, setting things straight for the next time he needed some help. Sometimes a little hiccup along the way was a good thing—it reminded bystanders like Brennigan of the artistry inherent in Snyder's work. Artistry that would finally earn him his spot on the Intelligence Action Network.

Snyder wasn't surprised to reach an assistant the first time he dialed; that was usually the way with the senators. He gave her his cell phone number and waited for Brennigan to call him back.

By the time Snyder was on his second glass of wine and third call to Brennigan, he was losing patience with the wall of administrative flunkies who seemed determined to keep him from reaching the senator.

"Tell him it's concerning four thousand jobs for his constituents," Snyder spat into the phone.

After about a minute, Brennigan's voice finally came on the other end of the phone.

"Snyder! Always great to hear from you."

"You'd never guess it," mumbled Snyder.

"What's that?"

"We have some movement on the coltan deal, Senator. I thought you'd like to know."

"About time. We have Congo back on board?"

Snyder felt exasperation ripple through him. Was Brennigan getting senile? "The Congo's already in, and Tanzania. It's Burundi who backed out, if you remember."

He paused and tried to re-create the sense of well-being he'd felt when he'd seen the fruits of his labor, his very own influence network, carving its path across OPRA's screens and shaping the course of future history. "We've created some additional pressure on Burundi. We'll be able to get them back in the deal before Shenyang Electronics makes its takeover bid for Capacitron."

"Ah, that's right. Capacitron. Well, good. Let me know when it's done."

"Wait!" Snyder nearly shouted, anxious not to lose Brennigan off the phone and back into the fog of bureaucracy. He calmed his voice. "We're going to need your help."

"Whatever you require."

"The Burundi government needs money to build up its border defense—which is good because it means they need our coltan deal—but their price has gone up since our last negotiations. We have to get Capacitron to kick in some extra funds, and they need to guarantee minimum purchase levels for the first two years."

Snyder paused and thought he could hear background talk at the other end of the phone. "Senator?"

"Ah, yes, that shouldn't be a problem. I've got a dinner with their CEO in a couple of weeks."

"We can't wait that long. Shenyang Electronics wants to announce their takeover bid at the electronics show next week." Snyder shook his head. It wasn't like the senator to forget the details of something that was so critical to his political standing. "If you can pull in a favor from Capacitron, we can get the contract signed before the weekend and lock up the coltan supply for the U.S. We'll announce the deal before the show, boost Capacitron's stock, and price Shenyang out of the market."

Snyder heard muffled talking. Then Brennigan's voice came back on the phone.

"The thing is, I'm a bit busy this week. I was just seeing if I could rearrange some things, but it doesn't look good."

Snyder pulled the phone away from his ear and stared at it, dumbfounded. *A bit busy?* They were about to lose one of the most strategically significant deals of the decade, and Brennigan was *a bit busy?* He moved the phone slowly back to his ear and tried to keep his voice neutral.

"Might I ask what's keeping you so busy?"

"It's this privacy thing. There are all kinds of demonstrations around the country this weekend." Brennigan's earlier vagueness was replaced with growing enthusiasm as he spoke. "The judiciary's putting together a new senate committee. I'm doing some grassroots work with both sides. It's fascinating you know, the way these Internet companies keep track of everything..."

"Yes, Senator, very interesting. But we really need to focus on the coltan deal. If it goes to China, we'll lose control over the cost of just about every electronic device you can think of. It will be easy to price the U.S. out of the market."

"I'll see what I can do, but the privacy work's got to take priority. It goes to the heart of American freedoms. You might want to take a look yourself—there might be some repercussions for the intelligence community. Well, it looks like I have a call coming in from those Electronic Frontier people, so I have to go. See what you can do about the Congo."

"Senator, I think—"

The line was already dead.

Snyder glared down at the phone, not quite believing that Brennigan had hung up on him. Since when did Brennigan give a fuck about privacy?

He took a deep breath. In one respect, the senator was correct: once Snyder was through with the coltan deal, he might also be able to turn the privacy fallout from Lenny's Blasht networks to his advantage. With OPRA's ability to project the scenarios forward, he could target the influence networks far more precisely than Lenny had ever been able to do. There was no end to what else Snyder could control—as long as he could keep control of Lenny.

Perhaps it was time to discuss those upgrades, and the sooner the better.

Chapter 31

Lenny felt something cold skim down past his ear and glance off the shoulder of his coat as he rummaged through his pocket for his door keys. He looked up at a row of icicles framing the porch above his head, with small gaps where several had succumbed to the forces of gravity and plunged to the steps beneath.

"Shit." Lenny clenched his gloved hand and smashed it through the line of ice. A few of the tips tinkled onto the steps, while the fatter stumps clung stubbornly to the overhang.

As Lenny pulled off his glove to resume his search for the keys, a buzz sounded from the metal grill beside the door. He pushed the door open and pounded up the stairs to his apartment.

"I brought someone here to see you." Roy was standing at the open front door.

Lenny frowned. He wasn't in the mood for visitors, whoever it was.

"Why did you buzz me in?" he demanded. "I could have been anybody. You can't just—"

"I knew it was you. I saw it on the webcam."

"Since when do we have—" Pushing past Roy, Lenny stopped short as he saw Mari sitting on the sofa. He turned back to Roy with a what-the-fuck glare. Roy smiled back and gave an encouraging nod in Mari's direction.

"What are you doing here?" Lenny couldn't bring himself to meet Mari's eyes as he shook off his jacket.

"I thought you said he wanted to see me?" Mari directed her question at Roy.

"He does. He's just not good at showing it."

Roy slipped onto the armchair, leaving only the sofa free for Lenny to sit on. Lenny lowered himself onto the opposite end from Mari and turned to face her.

"So, uh, how've you been?"

Mari snorted a soft laugh out through her nose. "Very well, thanks. And you?"

"I, uh..." What was he supposed to say? He knew Roy was furious with him for ignoring Mari's texts and calls, but really, what could he tell her? *Since we slept together, I've rewritten the algorithms I promised you I'd never use again, started a war in Africa, and tried but failed to turn myself into the police.*

"Sorry I didn't call you after... after..."

Mari shrugged and turned her face away. She looked as though she'd rather be anywhere but sitting on Lenny's couch.

"Mari called me because there's so much about the POP bill on the news. The protests and the counter-protests. I told her you might have some ideas, but she said you never answer your texts." Roy stabbed an accusatory finger in Lenny's direction.

"Nothing I can do. Not without my algorithms. Which I deleted."

"That's not what I meant." Mari turned to face him, with her chin jutted forward. "I thought we might be able to use normal social media, you know, just regular Blahst postings, create a middle ground somehow."

"And I thought if you actually bothered to return Mari's calls, the two of you could figure something out." Roy folded his arms across his chest.

Lenny felt a wave of anger at Roy's interference. Lenny never got involved in Roy's relationships, so why did Roy think he had the right to lecture Lenny?

"Well, thank you, Mr. eHarmony, but the privacy bill is the least of our worries."

Roy and Mari stared at him.

"What do you mean?" Mari said quietly.

Lenny looked between the two of them. Why had he said that? He had no intention of telling them what he'd done, of letting them both dump on him even more than they were doing already.

"Nothing."

"What do you mean, *the least of our worries?*" Roy was on his feet. "What are you not telling us?"

"Nothing, forget it. It's got nothing to do with you."

"Lenny, everything you do affects us now." Mari rounded on him. "We're all in it together. Roy's photos, that Blahst stock I bought, the fact that we knew and didn't say anything. We're accomplices."

"I thought the tech stocks were falling again." Lenny picked at a row of frayed threads across the knee of his jeans.

"They are. Blahst has crashed again. All those protests."

"So go ahead and sell it. Then you won't profit from the deal."

"That's not the point."

The room lapsed into silence as Roy and Mari glared at Lenny.

Lenny felt suddenly very, very tired. He closed his eyes and felt the weight of his body pressing into the threadbare fabric of the sofa. It was as though an invisible force had enveloped him and pinned him down, so that just the thought of moving a finger or a foot felt like a supreme effort. He wanted the last two months to evaporate. He wanted to wake up and find it had all been a weird dream that he could laugh about with Roy.

He opened his eyes and looked at Mari and Roy.

"I think I really screwed up."

Mari didn't know whether to yell at Lenny or to hug him. She could sympathize with why he'd gone along with Snyder's plans, but she was furious at him for not telling her. She felt a wave of relief that the reason he was ignoring her had nothing to do with his feelings for her, but then she felt guilty at feeling relieved when the real reason was so much worse.

In the end she packed Lenny off to the shower: one side of his hair was plastered to his head; the other side was sticking out wildly. His chin showed the early sproutings of a goatee, and his slim features didn't suit the designer stubble look. No wonder the police hadn't taken him seriously.

She wanted time to think things through with Roy without Lenny getting defensive every time they made a suggestion. She and Roy went around in circles on whether or not the FBI would believe them any more than the police had believed Lenny. Roy had faith that the authorities could fix everything, while Mari wasn't so sure.

"They have whole departments that deal with that stuff," pressed Roy.

"Yeah, but Lenny knows exactly how he did it. Our best shot is to keep him out of jail and see if he can figure out some kind of campaign to counter what Snyder's done."

"Thanks for the vote of confidence, but there's nothing I can do." Lenny came back into the room wearing shorts and a sweatshirt. He rubbed at his head with a towel and his hair sprung back into loose curls. "Once the campaign goes viral, nobody can stop it."

"You haven't tried," said Mari.

"I did. I put out that counter-campaign about Blahst's privacy initiative. Now they're rioting in the streets." Lenny threw the damp towel onto the floor next to the sofa.

"It worked for a while, before the two sides became so polarized. And you haven't done anything about the Congo."

"I *am* trying." The defensiveness had returned to Lenny's voice. With his freshly shaven face, Mari thought he looked more like a sulky high school kid than a master of global manipulation.

"Roy says you stay in bed all day."

"I'm thinking."

Mari shook her head, and the three of them lapsed into their own private silences.

"Roy, how long have we had a webcam?" Lenny slowly ripped a broken fingernail free and flicked it on top of the towel.

"I put it up right after our stuff went missing. It was a Christmas present from my dad, but I never figured out what to use it for. Why?"

"Do you record the video stream?"

"Yeah. It's set to store a frame a second," answered Roy.

"How long do you keep the recordings for?"

"I haven't deleted anything yet. It's only been a few days."

Mari could almost see the gears of Lenny's brain start to engage as his eyes darted between her and Roy.

"I don't know how to undo what Snyder did, but maybe we can stop him from doing any more. Slow him down, at least, till we figure something out." Lenny uncrossed his legs and leaned forward on the sofa. "Roy, can you show me the recordings from Wednesday morning?"

Roy looked puzzled, but he jumped up to get his laptop from his backpack. After a couple of minutes, he started scrolling through a series of photos of the empty space outside the front entrance to their apartment building.

"About eleven o'clock, maybe earlier. He was here." Lenny leaned over Roy's shoulder. "That's when he let himself in and made me agree to work with him. Woke me up and everything."

Mari watched Roy's screen as figures entered and left the building, some pulling out keys and others facing the camera as they hunted for a name among the rows of door buzzers. None of them seemed aware they were being recorded.

"There!" Roy and Lenny spoke at the same time. The face was full on toward the camera, the forehead creased with a slight frown above deep eye sockets. Mari thought there was something familiar about the face.

"That's Snyder?"

"Don't know if that's his real name, but yes, that's him," said Lenny.

"He's an investor," said Mari with a flash of recognition. "He came to Blahst to investigate the stock crash. He talked to me."

Lenny looked up from Roy's laptop. "What did you tell him? Is that how he found me and Roy?"

"What? No, I didn't know it was you. All the rumors were saying it was Clayton. Our team knew it wasn't him, but we didn't have any other leads. That was right before—"

"Before Clayton was killed." Lenny spoke over Mari's hesitation. "And when he realized it wasn't Clayton, he tracked us down at Healthway. He's not an investor."

Mari watched as Roy slowly clicked through the next few images. Snyder pulled something the size of a credit card from his pocket and leaned into the door handle, obscuring it from the camera. In the next shot he was opening the door, and two seconds later he disappeared from sight.

"Back up to where he's facing the camera. Here, let me do it." Lenny grabbed the laptop from Roy.

"What are you going to do?" asked Mari. She was glad that Lenny was showing some enthusiasm again, but the reality of their situation had been brought home: the man she had seen at Blahst was the one who had killed Clayton. She had sat there in her cubicle, chatting to a murderer.

"Remember what we did with the photo of Andrei?" said Lenny. "I'm gonna take a copy of this and—"

Music sounded from Lenny's pocket, and he pulled out his phone.

"Hi, this is Lenny."

Lenny's expression froze. Mari could make out a man's voice at the other end of the phone.

"Um, I'm a bit busy this week, could we—"

Lenny's mouth stretched into a grimace as he listened to the voice at the other end. "Yeah, of course I have the upgrades... Uh, yeah, I'll be there at four o'clock, then."

Lenny's face was pale as he put the phone back in his pocket.

"Was that him?" whispered Roy. "What did he want?"

"He wants to see me tomorrow at the hotel. Do some more work together."

"Are you going?"

"After what I'm going to do to him tonight? No way."

Mari felt her mind cloud with doubt. Should she really be encouraging Lenny to solve things himself, or were they crazy to even try? But he had created something incredible, for all its problems. There was no reason to think he couldn't work out what to do next, given time.

"We shouldn't stay here after tonight, or go to the office. Not if you're going to screw him over." Roy's face looked drawn, and his hands were clenched in his lap. "He knows we live here. And he planted those bugs you found. Your little spy detector device isn't going to help us if he comes around here with guns or poison darts or whatever."

Mari waited for Lenny's smartass response, but it didn't come. He stared into the distance with a deep frown on his face. She reached out to touch his hand, which lay slackly across Roy's keyboard.

"I'm way overdue to visit my parents," he said, wrapping his fingers around to catch her hand inside his. "I could head over to Albany for the next couple of days and keep working while I'm there. Once I've got everything under control, we can figure out what to do about Snyder."

Mari looked at the image of Snyder's face, still frozen on Roy's screen, and remembered the sensation of being studied by those deep-set eyes. She shuddered again.

"And if you don't?" she said. "Get everything under control?"

"Give me two days. If I don't fix it by then, we can turn ourselves in. To the FBI." He waved his free hand at Roy. "Or whoever you want. I promise. If we all tell the same story, the police will have to believe me this time."

Mari looked at Roy to gauge his reaction. Roy lifted his shoulders in a world-weary shrug.

"I guess I can stay at Mandy's for a few days. But what about Snyder? Even if you fix everything, we're going to need help getting him off your back."

"Yeah, I know." Lenny's frown suddenly turned into a smile. "Or maybe the grannies will take care of that."

"What are you talking about?"

Lenny released Mari's hand and captured a screenshot of Snyder's image.

"You'll see."

Chapter 32

SNYDER COULDN'T PULL HIS EYES away from the four short sentences of the police report displayed on his phone. He read them over and over with growing incredulity.

He glanced around the Langley parking lot to make sure he didn't have any observers. A couple of figures were making their way toward the entrance, hunched against the wind that cut across this side of the building. The fine snow was whipping into small swirls that darted around their feet as they walked. Snyder cupped one hand over the top of his phone to screen it from the cameras that were no doubt monitoring every movement around the building.

As soon as the name *Lenny Driver* had come to his attention those few short weeks ago, Snyder had added it to the list of search terms he used for his daily intelligence scans. His resources weren't as vast as OPRA's, but they included most of the intelligence, military, police, and other emergency service reports that were posted to databases all over the nation. The rest of his daily alerts had been what he'd expected: more border skirmishes in Burundi and the Democratic Republic of the Congo, and an interesting scandal about the chief executive of Shenyang Electronics, the company threatening the takeover of Capacitron. That one had made him smile—payoff from a side project he'd been working on for a while. But he hadn't really expected to see Lenny's name show up. Had Lenny got himself into a fight? That shouldn't be such a surprise. He'd been using Lenny for his coding abilities, not his sunny disposition.

Once he read the brief summary of Lenny's visit to the Cambridge precinct, he knew he'd never be relying on those coding skills again. *Self-initiated interview between Lenny Driver of Allston, MA, and DIs Plummer and Jensen. Subject reported government conspiracy and claimed to be controlling international stock markets. Possible schizophrenic episode? Gave recommendation for counseling.*

Snyder felt suddenly hot despite the icy wind. He forced himself to close his eyes and take several slow breaths, focusing on the cold air moving in and out of his lungs. When he looked back at the screen, he was able to examine the words with the level of detachment he prided himself on, even in the most unfortunate of circumstances.

The summary was too brief to be sure how much Lenny had told the police. Had he mentioned Snyder's name? If so, the officers hadn't thought it worthy of including in the report. They clearly hadn't believed what Lenny was telling them, and they didn't seem to be following up in any way. That was the good news.

But why had Lenny gone to the police at all? He'd thought Lenny had more guts than that. He'd been sure Lenny was a fellow puppeteer, happy to pull the strings that kept the world on track. Snyder was usually a good judge of character, but it looked like he had seriously overestimated Lenny. Based on this report, he doubted Lenny would be keeping their appointment that afternoon in Boston, but if he did—well, that would be an interesting meeting.

He glanced at the time on his phone—about an hour before he had to leave for the airport. Plenty of time to check in with OPRA on the latest gossip.

Snyder strode along the corridor toward the Office of Predictive Analytics, keeping one eye on his coffee to make sure it didn't breach the top of the polystyrene cup. Despite the news about

Lenny, he was feeling good about the day ahead. He was looking forward to seeing the dark lines of the influence networks snaking their way across Angie's screen, deliciously alone in the knowledge that he was the one who had put them there. With or without Lenny, the events Snyder had set in motion were now inexorably unfolding. He even felt a slight lightness of step at the thought of spending an hour in Angie's company. Now that he had convinced her of the purity of his motives, she always seemed enthusiastic to see him.

Snyder rounded the corner and nearly bumped into a young man he vaguely recognized as a collection analyst from the South Asia team. He raised his coffee out of danger's way and swung his body sideways to let the man pass, nodding a greeting as he did so. The young man did a double take and paused to peer at Snyder through thick glasses before hurrying on his way.

Snyder shook his head and continued along the blue linoleum floor. He was long used to the peculiar social skills—or lack thereof—of intelligence analysts and computer buffs.

His thoughts returned to his plans for developing his work with Angie. With Burundi and the Congo going so well, he might look at whether any of his other projects could benefit from Lenny's influence networks. Truth was, he felt an excitement he hadn't experienced since his early days at the Defense Intelligence Agency. He remembered when he first realized the unlimited potential of his chosen career. It was as though a veil was pulled from his eyes as he saw firsthand how the real forces in the world were the silent movers behind the scenes. While the country listened to the staged and scripted posturing of the politicians, the real power brokers like Snyder provided those politicians, their allies, and even their enemies with the right messages, the right deals, the right motivation, and the right direction. And the best influencers, like Snyder, made them think that they had come up with the plan themselves and that he was just the vessel to carry it out.

Now Lenny Driver had managed singlehandedly to update that force for the new era, right down to the subtlety of having people think the idea was their own. The joint potential of Lenny's algorithms and OPRA's simulations was unbounded. Just look at the forces Lenny had unleashed with no real understanding of what he was doing or where it would lead. He was blundering around like a kid with a rocket launcher, but Snyder could focus that firepower where it really mattered. He thought wistfully of Lenny's skills. Would it have been different if Snyder had paid him more attention, kept him closer? But there was no going back.

Angie was in her office concentrating on her computer screen. Snyder watched her for a moment. Her smooth brown hair draped loosely down the back of her tweed jacket, and she jiggled her foot as she worked. As soon as she realized Snyder was there, she jumped to her feet.

"Good morning, Sir."

Snyder frowned. The *Sir* was back, and her face was solemn.

"Everything okay?"

When she didn't answer, he tipped his head quizzically. She remained standing, watching him, her shoulders tensed forward.

The thought of Lenny's police report lurched into his mind. Was there another version that had his name in it? Had OPRA's intelligence analysis uncovered something about him? But he didn't want to assume the worst and give Angie any unnecessary suspicions. This could be about something else entirely.

"Is there something I should know?" He took a step forward and caught a brief look of surprise on her face before she lowered her eyes.

"You mean you haven't... I would have thought security..."

Snyder felt his own eyes widen but quickly brought his panic under control. He needed information from her without giving anything away. Options flashed through his mind, and he settled on milking the connection that he and Angie seemed to have forged over the last couple of weeks. He softened his expression.

"Angie, help me here. What's going on?"

She glanced both ways along the corridor and closed the door.

"You haven't seen the photos? The postings?"

"Show me." He kept his voice even.

Angie sat hesitantly in front of her screen. "Joan over at the Asia desk was showing them to everyone. I mean, it's obviously some kind of joke. But who would want to... ?"

She trailed off as they inspected the first of the Blahst postings she pulled up. The photo was grainy but clearly recognizable. *This man strangled my puppy*, read the caption. As Angie scrolled through the postings, the stories were varied and highly creative, but the photo was always the same.

"I hope you don't mind, but I started an analysis of the connections between the postings. It's not just Blahst—it's most of the major social sites, and there's no clear source. I'm sure when you talk with security, they'll be able to tell you more, but, well..." She peered at him nervously. "I guess you've gone viral."

Snyder had felt his fists clenching tighter with each link that Angie clicked through, but all traces of anger suddenly evaporated from his body. Anger came from uncertainty, frustration, a lack of control. Right now there were no uncertainties left in Snyder's mind.

He spun away from the screen and swung open the office door. He walked along the corridor with his eyes focused on nothing but the linoleum floor until he reached the security desk. He retrieved his phone from the locker and exited the building with a nod to the guard and no hesitation in his step.

Chapter 33

LENNY WAS HOLED UP IN his old bedroom at his parents' house in Albany when he got the call from Mari. It was his first trip home in two years, and he'd been disturbed to find his Marvel posters and bedspread had been replaced with a generic spare-room leaf motif. He'd talked to his parents just long enough to keep them off his back, and then sunk back easily into his teenage habit of surfacing for food between marathon coding jags. He'd worked through the night but was no closer to reining in the power of his algorithm.

The sound of his phone was a welcome break from the cycle of well-worn but dead-end paths he kept turning over. He could tell it was Mari's voice—they'd agreed to check in twice a day to see how Lenny was progressing—but the reception was poor and he couldn't make out what she was saying. He centered the phone's speaker tightly against his ear.

"Mari, what's up?"

The signal locked briefly into place and Lenny heard her next words all too clearly.

"Lenny, you've got to get back here. Roy's been in a car crash."

"What?" Cold dread played across Lenny's scalp. "Is he okay?"

He strained to hear Mari's response. He could decipher the words *intensive care* and *Mass General Hospital* but not much else. At least that meant Roy was alive.

"I'm on my way. Be there about noon," he yelled into the phone, but he heard only the faint beeps of a disconnected call.

He said a quick goodbye to his surprised parents, and eased his old Explorer as fast as it would go before the juddering grew too disconcerting. He'd checked the route and the traffic was light, but the forecast said Boston was about to be hit with six to eight inches of snow. He was anxious to be off the exposed highway when it arrived.

By the time he hit the outskirts of Boston, fat snowflakes were patting onto the windshield. The cars around him had slowed to a crawl with the reduced visibility, and Lenny ground to a halt behind a sedan fishtailing up the incline of the Mass Pike exit ramp as its tires failed to find traction against the thickening carpet of white. It was after one o'clock when he finally found himself confronting the receptionist outside the intensive care unit of Mass General Hospital.

"I'm sorry, but we can't discuss patients with anyone outside the immediate family." The receptionist smiled brightly from her seat behind the counter and hooked her chin-length brown hair behind one ear with her middle finger.

"I'm his brother."

The receptionist raised her eyes away from Lenny for a second before looking back at him. "You just said you were his friend." Her smile didn't waver.

"Yes. Both. We're a very close family."

"Do you have some I.D. that shows the same last name?"

Lenny looked across at the thick, frosted-glass doors that were separating him from Roy. He could tell this conversation was going nowhere. They wouldn't even tell Lenny what condition Roy was in, let alone allow him to visit. Perhaps he could lock a janitor in a supply cupboard and steal his clothes, like in the movies...

"His parents are flying in from Seattle." The receptionist's smile was gone, and she was watching Lenny with what might have been a hint of sympathy. "Once they arrive, they can give permission for you to see him. It's going to be at least two or three hours, but you're welcome to wait in the public reception area."

Lenny found a seating area out of sight of the receptionist. He hunkered onto a square black armchair and tried calling Mari. They'd spoken again on his drive down, but he couldn't remember if he'd said he would go to her apartment or meet her here at the hospital. He got no response to his call, so he left her a text.

He stared at the blank screen of a TV on the opposite wall, thankful that it was off so that he didn't have to watch some soap opera or, even worse, the news. He'd been trying to avoid all media input for days, but he had caught glimpses of headlines and photos of the privacy protests and debates that were now consuming Washington. Wars in Africa didn't seem to warrant the same attention, but he didn't need reporters to tell him that the fallout from his algorithms was still raining its poison into the Congo and Burundi. He pulled up the listings of his programs on his phone, trying once again to jolt his brain into that elusive flash of insight that would allow him to end, or at least control, the chaos he had set in motion.

The sound of voices made Lenny jerk upright in his seat. His neck felt stiff and he realized he'd been dozing. He peered groggily around the corner of the waiting room and saw two men standing at the reception desk. One wore a doctor's white coat, the other a casual light-grey suit. They shook hands, and the doctor disappeared into the ICU.

Lenny hovered at the corner of the waiting area. He was sure he'd heard Roy's name in the exchange between the men, but he didn't want to strike up a conversation in front of the receptionist. He waited until the man in the grey suit headed toward the elevators before confronting him.

"Excuse me. Are you Roy's father?"

The man looked Lenny up and down. Now that Lenny saw him close up, he could see he was too young to be Roy's father—in his mid-thirties at most.

"I'm a friend," Lenny added.

The man shook his head. "No, his family hasn't arrived yet. I work with him."

"No, you don't." Lenny hadn't meant it to sound like an accusation, just a fact, but the man pulled his head back with a frown. "I mean, *I* work with him, at the office, and I've never seen you," he added.

"Sorry, I should have introduced myself. Doctor Sprague, pleased to meet you." The man nodded at Lenny. "I was on a tour of Burundi with Roy a year or so back. He was doing a photo shoot. Very talented. I follow his photos on Blahst, and his brother posted the news of his accident there. I came straight over."

"Did they tell you anything about how he's doing?"

"Yes, I saw him. He hasn't regained consciousness yet, but the bleeding's been stabilized."

"You saw him? How come they let you in?"

Sprague's eyebrows twitched. "Being a doctor has its privileges, I suppose." He glanced at his watch and hit the elevator call button.

"No, wait." Lenny swore silently at himself for wasting time interrogating the man's credentials when he still didn't know what had happened to Roy. "I didn't see the Blahst post, and they won't tell me anything. How did Roy crash? How badly is he hurt? Is he going to be okay?"

Sprague looked at his watch again. "I have to get going, but I'm heading to the cafeteria downstairs before I leave. You can join me if you like, and I'll bring you up to speed."

The two of them travelled silently down in the elevator as Sprague responded to text messages on his phone. Lenny was itching for news but didn't want to interrupt after his less-than-impressive introduction. At the cafeteria, Sprague bought a chicken Caesar salad, and Lenny selected a cardboard sleeve of French fries. They easily found a table among the scattered families and health workers in green scrubs or patterned coveralls.

"His left side is worst." Sprague gestured to his own body as he enumerated the injuries. "The arm's crushed and his left leg's broken in multiple places. Fractured ribs and internal bleeding. The other car broadsided him."

Lenny let the words sink in as he tried to imagine Roy's messed-up body. "Is he going to be okay?"

"Yeah." Sprague paused with a fork of grilled chicken halfway to his mouth. "Yeah, he'll be okay."

Lenny plucked a fry from the packet and nibbled one end before returning it to the packet. He watched Sprague eat with hearty mouthfuls.

"What kind of a doctor are you?"

"I'm a virologist. I was working on Healthway's HIV program for a while."

"Virologist?"

"Yes." Sprague finished crunching his mouthful. "We were looking at how we could increase patient compliance with taking their antiviral drugs."

"Huh." Lenny slowly snapped fries in half and lined up the pieces side by side. "How does that work? If I needed to kill a virus that's spreading?"

"Not an easy problem, I'm afraid." Sprague paused as he speared the last few pieces of lettuce. "Right now we don't know how to kill a virus without destroying the cells that the virus lives in. So, instead, the antivirals have to target the whole system and remove what the virus needs to replicate." He snapped the empty plastic salad container shut and stood up. "Now if you'll excuse me, I have to get back over to Beth Israel Hospital."

Lenny swept his fries back into the packet and followed Sprague toward the exit, mulling over the obvious parallels of the human virus and his algorithm. The people who forwarded the planted ideas were the infected cells, and even if he could track them all down—which he couldn't—killing them was hardly an option for him either.

"You know what really sucks?" He tossed the fries into a trash can. "It shouldn't have been Roy. He's such a careful driver."

"Not this time. He ran a red light. And they found a massive amount of OxyContin in his blood. But no prescription." Sprague shook his head. "Such a waste. You said you worked with him? How long had he been... was he going through a rough patch or something?"

Lenny froze, his arm still stretched over the trash can. "No. I mean yes, but not..."

OxyContin? From a guy who refused to drink so much as a Bud Light if he was going to drive? It made no sense. Maybe someone had slipped it to him by mistake at a party.

Unless it wasn't a mistake.

Lenny pulled out his phone, barely noticing Sprague take his leave and head out through the revolving doors.

He hit the *Redial* button and listened with creeping panic to the slow rings of Mari not answering her phone.

Chapter 34

MARI THREW HER SPORTS BAG and softball bat on the bed and flopped face down next to it, rubbing her check against the soft caress of the comforter. She'd hoped that some lunchtime indoor softball practice with the guys from work would take her mind off things, but she'd been so distracted that she struck out half the time. None of her colleagues knew Roy, so they were sympathetic at the news of his crash, but then they quickly became caught up in the energy of the competition. And of course she hadn't been able to mention Lenny at all. She'd decided to leave early, and nobody had blinked an eyelid when she'd said she was taking the afternoon off.

A car horn sounded in the street outside. She sat up on the bed—was Lenny here already? She sprang into the living room and pressed her nose against the window that faced over the front courtyard and the street below. The snow was starting to fall heavily and settle on the ice-covered sidewalk. In the center of the road a taxi was discharging a passenger and blocking the car behind it. The horn sounded again before both cars drove off along the street. Mari strained to see if Lenny's car was among the parked vehicles, but she saw no sign of it. She hoped he'd arrive before the snow made the roads too treacherous.

She watched the passenger from the taxi pick his way across the sidewalk toward her building. The snow was flecking his fur-lined deerstalker hat and forming white epaulets on his heavy grey overcoat. As he passed the stone lion pillars, he paused and looked up at her building. Most of his features were obscured by the peak of his hat, but an odd familiarity tugged at her subconscious. One of her neighbors, no doubt, but she couldn't place him.

She rolled away from the window and leaned against the cotton drapes. Her anticipation at seeing Lenny was dulled by the knowledge that she would have to tell him the decision she'd made. While she'd been sitting next to him in his apartment, smelling the fresh aroma of his shower-damp hair and feeling the warm touch of his long fingers, it had seemed natural that she and Roy would trust him to find a way to fix the trouble he had caused. But the more she read the incessant news reports about how the POP privacy bill was torturing the U.S. economy, not to mention the coverage of the escalating violence in Africa, the more she was regretting her decision to play along. Even if Lenny's two days weren't up, they needed to go to the police as soon as possible, especially now they had Roy to worry about. She didn't know how it would play out, but she knew it was the right thing to do.

In the hallway outside, Mari could hear the faint sound of footsteps on the marble floor. They came to a stop outside her door.

Finally, Lenny. But how had he got up here without her buzzing him in? One of the other residents must have let him in, even though the management kept sending out security reminders. She reached for the door handle, but a sudden feeling of disquiet froze her hand halfway. She peered through the peephole in the door and saw the man in the deerstalker. This time she could see his face—the same features she'd seen hovering over her cubicle at Blahst and staring from the security footage on Roy's laptop.

Snyder.

She started to tiptoe toward the coffee table, where her purse was sitting with her phone inside. But before she reached her purse, she froze again.

The latch of the deadbolt was turning slowly toward the open position.

Snyder inspected the neat, Ikea-grade living room. Her boots sat in a damp puddle next to the door, and a small leather purse lay on the coffee table. He'd expected her to be at work, but the evidence said otherwise. He'd have to proceed more carefully. If he was lucky she'd be sleeping, or maybe showering. That would be a double treat. He imagined her turning toward him in the steamy confines of the bathroom, the water beading over her naked body, her face registering first surprise then terror as he moved in.

He tried to focus his thoughts back on the task he needed to accomplish. He knew the importance of maintaining professional distance, no matter how much the circumstances threatened to cloud his emotions. The ridiculous rumors captioning his photograph flashed through his mind, the rumors still spreading all over the Internet. *Do you know this guy? He raped my girlfriend.* Some of them were downright ludicrous: *The man who swindles grandmothers out of their life's savings.* And the one that irked him the most: *The face of a Chinese superspy.* Angie had said she hadn't tracked down the source, but Snyder didn't need to look at analytical models to figure this one out. Lenny Driver and his friends had far outlived their usefulness.

He stopped next to the sofa and listened for a minute, trying to hear the little sounds of movement that would guide him to her. Nothing. No water running, no television mumbling its inanities, not even the rustle of a page turning. Perhaps she really was sleeping.

A blare of music cut through the silence, startling him momentarily. It was coming from the bag on the coffee table. Her phone, he realized, and she'd be in to answer it any second.

He slid behind the sofa and crouched down. From here, he couldn't be seen from either the hallway or the kitchen door. He slipped a hand into the pocket of his overcoat and felt the reassuring outline of his Glock. He had other ways that he would prefer to use, quieter ways, but it was good to know it was there if he needed to hurry.

The music continued to play, and Snyder widened his crouch, ready to move when the time was right. Then the music stopped, and the room was as silent as before. Snyder waited a moment longer before raising his head above the back of the sofa. The room was still empty.

He rummaged around inside her purse, his thin latex gloves helping to maintain a mindset of clinical, impersonal efficiency. He found her phone and saw a missed call from Lenny through its cracked screen. He felt anger swirl through him as he read the name. He took a slow breath and reminded himself it wouldn't matter after tonight—when he was done here, he'd be paying a visit to Albany to finish things off.

Of course, he'd have to keep an eye on Roy, just in case he pulled through and needed further attention. Crashes were unreliable, but they were easy to pull off without raising any suspicion. He'd seen the flood of comments from well-wishers on Roy's Blahst page that morning. Very touching. Snyder would just need to nip any potential medical miracles in the bud.

Snyder inspected the list of Mari's incoming texts and read the most recent message from Lenny: "leaving hospital see u at ur place 30 mins." The corners of his mouth twitched upward. This was turning into a good day, a very good day indeed. No need to chase Lenny all around the country—he could take care of everything right here. He might even be a little creative. Two victims were almost easier to deal with than one, especially a man and a woman. Would a murder-suicide be too Hollywood? There were so many motives for that one. And it was all about the motive. If the investigators thought they understood why it happened, they'd wrap the case up quickly and move on, no lingering doubts or questions.

He glanced at the time on Mari's phone. Better get things started before Lenny arrived. He slid the phone into his overcoat pocket, curled his hand around the grip of the Glock, and moved slowly toward the hallway.

Through the open door on the right, he could see a mirror over a sink, reflecting pictures of cartoon ducks on the opposite wall. He stepped into the opening and confirmed that the bathroom was empty. The only other door was opposite, slightly ajar but not enough to give him a view of the room. It had to be the bedroom, with the girl inside.

He pushed the door open just enough to give himself space to slide through sideways. The drapes were pulled shut, and as he moved into the room, he paused for a split second to let his eyes adjust to the lack of light. His guess about the nap must have been right.

As he turned to find the bed, a solid object crunched into his stomach and slammed him against the wall. He doubled over with the pain. He saw a flash of movement and instinctively reached out toward it. His fingers started to wrap around a tube of smooth metal before it was wrenched from his grip. A second later he felt more pain sear across his jaw, and the world went black.

Chapter 35

LENNY FELT HIS REAR WHEELS slide across the soft snow as he rounded the corner into Mari's street. The last part of the drive had been slow going as the flakes spattered silently across his windshield at a rate that defied even the fastest wiper speed.

Following some distantly remembered rule from driver's ed class, Lenny cranked his steering wheel in the direction of the skid, and the car found its traction once again. Mari's street was strangely deserted. He hadn't seen many cars on the ride over from the hospital, just a few SUVs mashing through the thickening white blanket.

He pulled up next to the sidewalk in front of Mari's apartment, relieved not to have to hunt around for a parking spot for a change. He tried calling her again, but still no answer. His panic at the hospital had subsided when she'd responded to his earlier text, telling him she was on her way back from batting practice. He looked out the side window at the snow gusting around the open courtyard and decided he might as well wait in the warm car until she returned.

He wondered if he'd been overreacting about Roy's crash, too. His first reaction had been to blame Snyder—Lenny was sure the guy could do something like that and make it look like an accident. But Roy had certainly been stressed out, so maybe he really had taken something at a party and unwisely decided to drive home. But whichever way you looked at it, he—Lenny—was the cause of whatever had happened to Roy. His heart accelerated and a wave of nausea started to rise slowly from his stomach. He closed his eyes and willed it back down. This was no time to wallow in self-recrimination. He still needed to stop his algorithms and maybe, just maybe, he could see a way forward.

An idea had been buzzing around in his head since the conversation with the virologist, something Sprague had said about treating the whole system. What if Lenny *could* remove what the virus needed to replicate? Might that make the whole thing fade away?

He tapped an icon on his phone and dived into his development tools. His fingers flitted over the tiny onscreen keyboard as he jotted down some ideas and started to outline a code fragment. His excitement grew—the approach might actually work. Thick white flakes began to obscure the windows until the only light inside the car came from the glow of Lenny's screen.

The sound of a door slamming close by broke his attention. Was that Mari arriving home? He had to tell her about the OxyContin in Roy's blood and his suspicion that Snyder might be behind the accident. If he was right, they might not want to hang around too long at her apartment. They could head back to the hospital—they'd be safe there—and wait for Roy's family while he worked some more on his antiviral idea.

He pushed open the car door. A shock of wet snow dislodged itself from the roof of the Explorer and hit the back of his neck. He shook himself off and started toward Mari's building. He stopped as a figure hurtled out between the courtyard's stone lions.

"Mari? That you?" he called.

She appeared not to hear him, so he called again, louder. This time her head turned toward him. It was Mari, eyes wide and wild. She was dressed in yoga pants and a sweatshirt, with fur-lined Ugg slippers on her feet. A softball bat was clutched in one hand and a purse in the other. She ran toward him and wrapped both arms around him. The bat dropped with a soft thud onto the snow-covered sidewalk.

"He's up there, in my apartment. We've got to call the police." She released Lenny and started rummaging through her bag.

"Whoa, Mari, who's up there?" Lenny gripped her shoulders. His earlier panic resurged in full force. "Is it Snyder? What happened?"

"I might have killed him." She shook her bag and thrust her hand in again. "Shit, where's my phone?"

Lenny stared at her for a second. His eyes dropped to the softball bat.

"You killed Snyder?"

"I don't know. I hit him."

A tumult of emotions flashed through Lenny's head. Confusion about how Snyder had found Mari faded rapidly—Snyder could find anyone he wanted. It was replaced by anger that Snyder would involve Mari at all, followed by a glimmer of hope that Mari really had got Snyder out of the way.

"What did he want? Did he hurt you?"

"No, I hid. He didn't see me." Mari quickly recounted the story of how Snyder had broken into her apartment. Tears hovered in her eyes but her voice was steady. Lenny listened with admiration. If Snyder was dead, that changed everything.

"Did you check for a pulse?"

"Are you crazy? I ran." Mari turned her attention back to her purse. "Do you have your phone? We have to call the police."

As Lenny pulled out his phone, he heard the sound of a door slamming, the same sound he'd heard a few minutes earlier. One of the stone lions obscured his view of the building's entrance, so he took a step closer to the opening into the courtyard. Before he could take another step, he felt a hard tug on his arm. He staggered as Mari pulled him backward and yanked him down behind the rear of his car. They crouched together,

Mari still grasping his arm, as a muffled curse drifted over from the building's entrance.

Lenny shifted his weight slightly so he could peer around the corner of the car. Through the curtain of snow, Lenny could see a man leaning with his back against the pillar. One arm was held across his stomach; the other hand was spread over his face. A deerstalker hat was lodged crookedly on the back of his head. Even with half of his features hidden, Lenny recognized him immediately: it was Snyder. And he definitely wasn't dead.

As Lenny continued to watch, Snyder pushed away from the pillar with a grunt. He looked away down the street and then turned his head toward them. Lenny pulled back sharply and bumped Mari, sending her sprawling into the snow. She righted herself quickly and the two of them listened for Snyder's next move. Lenny tensed as he heard the whisper of footsteps in the soft snow. They edged into the center of the road, putting Lenny's car between them and the sidewalk.

Lenny held his breath until an engine revved loudly a short distance away. He and Mari crept back behind the rear of the SUV and listened to the sound of tires spinning against the ice as Snyder's car skidded off down the street. He waited until the sound of the engine faded and he could hear nothing but the pounding of blood in his ears. By the time he looked out from behind his car, the street was deserted again.

He helped Mari to her feet and brushed at the wet clumps of snow that were plastered to her back and caught inside the hood of her sweatshirt. Her pants and slippers were soaked.

"You want to go inside and change?" he asked.

Mari looked at him as though he'd asked her to tango through the snow.

"What?" Lenny asked, even as he realized it hadn't been the brightest of suggestions.

"I want you to call the police, and then I want us to get the hell out of here," she replied. "I'm not going back up there—what if he decides to pay another visit?"

Lenny looked down at his phone and thought about the implications of his next move. If they called the police, it would all finally be out of his hands. He had another witness who could confirm his story, so they'd know he was telling the truth. They'd find Snyder and arrest him. They'd probably arrest Lenny too, but at least it would all be over. Lenny would tell the computer experts at the FBI everything he'd done, and they'd figure out a way to fix it, eventually.

Eventually. But in the meantime, what about the people in Burundi and the Congo? What about the kids getting caught in the crossfire as the rebels fought over Snyder's vicious lies, lies that Lenny had helped him to spread? Lenny knew how to stop it all in its tracks. If he called the police, he had no idea when he'd be able to finish off his program. It could be days. Weeks. They would never let him keep his phone in a prison cell.

"Lenny?"

Lenny shook his head slowly as he continued to stare at the black screen of his phone.

"I know how to finish it, Mari. I just need some time."

Mari raised her eyebrows in disbelief. "Well, you can tell the police how to do it, and I'm sure they'll take care of it."

She reached toward his phone. Lenny clamped his hand tighter around the smooth casing and twisted it out of her reach.

"No. Why would they trust me? They'd have no reason to think I could fix anything. Last time I tried to talk to them, they thought I was insane."

"Maybe they have a point." Mari's glare was tinged with fear, anger, and impatience. Lenny tried to think of a way to make her understand that he had to finish this off once and for all, and that this time he really knew what he was doing.

He dropped his head as he realized there was no reason on earth why she should believe that this time would be any different from all the other screwups.

"How long do you need?" Mari's tone was grudging, but the words were a jolt of energy to Lenny.

"I don't know. Probably just a few hours."

Mari crossed to the passenger side of Lenny's car. "Let's go. Somewhere Snyder can't find us."

Lenny climbed into the car and started up the engine. The wipers struggled against the thick white layer on the windshield. Mari tugged her sweatshirt sleeve down over her hand and cleared clumps of snow off the windows before sliding into the car next to Lenny. White flakes glistened in her hair like confetti. Her eyes mirrored his own feelings of alternating fear and hope. He reached out and wrapped his hands around her ice-cold fingers.

"It's going to work this time," he said. "I know it will."

Chapter 36

THE DESIGN WAS SCRAWLED ON napkins spread across the round table. The short, curly haired barista, whose nametag said *Owen*, had seemed mildly put out when Lenny and Mari ordered a single bottle of water between them, and even less impressed when Lenny paid for it in small change and fluff from his jeans pocket. But he had lent them a pen with good grace, warned them that they'd be closing early because of the snow emergency, and proceeded to sneak glances in their direction as they worked.

There wasn't much clientele for a late afternoon at Starbucks. The only other people in the place were a couple in matching MIT sweatshirts. They were draped across an outsized armchair, holding hands and gazing alternately at each other and at the swirling flakes on the other side of the window.

"I can work on this section." Mari pulled together three of the napkins. "I think I get what you're doing, I'm just not sure what this part here—"

"I don't know, Mari. It'll take just as long for me to explain it as it would for me to do it." Lenny eyed the dark patches covering her yoga pants and sweatshirt. "Why don't you see if they've got any hand dryers in the bathroom to dry out your clothes."

"That can wait." Mari's voice was insistent. "We've got to get this done before he finds us. I can help."

Lenny watched the impatience flash in her brown eyes, and he knew she was right. Mari was as good a coder as he was—well, almost. In any case, he owed her this much after all the trust she'd placed in him.

"I guess I can find some easy parts for you to help with," he conceded.

He recapped the design that had been inspired by his encounter with the virologist. Mari nodded as she listened.

"So we've got to eliminate the conditions that let the virus replicate," she said.

"Exactly. There are three elements: finding the right hub, personalizing it, and making people think it was their own idea. It's the third part I'm going after. I'm going to notify everyone who's ever been targeted through my algorithm. Once they know they've been influenced, it won't work anymore—I hope."

Behind the counter, the barista had given up all pretense of cleaning the espresso machine and was watching them with unabashed interest.

"But how are you going to find the people you targeted? You've deleted all the links." Mari pulled her purse onto the table and sorted through it methodically while she spoke. "I thought you said it's impossible to trace the message flows, in either direction."

"That's true. It's like you've cut a string, and if you're at one side of the cut, you can't find the other side anymore. But if you can rise up and look at the big picture from above, you can still see the patterns of all the disconnected strings, of the..." Lenny tried to remember what Snyder had called them, back when he'd first visited Lenny and Roy at Healthway. "The influence networks. This antivirus code, it's going to find anyone who's part of an influence network and alert them. Any influence network— mine, Snyder's, anyone's—I'll be able to—"

"Are you launching a startup?"

Lenny turned to see Owen hovering next to the table with a damp cloth in one hand. He glanced around the empty seats. The other couple had left while he'd been talking.

"I'm a website designer, but my last company went belly up." The barista twisted one end of the cloth between his fingers. "You hiring?"

Lenny tried to think of a way to tell the barista to mind his own business that wouldn't get them thrown out of the café, but before he could speak, Mari spun to face Owen.

"Maybe," said Mari. "Let's see what you can do. Do you have a browser on your phone?"

"Sure." Owen disappeared behind the counter and came back with his phone. "What do you want me to do?"

Lenny shot a frown at Mari. Having Mari help was one thing, but this guy was a total stranger. What was she thinking?

"It'll take a while to set up. Give me half an hour or so."

Owen glanced at his watch. "I'm supposed to be closing up soon. The storm." He nodded toward the window. "But I guess it doesn't matter. I don't live far away."

He handed Mari the phone and watched over her shoulder while she brought up a web browser on the screen.

"Why don't you finish clearing up. Then we can tell you all about the startup." Mari flashed a smile at Owen.

As Mari started typing in the logic flow for one of the functions outlined on the napkin, Lenny understood. She didn't have her phone, but she'd procured another one so that she could help him out. Plus she'd bought them some time in the relative safety of the Starbucks. Against a background hiss of compressed air from the coffee machinery, Lenny showed her how to save her work into one of his online accounts. Between them, they worked through the designs on the other napkins. He was surprised at how quickly she understood what he was trying to do, and how few questions she asked.

Owen emerged from the counter with a mop and cleaned around them, lapsing into companionable silence when his attempts at small talk were met with monosyllabic responses.

As they both typed into their phones, Lenny felt the soft pressure of Mari's shoulder leaning against his upper arm. He shifted in his seat so that his head rested gently on hers. The deaths in the Congo, Snyder's threats, the trouble at Blahst, and even the snow whirling outside suddenly seemed very remote compared to the softness of her hair against his cheek and the sense of achievement as the lines of code formed beneath his fingertips.

As he linked one of Mari's functions to his own, he became aware of a soft orange light pulsing at the edge of the window. It had grown dark while they worked, and the light caught the snow in a strobe effect of freeze-framed flakes suspended above the sidewalk.

Lenny craned forward, but the source of the light was out of sight along the street. Some kind of emergency vehicle, no doubt. Would the police be there, too? His heart cranked up a notch. If Mari knew the police were outside, might she be tempted to tell them about Snyder's attack after all? They were so close to the finish line, he didn't want to risk it.

He glanced at Mari, but she didn't seem to have noticed anything. She was wrinkling her nose in thought as she tapped at Owen's phone.

Lenny slid out of his chair and crossed to the door, but he still couldn't see past the corner of the steamed-up window. He pushed the door open a couple of inches and a blast of cold air swept in. Mari looked up distractedly. Lenny mumbled something about clearing his head and stepped out into the snow.

The wind whipped snow into his eyes as he peered toward the source of the light. Halfway down the otherwise deserted block, a truck was parked in front of Lenny's car. He could just make out the shape of the driver climbing into the truck's cab. The door slammed and the truck eased away, its orange light pulsating across the settling snow like a spaceship illuminating an alien landscape.

From this angle, some illusion of the light made it look to Lenny as though his car was following the truck. He watched for a moment before he realized that his car really was moving forward, following the truck's every move as though locked in a tractor beam. His frown of puzzlement turned quickly to a curse of frustration as he lurched after the tow truck.

His shouts were lost in the gusting air. The snow was past his ankles, and he had to lift his feet as he ran. He gained some ground as the truck slowed down for the corner and made a right turn. But by the time Lenny rounded the corner, the truck and his car were fading into a dense veil of snow.

Just as his car disappeared from sight, Lenny noticed a figure moving on the sidewalk, hazy at first and then resolving into solidity with each slow step forward. The figure turned to face the wall of the building next to him. As Lenny peered through the driving snow, he saw that the man had his head bowed over something in his outstretched hands.

Lenny caught his breath. Even from that distance, with the snow stinging his eyes, he recognized the unmistakable profile. He took two silent steps back out of sight around the corner, then turned and ran back to Starbucks.

Mari looked up as Lenny ran into the coffee shop in a bluster of snow. Owen was sitting on the armchair nearby, his eyes glued to Mari.

"It's Snyder," gasped Lenny. "He's here." He told her what he had seen outside. She gaped at him for a moment before jumping to her feet, still typing on Owen's phone.

"Owen," she said, "is there a back way out of here?"

"Sure. The kitchen entrance goes out into the alley. It connects to Boylston Street."

Lenny scrunched his eyes shut and tried to visualize his location.

"That's perfect. It's the opposite direction to Snyder. Let's go."

"One sec." Mari raised a finger in the air and finished typing something with the other hand. She handed Owen his phone back and grasped his hand in hers.

"Now would be a great time to lock up. An old boyfriend's after me, a very nasty piece of work. Thanks for everything."

"But the startup—" Owen began.

"We'll call you!" she said. "Just lock this place up!"

Lenny grabbed Mari's hand, and together they ran behind the counter and through the back door.

The alleyway dead-ended to their left, which by Lenny's calculations was where Snyder was standing staring at the wall. They turned right and waded and slipped through the drifting snow until they emerged onto Boylston Street. They ran down to the next cross street and ducked into a shallow doorway in front of a shuttered jewelry store.

Mari had been trying to tell him something as they ran, and he turned to listen to her now as they stood panting.

"Your phone," she said insistently.

"It's okay; it's in my pocket," he reassured her.

"No, I mean it's how he found us. Location tracking." She paused for more deep breaths. "You said he was staring down at something. I bet he was tracking you."

Lenny pulled his phone out of his pocket. Of course she was right. They would never be able to escape Snyder while he had his phone. But how could he finish his program without it?

"Quickly, Lenny, before he finds us again."

Lenny rubbed one hand across the smooth screen in a final caress and let the phone slide from his open palm. It sank soundlessly an inch into the snow. Lenny stamped down with one foot and ground the device under his boot until he heard a crack.

He stepped back and surveyed his work. His phone lay in the center of an outsized boot print, a piece of circuit board winking reproachfully from behind a shattered screen.

Mari cleared her throat.

"Couldn't you have just switched off location tracking?"

Lenny's skin felt hot against the cold air. "Doesn't it still transmit something? Even when the whole phone's off?"

"I don't know." Mari looked down at the device. "I'm sure you're right, it probably does." She took his hand and gave it a squeeze. "You did the right thing."

Lenny reached instinctively into his pocket to fire off a search on his phone about how location tracking worked. His hand flailed uselessly as he remembered that his phone lay on the ground right in front of him. He felt a sudden and overpowering sense of disconnection from the world. He gripped Mari's hand more tightly.

"What do we do now? We can't finish the antiviral code without a phone."

"What about an Internet café?" suggested Mari. "There used to be one close to BU."

Lenny reached toward his pocket for directions, but found only soft fabric where the hard outline of his phone should have been. His hand formed into a fist as he and Mari ran through the deepening snow to where his rusty memory told him the salvation of twenty-four-hour Internet access was waiting.

Snyder rubbed a hand across his swollen jaw and swore silently as he stared down at the broken device abandoned in the snow. He spent a moment trying to figure out if it was a monumentally unfortunate accident that Lenny had broken his phone right now or if they'd somehow detected that Snyder was tracking them. He quickly dismissed the question as irrelevant to his current predicament, which was how he was going to find Lenny Driver and his smartass girlfriend and put a permanent stop to their interference.

He'd calculated that they were most likely together, given that Lenny's phone had passed by Mari's apartment at exactly the time she was whacking him in the head. He'd tracked the phone successfully to this location, and now he understood why the signal had suddenly stopped.

Snyder had a hunch that Lenny wouldn't be able to stay away from a computer for long, which meant that he'd be leaving a digital trail again. With a little bit of time, Snyder could find Lenny's online accounts and the location of the computers that were accessing them. But Snyder didn't have time on his side. He needed to remove Lenny and his friends and start some serious damage control on the rumors that were still spreading about him.

He didn't know if he'd still have access to the OPRA systems—most likely not based on his conversation with Angie—and there might even be repercussions in his own department at the Defense Intelligence Agency. With his photo all over the Internet, his value as a covert operator had plummeted to zero, along with his chances of being appointed to the Intelligence Action Network. Even Brennigan couldn't be trusted—he'd actually had the audacity to call up Snyder asking about the Chinese spy rumors, hinting that these things didn't happen without reason. The nerve of the man. As though Snyder hadn't been the one protecting the Senator's interests from that particular threat for all these years. No, the only course left for Snyder would be to go independent.

The idea actually had a lot of appeal to him, though he never would have taken the plunge voluntarily. But now he had no choice. The thought of picking and choosing projects for himself, perhaps carefully building a network of like-minded thinkers, set his heart beating a little faster. It would be harder without the massive data tracking capabilities of his agency, and especially of OPRA, but if he could replicate even one tenth of one percent of that information from alternate sources, he'd still be able to target Lenny's viral algorithms with razor precision.

He spat out the blood that had been pooling in his mouth and groaned at the stab of pain that the movement caused. Beneath the streetlamp, the splash of red was startling against the purity of the snow.

He shook his head at the sight of Lenny's phone rapidly disappearing under a fresh layer of flakes. His life would have been so much simpler if he'd never found Lenny, if he'd let the kid implode under his own stupid schemes.

As his eyes followed across the patterns of bumps and indentations in the snow beyond the phone, he suddenly straightened up. He placed his foot carefully into one of the indentations, and his mouth curled into a smile.

Heading off down the street were two sets of perfect, beautiful footprints.

Chapter 37

LENNY HAD TO THUMP THE *Enter* key twice to save his code to his online account. He twisted the keyboard upside down and shook it, hoping to dislodge whatever was making the key stick. He whacked the plastic case with more force than necessary before righting it and returning it to the counter.

He glanced behind him at the rows of empty terminals, surrounded by bookshelves stacked with periodicals. It was Mari who'd remembered that the Boston Public Library offered free Internet access, albeit in fifteen-minute increments.

The good news was that the building was still open, and the even better news was that the usual hordes of students and tourists were sensibly ensconced in their homes and hotels because of the blizzard, so nobody was going to stop him from using as many fifteen-minute slots as he needed. The bad news was that he couldn't start a new session until Mari came back from the restroom with her library card. She'd finally agreed to dry off her clothes and slippers with the hand dryers, which, judging by how soaked she was, would take a while. He wasn't sure if his tests would finish before his current fifteen minutes expired.

He poked his head around the archway that connected the computer area to the main library, but she was nowhere in sight. He flopped back in front of his terminal to watch the test routines activate one by one. Before he set the code loose on the Internet, he wanted to make sure that none of the functions were going to crash and bring the program to a grinding halt. He blinked and tried to focus his eyes on the small font. The combination of hunger and lack of sleep made it hard to concentrate, and he felt his eyelids becoming heavier as he stared at the test routines making their precautionary pass through the code.

A shadow fell across his screen. That was good; now he could get Mari's library card and open up a new terminal for the final launch.

"It's just about done." He stretched both arms upward to free the tension in his shoulder muscles. "I hope it works."

"You hope what works, Lenny?"

Lenny whirled round to see a face looming above him. The jaw was lopsided and swollen, but the sneer was unmistakably Snyder. Purple bruising pooled in puffy stains around his eyes, and dried blood smeared outward from one corner of his mouth.

Lenny jumped to his feet and backed away, realizing too late that he'd just put Snyder between himself and the exit.

"You used it against me, didn't you?" Snyder's mouth barely moved as he spoke, giving the words a guttural tone. "You spread those dumb stories."

"What are you talking about?" Lenny glanced around for an escape route, but the corridor was the only way out.

"I'm talking about my newfound notoriety. My photos all over the Internet." Snyder lunged forward and grabbed Lenny's shirt with one hand. The other hand clamped itself around Lenny's chin and forced him to look up into Snyder's face. His lips were drawn into a tight line. "I thought we were working together."

Lenny felt Snyder's fingers dig into the sides of his face and felt a glimmer of satisfaction beneath his fear. He'd been so preoccupied with the antivirus code, he'd almost forgotten his feeble attempt to slow Snyder down. Maybe it hadn't been so feeble after all. Despite everything, he found himself smiling.

The parts of Snyder's face that weren't already purple flushed a deep red. Lenny felt Snyder's fingers dig harder into his cheeks and feared for a moment that his own jaw was going to crack.

Suddenly, the pressure released. Lenny watched as Snyder unbuttoned his overcoat and started to reach for something in his jacket pocket. Flashbacks of detective movies pulsed through Lenny's mind. Was that really how somebody pulled a gun? He decided he didn't want to wait to find out.

"I have a reason," he blurted.

Snyder's hand paused at his side.

"A reason for what?"

"A reason to keep me alive."

"Upgrades?" Snyder huffed what might have been an attempt at a laugh.

"A way to control it."

"Sure." The word was dripping with skepticism, but Lenny saw a hint of interest in Snyder's face. Snyder relaxed his arm and looked around the empty room. "Where's your girlfriend?"

Lenny willed himself not to look toward the corridor that led to the restrooms. "She went to the hospital. To visit Roy."

The curl of Snyder's lips above his crooked jaw told Lenny everything he needed to know about the cause of Roy's accident. He caught his breath but forced his mind to focus back on stalling Snyder. He had to finish the antivirus.

"I can stop your photo spreading around."

Snyder's narrowed eyes continued to watch Lenny.

"I've created an antivirus." Lenny glanced over his shoulder at the terminal he'd been working on. A thin black bar advancing across the screen announced that the tests were close to complete. He just needed to hold Snyder off for a few more minutes. The truth had seemed like a good gambit, but he couldn't let Snyder know he was about to destroy all their work or Snyder would stop him on the spot. Perhaps he could make him believe he could stop an individual influence network, rather than killing all the networks at once as his code was set to do.

He had to tread carefully. Snyder was too perceptive for Lenny to bluff outright, and he'd been burned before when he thought he could play bait and switch with Snyder. The war between Congo and Burundi was testament to that. He took a deep breath.

"Remember the three factors that make it all work?"

As Lenny explained how he'd removed the power of the third factor by making people realize they'd been secretly influenced, Snyder pulled out a chair from the adjacent terminal. He leaned heavily on its back with both hands, still blocking Lenny's exit.

The blazing anger in Snyder's face slowly flattened into a mask of contempt as he quizzed Lenny about the details. Lenny answered truthfully, although he omitted Mari's involvement.

"But people will have to trust the source of the antivirus alert," said Snyder, once Lenny reached the end of his explanation. "Otherwise, it won't work. That means you can't make it anonymous. You'll have to expose yourself. And me." Snyder's words were becoming more distinct, but it still sounded as though each one cost him extreme effort.

"It's still anonymous. It'll work."

"And how do you identify the right influence network to target, so that the antivirus doesn't wipe out everything?" asked Snyder.

There it was. The question for which there was no answer.

Lenny rubbed his hand across his face and tried to think of something plausible. He sneaked another look at his terminal. The tests were complete, and a prompt box was asking him whether to continue. If he confirmed the prompt, his antivirus code would launch. It would notify thousands of people, maybe millions, that they had been part of an influence network. If it worked, all of the consequences of his viral algorithm would fade away—the fighting in Burundi and the Congo, the privacy demonstrations, even his original fundraising and the fake photos and stories about Andrei—and Snyder. He'd set it up so that the antivirus code would keep launching, over and over. Nobody would be able to use his algorithms again.

He looked back at Snyder, who was still leaning on the chair with one arm. The other was held loosely across his body, the hand obscured by his overcoat. As he shifted his grip on the chair, the overcoat flapped forward to reveal his fingers, which were wrapped around the black metal handle of a gun.

Lenny felt like his mind had been suddenly erased. He couldn't even remember what question he was supposed to be answering. His head jerked up to stare in panic at the swollen face in front of him, but Snyder seemed not to notice. He was frowning in thoughtful concentration

"I get it!" Snyder's stare snapped back into focus on Lenny. "Each influence network has its own unique pattern—a signature, right?"

"Uh, yeah." He took a small step back toward the terminal, trying to figure the distance to the keyboard. Perhaps he could make the four or five steps to the computer before Snyder could shoot him. He could stop Snyder and others like him from using this power ever again. Was that worth dying for? A shudder rippled the length of his body. He was no hero.

"Yes, I've seen it on the OPRA system. They're all recognizable as influence networks, but each one has a distinctive pattern. If you can identify those..." The frown returned to his face. "But how did *you* find the signatures? Without the OPRA system?"

Lenny felt his sense of reality receding. He had no idea what Snyder was talking about. What system? The world around him seemed to be dissolving into pixels, the objects losing their definition and fading into insubstantial smears of color.

"It's like you said... the signatures," he heard himself say. "They look different. When you look at them."

"Go on."

Lenny looked blankly at Snyder. He had nothing more to offer. His ability to feign knowledge had slipped away at the sight of Snyder's gun. All he could think of was Mari, drying her clothes in the ladies' room, and the fact that he might never hold her again.

Snyder watched Lenny with a frozen stare before emitting a single mirthless bark. His lips opened into a twisted smile, causing the rest of his face to flinch. "You nearly had me there, Lenny.

Good try." His expression returned to one of blatant contempt. "It's all bullshit, isn't it? You can't stop the influence networks with your cheap little online accounts. You can't control anything."

Lenny waited for the familiar panic to return at the revelation that Snyder didn't believe a word he'd been saying. But instead of rampaging adrenaline through his body, his insides stayed empty, a dull hollow where his emotions had no more fuel to burn. It was over. He'd influenced millions of people around the world to do his bidding, but the one time it mattered, he couldn't use his powers of persuasion against one man to save himself and a whole lot of innocent people. From the anonymity of his keyboard he was a god—face to face, he was a nobody. A few feet away, the prompt on the computer terminal mocked his impotence. *Do you really want to continue?*

From the corner of his eye, Lenny caught a flicker of movement behind Snyder. Mari was rounding the corner from the corridor. She saw Snyder and froze. Lenny fought the urge to call out, to run to her, to warn her that Snyder was armed. He kept his eyes lowered and shook his head slowly from side to side, trying to send a telepathic alert while hoping that Snyder would interpret his movement as one of defeat.

"You're right, I can't control anything." Lenny's heavy sigh was almost genuine. "I was just starting another influence network. It's for a friend who wants his music video to go viral. Mind if I send it out for him?"

Snyder cocked his head and looked at Lenny's terminal as though considering the proposition. Almost absently, he raised the gun in one smooth motion and leveled it at Lenny's chest.

"I don't think so, Lenny."

Over Snyder's shoulder, Lenny saw Mari moving slowly in their direction. His eyes widened; he looked quickly back down at the gun. What was she doing? Didn't she recognize Snyder? He realized with a stab of alarm that she couldn't see the gun from where she was standing.

"Are you going to shoot me?" Lenny spoke the words with exaggerated clarity.

"I'd rather not do it here. Let's go for a walk, shall we?"

"Um. Sure."

Mari was no more than a few feet behind Snyder and still closing in. Why wasn't she running for help, or at least getting the hell away from here? The time for subtlety was over.

"Run, Mari! Run!"

He raised his foot to the seat of the chair that Snyder was leaning on and kicked it with all his strength. The back of the chair slammed into Snyder's stomach. He hoped that would give Mari time enough to flee.

He spun round and lunged toward the terminal. Just as he reached it, he felt something thump into his back and knock him to one side. His shoulder landed heavily against the counter, but he managed to reach out an arm to grab the edge. His eyes were level with the keyboard. He picked out the blue square of the *Enter* key and pushed it with his free hand.

With a groan Lenny, looked up at the screen and confirmed what the feel of the key had already told him. The *Enter* key was stuck. The confirmation message glowed stubbornly on the terminal. Before he could hit the key a second time, the message faded to black and was replaced by a green box telling him he needed to authorize another fifteen-minute session at the service desk.

He smashed his fist down on the useless keyboard and braced himself for the shot.

Chapter 38

SNYDER HAD BEEN EXPECTING LENNY to make a move, and he was only surprised that it had taken him so long. Lenny had looked like a trapped animal, panic in his face and his voice, and eyes darting in all directions. It was true that Snyder had nearly fallen for Lenny's story about controlling the influence networks, and he recognized now that his own wishful thinking had temporarily blinded him to the obvious fabrication.

He had no idea, in the end, what new programs Lenny was finding so important to launch here in the library in the middle of a blizzard, but Snyder was sure that whatever they were, they would not be beneficial to his plans. So when the chair slammed him backward, he was torn between preventing Lenny from reaching the terminal and making sure that Mari—apparently somewhere in this room—wasn't planning to slug him again. His options were limited by the fact that he really didn't want to shoot either of them right here. He'd positioned himself to hide the details of his confrontation with Lenny from the two cameras he'd spotted, but if bodies started dropping, someone was bound to come and investigate.

Ignoring the rip of pain that shot up from his damaged rib, he raised a foot to send the chair back in Lenny's direction. It caught Lenny squarely in the back and knocked him to one side. Snyder let the momentum of the kick spin him around, just in time to see Mari stepping toward him with something in her raised hand.

It was something metal. Not a gun or that goddamned baseball bat, something smaller... His left hand acted by instinct, sweeping up the front of his body and deflecting her arm with the outside edge of his palm, then twisting to lock on to her elbow.

He heard a sudden hiss, and a mist formed across his vision. He closed his eyes against what felt like a hundred bee stings, and smashed the butt of the gun in his right hand into Mari's fist. He felt her release whatever she was holding and heard it clatter to the ground.

He opened his eyes as his brain caught up with what she'd done to him. Pepper spray. The vision out of his left eye was blurred, but if he closed it, he could see clearly out of the other. Her aim was wide—she'd caught the side of his head. He'd managed to keep the worst of the stream away from his eyes, but if he hadn't seen her in time, she would have totally disabled him.

He blinked his left eye, and her face came into focus. She was looking up at him, her dark eyes wide with fear. He wondered briefly why she was standing there, why she didn't run from him, before he realized he was still gripping her arm. Her forearm was twisted awkwardly in front of her body, and her face was tilted up. Waves of dark hair fell back to expose the smooth skin of her cheek and the delicate curve of her neck. He thought of the satisfying crack that his fist, still wrapped around the heavy weight of the gun's handle, would make as it connected with her jaw. But he needed her on her feet, so he contented himself with a backhanded swipe across the side of her face He pushed her shoulder around so that she was facing away from him and shoved the barrel of the gun hard against her back.

He turned his attention to Lenny, who pounded his fist with evident frustration on the keyboard before turning to face them. Snyder shifted so that Lenny could see the gun against Mari's back, and Lenny's face contorted in panic.

"Let's take that walk," said Snyder.

Lenny's eyes flicked between Mari and Snyder, and his face gradually fell into the slackness of submission. Snyder took a breath of relief—he wouldn't be forced to kill them both here.

He gesticulated with his gun toward Lenny's jacket, which was draped over the back of a nearby chair. No point in leaving unnecessary evidence. Lenny pulled the jacket free, stuffed it under his arm, and obediently fell in step in front of Snyder and Mari. Snyder swooped down to pick up the pepper spray canister and dropped it into his pocket. He draped his arm loosely around Mari's shoulder in what he hoped looked like a fatherly hug and nudged her forward with the gun.

They walked in silence toward the door of the center courtyard. Snyder was grateful that the talking was done, as each word sent a stab of pain across his jaw. He needed to get Lenny and the girl into his car and out of the picture, and then get himself to a discreet doctor he knew.

As Snyder watched, Lenny struggled to open the door to the center courtyard, until the wind caught it and flung it away from him. The three of them filed along the covered path, with the snow in the open center whirling beside them. Snyder felt the freezing air biting at his face and concentrated on keeping steady footing where the snow had encroached onto the walkway.

In the opposite corner of the courtyard, a man emerged from the front wing of the library and started along the path opposite them. Snyder tensed and watched Lenny's reaction. Might he try to mouth a request for help, or give some kind of gesture? But Lenny continued to lumber along the path with his head down.

Snyder let Lenny hold the door for them into the front wing, and then he maneuvered himself and Mari to one side so that Lenny could once again lead the way. As far as he could remember, there was one more obstacle before their safe exit into the street: the front desk at the entrance, which had been occupied by a young security guard.

He watched Lenny's head bobbing steadily forward with an occasional glance back at Mari, and felt a wave of regret at what could have been. If only Lenny hadn't betrayed him. Why hadn't the boy been able to see the incredible potential of the two of them working together?

Snyder sighed. He was kidding himself, of course. He knew he was too softhearted sometimes, had too high expectations of people. Like so many of his generation, Lenny had no vision beyond his own selfish needs and certainly no appreciation of the value that invisible heroes like Snyder provided to his country. It was a waste of time thinking Lenny could ever understand what it took to keep the world on an even keel.

And spreading those rumors about Snyder being a spy for China—that was unforgivable. The people who knew him well wouldn't believe it, of course. Still, once the seeds of mistrust were planted, the roots spread quickly and deeply. Even those in Snyder's debt might feel compelled to turn their back on him. Including Brennigan, if that last phone call was anything to go by. All in all, Snyder was more than ready to put a bullet through Lenny Driver's too-smart-for-its-own-good brain.

Snyder braced himself as they approached the turn for the front desk. From what he'd noticed of the guard's posture on the way in, the man most likely didn't have a gun, but that was something he never took for granted. He took a breath, positioned his body tighter against Mari's, and stepped around the corner.

The guard's desk was empty. Snyder released his breath and relaxed his grip on Mari. Sometimes fate was on the side of the righteous.

They exited the library and again he felt the force of the wind whipping the snow into their eyes and faces.

"Keep going, Lenny. Down the steps and to the left." Snyder had to shout the words. Now he almost enjoyed the pain gnawing at his jaw, reminding him he was alive. He just had to get them to his car and he'd be home free. He pictured himself back at his desk in the front room of his apartment, finally rid of all these distractions, back at work with Lenny's viral algorithm. He'd be the only person on the planet with the power to influence world events so precisely. The only one who even knew that such power existed.

The smile that this thought brought to his damaged face was replaced by an "o" of surprise as an unbearable pain exploded inside his head. He felt himself stagger to one side and pitch forward as his brain's ability to send his body instructions was terminated.

Chapter 39

LENNY FELT A SUDDEN FORCE from behind clip his legs and push him forward. He threw out a protective hand as he slid face first down the steps of the library. He managed to twist sideways, and felt the hard stone edges beneath the wet snow bump against his torso before he glided to a halt.

"Mari!" He got back on his feet and pounded up the steps. Two bodies lay motionless. Snyder was sprawled on his front, facing down the steps, and Lenny could see Mari's arms and legs splayed beneath. The bottom half of Snyder's overcoat was flipped back on itself.

"Mari!" he yelled again, trying to push Snyder off of her with his boot. Snyder's shoulder rose a couple of inches before falling back in place. Lenny stepped over to straddle Snyder, pulled with all his might, and rolled him onto his back.

Now that Mari was free, Lenny could see that her head was twisted sideways against the stone. His heart froze as he realized that the back of her head was matted with blood. He slid one hand under her cheek to lift it off the ground and gently brushed the snow from her mouth and nose. He heard a faint groan in the back of her throat.

"Mari, are you okay? Say something."

"Fuck." Mari drew her arms in underneath her body. As she lifted her head and shoulders, a movement on the far side of the steps drew Lenny's attention. He caught a glimpse of a man's face turning away from them, its features indistinct beneath a dark, close-fitting hat. The figure thrust his hands into his pockets and set off in a brisk pace along the sidewalk. Lenny pushed Mari back down and leaned his body over hers until the figure disappeared around the corner of Boylston Street.

He released his hold and Mari threw her arms around his shoulders. He held her head against his cheek, unsure if the wetness he felt on her face was snow or blood, but for the moment not caring.

"Who was that?" she whispered.

Lenny shook his head. "No idea, but he shot Snyder. And probably saved our lives." He pulled her face back to inspect it. A red circle flared on one cheekbone, and blood-encrusted ice clung to her hair. "Are you hurt?"

Mari inspected the swollen knuckles of her right hand and ran her other hand across the side of her head, where Snyder had cuffed her. "I'm okay. What about..."

They released their embrace and turned to look at the motionless figure next to them. One arm was twisted under his body, and his head was a mess of blood.

"He's got to be dead," said Lenny.

"Do you think we're safe?" Mari glanced over her shoulder at the street below.

"I guess so. If that other guy wanted us dead too, he had time for another shot. No, he was just after Snyder."

Lenny moved toward the body and felt something roll under his boot. Mari grabbed his elbow. With one eye still on Snyder, he reached down and picked up Mari's pepper spray.

"You've got blood on your ear." Mari sounded alarmed.

"I think it might be from... um..." Lenny ran a finger over Mari's hair and held out his hand to show her the smear of dark red. "Are you sure you're not hurt?"

Mari's hands flew up toward her head but stopped short of touching her hair.

"It's his." Her face grimaced in disgust, and she froze with her fists clenched a few inches from her ears.

"Here, let me try." Lenny scooped up handfuls of fresh snow and clumped them on either side of her hair, pulling them down from her scalp to the roots. He threw away the soiled snow and picked up some more. Mari flipped her head to one side so that her hair fell away from her body, and Lenny rubbed at the worst of the muck.

"Look, there." Mari pulled upright and pointed at the clearing where Snyder's headfirst dive appeared to have ejected the contents of his pockets. Against the flattened snow lay a set of keys and two phones, one of them emblazoned with a green-and-purple spiral. A couple of feet away, its barrel elongated with a silencer, was Snyder's gun. Lenny reached a hand down toward the dark shape.

"Is he okay?" Lenny startled at the sound of a man's voice. He looked over his shoulder to see two men and a woman approaching from the bottom of the steps. The woman wore a yellow-and-black Bruins hat and a parka; the men wore baseball hats above padded windbreakers.

Lenny's hand hovered over the gun a moment before reaching down to grab the two phones.

"No, he's hurt bad. I think he's been shot."

Lenny spun around to face the newcomers, deftly lifting the hood of Mari's sweatshirt up over her blood-streaked hair as he turned. "You should call 911. We're going to go..." He looked around at the open park opposite and the broad streets on either side, so deeply covered with snow that he couldn't tell where the sidewalk ended and the road began. His eyes came to rest on a familiar black T in a white circle. "We'll see if there's someone in the subway who can help."

Lenny grabbed Mari's hand and left the three Samaritans staring open-mouthed at the motionless body on the steps.

"He's really dead." Lenny huddled next to Mari at the bottom of the subway escalator and waited for the relief to flood through him at the finality of those words. He no longer had to fear for

Mari's safety, or his own. If Roy could just pull through, everything could be the way it was before. But the words triggered no release. He knew the journey wasn't over yet.

The subway speakers announced severe delays on the Green Line. In front of the empty MBTA ticket office, a homeless man draped in a blanket sat hugging his knees. The hood of his stained sweatshirt was pulled forward over grey stubble, and his head bobbed every few seconds as he mumbled expletives at an imagined companion. The rest of the station appeared deserted. A perfect spot to finish what had to be done.

Lenny pulled Mari's phone out of his pocket. With practiced strokes, he pulled up the browser and opened the accounts where his code was stored on a distant server. His session picked up where he'd left it in the library, with the single, insistent message etched on the screen. *Do you really want to continue?* Beyond that screen, the messages that he and Snyder had sent out were still flying around, driving people to action. Snyder might be dead, but his influence lived on.

"It's not anonymous this time, is it?" He felt Mari's breath against his cheek. "The code we just wrote? I heard what you told Snyder, but it's not true."

"No, it's not anonymous."

"Now that Snyder's... gone, you could spend more time on it. Rewrite it so that it won't point back to you."

She was right. They could go back to his apartment and take their time, the two of them, to do it right. He imagined them curled side by side on the sofa, their laptops warm on their knees, drinking slow cups of coffee while they coded. And there was more. He remembered the excitement in Snyder's eyes as he'd spoken about the distinct signature of each influence network. If that was true, then Lenny could redesign the antivirus so that it could target a single influence network. He'd be free to pick and choose, to experiment and back off, and if anyone else got hold of his algorithm again, he could shut them down whenever he wanted.

But they didn't have time. How many more people would be hurt by those influence networks as he refined his code? And what if anything happened to him? He couldn't risk another Snyder getting control if he wasn't around to fix it. Even if the algorithm ended up in the hands of the good guys, what gave them—or himself for that matter—the right to play with human lives?

Then there was the question he should have asked himself a long time ago, before he sent out his first set of messages. Was it fair to influence people who didn't know they were being influenced? Sure, none of his targeted opinion leaders acted against their natural tendencies—that was the beauty of the targeting—but still...

"It has to be this way." He stared at the bobbing head of the homeless guy.

"Lenny, they'll put you in jail."

"Everything has consequences." He held his finger over the screen. *Do you really want to continue?*

He placed his finger onto the *Yes* option and held it there, waiting for the electrons from his fingertip to complete the circuit. The prompt disappeared from the screen, leaving a void. Behind the dark screen, Lenny imagined his code spidering out between the millions of web servers around the globe, each time spawning a thousand new processes that would find their way to yet more servers. Each new process set about tracking down the telltale patterns of the influence networks—the hubs of the key influencers, the sudden shifting of opinion in a unified direction, the chains of cause and effect. If it was working as planned, his antivirus code would be reestablishing the severed links to warn the recipients about the messages he had forced on them, alerting them that they had been played as part of an influence network. Lenny could almost feel the links forging back together. He felt as though he was a part of the software, slowly being connected to a billion different consciousnesses. He was no longer a separate entity, playing out his individual will, but an integral part of the interplay of actions and reactions, decisions and consequences. So many consequences.

The sound of an incoming message chime pulled Lenny from his vision.

"Look. Look at that!" Mari was pointing at her phone, still clasped loosely in Lenny's hand.

It was there. His message, right on the screen, with a link to a website promising further information.

Lenny closed his eyes. If his program, launched from distant servers, had found its way back to Mari, then there was no reason it hadn't reached every person he and Snyder had influenced. His antivirus worked. It was really over.

A distant sound of sirens played against an announcement about an approaching Green Line train. He placed his arm around Mari's shoulder and they rode silently up the escalators, feeling the force of the wind gather as they moved closer to the exit.

As they crossed the road toward the library, the sirens blared insistently. Two police cars and a fire truck had planted themselves haphazardly in the street. Another police car turned in front of them, its back end sliding out wide before coming to a stop inches from the fire truck. On the library steps, two firemen guarded Snyder's body while a windbreaker-clad policeman tied black-and-yellow crime-scene tape between orange cones. A few steps below, two policemen stood talking to the group that Lenny had told to call 911. The woman in the Bruins hat caught sight of Lenny and Mari and raised an arm to point at them.

Walking through the swirling snow, Lenny felt a lightness in his shoulders. For the first time in months, his head wasn't racing with the next line of code in some program that was supposed to fix everything—but never quite did. At the bottom of the steps, a fireman was asking a group of teenagers to stand back. The fireman's large frame was bulked out even further by his protective clothing. Lenny glanced down at Mari's fur slippers caving deep prints into the snow, and tightened his arm around her.

Most of the teenagers stared freely at Lenny and Mari as they passed, although one was too busy frowning down at the screen of her phone. The policemen watched Lenny and Mari come closer. One called out to him, but the wind snatched his words away. Instead, Lenny heard the voice of the frowning teenage girl, and it wrapped him in a glow of warmth even as the brutal force of the storm whipped against his face.

"What the heck is an influence network?"

Chapter 40

"WELL THIS FEELS LIKE DÉJÀ VU all over again." Roy looked from one end of the sofa to the other. "Lenny, anything you want to say to Mari?"

Lenny glanced at the opposite end of the sofa, where Mari was studiously not looking at him. Her chin was cupped in the palm of her hand, and her leg was crossed away from him.

Lenny was determined not to be the one to break the silence. Admittedly, he'd told Roy he was going to be out all day before he'd changed his mind and come home early, but Roy should have warned him that Mari was here. After two months of FBI questioning, he'd only been back home for a week. He wasn't ready to see her.

Roy sighed loudly and pushed himself out of the armchair with both arms.

"I gotta go to physical therapy. Mari, make yourself at home. There's more coffee in the pot."

"I thought you said your appointment's at noon?" Lenny tipped his head and glared at Roy.

"I'll drive the long way round."

"Your arm's looking stronger, dude. That exercise stuff is working." Lenny watched Roy pull on his coat with a lingering hint of stiffness in his left arm. He was impressed at how quickly his friend had recovered from his injuries. "Tell you what. I'll give you a ride."

Lenny started to rise from the sofa, but Roy turned and pointed a finger straight at Lenny.

"Stay!" he said with a ferocity that froze Lenny back into his seat. Roy swept up his keys and slammed out of the front door.

Lenny stared down at his knees. He was still wondering how to extricate himself from this embarrassment when he heard a rapid series of short breaths from Mari.

Great. Now he had to deal with tears on top of everything else.

The breaths gave way to a lighter sound that Lenny realized wasn't sobbing. In fact, it was more like...

He looked sideways to see her watching him, the back of her hand held over her mouth to hide her reaction to something she clearly considered very funny.

His embarrassment turned to annoyance. "What?" he snapped.

"I'm sorry, I shouldn't..." She dropped her hand and turned her head away, her whole body shaking with laughter. "It's just Roy. He sounded like he was talking to a dog, and then you..." She turned back to face him and wiped under her eyes with slim fingers. "I'm sorry, I couldn't help it."

Lenny studied her face as she brought herself under control. Her skin was free of makeup, and her hair was swept back loosely over her shoulders. Her clear brown eyes were watching him back, questioning—or was it accusing?

"Yeah, well, he's always on my case." He pulled his feet up onto the sofa and hugged his knees. "The FBI told me they didn't bring you in. Is that right?"

"Yeah. They came to my apartment and questioned me. Three times, the same woman and a guy. They wouldn't tell me anything about you."

"I'm sorry you had to go through that. Because of me." Was that what she wanted? An apology? Lenny could feel her eyes still on him as he focused on a small hole in his sock.

"That didn't bother me."

From the corner of his eye, he could see her fingers twisting around each other on her lap.

"It was after, Lenny. All those weeks the FBI had you, I couldn't sleep. I stayed up half the night binging on Netflix series and went to work each day like a zombie. I was so relieved when they let you go. But then you wouldn't even talk to me."

She slid her legs up onto the sofa and crossed them underneath her body. "Did they hurt you?"

"What?"

"The FBI. When they had you inside."

"No, it wasn't like that." Lenny hadn't talked with anyone, not even Roy, about his experiences in Washington. He wasn't sure he ever would. But there was something about Mari's matter-of-fact tone that made the words easier to form. "They just asked me the same questions, like fifty times, every day. It was more like a hotel room than a prison, except they didn't let me out."

"So why... why don't you want to see me?"

Lenny pulled his knees closer. How could he explain the agonizingly long hours alone in Washington, with nothing but his thoughts for company? Thoughts that kept turning to how, when it really mattered, he'd failed her.

He took a deep breath, unsure of how to articulate the guilt that was holding him hostage.

"That night, in the library," he began slowly. "When he had the gun on you. I was planning how to get us both free. I thought maybe when we reached his car, there'd be some kind of opportunity, that I could catch him off guard... you know, be a hero." The words tumbled out faster as he vented his frustration. "But then he got shot and we launched the antivirus, and suddenly it was all over. Big relief. Happy ever after."

Lenny studied the bands of patterned color on Mari's socks, each one different but complementing the one next to it.

"I know it's stupid, but I feel like I got cheated," he said. "Snyder's dead, but it's nothing I did. Just some random fluke."

"Maybe it *was* you. You know, the stuff you sent out about Snyder. Some gang of pissed-off grannies hired an assassin."

Lenny couldn't help but smile at the vision. "Yeah, right."

Mari moved closer. He flinched as he felt her hand on his knee, but then he relaxed and placed his hand on top of hers. It felt good to talk through the recriminations he'd been beating himself up with for the past two months—as if the FBI hadn't made him feel insignificant and selfish enough without him adding to it.

He'd played right into their hands, too: boasting about what he'd done and how he'd done it as they sat listening with what he soon realized was completely fake admiration. They'd seemed to understand his every motive and move, had sympathized with his predicament. *Yeah, I can see how that must have felt. Of course you had to do that.* Egging him on until the tone changed and the accusations began. They read him back his own words but twisted the motives. *Had he traveled outside the U.S.? Joined any groups or organizations? What did he read online?* He'd woken every night in a cold panic, sure he was digging himself in deeper with every denial that he wasn't a terrorist or part of some international plot. Then suddenly, unexpectedly, they'd let him walk out the door with a ticket back to Boston and a warning that they'd be monitoring his online activities.

"The news reports wrote off Snyder's death as a mugging," said Mari.

"Roy showed me. They didn't even mention us."

"Well, I'm not going to put them right about that one." Mari paused, and Lenny felt a soft squeeze on his leg. "You did make the antivirus work, though."

"Yeah, I did." Lenny nodded. "No, *we* did." He looked up and met her eyes as she smiled at him.

"Let's go for a walk." Mari tugged on his hand, and he let her pull him to his feet. They slipped on jackets and boots, and Mari switched off the coffee machine on the counter before they left.

The street was sodden with the melt-off from a late spring snow. Lenny took Mari's fingers loosely in his own as they picked their way around brown puddles and headed toward Harvard Square.

"Have you thought about what you're going to do next?" asked Mari, launching herself over a pile of slush. "They might still take you at Blahst, you know. They've bundled your antivirus in every product."

Lenny frowned as they slowed to a stop behind a crowd waiting to cross the intersection. "I'm probably not the corporate type."

"Good insight."

Lenny found himself wanting to tell Mari the crazy idea he'd been mulling over for the last few days. Before all of this, he'd never considered other options besides Blahst, but suddenly it seemed like there were a million directions he could go.

"There's this new program that Healthway's sponsoring. It's a malaria vaccine, and they need some analysis on how effective it is."

"That sounds great."

The WALK signal lit up, and they filed across the road with the crowd, dancing out of the way of the pedestrians crossing from the other direction.

"It's onsite," said Lenny.

"In Africa?" Mari stopped in the middle of the crossing. "You're going to Burundi?"

"Um, probably not. I talked with Professor Ramsey, and he doesn't think Burundi or the Congo would be such a good idea for me. They haven't been very friendly to Americans since the antivirus sent out the alerts. If anyone found out who I was..."

Lenny trailed off as they continued onto the sidewalk. It still seemed too unreal. How could he have two whole nations mad at him?

"Where, then?"

"Probably Malawi."

Lenny sneaked a glance at Mari. She was biting at her bottom lip as she looked distractedly at the green-and-gold Panera Bread sign.

"Can I come visit?"

"Are you serious?"

Mari shrugged. "Maybe."

Lenny felt his heart race. She hadn't laughed at him and told him what a dumb idea it was. Perhaps he could really make it happen. Maybe she'd even visit.

"They don't have Whole Foods or Trader Joe's, you know," he said.

"I can survive that."

"And it's a really long walk to Starbucks."

"Do you want me to come or not?" Mari turned to face him with her hands on her hips.

Lenny grabbed around her waist and swung her over a patch of dark-brown slush that had pooled outside the Panera entrance. He realized he had no real idea what it would be like once he got to Africa—it was just something he knew he had to do. The thought of having Mari visit made it suddenly more real. He wondered if he'd really be able to make a difference there, whether he could make up for what he had done in some small way.

At least he couldn't do any more harm, could he?

Epilogue

ANGIE FELT THE WIND GUSTING up off the Potomac, nullifying the effect of the weak sun trying to eke out another hour of daylight. She hadn't dressed for a long walk, assuming that Senator Brennigan's invitation to "have a quick chat about recent events" would take them to the senator's office or some other indoor venue with a heated walkway from the Metro station. But as the senator slowed to lean against the bridge, Angie flipped up the collar of her suit jacket and resigned herself to the cold.

"Did he tell you anything about his projects?" Brennigan tucked a stray scarf end back inside his overcoat. "Any of his... special interests?"

Angie thought back to her conversations with Snyder. She was trying to answer the senator's questions as frankly as possible, but she realized she'd learned very little about Snyder in the weeks he'd spent at OPRA. He, on the other hand, had learned everything about the OPRA systems and her research on influence networks, thanks to her excitement at having found someone who cared. Of course, she'd downplayed that aspect of her interactions with Snyder during the multiple debriefing sessions that followed his death.

"He was very interested in Burundi, and the influence network that started there. I got the impression that was why he'd been sent over. To learn more about it."

"Nobody sent him." Brennigan leaned both gloved hands against the railing. A barge passed below, leaving a trail of white-capped ripples in its wake. "He made his own choices."

Angie frowned. What was Brennigan talking about? You had to have at least three levels of signature for an interagency transfer.

"But somebody must have authorized..." Angie trailed off. Sometimes she felt there was another world coexisting in the same corridors and buildings that she inhabited, a hidden parallel universe where the rules worked differently. Once in a while she'd catch a glimpse of it—a knowing look between two directors, a project that became top priority for no apparent reason—but when she tried to pin it down, it flickered out of sight.

"How about China? Did he seem to have any interest there?" The senator continued to gaze at the river below.

Was that what this was about? Rehashing the rumors about Snyder being a spy for China? Angie had been taken aback when she'd got the call from the senator. She was aware that Brennigan was on the Senate Select Committee on Intelligence, but as far as she knew, Brennigan had never visited OPRA. Angie had certainly never met him before. She'd accepted the invitation, of course, but as she'd hung up the phone, something had clamored inside of her that this wasn't like the other departmental debrief-ings she'd endured. Senators didn't ask for private meetings with lowly intelligence analysts.

"You mean those rumors that were spreading with his photo? You think they might have been true?" she asked.

"What do you think? Did he say anything that might hint at that conclusion?"

Angie recalled the conversations she'd had with Snyder. The way those deep-set eyes seemed to pierce inside her head. He was certainly passionate about his work, maniacal even. But for what cause?

"He did mention that he thought the U.S. wasn't doing enough to hold off Chinese investments. I covered that in my debriefing." A connection popped into Angie's head from the endless pages of Brennigan's press coverage she'd pored over in preparation for this meeting. "Sorry to hear you lost that tantalum plant," she added. "I heard that went to Shenyang. Maybe Snyder was right."

Brennigan's head jerked toward Angie, his eyes narrowed with suspicion. She drew back from his stare. What had she said? Was he really that sore over losing the plant, or was it something about Snyder? She felt a crack opening into the parallel world.

Brennigan recovered his poise. "Those jobs would have been good for the region, no doubt about that." He drummed his fingers against the railing. Angie resisted the urge to jump in with questions, and waited instead to see where he would take the conversation.

After a long pause, Brennigan continued. "That Driver kid claims he started the rumors about Snyder. He says he also started the rest of it: Blahst and the financial crisis, the POP bill, Burundi and the Congo. Is that possible?"

This question had been consuming Angie's every waking hour—and many of the hours when she was supposed to be sleeping—for the past two months. She hadn't yet come up with an answer. Every day she watched the remaining trails of the influence networks breaking apart into ever smaller branches, fading and dispersing into insignificance. Every day she rolled the time-lines back to when the influence networks were at their most intense. She drilled into the heavy lines gashed across the globe, searching for some new glimmer of insight into how they had formed. Could one person—not a president or a king or a general, but a twenty-two-year-old computer programmer—have caused all that disruption? Could he have created economic and political shifts on a scale few world leaders had managed to achieve?

"It seems unlikely," Angie said. "But I haven't seen the detailed reports from the FBI yet."

"The reports are inconclusive. Nobody's been able to replicate the effect, now that his influence antivirus is part of every operating system around the planet. That much he did do. Played to everyone's paranoia."

Angie turned her head away to hide the frustration that she could feel twisting across her face. She'd been trying for a month to get access to the transcripts of the FBI's interviews with Lenny Driver, reports that her department should have received as part of the routine inflow of intelligence data. She'd even asked Colonel Egham to pursue it, though his bull-in-a-china-shop approach had probably done more harm than good. If the FBI was being so cagey about the material, then how did Brennigan get to see it? Perhaps if she played her cards right, she could get some value out of this meeting.

"On the other hand, the strength of any one of those influence networks was unprecedented." Angie turned slowly back to face Brennigan. "I can't believe they all started at the same time by coincidence. In the FBI report, did it say anything about how Lenny Driver might have—"

"How about Snyder?" suggested Brennigan. "He was well connected, and Driver said he was involved. Could he have been the one behind it all?"

Angie thought back to her own suspicions on that topic, and the easy way Snyder had reassured her that it had nothing to do with him. But his cold fury at his own photos and the rumors that were making the rounds had seemed genuine enough.

"Why would Snyder spread those rumors about himself?" she mused.

"Who knows. A red herring. A double bluff."

"So you do think he was working for China?" The words were out of her mouth before she realized how abrupt they sounded, like a conversation between equals. She waited for the rebuff.

Brennigan lifted his gaze toward the Capitol building on the far bank of the river. A line of low clouds glowed faintly pink behind it. "I think you have to err on the side of caution in these matters."

Angie felt a chill travel up her back and spread across her shoulders. What was Brennigan saying? Nobody at OPRA believed the news reports that Snyder's death was a random mugging, but was Brennigan implying that somebody had believed the Chinese spy rumors enough to...? No. She shook her head against that line of thought. She was letting her imagination run away with her.

She realized that her arm was numb where the railing had leached the warmth through her thin jacket, and she clenched her fist to get the blood moving.

"Angie, you come highly recommended." Brennigan nodded toward her. "You have a knack for seeing patterns, for working out what's important. You have good instincts."

Angie returned the nod cautiously.

"Are you a patriot, Angie?" continued Brennigan.

"Yes, of course. I have SCI clearance."

"How far would you go? For your country?"

Angie met the senator's eyes as she tried to figure out where he was headed. She knew that her instincts were actually less than stellar without a room full of analytical software to help her out. She was being tested—that much was clear. She could feel the gateway to the hidden world opening wider.

"Sir, I would never betray my country. I'm not a material-istic person, and I have no dark secrets, so I'd be hard to bribe or blackmail."

"How about your work at OPRA? If it was in the best interests of our country, would you be prepared to... bend the rules a little?"

So that was what this was about. Naturally, Brennigan was nervous after the publicity around Snyder. It must be hard for a man in his position to know whom he could trust.

"No, Sir. I know the bounds of my authority, and I always operate within it. You can count on me."

Brennigan's eyes locked on Angie's, and they stayed there until Angie felt her feet shuffling with discomfort. Finally he released her from his gaze and clapped his hands together.

"Good. That's good then." Brennigan pulled his phone out of his pocket and glanced at the screen. "Well, Angie, it's been a pleasure meeting you. I appreciate you coming out here like this."

Brennigan reached out a gloved hand. Angie shook it, feeling a momentary warmth as the smooth leather wrapped her cold skin.

Angie watched the senator turn and pick his way along the sidewalk, avoiding the patches of ice that formed black mirrors on the concrete.

Was that it? Somehow Angie had expected more from this meeting. Perhaps Brennigan hadn't believed her. Perhaps she should run after him and protest her integrity, but how could she do that without sounding defensive? She realized with dismay that she had learned nothing new about Lenny Driver and the influence networks, and her opportunity was receding with every step the senator took.

"Sir, any chance you could forward me those FBI reports?"

Brennigan paused and turned his head back toward Angie. "I only saw a hard copy, and I had to return it. I'll see what I can do, but don't hold your breath."

As she walked back across the bridge with the whistle of the wind in her ears, Angie could hear the rift resealing itself as it once again shut her out.

She blew on her hands and consoled herself with the thought of her own parallel universe of models and simulations back at OPRA. She was looking forward to a couple of hours of uninterrupted research. She thought she might have found some common traffic patterns around the original Blahst influence networks, and she was planning to run some experiments in a protected microcosm free of the antivirus code. She knew it was only a matter of time before she figured it out. And once she knew how it worked, maybe—just maybe—she could run some other experiments. Something from her discussions with Snyder had stuck in her head—something she'd chosen not to share in the debriefing sessions. *What if you could combine the deliberate initiation of an influence network with OPRA's predictive modeling? A killer combination.* Why should OPRA always, only, be the watchers? What if, once in a while, she could nudge things in a more desirable direction?

Just as an experiment.

ACKNOWLEDGMENTS

An essential source of motivation and constancy in my writing life has been the Writes, a wonderfully supportive writer's group that has provided me with feedback and encouragement for over ten years. Thanks to Kitty Beer (author of the *Resilience* trilogy), John Amiard (author of *Swedish Blood*), Marty Levin, David Rich, Shelby Allen (author of *Crack Willow: Poems of Transformation*), Wayne Soini (author of *Deep Snow*), Terry Kitchen (author of *Next Big Thing*), Jeanne Harnois, and Paula de Fougerolles (author of *The Chronicles of Iona* trilogy.)

Many authors have informed my thinking around the way that ideas spread through society. In particular, the concepts behind the viral algorithm were inspired by Everett M. Rogers' *Diffusion of Innovations* and Malcom Gladwell's *The Tipping Point*. For the crashing realizing that that nobody is in charge of the world, I am indebted to Thomas L. Friedman's *The Lexus and the Olive Tree*.

I would like to thank the following for their reviews, suggestions, and support: June and Mike Leaney, Parul Vakani, Nancy Roosa, Sue and Larry Ramin, Angelika Linden, Tracey Haber, Mary Mesaglio, Rand Leeb-du Toit, Kimberly Davis, and Laura Gross. Thanks to Renee Nicholls for her sterling editing, and to Ari Choquette for the book design. All errors, inconsistencies and logic bombs that remain are mine alone.

Made in the USA
Lexington, KY
02 September 2018

3 1270 00839 6345